Extraordinary Creatures:

A Compilation of Short Stories about Remarkable Beings

Brieanna Robertson

Tex Leiko

Whimsical Publications, LLC

Florida

To purchase the authorized electronic edition of *Extraordinary Creatures: A Compilation of Short Stories about Remarkable Beings*, visit www.whimsicalpublications.com

Cover art by Shyanne England
Editing by Janet Durbin

ISBN-13: 978-1-63495-008-4

Published by
Whimsical Publications, LLC
Florida

Dedication

This was a labor of love and remembrance.
Your work was always so amazing.
I am happy we can be published alongside one another.
I love you so entirely.
You are and always will be my love story.

Also:
To The Lifecoach and The Enigma.
You helped heal a broken phoenix,
Consumed her in fire so she may fly again.
You are the color and the adventure in this world. Thank
you for gracing my life with your beauty, however fleeting.

Honey Wine
By Brieanna Robertson

Chapter One

The Complete Guide to Understanding the Mythical and Paranormal Creatures Commonly Occurring but Rarely Found in Our World, Volume 4 by Dr. Lawrence Lowenstein.

Autumn peered at the cover of the old book incredulously. It was thicker than the Bible and had been thumbed through so many times that the pages were yellowed and frayed. Many were dog-eared, with her uncle's notations in the margins.

With a weary sigh, she flung the book aside. It landed among where she had already thrown Volumes One, Two, and Three. "Sorry, Dr. Lowenstein," she muttered, "but there just isn't room for you in my new bed-and-breakfast." She stood and dusted her hands off on her pants as she moved over to the bookshelf. She hauled another armload of books down and carted them back to her spot on the floor. "Good lord, Uncle Sal," she said, dropping the load onto the hardwood. "How many paranormal creature handbooks does one man need?" The more important question would be how many paranormal creatures were supposed to actually *exist* in the world? According to Dr. Lowenstein, at least four volumes worth.

Autumn sat back down and started to flip through the new stack. At this rate, it would be the turn of the century before she finished sorting through all of her uncle's belongings.

Sal Jasper had been a world-renowned historian, as well as a much-adored professor at Oxford. Unfortunately, Autumn's crazy uncle had also had a bit of a preoccupation with mythology and lore. And he'd apparently thought he was Indiana Jones. So when Autumn had gotten the call a month ago at four in the morning that her only living relative had been eaten by a hippo out in the middle of the African wilderness, she'd been upset, but not all that surprised. Uncle Sal had been her guardian from age thirteen up. During her teenage years alone, he'd almost been killed at least a dozen times. It was amazing to her that he had lasted as long as he had. And if he had to go, at least gored and eaten by a hippo was memorable. That was how Uncle Sal had always wanted to leave the world. "Dramatic and memorable" was what he'd always said.

Uncle Sal had been living in Ireland at the time of his death, and being how Autumn was his only family, he'd left everything he owned to her. She'd flown in from the States to sort through his things and had instantly fallen in love with his home. It was nothing short of a castle really. Gothic, medieval, historic—definitely Uncle Sal. She'd had no idea what an aspiring restaurant owner was going to do with a castle, but after giving it some thought, she realized she could turn it into a unique bed-and-breakfast. There were definitely enough rooms, and it would make for an awesome tourist attraction.

She had plans to make the whole thing historical, have all the employees dress up in medieval garb, and treat all the guests like ladies and lords.

But before she could do any of that, she had to sort through Uncle Sal's treasure trove of bizarre possessions. She'd already found an entire collection of shrunken heads, some sort of sick stuffed dog-thing that was supposed to be a chupacabra, enough alien paraphernalia to make the CIA suspicious, and so many strange books she didn't know what to do with them all. She'd loved her uncle very much, but going through his things was painful on more than one level.

Autumn threw the book she'd been perusing back into the *to-go* pile and stood up, deciding to leave the books for a while. There were a billion other things she could sort through. The books were giving her a headache. She started toward the far side of the room, intent on removing the two lines of African tribal masks from the wall. They were giving her the creeps.

She passed by her uncle's desk on the way and paused. There was a framed picture of the two of them when he had flown out for her college graduation. She picked it up and studied it, tears gathering in her eyes. Uncle Sal had been the only family she'd had after her parents had died in a car accident. He'd been eccentric and zany, and even a little bit nutty sometimes, but he'd always supported her in everything, and she had loved him tremendously. She felt his absence like a gaping hole in her heart.

With a sigh, she set the picture back down and returned to the task at hand. She removed most of the masks with little trouble, but the second-to-last mask had let loose a cloud of dust that she inhaled as she tried to take down the last one. She sneezed violently, causing her to drop the mask, which crashed down on top of her head and sent her black, square-framed glasses skittering across the floor.

She sneezed three more times, rubbed the spot on her head where the mask had conked her, and went to retrieve her glasses. As she bent to pick them up, she noticed something extremely large lodged into a dark corner of the room. She frowned, shoved her glasses back on, and looked over the discovery.

It had to be somewhere around six feet tall, maybe taller, and it was covered with a large white sheet. Curious, she grabbed the end of the sheet and flipped it over the object. More dust exploded into the air, which caused her to choke and wheeze and stumble back in order to avoid it. She fanned at the cloud, and when the dust finally settled, she sucked in a breath and blinked rapidly.

"Whoa," she murmured.

It was an enormous stone statue of a man, but not just any ordinary man. This guy was so detailed she almost expected him to start moving. He stood proud and powerful, wearing something resembling a loincloth and nothing else. Every inch of his body had been chiseled in muscular perfection, and his face was absolutely breathtaking. The artist must have taken great care with it. It was nearly flawless in its beauty. A strong jaw, full lips, straight nose, high cheekbones. He even had a small cleft in his chin. His hair was carved in intricate, subtle waves that rested at his shoulders, and from his shoulder blades were the two most amazing wings she had ever seen. For a second, she thought maybe he was supposed to be a rendition of some kind of angel, but upon closer inspection, she realized that the wings weren't typical.

Most angel statues tended to have very straightforward feathered wings, like swans. These seemed to span out at a slightly lateral angle, and the feathers were more wispy and intricate. They were graceful and elegant, like feathered flames.

Autumn shook her head, but couldn't bring herself to look away from the mesmerizing statue. The thing that intrigued her the most was the fact that he didn't even have a pedestal to stand on. He'd been created to stand on his own, like a person, two feet firmly on the ground. She wondered how in the world it had lasted this long without falling over. Maybe that's why her uncle had kept it in the corner.

She blew out a long, slow whistle. "Man, aren't you beautiful. Someone must have really loved you to put so much detail into you." She reached her hand out and placed it on the sculpture's forearm, running her fingers along the lines of muscle. She smiled. "Too bad you're made of stone, right?" She giggled, feeling silly in a delightful kind of way. She rolled her eyes and leaned in like she was having a conversation with the statue. "I know, I know. I'm a geek. No need to tell me what I already realize. I didn't stand a chance growing up with Uncle Sal."

Just then, a loud knock sounded from downstairs and made Autumn jump. She let go of the statue and frowned toward the door of the office, wondering who would even know she was there.

Dusting her hands on her pants once again, she strode out of the room, down the long corridor, and descended the stone staircase. She pulled the heavy front door open to reveal a tall, somewhat gangly young man with dark, immaculately placed hair and wire-rimmed glasses.

He flashed her a bright, nervous smile. "Hello!" he greeted cheerfully.

Autumn arched an eyebrow and folded her arms over her chest. "Um, hi."

"You're Autumn Jasper, right?" he queried, his accent very British. "Professor Jasper's niece?"

She frowned and nodded. "Yeah, why? Who are you?"

He grinned again and extended his hand. "I'm Curtis Jenkins. I was your uncle's apprentice. I'm so sorry for your loss. Professor Jasper was a brilliant man."

She shook his hand, but still felt confused. "Apprentice? For what?" The thought of her uncle training anyone in anything at all made her somewhat squeamish. He may have been brilliant, but he'd met his end by a hippo, for crying out loud.

"Oh, well, I was one of his students at Oxford, and we shared a love of mythology and such..." He glanced up at Autumn with a guarded expression, as if he was afraid of revealing too much.

Autumn rolled her eyes. "Oh, you mean you're a paranormal freak, too?"

He let out a breathy laugh and blushed a faint pink. "Yeah, I guess you could say that. Professor Jasper was teaching me about the different kinds of creatures, the legends and the myths and so forth."

She waved her hand. "Right, right. Well, I have about eight gazillion manuals on every paranormal creature known to man in here, as well as a stuffed chupacabra if you want them."

Curtis's smile faded and he stared at Autumn in something close to sorrowful shock. "You're getting rid of Chewy?"

She frowned. "Chewy? You trying to tell me you named the chupacabra? Or did my uncle manage to find out where Wookiees lived?"

Curtis shrugged self-consciously and gave her a shy smile. "It was my idea, actually. And, no, we never did find any Wookiees. I'm sure they exist, though."

Autumn couldn't stop her smile. "I'm sure you'll find them someday. Just use the force." She put her hand up in the *Live Long and Prosper* sign.

Curtis burst out laughing and shook his head. "Wrong alien race. That's from *Star Trek*."

Autumn glanced at her fingers, still poised in the sign, and wrinkled her brow.

"That's from the Vulcans," Curtis continued. "Completely different sci-fi universe."

"Oh." She dropped her hand with a sigh and shrugged.

"Well, that shows how much I know." She shoved her hands in her back pockets and smiled at Curtis. "At any rate, I really do have a ton of stuff I need to move along. I'm planning on turning the castle into a bed-and-breakfast. Can't exactly do that with aliens and goblins hanging around to freak out all the customers. If you want to come in and take a look, I'd be more than happy to let you have most of it."

Curtis's eyes lit up like a little kid at Christmas. "Brilliant! I'd be honored to have some of Professor Jasper's things."

Autumn's heart filled with warmth at Curtis's obvious enthusiasm. At least she knew her uncle's possessions would be going to someone who would love them as much as he had. She stepped away from the door and motioned Curtis inside. "Most of the stuff is up in Uncle Sal's office," she said, heading toward the staircase. She glanced back over her shoulder with a smile. "But I imagine you knew that already."

Curtis nodded as he hurried after her. "Oh yes, Professor Jasper and I spent many nights in there, poring over books and trying to find leads."

She frowned. "Leads?"

"Yes, Professor Jasper had decided he'd had enough with merely doing research about the creatures that are rumored to exist. He wanted to find them for himself. He said he was getting too old to sit cooped up in a room looking at dusty books."

Curtis went quiet, and Autumn turned to face him as they entered the office.

He stuffed his hands into his pockets and hunched his shoulders sadly. "That was what he was doing in Africa. He'd gone on an expedition to find a creature from the local lore. I wanted to go with him, but he said I wasn't ready yet, that it was too dangerous." He chewed on his bottom lip. "Maybe if I'd been there..."

Autumn sighed, and her heart softened at the distraught look on Curtis's face. She put her hand on his shoulder in consolation. "If you'd been there, you would have been the hippo's dessert. What happened to Uncle Sal was a tragedy, but he knew what he was getting into. He was always a daredevil adventurer." She forced a smile even though emotion clogged her throat. "At least he died doing what he loved."

Curtis nodded and sniffed, blinking back tears that had gathered in his eyes. "How come you never followed in his footsteps? He always bragged about how brilliant you are. I imagine you two could have been unstoppable. Probably could have found Wookiees too."

She laughed and shook her head. "My uncle was biased, and unlike him, I do not have a preoccupation with the strange and bizarre things of the world. I have a degree in business. I want to own a restaurant. The only reason I'll ever go to Africa is if there's some kind of rare spice that will make the food I serve more appealing to my customers."

He smiled. "I imagine it was odd for you to grow up in this kind of environment." He swept his arm around to indicate the room full of idiosyncrasies.

She shrugged. "Nah, it was just home, y'know?" She caught Curtis's eye and smiled.

He gave her a boyish, bashful grin and averted his gaze to the ground. "Well, I'm sure Professor Jasper would be honored that you're going to turn his home into something that will help you accomplish your dreams. All he ever talked about was you and how proud he was of you."

Emotion clogged her throat again, and she waved her hand as tears stung her eyes. "All right, Curtis, come on. I've cried enough already. Don't make me start again. Let's get going on some of this stuff."

He snapped to attention and saluted playfully. "Aye, aye, sir!"

Autumn smirked and got down to the business at hand, sorting through the remaining books and things strewn about the office. Curtis was friendly and easygoing, and she was happy for the company. They shared stories about her uncle, and the afternoon passed by much quicker than she had anticipated. After they'd managed to get through the entire bookcase, she stood and stretched out her stiff back with a groan.

She glanced at the empty bookshelf and sighed. "Man, I can't believe we got through that today. Thanks, Curtis. You're a lifesaver."

He gave his shy smile again and shrugged self-consciously. "No problem. I'll start loading some of these things into my car so you can go and have some dinner." He cleared his throat. "Have you been to any of the pubs around here? I could show you, if you wanted to go."

Autumn raised an eyebrow and smirked playfully. "Are you asking me out, Curtis?"

His face turned a bright shade of red, and he looked away. "Oh, uh, no, I was just...I just thought maybe you'd be hungry and..."

She laughed softly at his obvious embarrassment. "Maybe some other time. I'm really tired and think I'm just going to stay in tonight."

He nodded and darted his eyes around the room as if searching for anything to get him away from the current topic of conversation. He pointed over to the pile of tribal masks on the floor. "Hey, can I have a couple of those?"

"Go for it. They give me the willies."

He headed toward the pile and started to gather a few of the masks up in his arms when his gaze strayed to the corner of the room. He sucked in his breath and stood abruptly, dropping the masks to the floor. "Bloody hell!"

Autumn frowned over at him. "What?"

He cleared his throat loudly and stole a sidelong glance over at her. "Oh, uh...I didn't know that Professor Jasper had one of these."

"Oh, that statue?" She went over to him and glanced over at the stone man. "Yeah, it's cool, huh? So much detail."

"Yeah." He worked his bottom lip with his teeth for a few seconds, then cleared his throat again. "I can, uh, take that off of your hands too, if you like."

She scowled furiously. "No way! I actually like this one. You can help me lug it to my room, though. I want to clean it up a little bit."

"Uhh..." His voice wavered and he scratched at the back of his head. "Are you sure? I mean, wouldn't it freak out your customers? He looks almost real and all."

She snorted and gave him a questioning look. His voice had gone up in pitch, and he was sort of screeching like a pubescent teen. "Um, yeah, that's why I like it. And it's not going to freak out my customers if I keep it in my room. Come on, give me a hand. I'll give myself a hernia if I try to cart it down the hall all by myself."

He swallowed audibly and scratched at his head some

more.

Autumn raised an eyebrow at his hesitance. "What's with you? You afraid of stone?" She reached over and knocked on the statue's chest. Curtis winced. "He's not going to bite you. Come on. You take the head, I'll take the feet." She went around to the statue and started to tip it over, giving Curtis no choice but to catch it before it fell. He looked pained as they toted it down the hallway to her bedroom, but she got the feeling it had nothing to do with physical exertion.

They set it upright by the fireplace, and Autumn stood back and brushed off her hands, admiring the statue's beauty even more now that it was out of the dingy corner. She smiled. "There, that wasn't so hard." She shot Curtis a chastising look, but he was still gawking at the statue with a sort of queasy expression. "Are you all right?"

He snapped his gaze to her and wheezed out a breathy laugh. "Yeah, I..." He cleared his throat for probably the hundredth time. "I'm just gonna go. I don't feel so well all of a sudden."

"Oh, okay. Well, did you want to take those books, or..."

"I, uh, I'll come back for the stuff tomorrow, if that's okay. I just want..." He darted out of the room.

Autumn poked her head into the hallway just as he emerged from the office again with one thick book.

"I'm just gonna take this one for now. Is that all right?"

She blinked in bewilderment at him and glanced at the title of the book he had chosen. It was Dr. Lowenstein's Volume Two. "Yeah, okay, you sure you're all right?"

He was so pale that he almost looked gray. He nodded a little too vigorously. "Yeah, I just think I ate something bad or something. Anyway, I'll just see you tomorrow." He waved and all but ran down the staircase.

Autumn watched him in stunned silence. She shook her head at his odd behavior, sighed, and then turned back to the statue with a smile. "All right, mister. Let's get you cleaned up."

Chapter Two

It was probably silly to think that a statue was hot, but he was. She wasn't even going to deny it. For a hunk of stone, he really was the most gorgeous thing she had ever seen. She wondered if he'd come straight out of the sculptor's imagination or if he'd been based on a real person. If the latter was true, Autumn wanted to meet the inspiration.

She continued to run a damp cloth over the intricate lines of the statue to rid it of all traces of dirt and dust. She'd never really had that great of luck with men. She was decently attractive, so she got a lot of attention, but her glasses seemed to make guys think that she was the naughty teacher type or something. She'd go out with men and spend the evening intimidating most of them with her intellect, and then when she wouldn't put out on the first date, she never heard from them again. She didn't know why everything male just seemed to assume that she was easy. Apparently, ninety-five percent of the population didn't think that a woman could be both intelligent *and* pretty.

As she finished the last of the dusting, Autumn leaned back on her haunches to assess her handiwork. She smiled and reached up to brush back several strands of her dark brown hair from where they had escaped her messy ponytail. "You look better already! Much better than me, anyway." She looked down at her khaki cargo pants. There were dirt smudges everywhere, and an equal amount of white dust patches decorating her black shirt. "I need to take a shower," she muttered. She glanced up at the statue and pointed at it. "Don't go anywhere."

She giggled at her own silliness, and a pang shot through her heart as she thought of Uncle Sal. She tried to push the sadness away, but she had been ignoring it ever since she'd gotten the call. It was her way. Take care of business first, worry about emotion later.

The sorrow was persistent now, however, and by the time she was in the shower, her tears surged in a torrent. She washed her hair and tried to go about the task at hand until the grief overwhelmed her and she eased herself to the shower floor and sobbed as the hot water cascaded over her back. She couldn't stand the thought of not having her uncle in the world. He was all she'd had for so long. And even after she'd gone off to college and he had moved overseas to travel and teach, she'd loved him just as much. They had talked at least three times a week, and she had enjoyed his jubilant Skype conversations. He had always made her laugh, had brought lightheartedness to her otherwise serious world. Her uncle had dared to believe in the impossible and the extraordinary. That was a quality hardly anyone had anymore. And no matter how crazy he'd seemed, she'd adored him for his eccentricity and individuality.

Autumn stayed in the shower, crying until the water started to get cold. Finally pulling herself together, she stood, switched it off, and got out. She dried off and wondered about her future now that Uncle Sal was gone. She'd never not pictured him in her life. Now, she had no one. Her world suddenly seemed like a lonely, empty chasm.

She slipped into her pajamas and made herself a cup of tea, then headed back into her bedroom. A blast of cold air assaulted her as she stepped in, and she shivered violently. "Geez," she muttered, setting her mug down and going over to the fireplace. "Drafty old castle." She made quick work out of starting a fire, freezing almost the entire time she was doing it. It was odd. The rest of the castle hadn't seemed this cold, but then again, her room did face the sea. There must have been more fog than usual.

Once the fire was blazing hot and the chill started to disappear from the room, Autumn grabbed her tea again and pulled an antique chair over to the fireplace. Feeling exhausted, she sighed and took a sip. She made a face because the liquid was ice cold. She frowned down at her cup. "Gimme a break." She rolled her eyes, set her mug on the floor, and pulled her knees up to her chest as she gazed into the fire. Her nose and toes still felt frigid despite the warmth of the flames.

She didn't understand why she felt so lonely now that Uncle Sal was gone. She was independent, was used to doing her own thing and being by herself. She hadn't seen him in person but once a year for the last five, but she'd always known he was there. Just a phone call or e-mail away. Now, nothing. No more Skype. Just a bunch of useless possessions and a castle made of stone.

She shook her head and looked away as tears threatened to come again. She turned her attention back to the statue. "What am I complaining about? You're made of granite or something. You have to be lonelier than I am..." Her eyebrows drew together in curiosity. He looked different. The color of the stone was not as gray as before, but more of a white with a bluish tint...like ice. She blinked at it in contemplation for a couple seconds before two thoughts went through her mind. One was that she must have cleaned him a lot better than she'd given herself credit for. The other was that she really needed to go to sleep.

Leaving her cold cup of tea where it was, she stood, went over to her bed, climbed beneath the covers, and pulled them up around the bottom part of her face. If she could have moved her entire bed over to the fireplace, she would have. She felt like she was in freaking Antarctica.

After several minutes of shivering, warmth finally began to seep back into her tired body. Within seconds, she was asleep.

She was hot. So deliciously hot. Waves of warmth cascaded over her skin in sensual ripples, making her writhe in fantastic torment. She tossed her head restlessly on her pillow, her mind filling with a hundred wanton images. Blindly, she clutched at her shirt. It was stifling her. She tugged on the collar, then gasped as a trail of erotic fire ran from her neck all the way down to her stomach. It felt like the lightest touch of fingers, but so much more sinful, exploratory, curious...*hot*.

She tossed her head again and frowned as consciousness pulled her out of her bizarre dream. She blinked away the remnants of sleep and opened her eyes to find herself staring at the most amazing face she had ever seen. Full lips, strong jaw, cleft chin, and eyes that burned blue like the hottest part of a flame.

She screamed bloody murder.

The intruder backed away from her, but she screamed again, panic causing her adrenaline to take charge. She scooted up toward the headboard and swung her fist on reflex. It made contact with his eye, which sent him tumbling backward off her bed. Scrambling for any kind of protection, she snatched up the only thing on her nightstand that looked formidable, which happened to be a carved, downsized rendition of a Native American totem pole. She grasped it tightly in her fist and held it up, ready to swing away if he came anywhere near her. "Who are you?" she shouted at the top of her lungs. "What are you doing here?" She got up on her knees, preparing herself in case he tried to attack.

He was sitting in a heap on the floor, cradling the eye she had belted, and he glanced up at her with a pained, bewildered expression. She drew in a breath that was so far past a gasp that she wheezed. The hand clutching the totem pole started to shake uncontrollably at the sight that met her eyes.

His entire body looked like it was glowing, and his wavy, shoulder-length hair was made up of variations of red and orange. Crimson, amber, and gold were all interspersed, like he'd had some really expensive highlights put in. But all of that could be overlooked. It was the two large red-orange wings flaming out from his shoulders that really did her in. They didn't look like feathers. They looked like fire.

She let out a wavering whimper and instinctively glanced to where her statue had been. It was no longer there. She screamed again for good measure, and her heart started to pound even harder.

He winced. "Where am I?" he murmured.

"Where are *you*?" she bellowed. "Where am *I*? The freaking *Twilight Zone*?" She brandished her totem pole even higher, gripping it with both hands like a baseball bat.

His amber-colored eyebrows drew together in a frown. "The *Twilight Zone*? I am unfamiliar with that realm."

Her eyelids spasmed, and she shook her head. "You're unfamiliar with that *realm*?"

He frowned harder and glanced around the room. "Please, who are you?"

"Who am I? Who are *you*?" she screamed, and it seemed like repeating everything he said was the only thing she was capable of doing at the moment. That and gripping her wooden weapon like her life depended on it.

He flinched again at the volume of her voice. "I'm Gabriel," he said, his voice never rising above a soft, velvety tone.

Her eyes widened, and she stared at him for a moment. "Like the angel?" she squeaked.

He looked up at her. "What? I'm not an angel. I'm an Elemental." He cast another confused glance around the room. "Tell me, am I in Algoria?"

"Al-whatthewho? No, you're in Ireland!" She was still fairly yelling the information at him.

"Ire-what?"

"Ire*land*. You know, Europe! Planet Earth!" She shook the totem pole at him.

He looked so confused that she thought she might have to smack him, but then a slow look of realization crossed his flawless features, followed by one of horror. "I'm in the human realm?" he whispered.

"Yes! The human realm."

He held his hand up as if doing so might ease the force of her volume. "Why are you screaming at me?"

"Because six hours ago, you were a work of art! What are you doing here?"

"I don't know," he stated emphatically.

"But you're not human?" She lowered her totem pole just slightly, clutching it to her chest instead of brandishing it at him. He wasn't making any threatening moves toward her, but she wasn't going to take any chances.

"I'm an Elemental," he repeated. "I'm made up of the four elements. Fire, wind, water, earth. My body is human because humans are made up of all the components of earth."

She pointed at him. "But you look like fire."

He nodded. "It is my element of choice, but I can change if I wish. Please, I'm sorry that I frightened you."

He met her eyes and she stared at him for a good long time. He looked disoriented, lost, and confused. It made her heart reach out to him, even when her mind refused to wrap itself around this situation in any kind of logical way. After several moments of her brain and heart wrestling with one another, Autumn just decided it would be best to accept the situation and try to deal with it. She couldn't deny that he was there, however unreal it may have seemed, and years of living with Uncle Sal had taught her to embrace the unexpected and bizarre.

Slowly, she lowered her totem pole, and her heart began to slow its pace. She let out a shaky breath and pushed herself off the bed, approaching him tentatively. "Your name is Gabriel?"

He nodded as she came to sit cross-legged in front of him.

"How did you get here, Gabriel?"

He shook his head, which sent tendrils of his multicolored hair falling roguishly around his face. "I don't know." He met her gaze with a desperation that stabbed at her heart. "When I was a youth, war ravaged my homeland. My people were scattered to the four winds. I was separated from them. For many years, I traveled the realm, but I could never find my people. Then, one day, I started to get cold, unbearably cold, until the only way I could handle it was to sleep. That's the last thing I remember, until I awoke here...with you."

She stared at him, at a loss for what to say. She finally settled for the only thing that came to mind, which also happened to be completely stupid. "I'm sorry I decked you in the eye."

One corner of his mouth lifted in a sexy, lopsided smile, and his eyes filled with a measure of warmth. "I've suffered worse."

She twisted her fingers in uncertainty as the silence stretched out between them. "Uh...well, are you hungry? You want something to eat or drink?" Being a hostess was a good choice. Nice and safe. Still stupid, though.

His eyebrows drew together and he pursed his lips in an expression that looked crossed between confusion and pain. "I...ache," he stated.

"You ache? Like...like a stomachache? A headache?"

His frown deepened and he glanced up at her. "No. Here." He put his hand on his chest, over his heart.

She drew in a soft breath and stared at him, her heart

breaking at his mournful expression. "You're sad?"

He gave a slight nod. "And empty...alone."

His words stabbed at her, for she remembered what she had said to him before she'd gone to sleep. "You're lonely?" she queried softly.

He nodded again, then shook his head in frustration. "I'm sorry. Forgive my foolish words. My mind is clouded."

She gave him a gentle smile. "No, it's okay. I understand. This must be just as weird for you as it is for me. Besides, lord only knows how long you were...well, stone."

He said nothing more, just sat there, hunched, looking lost and isolated, nothing like the proud, commanding statue he had been—she could hardly believe he had *actually* been stone.

Go with it, Autumn. Just go with it.

Autumn let her gaze rake over his fantastic physique, all hard lines and sculpted angles. Instinct had her reaching out to touch him, but she hesitated. She was curious, wanted to see if his glowing skin was hot like it looked, but that was very forward, and the man was not a science experiment. He didn't need to be poked and prodded because he was foreign to her.

Gabriel's gaze slid up to hers and he glanced at where her hand was poised in midair. He slowly lifted his own and mimicked her position, facing his palm toward her. He gave her a look that was as uncertain as she was sure hers was. It brought a small smile to her lips. Maybe he was just as curious about her.

She extended her hand forward until her palm lightly touched his. That delicious warmth from her dream coursed along her skin and down her arm, making her suck her breath in and pull away.

"I'm sorry, am I too hot? Did I burn you?"

He both looked and sounded extremely concerned, and she giggled at his choice of words. Too hot was an understatement. She shook her head and placed her palm back on his. "No, you just surprised me."

"I frighten you."

He still sounded so sad, and it made a lump rise in her throat. She shook her head and met his eyes. "No, Gabriel, you don't frighten me. You're just...different. I'm not sure what you are, and I have no idea what to do with you. But you're not alone."

He regarded her with his burning, baleful eyes.

"I'll figure this out," she declared with more conviction than she actually felt. "I promise." What was she going to do? She had no idea, but she couldn't just kick him out of her home and let him wander around the European countryside. He'd scare the living crap out of everyone, and then the government would think he was an alien and do tests on him.

She shook her head and squeezed her eyes shut for a second, wishing with everything in her that Uncle Sal was still alive. He would know what to do.

"You ache, too."

His voice was warm, soothing, and gentle. It chased away the wave of grief she was feeling with a wave of something else entirely. She looked back up at him and forced a smile. "I'm all right," she said, lying.

He kept his palm to hers and stared into her eyes for one intense moment. "You're not alone either."

Tears stung her eyes and she fought a shiver. He was, by far, the most beautiful creature she had ever seen. Maybe he didn't make sense. Maybe he freaked her out on the highest level. Maybe he went against all the rational laws of her universe. It didn't matter. None of it mattered. At that moment, he was a companion. And he was just as lonely, if not more so, than her.

"I'm Autumn."

His captivating mouth curved in a smile that lit up his face and made his eyes sparkle. He dipped his head slightly. "It is my privilege and extreme honor to meet you, Autumn."

Tingles worked throughout her body, and she turned her attention back to where their hands still touched. Slowly, she twined her fingers with his, unable to stop herself, and he responded in like kind. Warmth spread up her arm, and he closed his eyes in something close to rapture. If it was possible, Autumn almost felt a sizzling current run between them, seductive and electric. It made her shiver despite the warmth of his touch, and closing her eyes, she tried to will her heart to beat normally.

A sudden, extreme, and howling wind sounded outside, rattling the glass in the windows. Autumn opened her eyes and frowned, then jumped as a flash of lightning illuminated the darkness. She glanced back at Gabriel, who yanked his hand away and turned his full attention to the window. He sat up straight, alert and focused.

She opened her mouth to ask him what was wrong, but tremendous pounding on the front door made her already frayed nerves spasm. She put her hand to her chest as her heart made a somersault, and she rolled her eyes. "Good grief. Who could that be at this hour?" She pushed herself into a standing position and looked at Gabriel, who still had his attention on the window. "I'll be right back. Stay here."

She ran downstairs because the pounding was insistent. She pulled the heavy door open and let out a squeak of surprise as torrential rain barraged the countryside, sending cold, wet sprays of water her direction. She blinked in bewilderment to see Curtis standing there, completely drenched and looking really irritated.

"You cared for him, didn't you?" he shouted over the gale force of the storm.

She frowned and tried to retreat farther into the castle to get away from the cold. "What? Who? Curtis, what are you doing here? It's the middle of the night!"

He shoved his way inside and pushed the door closed, then turned to her with a flabbergasted expression. "The statue! You woke him up, didn't you?"

She gasped and her eyes widened. "You *knew* about him? You know what he is?"

He ran his fingers through his drenched hair a couple of times and shook the excess water off of his coat sleeves. "He's an Elemental," he cried. "Nice and safe while in statue mode, but completely dangerous for our world while he's moving and breathing. We have to get him out of here."

He started for the staircase, but Autumn grabbed a hold of his arm. "Hold on, wait a second! Where are you going to take him? How did he even get here?"

Curtis shook his head. "I don't know. I had no idea Professor Jasper even had one, and I have no clue as to where he could have acquired one, but he can't stay in the human realm, Autumn. Look at the weather!" He stabbed his finger back toward the door. As if on cue, thunder rumbled ominously.

"You mean Gabriel is causing the storm?"

He snorted. "Oh, so it's Gabriel, is it? Yes, *Gabriel* is causing the storm. It's as if you took a compass and went into the middle of, let's say, New York City. There's so much magnetic activity that all the compass does is spin around. It's the same with him being here. He's made up of the elements. He can control them. They react to him. Our world does not support the kind of creature who can do that. Therefore, his abilities are making our entire weather system completely wonky. If he stays here long enough, we'll have typhoons in the Sahara and ice storms in the Bahamas!"

He tried to stride away, but Autumn caught his arm again. "Well, what are you going to do, Curtis? Do you know how to get him home?"

He stared at her for a moment before his eyebrows drew together. "Well, no, not exactly. But I was hoping that I could have some time to figure out what to do with him before you went and brought him to life. Elementals thrive on companionship. When they are alone and isolated, they turn to stone. It's like a kind of hibernation. I was trying to take him from you earlier to prevent something like this from happening."

She sucked in a horrified breath and stared at him, aghast. "So, you were just going to stick him all alone in a corner like my uncle did? He's a living creature!"

"He was unconscious! He wouldn't have known any better!" He reached up and tangled his fingers in his hair with a groan. "Seriously, Autumn, this is really bad. We have to get him out of here."

"And do *what* with him? Curtis!" She barreled after him as he started up her staircase. She grasped on to his sleeve, but he shook her off. "Curtis! Just hold on a second. Stop freaking out."

He continued to ignore her protests and flung the door to her room open. Autumn screamed and stumbled back as an enormous fireball shot through the doorway. Curtis shielded his face with his sleeve and avoided the flames, but no sooner had he stood back up than a spear was swung full force at his head. He managed to duck to evade it, and Autumn ran into the room, shoving herself in between Curtis, who was now hunched in a ball on the floor, and Gabriel, who had apparently remembered how to fight while she'd been gone. He stood like a warrior, clutching the spear tightly in his hand, poised to throw it. His face was grim, determined, and every muscle in his body seemed coiled tight and ready for action.

"Whoa!" Autumn screeched, holding out both of her hands. "Whoa! Just stop! Everybody *stop*!" She put her hand to her chest, panting as her heart hammered. She turned her shocked gaze to Gabriel. "What are you *doing*?"

His eyes never left Curtis, who had managed to uncurl himself enough to stand in more of a crouch, and his face barely belied any emotion. "You sounded distressed."

She stared at him in bewilderment for a second before she huffed and stood tall. "I'm not distressed, I'm *pissed off!*" She grasped hold of the spear handle and yanked it out of Gabriel's hands. "Gimme the spear!" She spun and pointed it at Curtis, who was advancing again. "Back off!" He stumbled backward a few steps, and Autumn turned to point it back at Gabriel, shooting him a warning glower. He held up both of his hands in a sign of peace. His glowing skin now looked as if he had flames dancing across the surface.

Autumn flung down the spear and it hit the floor with a clamor. "What is *wrong* with you people?" Curtis started to wheeze, and she looked over at him. He placed one hand on his chest and braced the other on his knee as he bent over and tried to catch his breath. When that didn't work, he reached into his back pocket and pulled out an inhaler.

Autumn rolled her eyes. "Oh, for crying out loud. Curtis, here." She grasped his arm and led him over to the edge of her bed, where she shoved him down to sit. "Calm down."

She let out a long, slow breath and turned back to Gabriel. What kind of chaos had she fallen into? She'd gone to sleep in cold silence and had awakened to complete bedlam. "Gabriel, this is Curtis. He's not going to do anything to you."

Gabriel scowled and folded his arms across his chest. "I wasn't worried about myself. I was trying to protect you."

Autumn stared at him, stunned, while her heart did something funny.

Curtis sniggered. "Oh, how sweet," he grumbled, and took another puff of his inhaler.

Autumn ignored Curtis and went over to Gabriel. She placed her hand on his forearm, and he instantly uncrossed his arms so that he could take her hand in both of his. He stared down at her, his smoldering eyes holding a thousand unspoken things. She closed her eyes for a moment as the warmth enveloped her once again, and she marveled over the fact that his skin flamed but did not burn. When she met his gaze again, his eyes had grown warm, tender.

"Gabriel, you don't need to protect me from Curtis. He's my friend. He was very close with my uncle, the one who somehow managed to bring you here."

Gabriel shook his head slightly. "I am not safe for your world," he said softly.

Curtis snorted. "Well, at least you recognize that."

Autumn shot a sinister look back at Curtis. "Shut up," she snapped. "I thought you were supposed to like supernatural creatures."

His eyes widened. "I *do*. But I generally like them in their own environment! Not posing as Armageddon for our world!" He stabbed his finger at Gabriel. "You see? That's what I'm talking about."

Autumn turned her attention to Gabriel and noticed that the flames licking along his skin were now larger and burning brighter. Outside, violent lightning split the sky. She took one of Gabriel's hands and rubbed it soothingly between both of hers. "You have to calm down," she said gently. She looked at Curtis over her shoulder. "That'll work, right?" Like she freaking knew what she was doing.

He sat with a disgruntled expression. "It'll help."

She smiled in spite of herself and glanced up at Gabriel. "I have to go talk to him for a second. Can you refrain from trying to spear anyone while I'm gone? And no fireballs, avalanches, or earthquakes either."

His dark expression vanished as a smile lit up his face. The fire slowly receded back to its warm glow, and he nodded. She grinned and patted his shoulder reassuringly, then hauled Curtis up by the front of his shirt and dragged him out of the room.

She shut the door, turned to face him in the hall, and folded her arms. "Stellar move, Einstein," she muttered.

Curtis huffed. "He's the one who tried to kill me!"

She held her hands out to try to calm him. "Listen, all right, so this situation is weird, and insane, but we're stuck with it now, so let's start thinking like rational adults. We have no way to get him home because we don't know how he got here, correct?" He nodded dismally. "All right, then, what would my uncle do?"

Curtis met her eyes and heaved a sigh. "Well, he had him here, so he had to have known about him. And he had to have gotten him from somewhere. Maybe he had something written in his notes?"

Autumn nodded. "All right, that's a start. Do you know where my uncle kept his notes? His journals? Stuff like that?" She hadn't yet come across anything like that in her sorting.

He nodded. "Yeah, they're hidden in a secret compartment in his desk. I'll go rifle through them and see what I can find." He turned wearily and headed down the hall.

"Curtis." She jaunted after him and he turned to face her. She frowned in contemplation. "What should I do with him in the meantime? He said his head was cloudy."

Curtis rolled his eyes. "Well, sure, I would imagine. He's been basically in a coma for who knows how long." He sighed again in a defeated kind of way. "Just give him some food...and some clothes."

She nodded and started to head back down the hall.

"Autumn?"

She glanced back at him.

His shoulders moved in another rather large sigh of surrender. "And stay with him. Elementals thrive on companionship, and he...seems to like you."

Autumn tried not to smile at the note of irritation in Curtis's voice, but she couldn't help it. She nodded.

"If you need anything, I'll be in here, slaving away." He waved his hand airily.

She grinned. "Can I get you anything?"

He snorted. "An Irish coffee. Heavy on the Irish, if you know what I mean."

She giggled and turned back down the hall. She ran her hand through her messy hair as she headed toward the kitchen and tried to wrap her mind around everything that had happened. Thunder clapped outside in a deafening cacophony, and she jumped a little, her nerves just about shot. Maybe she would have an Irish coffee too.

Heavy on the Irish.

Chapter Three

When Autumn finally made her way back into her bedroom, several things were in order. She was much calmer, considering she'd had time to think while she'd sifted through her uncle's clothing in search of something suitable for Gabriel to wear, and she'd made him some of the teriyaki chicken and rice that was left over from the night before. She'd also taken a brief moment for herself in the bathroom, brushing her teeth and combing out her hair so she looked slightly more presentable. It was bad enough that she was wearing a pair of beat-up, faded pajamas with sheep all over them. She didn't need to make her sexiness score go down even further with her bedhead and dragon breath.

She padded softly up the staircase and pushed her door open. Gabriel was sitting in front of the fire, cross-legged, staring into the flames. He glanced up at her and smiled broadly.

His grin was contagious, and she winked at him playfully. "I brought you clothes and food," she declared. "You can decide which you want first." She set both the pile of clothing and the plate down in front of him on the floor.

He picked up the clothing and stood. "I believe I will dress first," he said. "I feel ridiculous in this thing."

You shouldn't, she thought to herself, but she was grateful she had managed to censor that before it came flying out of her mouth. She cleared her throat, embarrassed by her own bold attraction. "Yeah, what's with the loincloth anyway? Do all your people dress like that?"

An impish smile crossed his features, and he shook his head. "No, I was robbed, actually. While I slept, if you can imagine."

She arched an eyebrow. "Are you serious?"

He nodded. "That is one of my last memories." He looked up at her and met her gaze with mischief reflected in his eyes. "I was lucky, and so were you. I usually sleep naked."

Her cheeks burned, and she was thankful for the dark of the room.

"I'd been hunting that night and was exhausted. I don't wear much when I hunt because my body serves as good camouflage when I choose earth as my element. I wore only this while hunting and just left it on when I slept. When I awoke the next morning, vagabonds had taken all of my things. Shortly after that was when I fell into my deep sleep."

She rolled her eyes and folded her arms. "Geez, that sucks." She chewed on her bottom lip in contemplation, then took a step forward. "Hey, before you change. You said you could choose which element you represent in your appearance?"

He nodded.

"Can you show me?" She was hopelessly curious, and she'd just keep wondering about it if she didn't ask.

He grinned and set the pile of clothing down on the chair. He came to stand before her and held his arms out to the sides. "Fire."

"Obviously."

He chuckled, and before her eyes, the glowing of his skin began to diminish to a whitish frosty sheen. His hair turned from red hues to light blue, dark blue, and white, and his eyes turned a deep turquoise color. His wings, likewise, turned cobalt blue. "Water."

She stared at him in awe, for he was just as striking in a different way.

The colors began to change again until his skin was dark tan and his hair was brown, green, and green-yellow. His wings turned a mottled brown and green, and his eyes became an intense pine color. He looked primal and wild. "Earth."

She stared in fascination as he shifted once again. The browns melted away and everything turned white. His hair, his wings, his eyes. Even his skin became pale, almost translucent. "Air."

Her gaze roamed over him, and a small sigh escaped her

lips. He really did look like an angel in this form, but the white eyes were highly unnerving. She nodded. "I think I like fire best too, but earth was kinda cool."

His soft laugh was rich and warm and, slowly, the familiar orange and red coloring returned. He looked through the pile of clothing before selecting an item and untying his loincloth in one smooth, unabashed motion. Autumn's eyes bulged and she spun back to the fire to give him privacy, even though he didn't seem to need any, and to give herself the chance to tame the wild flush that assaulted her face.

"Autumn?"

Her name on his lips, spoken in his sultry voice, made her shiver. She glanced back tentatively.

"I need some help with this."

At least he had his pants on now. A pair of her uncle's re-laxed-fit jeans. She was glad Uncle Sal had been fit and decently in shape. Otherwise, there would have been absolutely nothing for Gabriel to wear, and he would have had to continue running around like a caveman. Autumn didn't think she would have been able to handle that, especially given his apparent lack of modesty.

He held up the gray, long-sleeved shirt she had chosen and gave her a questioning glance.

"It's a shirt," she stated.

His expression turned bland. "I know what it is, but how do you suggest I put it on?" He gestured to his wings.

She shook her head. "Oh! I hadn't even considered that." She frowned in thought for a moment. "What does your clothing back home look like?"

"They usually lace up in the back, with two openings for my wings."

She blew out a breath. "Well, that isn't going to work. I'm far from a seamstress. Here, let's try this." She went to her nightstand and grabbed a pair of scissors from the drawer. "All right, pull it over your head. I'll see if I can slash you some wing openings."

He looked skeptical but did it anyway. The material bunched up above his wings, which made it impossible for him to pull it down. He tugged it over his head, but the rest of the fabric gathered around his chest, right underneath his armpits, which caused him to not be able to lower his arms all the way. He narrowed his eyes at Autumn, and his lips drew into an unamused line.

Autumn burst out laughing, unable to help herself. He looked completely pitiful. She shook her head and started forward with the scissors. "All right, just hold on a second," she giggled.

"I'm glad you find this situation so hilarious," he grumbled as she tried to find the best place in the material to cut a hole. "You know, I was a warrior when I was back home. I was fearsome and powerful. I learned different styles of combat from the different peoples I encountered in my travels. I could conquer both beast and man. Now I find myself bested by a scrap of material and a woman with a mean fist."

Autumn laughed again as she carefully tore open a hole for his right wing. "Well, if it's any consolation, you almost murdered Curtis. And I'm pretty sure he had to go change his pants after he left, so that's something."

His rich chuckle rumbled through him once again and reminded her of the thunder outside. "I am sorry about your friend. I was very disoriented. All I knew was that you had helped me, were kind to me, and I did not want you hurt. You sounded upset. I only desired to protect you."

Her stomach flipped at his soft words, and she shook her head as she cut open a hole for the left wing. "It's all right. I know it must have been really confusing for you. Are you feeling better?"

"Yes, much. I remember myself again. My past, where I have been, what I know. And my ability to think and speak clearly came back to me, which makes things much easier."

She smiled softly and set the scissors down on the end of the bed. "Okay, let's see if this works. Hold still." She stretched the material down to try to position the holes over where his wings were, but she came to realize why his clothing had laced up the back. His wings were large and fanned out to the sides. How was she supposed to pull them through? The shirt would only stretch so far. Biting her bottom lip, she attempted to pull one side out to capture the right wing. The material protested, so she tried to maneuver the wing in a way that would help her get it through.

"Ow!" He recoiled. "That is attached, you know."

She grimaced and rubbed her hand across his shoulder in consolation. "I'm sorry. This is...difficult." She grasped the material once again and yanked with gusto, which caused him to lose his balance and stumble. The material ripped free from her hand, and she fell on her butt, stunned.

Gabriel turned to look at her with an expression that said very clearly, *Gimme a break!* The right side of the shirt had been torn all the way down, and it hung in two limp shards of cloth. The other side was still bunched up underneath his arm. Autumn started to laugh heartily, and she shook her head. "All right, this isn't going to work."

"No," he agreed, sharing in her laughter. He pulled the useless piece of fabric back off and flung it into the chair.

She pushed herself up and snatched his plate of food off the floor. "Here, eat this before it gets cold. You're just going to have to go shirtless until I can figure out how to modify some clothing for you."

He took the plate with a smile and lowered his head to press a tender kiss to her jaw. "Thank you for your kindness," he whispered.

Autumn closed her eyes, feeling dizzy, and hot prickles broke out all over her skin. Her stomach clenched at the unexpected contact and she leaned into him, the desire to be closer to his warmth almost overwhelming. She felt bereft when he pulled back.

He smiled at her and seated himself back in front of the fire, digging into his plate of food with enthusiasm. He'd eaten everything in a matter of minutes, and Autumn raised her eyebrows. "Did you want something else?" she queried. She imagined he probably was pretty ravenous.

He gave her a thoughtful frown. "Do you have any honey wine?"

She blinked. "Honey wine? Like mead? Uh, no, I can't say I have that on hand."

Disappointment crossed his features. "I remember I rather enjoyed that."

"All I have to drink is soda, water, beer, tequila, and whiskey."

He shook his head. "It's all right. You have done more than enough for me already. Please, come sit." He patted the floor next to him. "Talk with me."

She obeyed, anxious to be near him again and share some of the wonderful warmth he emanated.

"Tell me of humans," he said. "I have heard of you, have met a couple in my travels, but have never been to your world before. Crossing over into your realm is forbidden to my people."

She frowned. "But not to all the people in your world?"

He shook his head. "No, there are others who will sometimes travel between the two realms. And at times, humans have ventured into Algoria as well. Some prefer it to their own world. But, as you can see, it is dangerous for an Elemental to be here."

Autumn couldn't believe what she was hearing. So, Uncle Sal hadn't been insane after all. There really were paranormal creatures wandering around in the shadows. A thought struck her suddenly and she had to ask. "So, are vampires real, then?"

"Of course," he stated matter-of-factly.

Her eyebrows shot up. "And shapeshifters?"

"Yes."

"Unicorns? Dragons? Wookiees?"

"Yes, yes, and what is a Wookiee?"

She blew out a breath of relief. Well, at least Chewbacca was still fictional. "That's so bizarre."

He grinned down at her. "Why? Because those kinds of things do not exist to humans?"

She snorted. "No, definitely not. We're raised to think that things like that are imaginary. Probably because most humans don't have the ability to process the idea that anything exists other than themselves. Humans are self-centered creatures, and they like to fool themselves into thinking they are the superior race."

"You say they when you speak of humans. But you are human."

She shrugged. "I am, but I don't like to lump myself into the same narrow-minded category. My uncle was obsessed with the things that are from your world. He taught me to believe in the impossible and to respect all creatures, even the ones I thought didn't exist." She smiled as a memory of Uncle Sal's laughing face flashed through her mind. "I'm thankful for that."

He chuckled. "So am I. Otherwise you might have done much worse than punch me in the eye."

She laughed aloud, and doing so made her feel light and free for the first time in over a month. She shook her head with a sigh. "Man, he would have loved to see you, Gabriel. He would have been asking you all sorts of questions, I'm sure."

"None of which I have the answers to, apparently. What happened to this uncle of yours? If you don't mind my asking." His voice was kind and warm, not invasive, just curious.

She toyed with her fingers in her lap, her throat constricting as it always did when she let herself think of her uncle's death. "He was killed," she murmured. "A month ago. He was on an expedition, and there was an accident. I am his only family. I came here to go through his belongings."

He was quiet for a while before he said, "I'm very sorry."

A chill went through her due to the seriousness of the conversation, and she leaned closer to him. "At least it was me who found you, Gabriel. Otherwise, you might be stuck in an antique store or an art gallery somewhere."

"I am extremely grateful," he said, his voice full of soft sincerity.

"Do you remember anything about your people at all? Do you know why you turned to stone?"

He shook his head with a frown. "I was just a boy when the war happened. A tribe of wolf shapeshifters had a dispute with the Elementals, and they attacked. I was separated before I could learn many things about my own people."

"How many years did you wander?"

"Fifteen, at least, before the unbearable cold happened. I was seven and twenty when I fell into my deep sleep. I do wonder what caused the strange transformation you speak of, and I wonder how long I remained in that state."

"You've been a statue for five hundred years."

Curtis's voice came suddenly. Autumn glanced over to the door as Curtis, carrying a thick leather file folder stuffed full of papers, let himself in. He looked bedraggled and exhausted.

Gabriel stood. "How long did you say?"

"Five hundred years," Curtis repeated.

Autumn's eyes widened, and she stood as well. "Five

hundred?" she squeaked. She glanced at Gabriel, who looked kind of ill. She reached out to touch his arm in reassurance.

Curtis sighed. "And you turned to stone because you were lonely, Gabriel. Elementals can't be isolated for an extended period of time, or else they turn into statues." He turned to face Autumn. "Apparently, Professor Jasper did tons of research on Elementals." He waved the leather folder. "And he acquired Gabriel here from some kind of weird black-market trader who came from Algoria."

Autumn blinked in bewilderment. "Wait, the trader was from Gabriel's world?"

Curtis nodded. "There is a portal that allows humans access into Algoria and people from Algoria into our world. But it changes location constantly due to the planet's rotation. It's like a moon cycle, or the seasons. It moves while we do. Somehow, Professor Jasper found this trader from Algoria and managed to get his hands on Gabriel. He was keeping him safe in his office until he found out where the portal was. He knew Gabriel couldn't exist in our world without causing chaos, so he was going to transport him back to Algoria and wake him up there, hoping that Gabriel could then show him all of the fantastic creatures in his world that he'd always wanted to see. It's all in here. There's even a chart showing the course the portal travels on."

"Five hundred years..." Gabriel whispered. He took a step away and turned, wandering back over to the fireplace. "I've been a statue for five hundred years. My family...my people. I don't even know where to find them, if they even exist. Everyone who would have known me is...gone." His coloring gradually changed from fire back to the somber blue of water, and he hung his head.

Autumn and Curtis exchanged a concerned glance, and she crossed back over to Gabriel. "If my uncle knew the course the portal traveled on, there is a way to get Gabriel back home, right?" she queried, reaching out to take Gabriel's hands in hers. She looked up into his eyes, now full of sorrow, and her heart twisted.

"Yes, and as luck would have it, the portal is going to be right outside of the castle tomorrow."

She stared at him. "*This* castle?"

Curtis nodded. "Down on the cliffs. I think that may have

been the major reason as to why Professor Jasper moved to this place from London. According to his notes, he acquired Gabriel a year ago. He figured out the track the portal followed, and this was the closest available spot. His plan was to use the portal tomorrow."

"So, then we can send Gabriel home tomorrow." A stabbing ache shot through her heart at the thought of sending him away, but he didn't belong in her world. He was dangerous to the humans, and she knew that the humans were dangerous for him. She couldn't keep him caged up in the castle. He needed to be back in his own world, with his own people. Besides, she had no claim on him.

Sadly, she ran her thumbs across the backs of his hands. He responded by tightening his fingers around hers.

"It...isn't really all that simple," Curtis said.

Autumn frowned at him. "What do you mean?"

"As I said before, Elementals thrive on companionship. Gabriel came to life because you cared for him. You pulled him out of the corner, dusted him off. We can't send him back through the portal by himself. He hasn't been awake long enough. It's like charging a battery. He needs constant companionship for at least two days before he can even exist by himself. The loneliness that caused him to turn to stone was extremely intense. It doesn't just vanish. If we send him back through by himself and he gets lost before he finds civilization, he's done for. Even if he does find civilization, that doesn't necessarily matter. He needs a companion, not a bunch of random strangers."

"Gone..." Gabriel continued to whisper. "All of them."

Autumn looked up at him and drew in a sharp breath. He hunched his shoulders and put one hand over his heart as if he was feeling tremendous pain. His face contorted in grief, and she shivered as a wave of icy air blew off him. His skin began to turn that same shade of white that it had been before Autumn had gone to sleep.

"That's not good," Curtis remarked.

She glanced at him, saw the genuine worry in his eyes, and turned her attention full force to Gabriel. She placed her hands on his chest, which was ice cold. "Gabriel," she said softly. "Look at me."

He did so, and she almost recoiled at the sadness reflected in his eyes.

She ignored how cold his skin was and reached up to take his face in her hands. "Listen to me, I know you're in shock, and I know you're sad, but you aren't alone, remember?" She brushed back a fallen lock of his blue hair. "I'm here. And you told me I wasn't alone either, so you can't go back to that place where you felt nothing. I know you want to, but you can't. You need to stay with me, Gabriel. I don't have the luxury of turning into a statue to avoid my grief so if you disappear, I'll be all alone with it. At least if we stay together, we can be there for one another."

He stared into her eyes for several breaths, obviously fighting with his own emotions.

She forced a smile and gently rubbed her palm over his heart. "We'll find your people. I-I'll go with you." She swallowed, and her heart skipped a beat. What was she talking about? Was she insane? She was going to voluntarily go through some sort of portal to another world where vampires, shapeshifters, dragons, and unicorns existed? She shot a frantic expression over at Curtis.

"We'll both go," he volunteered, taking a step forward. "I would be an idiot if I didn't take this opportunity."

Relief flooded Autumn at the thought of Curtis going along to be their guide. He had studied with her uncle. He would be the next best person to have along. And she...

She was apparently going to go on the wildest adventure of her life, even larger than any crazy thing her uncle had ever done. For some reason, the thought warmed her heart and made her smile. It seemed like a fitting way to honor Uncle Sal's memory.

Curtis nodded. "All right, if we're going to do this, we need to get some sleep. It's going to be dawn in about two hours, and we need to be at the portal at exactly nine o'clock or we'll miss it. It'll only be open for about thirty seconds."

Autumn rolled her eyes. "Not a lot of time."

"Which is why we need to be prompt. I'm taking the luxury of sleeping in the guest room if that's all right."

She nodded. "Of course. Is there anything we need?"

He broke into a wide grin. "Everything we need would be right here. This place is a mythical world arsenal." He pointed at both of them. "You two need to get some rest also."

Autumn smirked at the way Curtis suddenly seemed to take charge of the situation. No doubt this was like a dream come true for him, no matter how disgruntled he had been in the beginning. "All right, Curtis. Let me see that folder, though. I'd like to look through it."

He handed it to her and looked at Gabriel. For the first time since meeting him, Curtis smiled at the other man. "Hey, don't worry about it, all right, Gabe? Everything will be fine. We'll get you home." He grasped his shoulder in a gesture of friendship before he left the room.

"I don't know where home is," Gabriel said when the door clicked shut. "I don't even know if I have one anymore."

Autumn couldn't stand how dejected he looked. She grasped his hand and pulled him over to the bed. "Here, sit down," she commanded. When he did so, she set the folder down and stood in front of him, placing her hands on his shoulders. "Now, listen to me, Gabriel—"

He looked up at her with a quizzical frown. "Why did you do this?"

She frowned. "What?"

"Why did you bring me to life? Care for me? What made you do such a thing? You didn't know I was real. You thought I was a statue. Why would I even matter to you at all? I was apparently in that state for five hundred years, and not one person cared the slightest bit. What made you different?"

"Well, I liked you. I thought you…" She cleared her throat and averted her eyes, feeling foolish. "I found you in my uncle's office, and I thought you were beautiful." She stole a glance at him and found him regarding her intently. She sighed and gave a helpless shrug. "All I did was bring you in here and dust you off, Gabriel. It wasn't much, really."

He shook his head and took her hands in his, standing back up so that he loomed over her. His coloring gradually began to change back to fire. "You set me free," he murmured. "Thank you." He pulled her gently into his arms and buried his face against her neck.

Autumn drew in a shaky breath and her arms went around his waist. His breath on her neck caused her skin to flame, and she closed her eyes. She relaxed against him and allowed him to tighten his grip on her ever so slightly. They held one another for several minutes of silence before he finally eased away, pressing the softest of kisses to her forehead. When she looked back up at him, he was smiling again.

"Curtis said we should get some rest," he said, "but I have apparently been asleep for a very long time and have no desire to sleep any more. If I may, can I read that information on my race that he had?"

Autumn nodded. "Of course." She picked up the folder and handed it to him.

"I will look this over while you sleep," he stated, heading for the chair by the fireplace.

"Uh, wait a second," she protested, the words flying out of their own volition. He glanced up at her, and she felt her face flame again. She sighed and decided to just continue with her line of thought. No sense in trying to deny the attraction she so obviously felt. "Curtis said you needed constant companionship right now," she said, trying to reason it out. "I don't exactly know what that entails, but maybe it would be best if you sat next to me on my bed." She pointed toward the queen-sized bed. "It's big enough. You sit and read. I'll lie down and try to sleep. At least we'll be next to one another. I don't need to wake up and find you made of granite again."

A slow, flirtatious, almost wicked grin blossomed across his lips, and he chuckled. "If you insist."

She bit down on her lip and turned toward her bed, wondering if she'd taken leave of every single one of her senses. She scooted under the covers and tried to remember how to breathe normally as he climbed up next to her.

He reached out and smoothed back some of her hair. "Sleep well," he whispered. "I'll be here if you need me."

Her heart somersaulted and she glanced up at him. "Likewise."

His eyes filled with a tender light, and he smiled softly. She curled on her side and heard him begin to turn pages. She enjoyed the feeling of having someone next to her. She'd been on her own for a long time. Contentment at his mere presence washed over her and she sighed.

She was asleep within minutes.

Chapter Four

Gabriel read three-fourths of the notes in the folder Autumn's uncle had kept, and he was thankful for the influx of information. Being a statue for so long had made his memories vague and his thoughts muddled. Her uncle had done an amazing amount of research on Elementals, and reading it had enabled him to get back in touch with his race.

He read for a good two hours before heaving a sigh and resting his head back against the headboard. He gazed at the dying embers in the fireplace and listened to the relentless, howling wind outside. His chest ached with the realization that he had been locked in stone for so long. He wondered if his world had changed, if Algoria was different, if Elementals even existed anymore. He felt so lost and so alone.

He closed his eyes and fought back the overwhelming wave of cold that washed over him. He glanced down at Autumn's sleeping form and sighed. Her dark hair fanned across the pillow, and he marveled over the soft lines of her face. Strong, striking, but feminine. Her eyelashes were long and thick, and her lips were the most tantalizing things he had ever laid eyes on. He had never known a human but had never imagined one to be as kind as she had been in the last few hours. He had invaded her life, frightened the wits out of her, and blown every theory on the world she'd been taught to believe. Still, she accepted him. She cared for him. She wanted to help him. Even amid the peoples he had encountered and could remember, he had never come across someone so selfless and giving.

Very slowly, so as not to wake her, he reached his hand out and traced just the tips of his fingers along her jawline. Her skin was so soft, so delicate. She chased away the gnawing pain in his heart. Her presence thawed the threatening ice. And regardless of what he'd read and what Curtis claimed, he did not believe that it was just because of his need for companionship. He had a difficult time believing he would have the same reaction to Curtis or to someone who was cold and aloof. No, he didn't crave the mere presence of a person. He craved *her* presence, her warmth and blind acceptance of who he was, what he was. And her beautiful smile was arousing on the highest level.

He turned back to the file folder, intent on finishing it before they made the journey through the portal. He couldn't deny that he was somewhat apprehensive about going. He had no idea what to expect. He had been gone for so long.

He opened the folder and skimmed over the notes regarding the portal, the different locations it appeared at, and the different times it would open. He glanced over the time chart and frowned when his eyes fell on the name of the place Autumn had said they were in. Ireland. He looked at the corresponding location and time that the portal was supposed to be open and peered closer at the number. At first glance, it looked like a nine, but the ink had been smudged, and upon closer inspection, he could see it was a seven.

Something Curtis had said echoed in his mind. *"It's going to be dawn in about two hours, and we need to be at the portal at exactly nine o'clock or we'll miss it. It'll only be open for about thirty seconds."*

Gabriel's eyes widened, and he turned his attention to the window, where daylight was beginning to lighten the sky. He turned to Autumn, and though he hated to wake her when she was sleeping so peacefully, he had no choice. "Autumn," he said with a shake. "Autumn, wake up. Curtis read this wrong."

She mumbled something incoherent and rubbed at her eyes. "What?" she grumbled with a frown.

"Curtis. He read this wrong. The portal doesn't open at nine o'clock. It opens at seven."

She fumbled for her glasses on the nightstand and shoved them on, then grasped the paper Gabriel was trying to show her. She blinked several times, then studied the chart. He knew the moment she came to the same realization as him because all the color left her face and her eyes bulged.

"Crap!" She flipped the covers off and tore out of bed, barreling out the door and into the hall.

Gabriel followed after her as she stormed into the room Curtis was in and flicked on a light.

"Curtis!" She shook his shoulder violently. "Wake up! You read the time wrong!"

Curtis rolled over, bleary-eyed and bewildered. "What are you talking about?"

She shoved the paper at him. "The ink is smudged, Curtis! It isn't a nine. It's a seven. The portal is going to open in"—she glanced at the bedside clock—"twenty minutes!"

If it were possible, he got out of bed even faster than Autumn had. "Get your shoes on and hurry up!" he ordered. "And grab a coat or something. I already have all the supplies packed. Get your stuff together and head outside ASAP."

Autumn turned and ran back in the direction she had come, grasping Gabriel's hand as she did so. "Come on, we have to hurry." She shoved her feet into a pair of strange, lace-up shoes and pulled some kind of thick shirt with a hood over the shirt she already had on. "We need to get you a coat and some shoes, Gabriel."

He shook his head. "Don't worry about me. I don't need a coat. I have my own way of staying warm." He flashed her a smile that he hoped was playful and encouraging even though his heart was racing with adrenaline. If they didn't make it to the portal in time, he would be trapped in the human realm. That wasn't ideal for him or for the human race.

"Fine, but you still need shoes. Come on." She hauled him down the hall in a different direction and searched through a closet until she'd managed to locate a pair of men's black boots. He didn't really understand them either because they closed by some sort of strange device on the side, but she apparently knew what she was doing because she fastened them quickly. The device made a *zzz* sound as it closed, and when she had finished, Autumn grasped a hold of his hand again and led them back down the hall.

They met Curtis running toward them, and they all headed down the staircase and out the door of the castle.

They were instantly blasted by a gale force wind that almost knocked them backward and rain that pelted like rocks.

Autumn screamed and stumbled back in shock. Gabriel wrapped his arms around her and pulled her close to his chest, trying the best he could to protect her from the harsh weather.

"Come on," Curtis shouted. "We have to go!" He plunged out into the rain and Gabriel followed, pulling Autumn along with him.

The storm worsened as they neared the cliffs, and the sea crashed angrily below.

"Oh my gosh," Autumn shrieked. "Curtis! Is that a freaking tornado?"

Gabriel glanced up to see a gigantic black funnel cloud making its way across the distant countryside.

"I told you," Curtis cried. "We have to get him out of here!"

They continued to follow Curtis until they reached the very edge of the cliffs.

"There it is," he shouted. "It's already open. Hurry!"

Gabriel saw the strange swirling mass of color through the rain and wind, and he pulled Autumn toward it. She slipped in the mud and went down with a shriek. Curtis shouted her name, but Gabriel pulled her into his arms and lifted his wings. He couldn't risk them not getting through. With three powerful flaps of his wings, they reached the entrance, and he touched back down to the ground. "Go, Autumn!" he commanded.

"Wait!" she cried. "Curtis! Hurry up!" She turned toward him and shielded her eyes against the deluge as he hurried to catch up.

Lightning crashed down from the furious sky, struck right in front of Curtis's path, and knocked him backward.

"Curtis!" Autumn shouted.

She started forward, but Gabriel grabbed hold of her arm. "We have to go through!"

She shook her head. "He could be hurt!"

"Autumn, go!" Curtis shouted. "I'm fine! Go now!"

"Come on!" she urged. "You can make it! Get up! Come on!"

He stood and began running in their direction, but he yanked the pack off his shoulder and grasped the strap. "You have to go! Gabriel, take her through! Now!" He threw the pack with all his force right as Gabriel grabbed a hold of

Autumn's arm and pushed her into the portal.

She screamed, and there was a strange sensation of falling and floating at the same time before they both landed on cold, hard, snowy ground. Autumn pushed herself up and turned to face the direction they had come. "Curtis!" she called, her voice panicked.

The pack came sailing through and skidded to a halt in front of them right before the swirling ball of color disappeared. Autumn gasped and stumbled forward. "No! Oh my gosh! He didn't make it through! How am I going to get home?" She spun to face him, and terror reflected in her eyes. "Gabriel!"

He stepped forward and took her by the shoulders. "Autumn, shhh," he soothed. "It's all right. You'll be fine. I'm here."

"And are you going to be able to get me home again?" she bellowed. She reached up, tangled her fingers in her hair, then looked around at the blowing snow and howling wind that was not that different from the storm they had just left. "Where are we? Oh, this can't be happening. This can't be happening."

Gabriel reached down and grabbed the pack Curtis had thrown through. He opened it up and saw many supplies that would serve them well, as well as the leather folder full of information. He smiled. "Lovely one, look." He showed her the folder. "This has everything you need to get you home again. You are not stuck here."

She stared at the folder, and a look of relief flashed across her face before she glanced up at him in bewilderment. "Wh-what did you just call me?"

He grinned and reached up to tuck back a wild, wet strand of hair. "I believe I called you lovely one." He had to shout to be heard over the wind so the moment was not as tender as he would have liked, but he let his fingers caress down her cheek, relishing the texture of her skin.

She closed her eyes for just a moment before she shook her head, folded her arms across her chest, and turned slowly in a circle. "Where the crap are we?"

"I think these are the Reynauld Mountains. They're treacherous, but I know how to get down. We need to find shelter from this storm first, or I'll get lost and you'll freeze to death."

She faced him with a look of shock. "Comforting!" She frowned for a second and looked as if she was focusing on something behind him before her eyes widened and she screamed.

A horrendous, hideous growl sounded behind Gabriel and he spun just in time to see a gaping mouth full of sharp teeth set in a white, furry, ugly head. He held his arms out in front of him and shot a ball of fire from his palms, illuminating the stark whiteness around them and driving the creature back long enough for Gabriel to grab a hold of Autumn and take to the sky.

It was difficult for him to fly with the wind and the blowing snow, but he managed to find a cave among some craggy cliffs that would serve as adequate shelter until the storm passed over. He took them inside and tried to set Autumn on her feet, but her knees buckled almost instantly and he caught her, easing them both down to the damp ground.

She was shaking, and tears coursed down her cheeks. The sight stabbed his heart and he took her face gently in his hands, removing her glasses and wiping her tears with his thumbs.

"What was that thing?" she asked, rasping.

"That was an abominable snowman," he stated.

She stared at him in horror. "An *abominable snowman*?" she cried. She shook her head violently. "What am I doing here? I can't stay here. Take me home, Gabriel! I have to go back! I don't belong here! I'm freaking freezing to death, and I don't even have any decent clothes! I'm still in my pajamas! I just almost got eaten by a child's nightmare! Get me out of here!"

Her voice bordered on hysteria, and Gabriel pulled her into his arms, rocking her while she sobbed. He summoned enough fire power to emanate comforting heat, and he searched through Curtis's pack with one hand while he held her close with the other. He located a blanket, which he pulled out and wrapped around both of them. "I'll keep you warm," he whispered against her hair. "I'll protect you, Autumn. I promise. Nothing is going to hurt you."

"My uncle was *insane*!"

He smirked to himself and continued to soothe her to the

best of his ability until her overwhelming emotions ran their course. When her sobs had abated into soft sniffles, he gathered her up close to him so that she was curled in his lap, her head resting against his shoulder. "Not all of Algoria is this frightening," he assured her. "After this storm passes, I'll get us out of the mountains. I'll show you the beautiful lush forests and spacious meadows full of wildflowers." He smiled down into her large brown eyes.

She squeezed her eyes shut in a wince. "Just don't let anything eat me, okay?"

He chuckled, squeezed her tight, and pressed a kiss to her forehead. "I won't. You took care of me when I was lost and confused in your world. I will do the same for you. You're in my world now, and everything you have done for me, I will repay one hundredfold."

Her eyes filled with a warm emotion that he could not name but tugged at his heart in a strange manner. It made his gaze stray to her luscious lips, and all he wanted to do was have his fill of them, kiss them until they were swollen and red. A wave of heat he was powerless to stop surged over and out of him, which made Autumn snuggle closer. He closed his eyes and tried to temper the blaze of his blood while he suffered silently.

"Don't let me go," she whispered. "I'm so cold."

He smiled and rested his cheek on top of her head. "I won't," he promised. And he meant it. What troubled him was the fact that he was positive he meant it in more ways than one.

Chapter Five

Autumn had to give Gabriel some serious credit. For a man who'd been a statue for the last five hundred years, he remembered his world remarkably well. The storm had passed over the night, and being exhausted from the events over the last twenty-four hours, Autumn had fallen asleep in Gabriel's arms. His warmth had permeated her, his gentleness soothed her, and the protective hold he'd had on her had chased away her fear of the unknown and terror of almost becoming an abominable snowman's midnight snack.

Gabriel had still been awake when she'd finally stirred. Like a diligent, alert sentinel, he remained stoic and strong. She also noticed that between passing back over into a world that was familiar and having more time to remember how to function as a living, moving creature, some of the poised, proud posture he'd had as a statue had returned to him. His broad shoulders were no longer hunched. His amazing face was no longer riddled with sorrow. He had a quiet strength about him that, if it was possible, made him even sexier than he had been before. Autumn secretly hoped that he didn't get any more desirable. She probably wouldn't be able to handle it if he did. She was having a hard enough time as it was.

He'd led them out of the mountains and down through a green valley that turned into a thick, dense forest. They'd wandered for much of the day while Gabriel told Autumn the things he remembered from his life before the loneliness had claimed him. The different people he'd encountered, the things he'd learned. She, in turn, told him of her life with Uncle Sal and all of the crazy things he had put her through over the years.

When they'd first started traveling, Autumn had been apprehensive and riddled with anxiety over what was so unfamiliar to her. Considering her first five minutes in Algoria had resulted in a blizzard and an abominable snowman attack, she really didn't know what to expect or what kind of strange creatures she was going to have to fend off. But as she followed Gabriel, who seemed so sure of himself, and shared stories and laughter with him, she found her nervousness abating. She started to pay more attention to her surroundings, the amazing, lush plant life and woodland creatures. She felt like she was traveling in some kind of fairy tale.

"Sword fighting was always my favorite," Gabriel said, continuing on a line of conversation they'd been having about combat. "I'm good with a spear also."

Autumn giggled. "Yeah, just ask Curtis."

Gabriel shot her a sly, playful smile over his shoulder before he continued leading them down the winding forest path. "It was never my first choice, though. I like the power of a sword, the way it feels in my hand. It feels strong, if that makes sense."

Autumn smiled as she followed, studying the ripples of muscle across his bare back and shoulders as he moved. "It makes sense. My uncle tried to make me do fencing when I was younger."

He looked back at her again with an arched eyebrow. "Oh?"

She nodded. "Yeah, but I almost put out my instructor's eye and then managed to stab myself in the head. How? Who knows, but it's a good thing I had protective gear on." His chuckle made her laughter surface as another memory came to the fore. "And then once my uncle tried to learn knife and axe throwing from this medieval combat guru. He tried to teach me that too, but I accidentally lobbed a knife straight into the instructor's foot."

Gabriel turned and smirked at her. "That either means you have no aptitude for any kind of self-defense or you really have a hatred for instructors."

She laughed and shook her head. "I was a disaster."

He turned back to the path and continued walking. "Of course, I also enjoy using the elements as my defense."

"As Curtis would also know," she pointed out. She glanced up when she realized he had come to a stop, and her breath caught in her throat. It was nearing twilight, and he was standing at the edge of a cliff. The trees broke, which afforded them a view of a spectacular mountain range. The sun was sinking just behind it, and its rays reached out and touched Gabriel as if caressing him. The sunlight danced across his skin and reflected off the golden, red, and amber hues in his hair and on his wings. It made him look like a glowing, radiant entity of light, and she stepped forward, unable to stop the overwhelming urge she had to touch him.

She'd never seen anything as magnificent as he was. He was power and strength and humble grace. He was a creature of myth and the extraordinary, something she had been taught to believe in but had never really thought existed. He was not of her world, yet she felt more at ease with him than she did with her own race.

"Gabriel." His name left her lips as her fingers touched his warm skin. Both things she did out of blind compulsion. She was not a bold person. She was not forward, but she had to touch him. It was a need she couldn't control even if she'd wanted to.

Her hands splayed across his back, feeling the lines of lithe muscle. She trailed them up in an exploratory caress, reaching her fingers out to lightly touch his wings. They looked as if they would burn, but they were as soft as regular feathers. She smiled, then felt foolish as he turned to face her. Was she out of her mind?

A warm flush crept into her cheeks and she tried to step away, but he captured her hands with his and held them to his chest, restraining her, keeping her pinned to him and his fire. She struggled for words, but found nothing. She glanced up at him to find his intense gaze on hers. It made her face grow even hotter, and she averted her eyes to the ground. Still, he held her hands.

She cleared her throat. "Um, how are you feeling?" she asked lamely. "I mean…"

He positioned one of her palms over the pounding pulse of his heart, and he lowered his forehead to rest against hers. "Alive," he whispered.

She closed her eyes, studied his heartbeat for a long, silent moment, then felt herself slip back into his warmth, back into the place she wanted to remain. It was so calm, so peaceful.

Her arms slid around his neck and she rested her head against his shoulder, enjoying the nearness and the way he cradled her close. She sighed in contentment and briefly wondered how she had managed to live her life in solitude for so long. Even as a teenager, when she'd lived with Uncle Sal, she had kept relatively to herself. She studied. She read. She'd never been extremely social or outgoing. She preferred her quiet time alone.

For some reason, Gabriel's presence made her realize how achingly lonely she had been, but never realized. Perhaps she'd convinced herself that she liked to be alone to avoid the pain of her solitude. She couldn't be sure. All she knew was, now that she'd experienced and enjoyed him, his company, his presence, his touch, she had no idea how she would be able to go back to normal, ordinary life once he returned home. She didn't know if she wanted to. She felt like she'd been asleep her whole life, only to have Gabriel open her eyes to what her existence could be like. A person couldn't return to ignorance after that. She understood a tiny bit of what Uncle Sal's passion had been all about. Who wanted nine to five, seven days a week when you could have new worlds and adventures? Who wanted a bed-and-breakfast when you could have a man made of the elements?

Gabriel combed his fingers through her hair, and she raised her head to look up at him. He smiled down at her and she lost herself in his incredible eyes, hot blue and bottomless. She pressed closer to him, and he lowered his head toward hers. She swore she felt the electric heat sizzle and spark between them. She closed her eyes, waiting, anticipating like a schoolgirl with a crush. Her heart hammered against her ribcage, enough, she was sure, that he felt it too.

"Well, now, I haven't seen an Elemental in this realm for well over four hundred years."

Autumn jolted at the unexpected voice, and Gabriel's arms tightened around her protectively. They both looked over to see an old, cloaked crone appear from the darkness of the trees just beyond. She reminded Autumn of the witch in *Snow White,* and she retreated farther into Gabriel's steady hold.

"You know of Elementals?" Gabriel questioned warily.

The crone let out a shrieking cackle. "Of course I do, young man." She pulled her hood down to reveal frizzy, matted hair of green and white. Her eyes were just as unnerving, one green and one white. "I'm half, you see," she croaked. "My father was one of the wandering people, the vagabonds. So I only ever managed earth and wind." She arched an equally frizzy eyebrow and shuffled closer to Gabriel. "The Elementals left this realm about...oh, four hundred years ago."

"And you're still alive?" Autumn shrieked, unable to stop the outburst.

The old woman turned her critical gaze on her. "I am half Algorian. Algorians live for thousands of years. You are human. What business have you here?"

Gabriel positioned himself in between Autumn and the crone. "She's here with me and none of your concern."

The crone let out another cackle and shook her mane of bizarre hair. "An Elemental and a human...how ironic," she said in a singsong voice. "We always want what is impossible."

Autumn frowned, but Gabriel spoke before she could ask what the woman meant.

"I have been a statue for five hundred years," he said, calm, poised, and firm. "I seek my people. Do you know where they are?"

"Oh yes, I just choose not to live there. I always fancied this realm above the other."

"You say they went to a different realm?"

She nodded. "Were forced to because of the wolves. The Elementals reside in Derynia now."

"Where is that?" Gabriel prodded.

"Beyond the red moon. There is only one doorway, and only two creatures have the ability to transport there. The Elemental chieftain, their leader, or the Great Dragon."

Autumn raised her eyebrows and glanced up at Gabriel. "Did she say dragon?" she squeaked.

"Yes, he is the king of all dragons and has the ability to travel between all realms. He resides on the Isle of Burkayall just south of the trader's village." She gave Gabriel a toothless sneer. "But be warned, young master, you must first best him in combat before he will take you anywhere. He only serves those who can beat him. And he has never lost."

Autumn swallowed hard, and a tremor of apprehension

ran along her spine. "Never?" She gripped Gabriel's upper arm.

The crone shook her head slowly, and a strange, satisfied grin twisted her wrinkled lips. "Many have tried. All have failed. But for you"—she stabbed her finger into Gabriel's chest—"it is the only way to get home again. The chieftain only comes to Algoria once a century, and he was just here fifty years ago. You're more than welcome to wait another fifty, but you might turn to stone again in that amount of time." She waved her hand airily and cackled again as she continued into the trees.

Autumn didn't realize she was digging her fingers into Gabriel's arm until he turned to face her and gently removed her hand, taking it in between both of his. She looked up at him with fear she couldn't conceal. "You have to fight a *dragon*?" she cried.

He smiled softly and pressed his lips to her knuckles. His eyes looked troubled, even though it was more than apparent that he fought to conceal it from her. "Forget the dragon for now," he said. "Let's go find the trader's village she spoke of. Maybe we can find something to eat."

She followed Gabriel as he started through the trees in the direction the woman had come from, but something wasn't setting right in her stomach. It was more than just the fact that, in order for Gabriel to find out anything about himself or his people, he had to fight the king of the freaking dragons. That was bad enough, but something the old crone had said kept ringing through her mind and it made her feel ill.

"An Elemental and a human…how ironic. We always want what is impossible."

Chapter Six

Uncle Sal had taken Autumn to several renaissance faires when she had been a girl, and that's exactly what the traders' village reminded her of. It was nestled among the trees, a gypsylike encampment of tents where musicians played lively tunes in the square and jugglers and fire dancers entertained. Most of the people Autumn saw looked human enough, even though they were probably something altogether different, and the two of them managed to find a clothier's shop. It took a bit of work to find Gabriel adequate garb considering no one had had to provide an Elemental with clothing for four hundred years, but a helpful tailor had managed to do some alterations to a shirt while Autumn found something for herself.

In all reality, she was extremely happy to get out of her sheep pajamas and black hoodie. She looked completely out of place, and they were getting enough stares because Gabriel was such an oddity. She didn't need to make it any worse. She opted for a simple one-piece, medieval-style maroon dress. It probably wasn't the most practical thing, and she knew she should have chosen more masculine clothing for more mobility, but there was something about the village and the atmosphere. She was caught up in the magic of it, and she was caught up in the magic of Gabriel. She didn't want to look like some tomboy wannabe warrior. She wanted to look…well…she wanted to look pretty. It may have been shallow, and it may have been stupid, but it was true all the same. And as long as she was stuck in Algoria, she figured she may as well fit in as best as she could.

She slipped the dress on, combed out her hair to the best of her ability, and left it down instead of putting it back up in the haphazard ponytail it had been in thus far.

Dusk had descended when she left the tent, and several torches had been lit around the village. They cast a warm glow, and the people seemed to be in full revelry. The music was boisterous, and people were dancing and laughing and talking. Autumn smiled and wove her way through the trees, taking it all in. She made her way into a small clearing where fireflies periodically glowed among the trees. It was slightly separate from all of the festivities and she took a deep breath, closing her eyes and letting the peace of the forest steal through her.

"You look beautiful in that."

She spun and drew in a soft breath as her gaze fell on Gabriel. He was dressed in a pair of black pants and a white shirt with brown trim around the V-shaped opening across his chest. It laced up with a black strap. He had on black boots, and at his hip was a sheathed blade of considerable size.

He chuckled as her eyes strayed to the weapon. "I figured I might need this."

He approached her quietly and she looked back up at him, amazed at how such a beautiful man could be even more beautiful in his natural environment. She smiled. "How did they get the shirt to fit?"

He grinned and turned so that she could see where the tailor had slit two openings for his wings, then sliced the shirt up the back and laced it back together in the same fashion as the front.

"You look very dashing." She had said it in good humor, but the way he turned and looked at her robbed her of breath.

"You look radiant," he murmured, taking a step closer. "Like you have always lived in this realm."

She giggled self-consciously and tucked her hair behind her ears in a nervous gesture. She shrugged. "I just wish Uncle Sal could see it. He would be in heaven."

"I'm glad it was you to bring me," he said softly. "Not that I wouldn't have enjoyed meeting your uncle, but...I'm happy it was you."

She held his gaze for several seconds before her heart made an uncomfortable flop and she had to look away. "Poor Curtis probably had a heart attack by now," she said. "He probably thinks we've been killed by something, and no doubt, he is extremely disappointed."

Gabriel chuckled. "He'll live, I'm sure. There will be other adventures for him. This one is ours."

The way he spoke made shivers work along her spine, and she gave a breathy laugh. "Yeah, fighting a dragon! What an adventure! Are you ready for that?"

His flirtatious smile faded and he sobered, his brow creasing just slightly. "I'm not sure I want to do it."

Autumn frowned. "Why not? It's the only way you can get home."

He met her eyes and stared at her for a long moment. "I don't know if I want to go home. I've been gone for five hundred years, Autumn, and I don't remember much from before I was separated from my people. I don't actually have a home. Why should I return to something that I've never really known?"

Narrowing her eyes in thought, she saw and understood his reasoning and his apprehension. Truth be told, she didn't want to see him go back either. Once he returned home, she would have to do the same. What did she have to go back to? An empty castle full of memories that would make her sad? A life of drudgery and isolation? It was one thing to live that life when it was all you knew. But how could she go back now? Now that she knew statues could come to life and worlds existed beyond her own? How could she go back to what she had thought was normal when she had been forced to see the world through Uncle Sal's eyes?

She looked up at Gabriel and sighed. But...

She placed her hand on his chest lightly. "You have to go home, Gabriel," she murmured, the words sticking in her throat. "If you don't, you'll always wonder who you are." Something flashed in the depths of his eyes, which let her know he understood that truth.

It was quiet for a few moments, the only sounds being the distant merrymaking of the village and that of the night birds and insects of the forest. Gabriel turned his attention into the trees, and Autumn studied his profile. His jawline was so strong, so defined. She fought the urge to reach up and run her fingers along it.

Suddenly, he heaved a sigh and turned to face her with a completely wicked grin. She raised her eyebrows and took a step back.

"Would you like to taste honey wine?"

She frowned, and he held up an ale horn that she hadn't even noticed he'd been carrying. She smiled. "Okay."

He stepped closer, making up for the step she'd retreated. "Close your eyes," he whispered.

She gave him a questioning look, and he feathered his fingers across her cheek.

"Don't you trust me?" he teased.

She was sure her expression was completely bland, but she obeyed and closed her eyes. For several heartbeats, she felt nothing, only the cool night air. Then she felt his warm, supple lips press very softly to hers. She gasped in surprise and he used it to his advantage, slipping his tongue in between her parted lips. Erotic sweetness filled her mouth, the taste of the drink he had sipped still clinging to his tongue. Fire raced throughout her, and she went pliant against him, kissing him back with a groan of bliss.

He cradled her face in one hand while he slipped his other arm around her waist, exploring her mouth in the most unhurried, deliberate manner. Autumn's head spun. She'd kissed men many times before, but this was nothing like anything she had ever experienced. This was passion, gentle seduction, and encompassing eroticism all rolled into one.

When he pulled away, she was leaning against his chest, her body pressed full up against his, and she had to keep her eyes closed and concentrate on dragging air into her lungs so she wouldn't pass out. He smoothed her hair with his fingers and pressed soft kisses to her forehead and face.

She sighed in contentment. "I think I like honey wine," she said, finally opening her eyes to look at him.

He chuckled, and his eyes twinkled with merriment. "Well, that's good. I was afraid you might hit me for that one."

She felt her cheeks flush, but she shook her head. "Hardly."

With a playful grin, he handed the ale horn to her. She took it with a bewildered frown, and he held up one finger as he took several steps back. Squatting down and peering at the moss-covered forest floor, he examined the ground. He smiled, then closed his eyes and held his hands out over the earth. His coloring changed to the green and brown tones, and he moved his fingers as if he was scattering seeds.

Autumn watched in enraptured silence as he then changed to the blues of water. He spread his hands in much the same fashion, only this time, tiny droplets of water cascaded from his fingers. In another second, he shifted back to fire, and he spread his hands a third time, producing a warm, gentle glow over the same patch of ground.

He stood, gave her a mischievous smirk, and changed back to earth. He drew his hands in an upward motion, as if he was dangling puppets on a string. Slowly, seedlings began to sprout from the soil and grow. They took shape, grew taller, and he directed them into a complex, weaving pattern that created nothing short of a canopy. Fat, gorgeous red roses budded and bloomed along the twining vines.

Autumn gasped in wonder and stared at his creation in fascination before she turned her attention back to him.

He looked extremely pleased with himself, and he reached above his head to pluck one of the lovely roses. He pulled it down and handed it out to her, his eyes reflecting gentle light.

She reached out to take it in her free hand and gazed up into his eyes. "Gabriel," she breathed, a smile tugging at her lips. "You're extraordinary."

His smile was soft and he morphed into the color of air, then turned in a semicircle while lightly blowing across one of his palms. The vines shivered and rained rose petals down around them until the ground was blanketed.

Autumn stared in silent awe as she watched them fall, graceful, elegant, beautiful. It was more romantic than anything she could have thought up in a fantasy. It was like a fairy tale—with dragons, old crones, and all.

Gabriel's fingers brushing against her cheek brought her attention back to him, and she smiled.

"This is for you," he murmured. "For your kindness, for your care. For all you have done and for all that you are. You're special, Autumn. I knew it from the moment I caught sight of you as you slept. I was so cold when I awoke, cold like I had been before I fell into my slumber. When I looked at you, when I touched you, that terrible, numbing cold abated."

He settled his palm against her throat, his fingers curving

around the column of her neck. She closed her eyes, knowing he must have been able to feel her pounding pulse.

"You brought me back, Autumn. You don't know what that means to me."

She shook her head, feeling foolish and self-conscious. "You didn't even know you were a statue. You had no idea what had happened to you. How could it mean anything to you at all when you had no idea what was going on?"

He took her chin firmly in his hand and forced her to look up at him. "I know that I was cold before I slept, and when I gazed upon you, I wasn't. I know I ached before I slept, and when I gazed upon you, I didn't. I know that you have bestowed more kindness and acceptance upon me in the past couple of days than most anyone else in your situation would, and I know that my heart comes alive within my chest when I am near you, when you touch me, when you smile at me.

"That is not nothing, Autumn. I may not have known what happened to me, but I'm not ignorant. Curtis explained well enough that I understand what you accomplished. You brought me out of a dormant state, breathed life back into me, then kept me from retreating into the cold. You have accomplished amazing things, and you have given me my life back, a chance to find out who I am, where I came from. You traversed a world just to help me. Your generous selflessness amazes me, and your radiant soul captivates me."

He took her face in his hands and feathered his thumbs back and forth over her cheeks. Autumn's heart beat erratically at his tender touch as well as his powerful words. His brow creased suddenly, and he averted his gaze. She frowned in concern and placed her palm against his chest. "Gabriel, what's wrong?"

He shook his head. "Nothing's wrong. I just..." He sighed and met her eyes again. "Autumn, this may seem like a strange request, but I'm only asking you to consider it."

She nodded, wanting him to continue.

"After this dragon business, when I am able to know where I came from, who my people are, would you ever think about...staying with me?" He shook his head. "I know it's wrong of me to ask you to turn your back on your world and your life, and I would gladly return there with you if I was able, but I can't. I am dangerous for your world. But...maybe you could stay with me in mine, if you wish it."

She stared up at him and felt tears burn her eyes. At any other time in her life, she would have balked at the idea he presented. She would have thought it irrational, insane, and completely out of the question. But that was before. Before Uncle Sal had died, and before she'd come to realize there was so much more than her carefully constructed world. Uncle Sal, in his death, had given her the greatest gift he ever could have offered. Because of his untimely accident, Autumn had discovered Gabriel. In discovering Gabriel, she had discovered an entire world she'd thought only existed in her uncle's imagination. Uncle Sal had bequeathed it all to her without even meaning to.

She had nothing now, not really. Now that Uncle Sal was gone, all she had was a useless degree and a trade that could only get her by in a world she felt out of place in. Maybe it made no sense, but she felt more at home in her medieval maroon dress, holding an ale horn and idly talking about fighting dragons with a mythical man, than she ever had back in New York. The thought of remaining with Gabriel was more appealing than thoughts of returning home. In all reality, everything that had been home to her had died along with Uncle Sal. She had nothing left to return to. Nothing that mattered, anyway.

Running her palm up Gabriel's chest, she looked into his eyes and smiled. "Do you know what I wish?"

He frowned in question.

Her smile morphed into a broad grin. "I wish I could have another taste of that honey wine."

He looked surprised for a second before a ravenously beautiful smile split his lips. He grasped the ale horn from her again and tipped it up to take a long drink. Then, he turned to her with a wicked smirk and lowered his lips to hers. She lost herself in the taste of the wine and in him, wrapped her arms around his neck, and pressed against him. Electric fire tingled between them, and she surrendered to the magic of everything that made Gabriel who and what he was. She knew in that moment that she would gladly turn her back on her sad excuse for a life in the real world to live something else at his side. A life that Uncle Sal would definitely have been proud of.

Chapter Seven

Gabriel swallowed hard. An overwhelming stench, originating from the immense cavern in front of him, twisted through the air. An orange-yellow glow pulsated from it, and the growls from within shook the cracked, parched ground he stood on.

"Gabriel." Autumn's voice was strained and fierce, and she gripped his hand with vehemence. "Are you sure you want to do this?"

He closed his eyes and tried to will some kind of calm to return to him. No, of course he didn't want to do this. Fighting a dragon was not on his list of plans, but if he ever wanted to find some answers about his life, and about what he was, he had no choice.

He hated the fear he heard in Autumn's voice. The night before had been exquisite. He had held her while they slept beneath the canopy of roses he had created, basking in the sultry light of the red moon. He had never before felt so content. His meager existence had awarded him few pleasures. Autumn was a treasure he never wanted to relinquish. He wanted to always feel her soft body pressed to his, her warmth against his skin, her lips on his own. He could never have any of those things if he became dinner for the king of the dragons.

"Gabriel?" she persisted.

Steeling his resolve, he drew in a deep breath and squared his shoulders. He was strong, and he was more than capable of handling himself. And if he really wanted to make some kind of lasting future for himself and Autumn, whatever that might entail, he couldn't do it as half a man. He needed to figure out who he was, completely, and in order to do that, he needed to find his people. This was the only course available to him.

He gripped the hilt of his sword tightly in one hand and turned to face Autumn. "Listen to me," he said. "I want you to stay out here where it's safe."

She snorted and gave him a ferocious scowl. "Like hell, Gabriel! I am not going to twiddle my thumbs out here while you fight a freaking dragon!"

He shook his head adamantly. "I won't be able to concentrate if I am worried about your safety. Please, Autumn, stay out here where it is safe. I promise, I'll be fine."

"You can't make that kind of promise! No one has ever beaten him before!"

"He's never had to fight an Elemental. I have advantages others don't." He took her firmly yet gently by the shoulders and stared into her eyes. "I would only be thinking about you if you came in there with me. You have no means of defending yourself." His lips turned up at the corners. "Perhaps if he was one of your instructors, your killer instinct would kick in, but as it stands now, I would be too concerned for you."

She did not look amused, and she folded her arms across her chest. "Nice, Gabriel. Make a joke. I'm laughing so hard."

He couldn't stop his chuckle, and he reached up to cup her cheek in his palm. "Please, lovely one," he said softly. "I need you to listen to me." Worry mirrored in her eyes, and she tugged on her bottom lip with her teeth. His heart twisted at her discomfort, and he took her face in his hands. "Do not fret. It will be all right." He really wished he believed his own words. He wished he could be more convincing, too, because she looked anything but relieved.

"Gabriel," she said, her voice raspy and thick with apprehension. "You told me last night you wanted me to stay with you when all of this was over. You made roses grow out of the ground in a second and swept me away in the intoxicating taste of honey wine. You seduced me with the thought of something so much more than the life I have known. How can I obtain that if you get eaten?" She grasped the fabric of his shirt in her fists. "There has to be a better way than this. There has to be some kind of other option!"

He sighed. "You want to wait around for fifty years for the Elemental chieftain?" Her eyes darkened, and he stroked his thumbs back and forth across her cheeks. "Autumn, you said yourself that I need to know who I am. You were right when you said it, but it's so much more important now. I want to be with you. I want to learn about you and teach you about me. How can I do that if I don't even know about me? How can we ever really know one another?"

Tears hovered on her lashes, and her bottom lip trembled. "I just don't want you to get hurt."

His heart melted and he gathered her in his arms, bringing his lips down on hers with tender passion. She reached her arms around his neck and kissed him hungrily, thrusting her tongue inside his mouth in an aggressive way that tore a groan from his throat and made his blood turn molten. Waves of heat pulsated off him and primal, driving instincts ripped through him, shouting to claim her as his, make her his mate. He didn't fully understand it, as he didn't fully understand himself, but it was all-consuming. Fire blazed through his veins, and he ached to the point that he trembled. It was different from the lonely ache he'd experienced before. This was need. Raw and unadulterated. He needed Autumn in his life. He needed her to survive.

She tangled her fingers in his hair, and he plundered her mouth while he felt each one of the elements that made up his body rage in turn. It was like a volatile tempest, releasing each and every one of his abilities in the most violent way, tearing through him. Infernal heat poured off him in a way that he feared would hurt Autumn, but it seemed to only heighten her passion.

She trailed her fingers down his neck and to his chest, then delved them beneath his shirt and caressed his skin. It was the final straw. He felt like something within him exploded. Flames burst from his wings and formed three columns that whirled around them like tornadoes, creating sinful, decadent, sultry heat that fanned their desire.

Just as quickly as it had happened, the fire was doused by torrential, driving rain that soaked them instantly. Pulling away from Gabriel, Autumn gasped in surprise and looked around in bewilderment. He growled low in his throat and felt empty without her lips fused to his. He needed to touch her, needed to feel her along every inch of him. His pressed his lips to her throat and tilted her head back so that he had free rein of her neck.

The rain abated, and wild wind whipped at their hair and clothing. He nibbled along her jawline, placed searing kisses to her flesh, and nipped at her earlobe before returning his mouth to hers. He felt a strange pulling sensation, like his heart was trying to climb out of his body and give itself over to her. He tightened his arms around her and she fit perfectly against him, melded to him until he felt like they were one person.

Slowly, his uncontrollable, insatiable desire dissipated into a warm glow that caused him to soften his kiss and hold her like the precious gift that she was. The burn of his craving for her simmered just beneath the surface. He had no doubt that, with a little coaxing, it would rage into an inferno once again.

When he finally pulled away, she let out a little sigh and rested her head against his shoulder. "What was that?" she whispered.

He shook his head as he stroked her hair. "I have no idea." He opened his eyes and tried to pull back, but something halted his progress. Bewildered, he glanced down to see that vines, not unlike the ones he had created for her the night before, had sprouted out of the ground and woven themselves up around their legs. They twined all the way up to their waists, binding them, tying them together.

"Whoa," Autumn murmured, discovering the same thing Gabriel had. "What's this all about?" She tried to step back, but the vines held and kept her connected to him.

"Again, I have no idea." This was why he had to fight the dragon. He knew nothing about his own abilities, his own heritage. What if he had hurt Autumn with his out of control display of passion? He never would have been able to live with himself. He *had* to get to his people. He needed to know about his past so that he had the ability to build a future.

Slowly, Gabriel reached down and snapped the vines binding them together. With each one, he felt like his heart was breaking. It was another thing he didn't understand, but deep within him, something told him that what had happened between Autumn and him was extremely important.

When he had freed them, he stepped back and took Autumn's hands in his. "Wait for me out here," he said, reaching up to caress her cheek. "I will return to you."

She looked terrified, and he couldn't deny that he wasn't feeling half as confident as he wanted her to believe he was. He hadn't fought anything in five hundred years. What if being a statue for so long had dulled his reflexes, or damaged his memory?

He shook himself mentally. He couldn't think that way. Failure wasn't an option. He needed to succeed so that he could find his people. He needed to succeed so that he could make a life for himself, without pieces missing. He needed to succeed for the wonderful woman who had set him free.

Pressing a lingering kiss to her forehead, he turned and strode toward the mouth of the cave while gathering his courage and pulling his blade free of its sheath with a resonating ring.

Chapter Eight

Gabriel was enveloped by heat as soon as he set foot inside the cave. It pulsated off the walls, matching in time to the deep, rumbling snores he heard from within. He swallowed hard, gripped his sword tight, and closed his eyes for a moment to tame the rapid thundering of his heart. He drew in a deep, calming breath and thought of Autumn, of the strange and fascinating exchange of passion they had experienced outside. This was for her. This was for them.

Sucking his breath in, he opened his eyes and squared his shoulders, drawing strength from the five-hundred-year-old warrior's heart within him. At one time, he had been a force to be reckoned with. He could be that again. He *would* be that again.

"Dragon!" His voice echoed off the walls around him. "You have a challenger! I am in need of your assistance!"

The rhythmic snoring ceased, and all was unnervingly silent for a long moment. Then, the ground began to shiver, and an enormous red and gold dragon, looking irritable and not amused, loped out of its hiding place. Blowing puffs of smoke out of his nostrils, he snorted in what sounded like disdain and sat down on its haunches. His beady yellow eyes scanned over Gabriel critically.

Gabriel gripped his sword tighter, waiting.

The dragon rolled his eyes and made a groaning noise. "Oh, not another one of *you*," he grumbled. "You are the third challenger in four days. I am getting too old for this. A dragon needs his sleep too, you know."

Gabriel raised his eyebrows in mild surprise.

"What is your name, young man?" the dragon yawned.

"Uh...Gabriel," he replied in bewilderment.

The dragon nodded and picked absently at his teeth with

a hooked talon. "I like to know the names of my victims before I devour them. It makes it, oh, I don't know, so much more personal."

Gabriel frowned and raised his sword in preparation. "If that is so, then I would like to know your name. Since it is you who will be defeated this day."

"Right, right," the dragon muttered, hoisting himself back up on all fours. "Well, tell me, what is your driving motivation to best the king of the dragons? Where are you trying to get to? The Far Shore? The Elven Wood?"

"I need to get to the realm beyond the red moon. It is where my people are."

"The Elementals, yes. I should have known. All right, then. Arm yourself!"

Before Gabriel could even think fast enough to move his weapon, the dragon shot a stream of fire from his nostrils. It engulfed him in a cloud of searing heat, and even though he was immune to the burning effects, it still felt like needles were stinging all over his body. He squeezed his eyes shut, gritted his teeth, and waited for the fiery prison to release him.

It stopped as abruptly as it had started and Gabriel shook his head, opening his eyes to see the dragon grinning at him. "Now, see, if you were a human, you would be burned to a crisp right now. Your sword would be useless." His grin faded and his eyes narrowed. "Don't underestimate me, boy. That was a warning. Rest assured, I have other things that can kill an Elemental just as quickly."

Gabriel didn't wait around to see what the dragon was going to unleash on him next. It was obvious that the conversation was a distraction technique. Realizing his elements were going to be much more beneficial in this battle, he lifted his sword and sent it hurtling hilt over point toward the dragon. The dragon had to dodge the projectile, which gave Gabriel the opportunity to slam his palm down onto the hard cave floor.

The earth shuddered violently, sending dirt and rocks tumbling from overhead. The dragon hissed and took a swipe at Gabriel, but a huge fissure split the ground, rending the cave in two and heading straight for where the dragon stood.

The dragon sidestepped the crevice easily and directed

another plume of fire toward Gabriel, this one hotter than the last. Gabriel held his hands up and shot a stream of ice toward the dragon to combat his flames. The fire melted the ice, and the ice caused the fire to turn to steam. Neither jet hit its intended target. The two elemental paths converged, held the other at bay, and created a massive steaming ball that grew the longer the two of them stood their ground.

Neither one of them backed down. Sweat began to drip down Gabriel's forehead from the strength he was exerting, and his arms ached. He squeezed his eyes shut and concentrated, trying to drive the power of his ice farther to neutralize the effects of the dragon's fire.

The ball of steam exploded and shot upward through the roof of the cave and into the air like a geyser.

Autumn jumped and let out a little shriek as steam erupted from the roof of the cave, sending debris and dirt crashing to the ground. The thunderous roaring from the inside of the cave did nothing to ease her frayed nerves. She stared in horror and tried to block out the image of Gabriel being ripped limb from limb.

How was she supposed to just stand out there and act like everything was fine? This was ridiculous! Gabriel was in danger! Her thoughts traveled back to the hot kisses they had shared right before he'd gone into the cave. Nothing in her life had ever felt as intense as that moment. She felt like he'd staked his claim on her, made her his in some unseen way. It was a strange, surreal feeling, but she also felt more complete than she ever had before. It was almost as if some part of her had been waiting for Gabriel.

Her eyes narrowed, and she squared her shoulders. She refused to lose him to a dragon! Not while she stood idly by!

Trying to ignore the sick churning in her stomach, as well as the horrendous noises coming from the depths of the cave, Autumn charged forward. She had to be able to help somehow, some way. She couldn't just leave Gabriel in there by himself.

Sweat dripped from Gabriel's hair and dampened his shirt. He was tiring quickly from the exertion it was taking just to keep himself alive. There was no chance of launching any kind of attack. The dragon kept striking fast and furious, giving Gabriel the only option to defend himself. If things kept up at this rate, the battle wouldn't last very much longer.

The dragon gave a snort that sounded very much like a laugh as he circled Gabriel slowly. "Did you honestly think you could best me, boy?" he scoffed. "Hundreds of creatures have challenged me. No one has ever succeeded. I am the king of the dragons! Your Elemental abilities hold no sway over me!"

The dragon lunged, and Gabriel jumped and rolled, narrowly escaping his snapping, hungry jaws.

"I will give you credit for valor and skill," the dragon continued. "No one else has ever lasted this long. Usually I'm feasting by now."

He snapped again, and Gabriel jumped out of the way, his chest hurting with his labored breath. There had to be some way he could get an opening, some tactic he could use to attack. He was just a creature. He wasn't invincible, even though he seemed to think that he was.

He scanned the area for his sword, but couldn't seem to find where it had landed. He dodged another lunge by the dragon, but his weariness made his reflexes sluggish. While he evaded, he missed the swiping claw that came from the opposite direction, knocking him to the ground with a powerful force. He landed on his back with a wince, and with his talons, the dragon pinned him in place.

The dragon lowered his snout toward Gabriel, sneering in a vicious kind of triumph. "Almost a shame to eat you," he snarled. "You at least gave me a decent fight."

Gabriel squeezed his eyes shut as the dragon opened its mouth and let out a hideous screech. A vision of Autumn flashed in his mind, and his heart ached with the knowledge that he had failed. He had failed her. He had failed them. The Elemental who had at one time been a warrior had failed to do the one thing that mattered to him. For five hundred years, he had existed in a state of nothingness. His loneliness had been so great that he'd turned to stone. Autumn had changed all of that. How many people had he must have encountered during his sleep? Only Autumn had been able to bring him back. She made him feel so much. He wanted to understand it. He wanted to understand everything about his own abilities that confused him. He wanted so badly to know about himself, to be complete, so that he could give her all of him. Now, he would never get that chance.

"Yield!" someone shouted in a frantic, slightly trembling, yet powerful, voice. "Yield or die, dragon. I will not hesitate to slit your throat."

Gabriel blinked his eyes open in confusion, and his heart stuttered and pounded in his chest as his gaze fell on the most breathtaking thing he had ever seen. Autumn stood with her foot on the back of the dragon's head and Gabriel's sword poised over the creature's neck. Her brown hair fell around her shoulders in wild tangles and her face was fierce, determined. She looked like the strongest warrior maiden, and desire swamped him like an ocean wave.

"Autumn," he murmured, concern for her safety causing his voice to waver slightly. "What are you doing?"

"Saving your life," she shouted. "Let him go. You're beaten. Yield!" She pressed the blade to the dragon's neck and scowled.

The dragon heaved a sigh and rolled his eyes, then glowered down at Gabriel. "You're in luck today, warrior. Even though two against one is hardly fair."

"You serve him now," Autumn continued to holler.

"No, actually I serve *you*, my lady," he drawled. "I know the rules. Now kindly get off me before my neck bends into this position permanently."

"Let Gabriel go," she cried, her voice losing some of its strength and taking on a slight note of hysteria.

"I can't until you get off of me," the dragon muttered. "I am pinned here, in case you haven't noticed."

She glanced at Gabriel, then lifted the blade and scrambled down the great beast. She kept the sword trained on him, but her hand started to shake so badly Gabriel didn't know how she was able to keep hold of it.

As soon as the blade had been removed, the dragon released his hold on Gabriel and sat back on his haunches, placid and bored-looking.

"Autumn!" Gabriel jumped to his feet and went to her.

She glanced up at him, looking mortified. "Gabriel." The power left her voice, and his name came out sounding watery and uncertain. The trembling in her hand migrated to the rest of her body.

Gabriel reached out, removed the sword from her grasp, then pulled her into his arms. "Are you some kind of crazy woman?" he breathed, stroking her hair and caressing her back in an effort to quell her awful shaking.

She buried her face against his shoulder and gripped his shirt in her fists as if she were afraid he might disappear. "I couldn't just let you get killed, Gabriel. I had to do something."

Awestruck at her bravery and touched by her concern for him, he sighed deeply and closed his eyes.

"Pity," the dragon mumbled absently as he set to picking at his teeth again. "I was hungry."

Gabriel looked up at him. "You serve me now, dragon."

He rolled his eyes. "My name is Falconroye, and no, I do not. I serve *her*." He stabbed one of his claws at Autumn. "She is the one who bested me. I only take orders from her." Slowly, he moseyed his way out of the cave and back outside.

Autumn blinked in bewilderment at the creature, then cleared her throat, moved out of Gabriel's arms, and followed him. She put her shoulders back and raised her chin in an effort to look commanding. Gabriel smiled at her undaunted attitude. So many others would have been cowering, or would have run away from all of this long ago. Not Autumn. She stared every challenge right in the face.

"Take us to the realm of Elementals beyond the red moon," she stated.

"I can't."

Gabriel's attention snapped to the dragon.

"What?" Autumn asked. "You have to. I command it!"

"Command away," Falconroye continued, "but humans cannot travel to the realm beyond the red moon. The atmosphere in that realm does not have adequate oxygen for you. Elementals can create their own air. You, however, will suffocate if you try to travel there."

Chapter Nine

A cold, sick dread slammed into Autumn's chest as Falconroye's words echoed through her mind. The old crone's words came back to her also and suddenly made sense. She looked up at Gabriel and tremendous sorrow, unlike anything she had ever experienced before, welled up within her. She reached out and took his hand, caressing her thumb across the back of it.

Gabriel's expression was so pained she almost couldn't handle it. "I won't go," he said. "There is no need for me to go. I will build my life with you here."

Tears filled her eyes, and she shook her head. "You have to go, Gabriel. You need to know about your people, yourself, your abilities! What about the thing that happened right before you came in here to fight the dragon? What was that? You need to know these things."

He shook his head adamantly and took a step toward her. "I can figure it out. I'm sure there are other people here who know about the Elementals. Just like that old woman who was half. I will find them, seek them out. They can answer my questions. It's all right. I don't need to go."

She huffed, and even though his words warmed her heart, she knew she could never allow him to actually do what he was saying. It would be wrong of her to deprive him of his right to know about himself, his past, his family, everything. It would be selfish and cruel. "Gabriel," she whispered, her throat constricting painfully. She reached out to take his other hand. "Listen to me. You have to do this. I will not ask you to turn your back on knowing about your past, knowing about *yourself.* This is something you need to do. I refuse to spend the rest of my life knowing that the sad look buried deep behind your eyes is because of me." He flinched, and she smiled forlornly, reaching up to cup his cheek in her palm. "Yes, I see it. You can't hide it from me."

"But, Autumn, you make me happy. The happiness you offer would completely overwhelm the one tiny spot of sadness."

"But for how long?" she countered. "How many years of eating away at you would it take before you turned to stone again? I won't have it. I can't do that to you. I won't." Somewhere deep within herself, she found a shred of stubborn strength and held on to it, knowing that she was doing the only thing she could. This was right. It was breaking her heart, but it was right.

"Autumn."

The tears threatened again, hovered just on her lashes, but she tried desperately to keep them at bay. At least for just a few more minutes. "Gabriel, you changed my entire life," she said. "You showed me that the world my uncle so desperately wanted to believe in was real. He wasn't an old crazy man. He wasn't a crackpot. His life was not wasted on silly things. That, in itself, is a gift." She shook her head and sniffed, fighting the tears that desperately wanted control. "You also showed me that my life could be more than what I envisioned for myself. I will never forget that. I will never forget *you*." She kissed the backs of both of his hands. "And I will never, for as long as I live, forget the taste of honey wine."

She attempted to smile, but didn't succeed all that well. Letting go of his hands made her feel as if someone was ripping her heart straight out of her chest. Taking a step away from him made the pain excruciating. She forced herself to meet his eyes, sad and confused. It was a look she knew would haunt her forever. "Thank you for everything," she whispered. "You really are so beautiful." She put her hand to her chest and the tears broke free, ripping out of her in a muffled sob.

Gabriel started toward her, but she shook her head and stepped back. She grabbed up the backpack full of supplies and her uncle's journal.

"Falconroye, take me home to the human realm. After you have done that, come back here and take Gabriel to his. Those are your orders."

The dragon nodded and moved to stand next to Autumn. "Climb on and hold on tight. I don't need you falling to your death."

"Autumn." Gabriel reached out to her again. "Please..."

She had never climbed up onto a dragon before. She'd never even climbed onto a horse. But she scrambled up onto Falconroye's back as if her life depended on it. She had to. She couldn't allow Gabriel to touch her or she would lose her nerve. It was almost more than she could bear to leave him, and the depth of that emotion frightened her. She and Gabriel had only known one another for a short time, yet her heart felt so permanently attached. She knew if she let him touch her, hold her, kiss her, she would never be able to let him go.

"Find your people, Gabriel," she said, looking down at him as she tried to get herself situated. "It was why we came here in the first place, remember? To get you home. At least I know I finished what I set out to do."

Biting her bottom lip, she tried to stay strong, tried to sound levelheaded, but felt as if part of her was dying slowly. She studied his eyes and knew she was hurting him, but had no other option. She tried to fix him into her mind so she could remember. Remember how powerful and strong he stood, all fire-colored with his amazing wings. The most extraordinary creature she had ever known. The most incredible man to ever live.

She forced a small smile and reached her hand out to him. She couldn't help herself.

He was at her side in an instant, reaching up to touch her fingers. "Autumn, you don't have to do this," he repeated. "We can figure out a way. I know we can."

She gave a bitter laugh. "Maybe in fifty more years when the Elemental chieftain returns to this realm, I'll come back. By then you should have been able to learn everything you need to know, although I'll probably look a lot like that old crone."

He shook his head. "You will always be beautiful to me. And I would love you then as I love you now."

His words made her chest tighten to the point that she could barely breathe. Her tears spilled over her cheeks silently. "I'm going to pretend you didn't say that," she whispered. "Otherwise, I'll never be able to leave."

His fingers tightened over hers. "In that case, I'll say it

again. I love you, Autumn. From the moment I first saw you. I always will."

She sniffled, not bothering to wipe her tears, and she met his blue eyes. "Know that, no matter where you are, I'll always carry you here." She put her palm over her heart and took one more long look at him. He had made her whole world special. He had given her a fantastic adventure. He had given her his heart. Even though she couldn't keep him, knowing she'd been able to have him at all was better than nothing. She would try to hold on to that. "Goodbye."

He tried to protest, but Falconroye lifted his wings and took to the sky. Autumn's fingers detached from Gabriel's. If it were possible, she'd have sworn she could both feel and hear her heart screaming in pain.

Gabriel was shivering by the time Falconroye returned. The cold had come over him almost as soon as Autumn had disappeared from sight. He tried to rationalize it away, tried to be strong, but it wouldn't subside. His chest felt like a cavern, like Autumn had flown away with his heart. It was worse than the first unbearable cold he'd felt so long ago. Much worse. It didn't make sense to him. Stubbornness was the only thing that kept him from giving in to the slumber his body so desperately sought. He *had* to find his people. They were the only ones who could tell him what was happening to him.

Falconroye landed and surveyed Gabriel with an inquisitive expression. "You seem a bit...blue," he stated.

Gabriel glowered at the creature as he pushed himself into a standing position. "I don't find your humor amusing, dragon," he grumbled. "Did Autumn return home safely?"

"I returned her. She was safe, but not looking much better than you. I imagine if she could change color, she would have been blue also. Get on. I don't have all day."

Gabriel snorted. "And what better things do you have to do? Sit around in your cave and eat challengers?"

"Exactly. I skipped a nice, hearty Elemental lunch because of an impulsive little human woman."

Gabriel smirked in spite of himself as he climbed onto

Falconroye's back. Autumn had saved his life. She had been so brave. An overwhelming wave of cold washed over him, and he clutched at his chest as he shivered. He squeezed his eyes shut and concentrated on staying awake while Falconroye flew. He had to make it to his people. He had to know what was happening.

Autumn barely had enough strength to make it down the dirt road leading up to her uncle's castle. Her legs felt like they were made of lead, and she was shivering uncontrollably. Falconroye had dropped her off about three miles away from her home to avoid being seen by anyone, and walking the distance had been almost impossible. With each step she took, she grew wearier, more exhausted, colder. Her chest ached. She just wanted to sleep. Sleep for about a century.

She climbed the few steps to the front door and rifled around in the backpack until she located a spare set of keys Curtis had packed. With tremendous effort, she managed to unlock and push open the door.

Once inside, she let the backpack drop to the ground, and she leaned against the door, laboring for breath.

"Autumn?" Curtis's voice came from somewhere near the kitchen, and he poked his head around the door frame. His eyes lit up. "Autumn! Oh, thank goodness you're all right!" He flew into the room and grasped her by the shoulders. "What happened? Did you get Gabriel back to his people? How did you get back home? You have to tell me everything."

All she could manage to do was groan and shove him away halfheartedly. "Later. I need to go to sleep. I'm exhausted."

He blinked in confusion and seemed to take in her appearance for the first time. "You look terrible. Your skin is…gray. What happened to you?"

His voice took on a frantic edge, and she pushed at him again, unwilling to tolerate his mothering at the moment. "Please, Curtis, just let me go to sleep. I need to go to sleep." She stumbled her way past him and managed to make it to the staircase, but all she could bring herself to do was stare at it. It may as well have been Mount Everest. Slowly, she sank down to the ground and leaned against the banister.

"Autumn!"

She had heard Curtis and knew he was approaching. She wanted to reassure him, but she couldn't even open her eyes. A vision of Gabriel flashed through her memory, and a pain shot through her heart so profound she wanted to cry. She felt Curtis heft her up into his arms, and she was dimly aware of him talking to her, saying something about a doctor, but she gave in to the beckoning darkness before her mind could even formulate a response.

Chapter Ten

"I think he's coming around. Noble sir? Sir? Can you hear me?"

Gabriel groaned and tried to open his eyes. That simple movement was monumental. The woman sounded so far away. He just wanted to be left in peace.

"Sir?" the woman continued. "You must arise!"

A surge of heat traveled over his body, momentarily dispelling the awful cold to the point where he could take a full breath and open his eyes to his surroundings. He was startled to see somewhere around seven Elementals standing around him, radiating heat in his direction. He imagined that was the reason for his being able to function. They were keeping the cold at bay, keeping him from slipping back into slumber.

He blinked several times to try to gain his bearings, and he pushed himself up on his elbow. "What happened?" he croaked. The last he remembered, he had been flying to the Elemental realm on the back of a dragon.

"You passed out cold," Falconroye's ever-drawling voice answered. "Right as we passed through the portal. Almost fell right off. It was a miracle I got you here in one piece."

Gabriel frowned. "What are you still doing here? You fulfilled your end of the deal."

He moved one of his massive shoulders in what appeared to be a shrug. "Wanted to see if you kicked off. I am still hungry, you know."

The corner of Gabriel's mouth twitched upward because he got the feeling that the dragon, in all his cynical sarcasm, may have actually been concerned for his welfare. Perhaps he had a measure of respect for the couple who had bested him when no one else had ever come close.

"You may dim your fires now," the woman's melodic voice commanded. "He is awake. Our companionship should be enough to keep him thus."

The other Elementals surrounding Gabriel diminished the glow they had been producing, and almost immediately the agonizing cold returned. Gabriel gasped and clutched at his chest while his head swam nauseatingly.

"Quick! More fire!" the woman ordered. She frowned and took Gabriel by the shoulders. "Sir, what is your name? How have you come to be separated from your people?"

"My name is Gabriel," he said, rasping. "I was separated long ago, as a boy, when the wolves attacked."

The woman's eyes widened in surprise. "That...that was over five hundred years ago."

He nodded. "I fell into a slumber. I was a statue for most of that time." As the resonating heat touched him, Gabriel found it easier to breathe, and the terrible ache in his chest subsided. He let out a long, slow breath and looked up at the woman. She was beautiful with long golden hair that sparkled with orange and red. Her eyes seemed wise. "A trader took me to the human realm. I remained there until a woman found me, cared for me..." He grimaced and doubled over in pain at the memory of his beautiful Autumn. The cold washed over him like a glacier.

He gasped as a jet of fire suddenly engulfed him, shocking him back to reality. When it abated, he blinked in bewilderment up at Falconroye. The other Elementals seemed just as surprised that he had interfered.

"Keep it together," he snapped. "You can't find anything out about yourself if you turn into a statue again. And I can't eat rock."

The woman Elemental facing Gabriel turned her attention back to him. "Gabriel, this woman, did...well, did anything happen while you were with her?"

Gabriel frowned. "Quite a bit, actually. My presence caused chaos in the human realm. We almost were eaten by an abominable snowman—"

She shook her head. "No, I mean, did anything happen between you and her? Anything strange?"

His thoughts immediately returned to the bizarre event outside of Falconroye's lair. "Yes," he answered. "I..." He swallowed hard as the pain threatened to consume him when he recalled Autumn's soft lips beneath his, her slender body in his arms.

"Did you fall in love with her?" the woman persisted gently.

He nodded. "And my elements...they went out of control."

The woman drew in a sharp breath. "Did your earth element bind the two of you in a very literal way? Did you feel like you were claiming her as yours?"

He looked up at her and gave a slow nod.

The woman looked distressed. "Gabriel, what you did is something only the ancient Elementals were able to do. Which makes sense, considering you *are* one of the ancients. It is how our people used to choose mates. Over the centuries, we have lost that ability, but it was very binding, very final. You chose her as yours, your heart chose her heart, and she obviously chose you in return. Everything within you, every element you hold control over, claimed her. You are tied together now, unable to be apart for any considerable length of time.

"You see, when an Elemental is alone, isolated, he turns to stone. You know this. It is tenfold when you have chosen a mate. One bound partner cannot exist without the other."

His eyes widened and his heart started to hammer. "Does that mean Autumn is suffering like this also? Autumn will...turn to stone?"

The woman gave him a concerned expression. "Unless you are able to be with her, yes. And..."

"What?" he prodded. "And what?"

The woman drew in a deep breath. "She is human. Her makeup is not like ours. We are equipped to hibernate as statues indefinitely. She is not. If she turns to stone, she will—"

"Die?" Blind, all-consuming panic filled Gabriel. This was his fault! What had he done to his beautiful Autumn? He had killed her with his ignorance! He swung his legs over the side of the bed he was lying on and jumped up. "I have to get to the human realm," he cried to Falconroye. "You have to take me back!"

"I don't take orders from you," he muttered. "You were not the one to beat me."

A terrible, otherworldly growl ripped from Gabriel's throat, and he approached Falconroye boldly. "I will fight you here and now if I have to, you miserable creature. I *have* to get to her. She's going to die!" Fire exploded across his body, leaping in out-of-control flames that he was powerless to stop. It was enough to drive most of the other Elementals back, even though they were immune to the fire.

Falconroye rolled his eyes. "Such drama. No need for the theatrics. I have no wish to see the woman die any more than you do. It would be a shame to waste all that bravery. I'll make an exception to my rule...once." He eased himself up so he was standing. "But you had better find some poor beggar for me to eat when we return. Otherwise, I might change my mind and devour you after all. I get unreasonable and cranky when I don't eat."

"I'll find you a nice fat abominable snowman," Gabriel grumbled. "Just shut up and take me to her."

"Gabriel, wait," the woman Elemental said. She placed her hand on his arm. "I wish greatly that you will return to us. You have much to learn, and we, as well, have much to learn from you. Our race has adapted in many ways since we were forced to leave Algoria. We could be very beneficial to one another."

He smiled softly but shook his head. "I'm sorry, but she cannot travel here, and my place is with her. You are my people, but she is my family. She is my everything."

The woman's smile was genuine and warm. "Perhaps I can make an exception to my station's rule as well."

He frowned.

"To only travel to Algoria once every hundred years. I might decide to make a special trip to visit a very old friend."

For a brief moment, the icy dread in his heart was chased away by a fleeting surge of warmth. "*You* are the Elemental chieftain?"

She nodded. "My name is Liara."

"I was led to believe you were a man."

She grinned and let out a soft, musical laugh. "And apparently your human woman bested the king of the dragons in battle when you could not."

He chuckled. "Point taken, Liara."

"My predecessor was male. Perhaps whoever told you

about me had met him at some point."

He nodded. "Perhaps. Thank you. I hope I will see you again soon."

She dipped her head in a regal nod. "I do as well, noble ancient. Now, fly to your mate while you still can."

Without hesitation, Gabriel climbed up onto Falconroye. The cold gripped at him as soon as they were away from the Elementals' comforting heat, but he steeled himself against it. He had to make it to Autumn. He would not stop, rest, or even close his eyes until she was safe and in his arms.

Chapter Eleven

Gabriel was so close to collapse by the time they reached the human realm that Falconroye landed right outside the castle. He didn't bother with discretion, and Gabriel was thankful. Underneath all the dragon's prickles, Gabriel had an inkling that he might actually care about the situation. Or perhaps he really was starving and just wanted to hurry up and get to his abominable snowman. Either way, Gabriel was grateful for not having to cover any ground to get to the castle. He wasn't sure if he could have anyway. His body was barely cooperating, and it was pure strength of will that he was still coherent and conscious. The cold exhaustion was almost unbearable. All he wanted to do was close his eyes so he no longer had to feel the awful icy pain.

He somehow managed to climb off Falconroye's back and stumble his way up to the door of the castle, where he pounded on it three times. Each raise of his arm felt like he was lifting a thousand pounds. Within seconds, a torrential storm had formed. Lightning split the sky, and ferocious wind whipped at Gabriel's hair, wings, and clothing as he leaned against the doorframe.

The door opened in only a few minutes, and Curtis stared at him in shock. "Gabriel," he murmured. His eyes traveled over him and concern came to life in his eyes. "What are you doing here?"

"Autumn," Gabriel croaked.

The concern in Curtis's eyes morphed into all-out fear. "She's really sick, Gabriel. I don't know what's wrong with her. She won't wake up. I was about two seconds away from taking her to hospital."

Gabriel shook his head and pushed his way, rather feebly, into the room. "Take me to her."

"What's going on?" Curtis asked frantically. "What are you doing back here?" He glanced outside as he started to close the door and his eyes bulged as his mouth fell open. "Oh dear lord," he breathed. "There's a bloody dragon in the front yard."

Falconroye rolled his yellow eyes. "Perceptive friends you have."

Curtis gasped. "He can *talk*?"

Falconroye fixed Curtis with a critical look. "Is that my dinner?"

Gabriel shook his head and slammed the door. "Curtis," he snapped. "Please! I need you to take me Autumn! Now!"

"What happened?" he persisted.

Gabriel ignored his questions and staggered toward the staircase, each step harder than the last. He gripped the banister and stared up at the fifteen or so stairs he had to conquer in order to get to Autumn. They seemed a billion times more daunting than fighting Falconroye had been.

"Gabriel!" Curtis grabbed on to his arm. "Tell me what's going on!"

"She's dying, Curtis," he exclaimed, hoping the man would understand the urgency of the situation. "I'll be happy to explain everything to you later, but I need to get to her *right now*."

Curtis paled and, without further argument, looped his arm around Gabriel's shoulders and lugged him up the stairs. "At first, I thought she was just tired," he said. "Exhausted from the journey, but the longer it goes, the worse she gets. Her skin is gray, and she's so cold. I started a fire and have about a hundred blankets on her bed, but it doesn't seem to be helping any."

Gabriel thought about how the Elementals had used their fire to keep him from turning to stone. He shook his head. "No, you did the right thing, Curtis," he said as they reached her room. "You probably saved her life." He let go of the other man and pulled himself together enough to stand without assistance. He stepped into Autumn's room, which was fairly glowing orange with the blaze of the fire in the hearth. His heart stopped when his gaze fell on her. She did, indeed, look gray, and she was so still it frightened him.

He approached the bed carefully, tentatively, fearful of

finding out he was too late. He drew in a shaky breath and reached out for her tiny hand. "Autumn," he whispered, sinking to sit beside her. Her skin was cold. Her lips were tinged with blue. Tears gathered in his eyes with the knowledge that he had caused this. He had done this to her without even realizing what was happening.

He reached out to brush back a strand of her hair, then trailed his fingers tentatively down her cheek. A tiny bit of the ice retreated from his heart. "Autumn, can you hear me?" She didn't so much as twitch, and he closed his eyes, leaning down to rest his head against her chest. Her breathing was shallow and faint, but her chest still rose and fell.

"I'm so sorry. I didn't know. Please, tell me I'm not too late." He took her hand and pressed soft kisses along the back of it. "Tell me you're still in there." The tears spilled down over his cheeks, but slowly, he felt some of his strength returning. His heart, which had felt desolate, began to beat with more power.

He took the hand he held and placed it over his heart. "Please, lovely one, listen to me. Hear my voice. Come back to me. I promise I'll never leave you again." He closed his eyes and concentrated all his might on making his fragile heartbeat grow stronger. He pressed her palm flatter against his chest. "Do you feel that, beloved? It beats for you. Only you." He kept his mind focused, trained on the sound of his heartbeat. He refused to let negative thoughts in and concentrated only on his love for her. It washed over him like the waves of the ocean, ripping away the cold and bathing him in a warm, tender glow.

He didn't know how long he sat there, but finally, he felt her slender fingers curl into the fabric on his shirt. "Gabriel?"

She sounded tiny, far away, but he heard it and felt it throughout his body. He expelled a breath he hadn't even realized he'd been holding, and his eyes popped open. She was still pale, but no longer ashen, and her lips were more white than blue.

She looked at him in confusion. "Wh-what happened? What are you doing here?"

He gathered her in his arms as his tears flowed freely. He pressed kisses to the top of her head, rocking her as relief chased away the black fear. "I thought I'd lost you," he said.

"I thought I'd killed you."

"Killed? What?" She pushed slightly at his shoulders until he moved back. She looked up at him with a frown. "I don't understand."

"That thing that happened right before I fought the dragon, it was an ancient binding ceremony. I chose you as my mate, Autumn."

She blinked rapidly as obvious bewilderment crossed her features. "Your mate?"

He nodded. "I didn't know what I was doing. It was instinctual. But I bound us together. We can't be without one another now."

"Is that why…why I felt so terrible? I was so cold." Understanding flashed in her eyes and she grasped on to his forearms. "Gabriel, is *that* how you felt right before you turned to stone?"

"It was similar, but this was so much worse."

"So, you mean…I was turning into a statue? Because you weren't with me?"

He nodded. "Only it would have killed you if I hadn't gotten here in time. Your body is not built to handle something like that."

Terror flashed through her eyes, and she pressed closer to him.

He held her tight and closed his eyes, relishing the feel of her against him. "I'm so sorry. I didn't know. Please believe me."

"Of course I do." She wrapped her arms around him and held on. "How did you get back here so fast?" she murmured after a long moment of silence.

"Falconroye. He brought me."

"He did?" She sounded completely surprised.

Gabriel smiled. "He did. And I met the Elemental chieftain. I'm pretty sure she saved my life. Seems like women keep saving my skin in this era." His words drew a giggle from Autumn, which warmed his heart. "She agreed to come to Algoria and teach me about my people, even though she is not supposed to for another fifty years."

Autumn pulled back to look up at him with a curious frown. "She's coming to Algoria? You mean you're not going back to your people?"

He sighed softly and took her face in his hands. "I don't think you understand the situation. I *can't* return there. You cannot breathe in that realm, and I cannot exist in your realm. Neither one of us will survive if we are apart. We have to live in Algoria. It is our only choice." She stared at him for a long moment while she digested the information. Self-loathing slithered through Gabriel, and he looked away. "I'm so sorry to rob your choice from you. I never would have done so knowingly. I understand if you hate me, but I have to take you back with me. I would rather have you hate me than have you die."

"So, let me get this straight," she said slowly. "In order to stay alive, I have to return to Algoria, and live there for the rest of my life as your mate. In other words, your wife."

He gave a dismal nod. "Please forgive me, Autumn. I wish your uncle had never brought me into your life."

She snorted. "Oh, gimme a break, Gabriel."

He blinked and looked at her in surprise.

She rolled her eyes. "Yes, I had so much to look forward to before you. A woman with no family and a dull life running a bed-and-breakfast all by herself, talking to statues and art because she was lonely. Don't be stupid." She ran her palms up his chest to his shoulders, then gazed intently into his eyes. Her color had almost returned to normal. "If whatever you did made it so that I am forced to live by your side for-ever, in a fantastic new world that my dear uncle would have loved to explore, then I think I should be thanking you."

His heart skipped a beat. "Do you mean that? You *want* to live in Algoria with me?"

She smiled. "I want *you*, Gabriel. I don't care where we live. All that matters is that you are with me."

His lips descended to hers with more force than he had intended, and white-hot, fiery passion shot through him and smoldered between them. All traces of the ice-cold pain and emptiness vanished, leaving only aching lust in its wake.

"Whew! All right! That was intense."

Gabriel pulled away and remembered that Curtis had been standing in the doorway the entire time.

Autumn peered over Gabriel's shoulder and grinned. "Curtis! I'm so sorry. I must have scared you to death."

He rolled his eyes. "That's the understatement of the

year. Look, I don't mean to be a bugger and break up the happy couple's makeout fest, but there's a bloody dragon outside the fricking castle, and I really want to know what just happened! So, I need a drink. I'm going to go get me one, and when I come back, you two better explain what all of that was."

Gabriel and Autumn both laughed. Gabriel nodded. "We will, Curtis. I swear."

Autumn giggled again. "Whatever it is you find to drink, just bring the whole bottle."

As Curtis disappeared back out the door, Gabriel returned his attention to Autumn. He smiled softly and cupped her cheek in his palm, feathering his thumb back and forth across her skin. "You know we can't leave him here by himself," he said. "It would be wrong, and he would be so lonely."

She smiled. "You want to bring Curtis to Algoria? Well, that would make his day."

He grinned. "Unless you want him to stay here to keep your uncle's castle for you."

She sighed and shook her head. "This castle is nothing but a bunch of stone without my uncle in it. It's much more fitting that we all end up in the world he wanted so desperately to see." She snuggled back into Gabriel's arms. "Thank you for coming back for me."

He closed his eyes and stroked his hands down her back. "I think I've always needed you to exist, Autumn," he said. "Even before I unknowingly bound us. I was a statue for so long, for centuries. I did not come back to life until you found me."

"You want to know something?" she said quietly. "I may not have been a statue, but I was stone in so many other ways, Gabriel. I was an emotional void. Something was always missing. You brought me to life too. I love you."

He tightened his arms around her, letting the potency of her words sink in and take root in his heart.

"All right, someone made off with all the whiskey," Curtis said as he returned to the room. "Oh right, that was me after I got locked out of the portal." He heaved a sigh that made Gabriel and Autumn laugh again. "Anyway, all I could find was this weird bottle of mead that your uncle had locked away."

"Mead?" Autumn squeaked.

Curtis looked up at her and frowned. "Yeah. You know, honey wine? I hope that's all right with you guys."

Autumn looked up at Gabriel with so many hidden messages in her brown eyes that his blood lit on fire. He knew his grin was one step away from being absolutely demonic. "That's fine," he said, his voice resembling a gravelly purr.

Autumn nodded, fisting his shirt in her hands and tugging playfully. "Honey wine is our favorite."

Touch of Black Velvet
By Brieanna Robertson

Prologue

There were exactly two things I knew about shifters.

One was that they were to be feared. I'd heard countless stories as a child about the shifters and how they were killing machines, nothing more than weapons that bled.

The other thing I knew was that they ruled our city, and no one dared cross them. To those who were loyal, the ones who obeyed, they protected. The ones who rebelled faced an entirely different fate. After all, shifters needed to eat too, right? No one had ever actually seen them eat anyone, but when people disappeared without a trace, others talked.

No one really knew where the shifters had come from. My mother said that they had been some kind of governmental experiment from before the Great War. I don't know if that was true. The shifters had already dominated most of the former United States well before I was born. Mother told me they'd been some kind of universal soldier project gone terribly awry.

I knew nothing of the Great War she spoke of, when all the nations of Earth turned against one another in the worst, most catastrophic and destructive war history had ever seen. All I knew was the anarchy and poverty the war had left behind. Disease, horrible things brought about by biological warfare, ran rampant during the whole of my childhood. My mother was a victim of such a disease. I had never known my father.

Somehow, I was one of the lucky ones to survive that period of tumult. But I say lucky lightly. The ones who survived colonized in the places that had seen the least amount of destruction. I was on my own from age eleven, existing in a filthy city full of filthy people who could never be trusted. It was every man for himself back then. I had no choice but to follow the course that led me to the shifter. I'd never really had an option.

When the shifter first found me, I had been almost dead. Starving, homeless, and so strung out on drugs I could barely function. My junkie boyfriend had beaten me up...again...and had left me on the deserted street of what had at one time been some great metropolis. I was black, blue, and bloody with my clothes torn to shreds. And I was about two seconds away from a complete overdose. It wasn't anything strange. It happened all the time in my world. I was no one special.

I really wasn't even aware of him when he pulled me off the street, and I was only vaguely aware of detoxing in a dingy hotel room while shaking and sweating and puking until I thought I was going to die. All I wanted was a fix. And it was the one thing he refused to give me.

Jack Snow, the man with the eyes of ice, and the touch of black velvet.

Chapter One

The first thing I saw when I managed to pry open my eyes was the silhouette of his body against the light of the window. He had one hand braced against the window frame and the other one on his hip. He was taller than any man I had ever met, and even though I couldn't see anything other than a black outline, I could tell he was strong. Power radiated off him even as he stood there so casually.

I lifted my head from the pillow and grimaced. My whole body felt heavy and stiff. I remembered how my boyfriend had attacked me, and I had bits and pieces of jumbled memories about being toted off the street and forced into being clean. One memory stood out above all the others. A pair of eyes so pale they were almost white, like blue ice.

I scowled and, ignoring the protestations of my sore muscles, forced myself into a sitting position. I ran my hands through my limp hair, which was dirty and matted, and shot a look over at the strange man at the window. "Where the hell am I?" I spat, the crassness of my lifestyle attaching itself to my speech. It was a defense. I was a woman alone with a stranger, and the people who ran in my circle could never be considered friends. I had no idea who this man was or what he planned on doing with me. Acting tough and brash was the only card I had to play.

He turned toward me slowly, every move of his body etched with elegant grace. "You're awake."

It was all he said and I stared at him. I still couldn't see his face, and I was not up to conversing with a shadow. I snorted. "No shit. Now, you wanna tell me where I am and who the hell you are? Or maybe at least let me see your freaking face."

He moved away from the window and came to stand at

the foot end of the bed. My abrasive bravado slipped, and I drew in a soft breath. He was the most stunning man I had ever seen. He was dressed in black jeans and a black muscle shirt that clung to every svelte line of his broad shoulders and toned arms. Sepia hair fell in subtle waves down to his shoulders and around a face made of defined lines and sculpted planes. And his eyes...his eyes were the ones from my convoluted memories. Pale, entrancing, intimidating. I felt as if he was staring straight into my soul.

Stifling a shiver, I pulled my legs to my chest and wrapped my arms around my knees. "Who are you?" I murmured, my voice losing all of its force.

"Jack Snow," he stated simply. His stance was casual and his hands were in his pockets, lending him a lazy, easygoing appearance. I wasn't fooled. I saw the underlying power in his strong body. I felt it like a presence.

"Jack Snow," I repeated, a little bit of edge creeping back into my voice. I arched an eyebrow. "Is that supposed to mean something to me?"

He shrugged. "Probably not."

He left it at that and continued to stand there and stare at me in unnerving silence. Still feeling kind of itchy, I rubbed at my arms absently and frowned, and I didn't like the foreign heaviness in my chest. "Hey, do you have any stuff?" I queried.

His posture changed in the blink of an eye. He straightened and his eyes took on a cold, steely look that made my heartbeat falter in apprehension. "No, I do not have any *stuff*," he practically hissed.

I scooted farther back on the bed until I was against the headboard and stared at him in strange, fascinated horror. He'd barely even moved, but the dormant power he possessed uncoiled to the point that it felt as if he took up the entire room. His presence was almost tangible, and it both intrigued and terrified me.

"How dare you even ask me such a question," he continued with a snarl. "When I found you, you were almost dead because of the poison you'd pumped into your body. I saved your life, and the only thanks I get is the desire to destroy yourself even more with some of the same poison?" He snorted and strode back to the window. "I knew this was a waste of my time."

I stared after him, the heavy, tight feeling in my chest growing to the point of pain. I realized it was fear. Fear and anxiety, feelings I didn't have to deal with when I was high. "Why?" was the only thing that came out of my mouth.

He glanced at me over his shoulder and frowned.

"Why did you save me?" In all reality, it probably would have been better if he'd left me to die. The world would have been rid of one more gutter rat, and I would have finally been at peace.

He sighed. "I don't know. Usually, I don't trouble myself with your kind." He ran a hand through his thick hair, then turned back to me. "What's your name?"

I wanted to fire a rude comment back to him about his "your kind" reference, but I was too afraid of what he might do if I provoked him. "Reya," I answered obediently.

He gave a curt nod. "Reya," he repeated. "Fine. If you wish to know any more about me or my purpose, you have to swear to me that you won't take anymore drugs."

I blinked, taken aback by his abrupt mannerisms. I frowned. "What are you talking about?" I cried. "I'm not going to promise anything to you! I have no idea who you are! I think you should just let me go!"

That cold look came into his eyes again and he fixed me with a dark glower. "I never said you were being kept here against your will," he spat. "You're more than welcome to go anytime you like. By all means, return to your life of squalor. No one's stopping you."

Anger replaced the fear I'd felt up to this point and burned through my veins. "I've had just about enough of you insulting me!" I shouted. "Some people in this life don't have a choice as to what they become and what lives they live."

"*Everyone* has a choice!"

His deep voice reverberated off the walls and I gasped, my anger diminishing back to the former fear. He moved toward me, bending so that he was eye-level. My fingers started to tremble. I'd never seen eyes so wicked. I felt as if he saw everything I was, like I was naked before him with all my secrets and foul deeds exposed. I couldn't hide from him. My armor was useless.

"There is always a choice," he said, his voice lowered into

a soft, menacing purr.

"I-I never saw one. Must have missed that part," I stammered. I sounded feeble and pitiful even as I attempted to come off as a smartass.

His beautiful face remained expressionless and he stood to his full height again and gazed down at me as if assessing my worth. I knew I couldn't be worth much.

"I'm offering you one," he stated.

I frowned in confusion. "I-If you want me to kill someone or something, you can just forget it."

He let out a rough snort of a laugh, the first sign of amusement he'd shown, and when he met my eyes again, a tiny amount of warmth reflected in his gaze. "I highly doubt you would be capable of doing such a task," he said in a slightly playful tone. "Judging by the way you had been beaten when I found you, you don't seem to know how to defend yourself exceptionally well."

I made a *psshh* noise and waved my hand in a weak attempt at humor. "You think I looked bad? You should have seen the other guy."

His gaze softened and one corner of his mouth twitched upward. "Of course." He let his eyes linger on me for a moment before he continued. "At any rate, no, I'm not asking you to kill someone. But I'm afraid I cannot divulge any more information until I know you can be trusted. Therefore, I will be back in exactly one hour." He pulled a plastic bag out of his pants pocket and placed it on the nightstand next to me.

I peered at the white powdery contents, and my eyes widened as I realized it was chock-full of my favorite drug. I snapped my gaze up to him in question and, I admit, excitement.

His icy eyes were back to being menacing. "One hour," he repeated. "If I return and this has not been touched, I will tell you what you want to know. If you fail this, I will return you to your...natural environment and you will never see me again. The choice is yours."

His words hung heavy in the air, and he fixed me with a long, purposeful stare before he turned and swaggered out of the room.

My instincts had me reaching for the bag the instant the door clicked shut. I didn't like feeling fear. I didn't like feeling anxiety and worry. Most of all, I didn't like feeling ashamed and weak. I felt nothing when I was high. It was the only way I could cope. It had been all I'd known since I was a teenager. How could he expect me to just change all that in a second? I didn't even know this man! He pulled me off the street, forced me clean, and then dangled some bizarre choice in front of me that I didn't even understand? What was my motivation to obey? He hadn't given me anything to go on. He could be offering me something awful. At least the life I knew was familiar.

I opened the bag and was about to reach inside when my entire life played out before me in a second. I remembered my mother. Up until her death, she had protected me, had kept me safe from the lowlifes I now called my companions. She'd told me to be strong, to always do what was right. If I did that, I would be safe. I would somehow forge a good life for myself out of the horror that the world had become. She would have been so disappointed to see what I'd allowed myself to turn into. How come I'd never thought of that until now?

I glanced down at the bag again and bit my bottom lip. The temptation was almost unbearable.

Jack Snow. Who was he? Why had he saved me? What was it that he had to share with me that was so important he felt the need to test me before he could divulge any of the information? I wanted to know. I wanted to know who the man with the pale eyes was. I wanted to know why he had thought I was something worth saving.

With an amount of self-control I didn't even know I possessed, I closed up the bag and set it back on the nightstand. I locked my arms around my knees and stared at it, then glanced at the clock. One hour.

I could do it.

Chapter Two

It was the longest hour of my life. Three times I'd opened the bag again, and three times I'd forced it away from myself. I'd smelled it, tried to lick the bag...I'd paced restlessly for a half an hour, then decided I would take a shower. At least that would kill some time.

Realizing I had no clothes to change into, and the ones I had on were destroyed beyond repair, I rifled through the hotel room until I found some of Jack's clothing hanging in the closet. Everything in there was entirely too large for my emaciated body, but I did manage to come across a hotel bath robe that would have to do.

I couldn't even remember the last time I'd had a real shower. The hot water felt incredible and I imagined it washing away all the filth of my life as it spiraled down the drain. Relishing the flowery smell of the shampoo, I took my time washing my hair. I scrubbed my body with the soap, trying to eradicate all traces of the debaucheries of the street. In the back of my mind, I still craved that high. I knew it was waiting for me in the other room. But my intrigue over the man who had forced me into clean status and what he may have to offer stayed my hand.

When I had finished, I dried off and slipped into the robe. I scanned over my reflection in the mirror. My face was gaunt, and I had dark circles under my hazel eyes. The remnants of a purple bruise marred my left cheekbone. Other bruises decorated the rest of my body. I knew I probably could have been attractive if I'd been healthier. What had I allowed myself to become? I felt disgust and loathing for the person I saw in the mirror.

Which immediately made me want to use.

Most of the technology of the past had been lost during

the decimation of the Earth during the Great War, but a few things remained. Military technology had survived, for the most part, even though there no longer was any military. Just renegades and bounty hunters, criminals, thieves, and mob bosses. Those were the people who ruled now. No government, no armed forces, just the men with the most power and the most equipment.

That and the shifters, who were the closest things to soldiers that remained.

Aside from the military technology, other strange devices had survived. Several hundred cars, a few select DVD players and random televisions that would play old movies, as well as strange, small things. Things like hair dryers and electric toothbrushes.

I was grateful for the beat up hair dryer in the hotel. I could at least make myself look somewhat presentable, and it was more time away from me thinking about the tempting bag on the nightstand.

I was astonished at the small transformation just my hair could bring about. Most of the time, my hair was up in a shabby ponytail, or hanging limp and boring. I never took the time to care for it. Who had the money for hair care when any small amount accumulated went to the next fix?

Studying my hair in the mirror, I ran my fingers through it several times. It was shiny despite my poor nutrition, and it fell in soft, delicate strands down to the middle of my back. Several golden highlights reflected the light from the bathroom. I smiled, and felt the first small measure of self-satisfaction I had in over a decade.

It was at that moment that I heard the door open. My heart thundered uncomfortably in my chest, and I left the bathroom in a rush. Jack set several bags down on the table in the corner, then turned to face me with a critical eye. He blinked in obvious surprise as he looked me over, and the expression made me feel a slight bit of pride. I must have looked better than even I realized.

The small moment of bewilderment in his eyes was chased away by sternness as he went over to the nightstand and picked up the bag of drugs.

"I'm not gonna lie. I did touch it," I stated. "Also tried to lick it. So I hope you weren't being literal about that. I didn't take any, though. You can check me." I took several steps toward him.

He threw the bag on the bed, then approached me. He took my chin firmly in his hand and studied my eyes, no doubt to see if my pupils were dilated. He checked my nose, probably to see if there were any telltale signs of residue, and he checked my arms, which made me giggle. He glanced up at me.

"You think I had a needle hiding somewhere in my shredded clothing?" I asked sarcastically. "Or some other kind of paraphernalia?"

The corner of his mouth twitched again and he let my arms drop. He said nothing as he stepped away. He grabbed the bag off the bed and disappeared into the bathroom for a minute. I heard the toilet flush, and some small part of me sighed in relief. At least that temptation was gone now. I folded my arms as he reemerged. "So, did I pass?" I still sounded sarcastic. That habit would probably be harder to eradicate from my being than the drug abuse.

"For now."

I frowned. "For now? What the hell is that supposed to mean?"

"Is that your favorite phrase?" he shot back smoothly as he looked through one of the bags. "'What the hell?' 'Who the hell?' 'Where the hell?'"

I blinked in bewilderment and crossed my arms over my chest before I glowered. "What are you, the moral police? There are a lot worse things I could say."

"This world is already a filthy place," he continued, his voice never rising above a velvety cadence. "I do not desire to make it more so by my speech and actions. If you wish to continue this journey with me, you must adopt the same philosophy. The place I'm taking you has no room for trash."

I knew my expression had to be a cross somewhere between confusion and irritation. "And where exactly are you taking me? What journey? You promised me that if I passed your stupid test, you would give me some information, so out with it before I kick you where it counts and make my escape!"

He pulled a set of clothing out of the bag and set them gently on the end of the bed. They were too small to be for him and I swallowed hard, knowing he had purchased them for me. It was a thoughtful gesture I didn't know what to do with.

"I told you, you're not my captive," he said. "You can leave anytime you wish. All I ask is that, if you do decide to leave, you keep the information I'm offering to yourself."

"What information?" I practically shouted. "You haven't given me any information!"

He turned and faced me in a slow, sinuous movement. "I am a shifter."

I felt the color drain from my face, and I stumbled back a few steps. I only knew two things about shifters, and neither one of them were things I thought were particularly good. My heartbeat stuttered before it began to race. "Wh-What?"

For the first time since meeting him, I saw him smile. It was a genuine smile that split his lips and showed his dazzling, white teeth. Every harsh line of his face softened, and there was one other thing I noticed that both frightened me and enticed me. His canine teeth were two glistening fangs. They were beautiful in the most dangerous way, just as the rest of him was.

He started toward me, and I backed myself straight into the wall, trembling against my will. I would have liked to pretend I was tough and strong, but I had been taught to fear the shifters. They were the most menacing force in my world. My reaction could not be helped.

He reached for my wrists and easily shackled both of them with his large hands. I let out a startled squeak, but he shushed me softly and ran his thumbs along the insides of my wrists in soothing, gentle circles. I let out a shaky breath and looked up into his eyes. Those, too, were much more tender than they had been.

He slid his hands down to capture my fingers and led me over to the bed. He sat me down on the end of it, then knelt before me. "Tell me, what do you think you know about shifters?"

I bit my bottom lip in apprehension. "Th-They…" I cleared my throat. "You were some kind of military experiment."

He nodded his head once. "True. The shifters were, at one time, normal human men. They were elite soldiers. The military was trying to play God, trying to create some kind of super soldier. They tampered with genetics, experimented with animal DNA. The result was the shifters. Men who can change their form into that of an animal. What you don't know is that two different things happened with the soldiers who were tested. Half of them responded favorably and were able to convert their shapes without any adverse effects despite the pain of the shift. They retained their humanity. The other half became extremely aggressive, more animal than man. They were violent and dangerous, operating more on instinct than anything else.

"In both cases, the soldiers were able to reproduce other shifters, and that is how our race was born. Tell me what else you think you know."

I swallowed hard and tried to push some of my fear away. He was explaining it very calmly, was not making any sudden movements, or looking at me as if I would make a tasty dinner. "You are dangerous."

"True. All shifters are dangerous, regardless of which group they fall into. Next."

"You rule the cities."

"True...in a sense. In the case of this city, my people protect it to the best of our ability."

"From?"

"From the others."

I stared at him, but when no more information followed, I arched an eyebrow. "And your people would belong to...which group?"

He flashed his amazing predatory grin again. "Well, I haven't eaten you yet, so which do you think?"

I gasped and my eyes widened in alarm. "So you do eat people?" I shrieked.

His chuckle was rich, warm, and made me feel funny in the pit of my stomach. "I do not. At least...not in *that* way."

The way he grinned at me made my face hot.

He laughed very softly. "The others, however, will eat whatever they can find. They are scavengers. We are protectors. Do you understand?"

I was trying to understand, but having a difficult time. "So, the shifters who dominate this city...they're the good guys?"

"In a manner of speaking. The others tend to stay on the

outskirts, in the No Man's Land. They prey on the travelers, the ones not protected by my kind. You see, even though the others received more of a violent temperament, their strength is not as great as ours. They fear us."

I shook my head. "What does any of this have to do with me?"

He took a deep breath and expelled a long sigh before meeting my eyes with purpose. "All you know of the world is the suffering and the rundown cities, the dog-eat-dog, but there is something more that most are unaware of."

I frowned and leaned toward him instinctively, curious and captivated.

"The Great War destroyed most of the earth, turned the planet into a barren wasteland, but about ten years ago, my people discovered something remarkable. About sixty miles south of here is a stretch of land located amidst some mountains. Somehow, it has remained untouched by the decay of the world. The soil is rich, the water is clean, and the forest surrounding it is thick and green. It's an oasis, Reya, a place that my people have cultivated and turned into a settlement. In the last several years, my people have started to bring humans into this exclusive place. Select humans. Our purpose is to build a civilization out of the rubble that our world has become, but we don't want to do it with the kinds of people you are used to running with. No druggies, no street trash, no traitors, or looters, or murderers, or thieves."

"You're building a utopia," I murmured in awe. I could try to envision the place he described, but it was difficult. I had only ever seen pictures of what the earth had once been. It seemed like a fantasy land to me, what he spoke of. I couldn't comprehend how any part of the corroded planet could still be beautiful.

His eyes twinkled with mirth. "Something like that, I suppose. I prefer to call it a beginning. The beginning of a new era that can change the course of the future if enough people believe in it."

"So…" I frowned at him. "Are you trying to tell me that you selected me for this?"

He dipped his head in a slight nod. "You have perhaps noticed other people disappear before. It is the fodder that fuels the horror stories surrounding the shifters."

I blinked rapidly as my mind started to click things into logical sense. "You mean, the people who vanished, the rebels...the shifters didn't eat them."

He chuckled. "No."

"But they were rebels! They didn't obey!"

"No, they were freethinkers. They were strong. They stood on their own, voiced their own opinions. They had something to fight for. That is what we look for in people. We have no use for cowering sheep. We need people who are strong, who will fight to keep what we have built safe and secure."

"But I'm not strong!" I cried. "I'm pathetic! I've never fought for anything in my life! Why would you pick me?"

His gaze grew serene as his eyes traveled over my face. "Because," he all but whispered, "you deserved a choice." He stood and stared down at me, his demeanor switching from understanding to all business in a split second. "Now, tell me, are you interested in the opportunity I have presented to you? Because, if you are, we have no time to lose. It is two days travel on foot to get to Pax, and the path is a treacherous one."

"Pax?" I questioned. "That is the name of your utopia?"

He nodded. "It is from an ancient language, Latin. It means peace...Pax."

I couldn't stop the shivers that ran down my spine as he spoke the word. He said it with such reverence, as if he loved it above all things. It made me want to believe in his vision, however absurd it seemed to my narrow, limited mind.

I took a quick trip through my life, tried to see if there was anything worth sticking around for. I came up short. The only good thing I'd ever known had been my mother. After her, all I'd known was survival. Giving peace a try might not be such a bad idea. Obviously, I'd have to stay clean, but that thought seemed slightly less unbearable than it had that morning. I'd been a junkie because getting high was the only way I could cope with the world I lived in. It had been an escape. Maybe, deep down, I'd always wanted more. Maybe Jack had seen within me what I had never even realized until now.

One thing was certain. The man had saved my life. And he was offering me a free ticket away from everything filthy I had always known and always loathed. He was offering me what I'd never had before.

A choice.

I would be stupid and completely ungrateful to refuse him. Besides, something about him—the way he moved, the way he spoke—made me want to believe that there was something else out there. Something better. Something worth living for, and fighting for.

I wanted to believe that shifters weren't evil as I'd been told. I wanted to believe the strange fairy tales Jack spoke of.

I wanted to believe in him. For, truly, he was the most amazing thing I'd ever set eyes on. He seemed not of my world, not of my time. He was something so foreign to me, an enigma, a complicated mystery. His icy eyes held depth to them, and I wanted to know what kind of secrets they had seen.

I squared my shoulders and looked up at him. He waited patiently, with his arms folded across his chest. "No drugs," I stated softly. "No trash. I'll even try not to swear."

His full lips quirked.

"Take me to Pax."

Chapter Three

He was trying to kill me. That was the only explanation as to why he had me jogging for miles across arid desert. No Man's Land, the most terrifying and deadly area of where I had grown up. It began five miles out of the city, and it stretched on for many more. It was a haven for bandits, thieves, mercenaries. The trader wagons had to come through it to sell their wares. Therefore, it was a hotspot for criminals looking for some freebies.

I had known that crossing it was going to be difficult, but I had imagined that having a big, bad shifter on my side would be adequate protection. What I hadn't expected was for Jack to hot-foot it like he was just as apprehensive about crossing it as I was. He'd said himself that the aggressive shifters wouldn't bother his kind because they weren't as strong, so what was the deal? I was going to freaking collapse.

As I wheezed and panted, my face dripping sweat and damp strands of my hair hanging in front of my eyes, I stared at him in both amazement and irritation. He didn't even look winded. We had been trotting along for hours in the blazing hot sun, and he didn't even look like he'd broken a sweat. He moved like a methodic warrior, never speeding up and never slowing down.

"What the...hell...are we doing?" I gasped as I stumbled after him. He threw a petulant glance back at me over his shoulder and I held up one hand. "Sorry...the swearing. Right. Just answer the stupid question. I'm going to die."

"No you aren't."

I glowered at the back of his head. "Come on, man! Seriously! What's with the rush?"

"We only need to run while we cross this stretch. Once we reach the caves, we'll be safe."

"And we're not safe if we walk?"

"Walking gives the others more time to pick up our scent. It's best if we hurry. Unless you feel like being dinner for a shifter tonight."

That didn't sound like a very appealing option, no, but at this rate, they'd be feasting on my carcass in a couple minutes anyway. "Look, man, I just almost overdosed and then spent several days ralphing and shaking all kinds. You didn't even give me any breakfast, and I haven't had a decent meal in weeks. You really think I am gonna last much longer? Because, in case you haven't noticed, I'm not an athlete over here, and I'm not in the best condition."

"Just a few more minutes, Reya, I promise." His voice had a snappy bite to it that I did not appreciate.

I tried to suck it up to the best of my ability, but by the time we finally reached the rock formation that housed the caves he was talking about, my legs were cramping up and my chest was on fire. As soon as he slowed down and came to a stop in the shade of an enormous hollowed-out boulder, I collapsed to the ground wheezing and gasping. Two seconds later, I had a lovely bout of the dry heaves.

His hands on my shoulders felt cool on my flaming skin, and I squeezed my eyes shut, continuing to gasp in great breaths of air that still didn't feel like they were filling my lungs.

"Reya, here, drink this."

His voice was almost as soothing as his touch and he pressed something to my mouth. I realized it was a canteen, and I grabbed it and gulped the contents so greedily that I made myself choke. He yanked the canteen back out of my hands, and I heard the sound of water splattering on the ground before a cool cloth was placed around my neck. It almost instantaneously eased my breathing.

"I'm sorry about pushing you so hard," he said in a tranquil voice. "There was no other alternative. It would have been extremely dangerous to take too much time crossing the No Man's Land."

"And...we'll be...safe here?" I panted.

He pulled the cloth from my neck, tipped my chin up, and smoothed the cloth over my face. "No place out here is completely safe, but the others don't tend to wander this far. It's too far away from the travelers and the merchants. Here, look at me."

I obeyed, and his eyes captivated me almost instantly. I blinked as I realized that the cloth he had doused in water was actually his shirt. My heart almost stopped at the sheer exquisite perfection that was his bare upper body.

He returned the shirt to my neck and pushed back a few straggly strands of my hair. "We will make camp here for the night and I will prepare something to eat. I'm sorry, I didn't stop to think about food."

"Didn't stop to think about food?" I rasped. "What's wrong with you?"

He averted his gaze. "Sometimes, it is best if I don't."

I frowned, but he didn't elaborate. I shouldn't have been surprised. He didn't offer much by way of information. It seemed so far like our relationship operated on a need-to-know basis, and there was apparently a lot of stuff I didn't need to know. I let my gaze roam over his sculpted chest and shoulders again, and I heaved a sigh as my breathing finally returned to normal. "Do you make all of your recruits do the death march across the sand?"

He turned his eyes back to me and grinned. "Yes. It builds character. Makes you strong."

"Makes you puke," I corrected. "I'm sick of puking, by the way."

His expression was almost teasing as he flung our meager bag of supplies deeper into the cave. "I'll keep that in mind. You should get some rest, regain some of your strength. I'll set up camp and have dinner cooking by the time you wake up."

I didn't even fight him. In all reality, I could have cared less about where we were and what needed to be done. I just wanted to lie down. I didn't care how he was going to miraculously produce food, and I didn't care how he was going to cook it. All I cared about was the cool, smooth rock that I splayed myself out on.

I closed my eyes and was dimly aware of gentle hands lifting my head and putting something soft beneath it, but I was too exhausted to pay much attention. I was asleep within seconds.

My dreams were terrible. They always were. I hadn't had anything other than a nightmare since my mother had died. I was used to the horrible things my subconscious conjured, but I wasn't used to anyone giving a crap when I cried out, when I screamed, when tears ran down my cheeks and I trembled. I wasn't used to the soft touch I felt on my face, the soothing motion that swept from my forehead down to my cheek.

"Reya."

The voice was sinful, perfect, totally different from any-thing I had ever known. I was used to harsh and cold. I was unfamiliar with tender. The word didn't exist in my vocabulary.

Trying to wake, I wrestled with the remnants of my nightmare while it tried to pull me back into its horrific depths. I tossed my head to the side and heard a strangled cry escape my throat.

"Reya, wake up. You're safe."

I had a memory flash through my mind as the last vestige of my nightmare passed away. It was a memory of my moth-er. I was very small, and I was crying. My mother picked me up from where I was sitting on the floor and cradled me in her arms. She whispered something soothing to me, kissed me on the forehead, and wrapped me up in the softest, most won-derful thing I'd ever felt. It was velvet, black velvet. It had been my blanket, my favorite thing as a child. Nothing had ever been more calming than the touch of that fabric. It felt like comfort. It felt like safety. It felt like home.

The touch on my face felt similar, only this also felt erotic, and it sent tingles down my spine.

"Reya."

It was just a whisper, but it brought me awake with a start. I gasped and blinked bewildered eyes up at Jack, who was looming over me. His face was very close, his eyes in-tent on mine. His dark hair fell forward and tickled the ex-posed skin of my neck.

The sun was down. I had slept away the remainder of the day. With a frown, I sat up and brought my fingers to my face. My cheeks were wet.

"You were dreaming," Jack said, reaching his hand up to

gently caress away the remainder of my tears.

I nodded and a shiver went through me. It was a cold shiver of loneliness, chased away by a hot shiver caused by his touch. I pulled my knees to my chest and met his gaze. "How long have I been asleep?" I queried.

"Several hours. Dinner is almost finished."

I glanced over to where a fire was burning not far away. A rabbit was roasting on a spit across it. My stomach roared, but I frowned. "Where did you manage to find a rabbit?"

"The desert is full of rabbits," he replied. "You just have to know where to look." He sat back and regarded me for a few moments. "What were you dreaming about?"

I looked away and gave a shrug. "Who knows? Awful things. Murder, blood, gore. I don't know. My brain has been concocting horror stories for me to experience when I sleep since I was a girl. Mostly I'm being chased, pursued by some unseen thing. I never know what it is, but I am filled with the worst kind of fear. All I know is that, if I stop, if I let it catch me, I'll be done for... I have that one a lot."

"Has it ever caught up with you?"

I shook my head. "Sometimes I wish it would, though. At least then it would all be over."

"It won't stop until you overcome whatever fear is fueling it. You have to conquer your fear, turn and face it, fight it. When you do, you will be free of it."

I snorted. "Yeah, but how am I supposed to overcome it when I don't even know what it is?"

"You have to take a journey within yourself," he said quietly. "And that can be the hardest thing for someone to do."

I looked up at him because his voice grew wistful, distant, as if he was thinking of a particular incident. I watched him stare off into the night for a few heartbeats of silence, and I was about to ask him what he meant when he moved over to the fire and checked the rabbit.

I became preoccupied with my ravenous appetite for a while, and it wasn't until I had obliterated over half the carcass that my mind strayed back to Jack. He ate very little, and was very silent in a serene way. I'd never seen anyone so powerful, yet so peaceful. Every move he made was slow, graceful, tranquil almost.

"Are you ever going to tell me anything about yourself?" I

asked as I tried to chew every last vestige of meat off of a bone.

He glanced back over at me with a small half-smile. "What would you like to know?"

I shrugged. "I don't know. Just, something. Where do you come from?"

"Nowhere and everywhere. I have traveled much of this world."

I blinked. That was the vaguest response I had ever heard. "Where is your home?" I tried again.

"Pax is my home."

"Before that."

"Before that doesn't matter." He met my eyes, and the firelight danced across his face, making him look ominous and fantastic.

I stared at him for a couple minutes, at a loss. How was I supposed to continue a conversation with a man who gave me nothing? I fixed him with a sardonic look. "What's your favorite color?" My words practically dripped with sarcasm.

His lips split into a grin and the light in his eyes as he looked at me was playful. "Black."

I snorted. "Go figure." I heaved a sigh, nibbled a little more, and then decided to steer the conversation away from his history. Maybe I could find more out about that at a later time. "What do you do in Pax? I mean, do you have a job?"

"I'm a recruiter. I search the cities for people worthy of living there, of making it prosper."

"Yeah, but, I mean, in your off time. When you're not saving junkies from OD-ing on the street, what do you do?" I gave him a teasing smirk.

He gave me a soft smile before he returned his attention to the fire. "I'm a fisherman."

That caught me off guard. Somehow, I had difficulty picturing him sitting on a pier somewhere, reeling in a fish. "A fisherman?"

He chuckled quietly and nodded. "I have an almost insatiable craving for fish."

Again, his statement was loaded with meaning that I did not understand, and again, he didn't elaborate. With a sigh, I gazed out across the desert plains. They looked white in the moonlight, eerie. "You know, you're expecting a lot if you just think I'm going to blindly trust you without knowing any information about you whatsoever. What kind of an idiot does that anyway? I must be out of my mind." I stood and, wanting to make a point more than anything, threw the remnants of my dinner down. I started to walk away from the cave and the fire, out into the night.

"Where are you going?"

I gave him a rude gesture with my middle finger. I knew it would get a reaction out of him, and I was right. Not even thirty seconds went by before he had caught up to me, almost soundlessly, and grasped a hold of my arm. He whipped me around harshly and scowled at me.

"What are you doing?" he spat. His eyes were cold, angry, and his jaw was stern.

"I'm making a choice!" I hissed, yanking my arm away.

"And what choice might that be?" he snarled. "To walk off into the No Man's Land in the middle of the night and get yourself killed?"

I folded my arms across my chest in challenge. "No, I'm making the choice to walk away from a person who expects me to do what he says without asking any question, and without telling me anything that will convince me that all the bull he spouts is true."

His icy eyes flashed fire for a moment. "You're deciding to question my intentions now? I saved your life! Shouldn't that be proof enough that I'm not out to harm you?"

I snorted. "You could be selling me into slavery for all I know! Look, I've tried to be compliant and understanding, but unless you give me some kind of answers right now, I'm turning my back on you and I'm walking back to the city."

"You would so willingly go back to that life of trash?" His voice rose to something that resembled a growl, and I blinked in surprise because I could have sworn I saw him begin to tremble.

I glanced down at his hands to see that they were clenched into tight fists at his sides. He was squeezing them so hard that the veins in his arms were protruding. Some kind of inner warning told me to tread carefully, that I was on dangerous ground, but I'd never really been that smart. The life I'd fallen prey to could contest to that.

I pushed just a little further. I narrowed my eyes and

stared him down. "Tell me who you are."

"I told you who I am," he snarled between clenched teeth. "Haven't my completely passive actions toward you proved that I am trustworthy? Why do you need to know my history? What does history matter? It is nothing more than a bunch of useless facts that are no longer valid."

"History is important because the past makes us who we are, Jack! You could be some kind of sick serial killer for all I know! The fact that you keep hedging is making me more uncomfortable as the minutes go by! You can't trust someone who refuses to divulge any information about himself! It makes you seem completely shady, and I've had it with being in the dark! I've spent too many years being kept in the dark. Don't ask too many questions and you won't be in danger. Just accept what goes on and pretend you don't see all the sordid junk that happens just out of your line of vision. That's been my life up until now, but no more! I'm done with sitting idly and just hoping things turn out okay, because they never do! You saved me and took me from the street. You forced me clean and made me make a choice to stay that way. When I did that, I turned my back on my old lifestyle. If I'm going to survive in this world without the help of an ever-present high, I need to be smart! And letting you guide me off to who knows where just because you say it's okay is not smart!" I spun on my heel and tramped away from him several more steps.

"Reya!" he bellowed.

My eyes widened, and I came to an abrupt halt as his voice echoed through the desert darkness. Chills went up and down my spine and the hair on the back of my neck prickled. It had been more than a shout. It had been a command. And not only that, it had sounded terrifying. I slowly turned my head over my shoulder to look back at him.

I frowned. He was pacing restlessly back and forth, his hands still clenched. My instincts told me that something was wrong. "Jack?" I called tentatively. I turned back toward him. "Jack, are you—"

A distinct rumbling growl came from his throat and my eyes widened. I took a slow step back and contemplated running for my life. Everything I'd ever been taught about shifters came rushing back to me. Something, however, made me stay put. "Jack," I called out again, my voice barely a whisper.

He held his palm up to me, signaling for me to stay back. He sank onto his haunches and braced his elbows on his knees. He tangled his fingers in his hair, held his head in both his hands, and squeezed his eyes shut tightly.

I stayed still, afraid to move, and listened to the beats of my heart. We stayed like that for what seemed like an eternity. In reality, it had to have only been about five minutes.

Finally, I heard him expel a long breath and he eased himself down so that he was sitting. "Reya," he whispered. "Please don't go."

"Okay." I'd never been great at arguing, and a voice inside my head told me that something bigger was going on here that I shouldn't test. His voice was completely defeated, quiet, void of any real emotion. "Jack?" I had no idea what to say. What had I just witnessed?

He held his hand out to me, and I stumbled forward. I slid my fingers into his and let him guide me down to sit across from him. Keeping his eyes downcast, away from mine, he stared at the dirt. I waited, because I was too afraid to do anything else.

"What did I tell you about shifters?" he finally asked me softly.

"That there are good guys and bad guys." It was a sad attempt at a summary, but it made the briefest of smiles flash across his lips.

"Yes, and what did I tell you about the bad guys?"

"That they are violent and aggressive, more animal than man."

He nodded and slowly turned his eyes up to mine. He held my gaze for several breaths. "It is very dangerous to challenge me, Reya. Or to make me angry. Or to surprise me in a negative way."

I frowned and, not understanding what he meant, shook my head.

"I also said that everyone has a choice. I made a choice, just as you did, but that does not mean that I am perfect and that does not mean that certain things about me are not as they have always been."

I stared at him as I mulled on his words and tried to

make sense of them. When I finally grasped his meaning, I gasped in alarm and my eyes grew wide. "Y-You're one of the bad guys," I squeaked in shock and fright. I scooted back away from him, terror coiling in the pit of my stomach. "You lied to me."

He shook his head adamantly. "No, I never lied to you, Reya. I *am* one of the good guys, but that doesn't mean I have always been so. I told you I made a choice. I chose to be something different, but it is difficult. Anger, frustration, pain, any negative emotion cries out to the beast within me. I have to remain completely calm at all times, avoid as much negativity as I can. I have to have strict control over my mind and body. I can never let myself slip. If I do, someone could get hurt. I could hurt someone." He squeezed his eyes shut and shook his head as if trying to rid his mind of a terrible thought. "I could have hurt you."

I just stared at him for several long moments. That explained why, since the moment I'd first seen him in the hotel room, he'd been completely placid, serene, unflappable. He couldn't afford to be anything else. "So, you used to be one of them," I finally said. "What made you change?"

He sighed. "All I had ever known was bloodlust and rage, this unquenchable hunger. I watched my companions do nothing but kill, eat, kill some more. It seemed so empty to me, to live an existence that consisted of only the hunt and the hunger. I had enough man in me, enough of a soul to know that it was useless and savage. I didn't want to live that way any longer. I tried to persuade some of the others to adopt my line of thinking. I was certain that we could all change what we were into something better if we tried hard enough. The others didn't agree. They turned on me and left me for dead."

"What happened?" The cool night air drifted over me, and I shivered.

"Someone found me, one of the civilized shifters. He was one of the men who had discovered Pax. He took care of me, took pity on me... He was kind to me." He met my gaze and the light from the moon made his eyes completely white and almost luminescent. "You have no idea what kindness can do, Reya. It can change worlds and reshape men. When I healed, I swore to myself that I would never again be the disgusting creature I had been. I forced myself away from that life, but that doesn't mean that the hunger ever goes away. I have just learned to ignore it."

One corner of my mouth lifted in a slight smile, and I played with my fingers in my lap. "So, what you're trying to say is that you're an addict too. And when I made you angry, I basically dangled your drug in your face the way you did to me." I shrugged in an attempt to look nonchalant even though my nerves still felt a little frayed. "I guess that means you passed your test also."

He kept his eyes on me, and his lips turned up ever so slightly. "More was at stake if I failed mine."

Right on the end of his sentence, a loud, mournful howl sounded in the distance. It was followed by two more and they raised goose bumps on my arms. Jack bristled, and he turned his attention to the east. He swore, which alarmed me more than the howls did, and he was on his feet in the blink of an eye.

"Come with me," he demanded, holding his hand out to me. "Quickly."

I obeyed and he pulled me into a standing position. "What's wrong?"

"The others were close enough to hear my growl. Shifters have extremely sensitive hearing." He started to lead me back toward the cave. "They don't know it's me, only that I'm one of their kind. They're looking for me. If they see you with me, they'll kill you."

My fingers tightened around his, and my heartbeat faltered. "Oh that's a comforting bit of information!"

He shook his head and doused the fire, then yanked a large blanket out of his bag. "Lie down."

I did so without hesitation and he threw the blanket over me, covering me completely. Minutes later, he lay down next to me, so close that it took my breath away. He aligned himself with me, and he pulled the blanket over himself as well.

"I am exiled from their kind," he said quietly, "so if they find me, they should leave me alone. Stay very still. The cave wall is at your back so the only view they have is of me. My body is blocking you from their sight. My hope is that they won't find me at all."

My heart thundered against my rib cage at his nearness,

at the sheer virility of him. He smelled like the desert. Like dust and the sun and the wind. It was a wild smell, a heady scent that intoxicated me. "Can I still talk?" I whispered.

"Quietly. They are still somewhat far off. I will warn you if they are near." He looked down into my eyes and guilt and self-loathing reflected in them. "I'm sorry, Reya. This is my doing."

I rolled my eyes. "No, actually, it's mine. I'm the one who stormed off into the night."

He shook his head. "You were right. I should have explained what I am to you from the beginning. How were you supposed to know otherwise? You were just trying to look out for yourself. Forgive me." His brow furrowed. "I don't like to think about what I once was. I don't like to think about the past."

"I understand." I debated on whether or not I should just shut up. It was apparent that he didn't like discussing his less-than-pretty history. But I was curious, and I figured I may as well learn all I could while he was willing to talk. "So, is it just the negative emotions that set you off? How can you live your life without feeling anger?"

"I do feel anger. I feel emotions just as anyone does. I just have to be extremely disciplined with myself. I can never let go of my control. When I'm caught off guard, it's more difficult, and when I'm in my animal form, it's almost impossible."

"Really?" I wondered what animal he was when he shifted. Some kind of powerful predator, no doubt. Obviously something that had large fangs.

He nodded. "The animal lives on instinct. The man in me almost completely disappears. All I see is red. All I feel is hunger. I don't shift very often because of that. Only when it's absolutely necessary."

It really was like being an addict. The constant craving, fighting thoughts of it out of your mind. I'd only been clean a couple days and I'd thought about my addiction more times than I could count. It was both encouraging and disheartening. It was encouraging to know that Jack had been successfully combating his problem for quite some time, but it was disheartening to realize that it would never completely go away. There was always the chance of slipping up again. Life would never be easy. For him or me.

I frowned in thought. "Is that why you saved me? You saw some of yourself in me?"

He heaved a sigh. "That was some of it, but I've run across many druggies before. You were not my first. I never rescued them." He gave me a gentle but pointed look. "You were different. Your situation was different."

"Why?"

"Because when I knelt down to see if you were alive, you grabbed onto my wrist. You looked up into my eyes, and with the most heartbreaking conviction I have ever witnessed, you muttered, 'Help me.' Now, tell me, how was I supposed to walk away from that?"

I stared at him, shocked, and tears gathered in my eyes. "I don't remember that," I whispered.

He shook his head. "I wouldn't expect you to. But as I stared down at you that night, I thought to myself, what would have happened to me if the shifter who'd found me half dead had just left me there because of what I was? I couldn't just leave you there, Reya. It was too similar. You were too much like me."

My bottom lip trembled, and tears spilled out of my eyes in an onslaught of emotion that I couldn't help and couldn't hold back. When was the last time someone had shown me real care? I couldn't remember any instance past when my mother had died. All I'd known since then had been cold, harsh, cruel. Jack had cared. He cared still. I buried my face against his chest and cried like a little child. They were years' worth of pent-up tears, and I imagined they were long overdue.

I felt his fingers in my hair and I shuddered, pressing closer to his unyielding body. He was like a refuge, a safe place, the only person to offer me any amount of security in over half my life. He'd taken me from the street, taken me out of my deplorable life. He'd given me the chance for something more, the hope for a future. I had only known him for roughly a few days, and already I owed Jack Snow more than I would ever be able to repay.

Slowly, my sobs abated, leaving an aching pain in my chest. I wasn't sure what it was from. Loneliness, maybe. I hadn't really realized how lonely I was. There are a lot of things we can ignore when all we're doing is trying to survive. Now that I wasn't doing that anymore, now that I had the possibility of a real life laid before me, and especially now that I wasn't escaping my emotions with the use of drugs, I realized how completely isolated I felt. It hurt profoundly.

I shook my head, still keeping my face against his chest. I could hear his heartbeat, strong, steady. "I don't think you want someone like me in Pax, Jack," I sniffled. "I'm a disaster."

He chuckled softly and nudged me back so that I was forced to look up at him. He gave me the gentlest smile, one that made his eyes seem so warm and inviting. He wiped my tears away, then traced the line of my jaw with his fingertips. "You're exactly the kind of person I want in Pax." At my confused frown, he reached up to smooth my hair. "You're real, your emotions are genuine. You have a real understanding of what you've left behind. You believe in something more, just as I did."

I studied his eyes for a long while and wished I could lose myself within their depths and never come out. His beauty was transfixing, and his kindness was infinite. I was awestruck by the man before me. He was a testimony to strength of will, and I hoped that, one day, I could possess half as much wisdom.

The chorus of howls echoed through the night again and I jumped. Jack tensed next to me and the peaceful light in his eyes vanished. He frowned and a hard edge set along the line of his jaw.

"How far?" I asked, my words barely discernable.

"Closer, but still a ways off. Sleep, Reya. You're safe."

Snuggling closer to him, I curled myself around him as much as I could. I wasn't ashamed or embarrassed. I was terrified, and he was the only thing standing between me and execution by a pack of ravenous shifters. Besides, he was warm, smelled good, and I got that strange black velvet memory again as he ran a soothing hand down my bare arm. I sighed. His touch was like heaven to me, and no matter how odd that seemed, I didn't care. I had known too much pain and suffering in my life. I wasn't going to deny myself just a little bit of heaven...however sinful it may have been.

Chapter Four

There was something wild about sleeping out in the middle of the desert with a shifter. It seemed dangerous, even though I knew he would keep me safe. He was precarious, and even though he kept himself in check, he was still an addict. An addict always had the possibility of slipping up. I knew it firsthand. I had tried to get clean before, several times. Jack hadn't been my first attempt. After a while it had just become easier to accept I was a junkie and be that junkie. It was easier than trying. It was mainly because I'd had no reason to, nothing to fight for. It seemed like I did now. Jack had given me that.

So, as I woke up that next morning, nestled in his strong arms, I knew I should have felt afraid. I should have been wary of the fact that he was one of the aggressive shifters, but I wasn't. I trusted him implicitly, which was so unlike me. It was probably exceedingly stupid too.

But all I really knew was how warm I felt. Warm and protected. It was a new and strange sensation, and I snuggled against him, wanting to capture as much of it as I could. His arm tightened around my waist and a strange, rumbling sound came from his chest. It was enough to make me raise my head in alarm and surprise. I thought he was growling at first, but when I saw that he still slept soundly, I realized it was more of a purr, like that of a contented cat. I raised an eyebrow and studied his face. His features were calm, placid. I smirked to myself and resisted the urge to laugh. At least now I had some sort of idea as to what his animal form was. It explained the fangs, as well as the fluid grace with which he moved.

Propping myself up on my elbow, I watched him for several minutes, studying the contours of his striking face, the fullness of his lips. I reached my fingertips out to touch them, to lightly trace them. They looked soft, decadent, tempting.

The purring abruptly stopped, and I pulled my hand away just as his eyes popped open. He was alert instantly. I could see it in the icy depths of his gaze. No blinking sleep out of his eyes, no trying to get his sluggish brain moving. He was immediately coherent and focused.

I smiled down at him. "Good morning."

He propped his head up and raised an eyebrow, no doubt confused by my mischievous expression. "Good morning." His voice held a slight question in it.

My smile morphed into a grin. "Let me guess, you shift into some kind of big cat."

He blinked in bewilderment. "How did you know that?"

"Well, the fangs are a good indication," I said, tapping on one of my own teeth, "but the purring was a dead giveaway."

He looked mortified. "I was purring?"

I giggled and gave a nod.

He rolled his eyes. "Well, that's embarrassing." He glanced down at where his arm rested around my waist and his brow creased. He moved his palm up to span across my side, slowly ran his fingers up to my shoulder, and then back down to my hip.

My breath hitched and, closing my eyes, I savored the gentle exploratory touch.

He sighed and I opened my eyes as he sat up. He had his elbows propped on his knees and a troubled frown on his handsome face. "What's wrong?" I asked, sitting up also.

He shook his head. "I haven't done that in a long time."

"What? Purred or run your hand along a woman's side?" I teased.

He gave me a wry smile. "Both."

I moved closer and rested my chin on his shoulder in an attempt to reclaim some of the nearness I had been enjoying. "Is there something wrong with that?"

He turned his head to look at me and a small, playful smile twisted his lips. "No, I suppose there isn't. It's just...hmmm."

I frowned and waited for him to continue.

After several seconds of silence, he took a deep breath.

"I don't purr unless I am extremely content. I haven't been extremely content in longer than I can remember, Reya." He gave me a pointed glance.

I chewed on my bottom lip in contemplation. "Not even in Pax?"

He shook his head. "Not even there." He continued to watch me with his unnervingly gorgeous eyes. He let out a small chuckle. "A man like me comes with his fair share of baggage. That baggage haunts me, even in my dreams."

"But then..." I let the sentence remain unformed, not quite understanding what he was implying. Why would he suddenly find his contentment in the middle of the desert, on the outskirts of the No Man's Land, after I had made him extremely angry and had an emotional outburst while he was trying to hide me from a bunch of evil shifters who would have eaten me for a midnight snack? Yeah, that just screamed of happiness.

"I don't know," was his simple answer, as if he could read my thoughts. "As for touching you, I don't know why I did that either." The crease in his brow deepened as if this thought troubled him. "It just seemed natural to do so."

The same way it had felt natural for me to sleep in his arms and to trace the outline of his lips. As far as I was concerned, there were worse things a person could do. But for some reason, this seemed to bother him. Maybe it was strange for a solitary man like himself to want to do such things. Maybe it was difficult for him because of what he was. At any rate, I didn't want him to feel like I was crowding him, so I reached my hand up and ran it down the length of his dark hair in a light, friendly caress. With a playful smirk, I tousled his hair.

He frowned down at me, but a tiny glint of sparkle had come to life in his eyes. I shrugged. "I thought cats liked their heads rubbed."

He shot me a bemused expression. "Very nice," he grumbled sarcastically.

I giggled. "The fish thing makes a whole lot more sense now too."

He chuckled and shook his head. "All right, all right, enough with the cat remarks. The shifters' howls stopped late last night. I think they might have given up in searching.

We should pack up and head out soon."

"Do I get breakfast?" I grumbled. I stood and yawned, stretching out my stiff back. "I know you don't eat much because you're afraid if you do you'll devour everything, but I still need food to survive, so..."

"I have some bread and cheese in my pack, as well as some water," he replied. "You can eat that before we start our journey."

I frowned and tried to straighten my disheveled hair. "What is this, the Middle Ages? Bread and freakin' cheese." I was saying it mainly to tease him. In all reality, bread and cheese was gourmet compared to what I was used to. I would take anything I could get. "You know, you might have mentioned the wandering gypsy meal you had hiding out in your pack yesterday when I was dying of starvation. Ever think of that?"

He smirked up at me while he started to fold the blanket that had been my camouflage the night before. "Why? You would have just thrown it back up. What a waste that would have been."

Both my eyebrows shot up and I put my hands on my hips. "Nice, thanks." I snorted and walked a few steps away, but his rich chuckle made me smile. I sighed and let the morning sun warm me as I wandered aimlessly out of the cave. It was still early, so it wasn't too hot yet, just comforting. I messed with my hair, combing it out with my fingers and securing it in a ponytail once again. I let my mind ponder on Jack, and I smiled at how easy it was to be around him. The more he let me see of himself, the more comfortable I became.

I was going to turn and head back, but the growl stopped me. It was low, menacing, and came from behind me. I froze instantly, my arms at my sides, not daring to move even an inch. It wasn't a growl like Jack's. This was different. This was sinister. Two more vicious growls joined the first, and my hands started to shake. My breathing became shallow, and I stood rooted to the ground, terrified of what would happen to me if I moved even a tiny bit.

Slowly, three wolves circled around to face me, their fangs bared, their eyes hungry. I slid my gaze over to where Jack was breaking camp, oblivious to my current predicament. I wondered if calling out to him would help. I decided against it. The wolves would probably have my throat ripped out before I could finish my scream.

As I stood there, staring in wide-eyed horror at the predators in front of me, an enormous golden eagle swooped down in front of the trio. The wolves ceased in their advance and remained stationary, salivating and snarling. I took a hesitant step back and glanced over to Jack again, only to find him gone. I blinked, horrified and bewildered, then turned my attention back to the eagle, who continued to stare at me with its piercing golden eyes.

As I watched, the eagle's shape began to shiver, and before my eyes, it morphed into the form of a tall, menacing human man. His eyes remained the same disturbing golden color, and he stood proud, unperturbed by his state of undress, with his mahogany-colored hair flowing in wild tangles around his shoulders. He crossed his arms over his chest and smirked at me, then directed his attention behind me.

"Did you really think you could throw us off your trail by dousing your fire and huddling against a rock face?" The eagle's resonant voice held taunting disgust. "Please, Jack, you insult my intelligence, as well as that of your old brethren. We could smell this human woman miles away."

His attention shifted to me, and I suppressed a shiver. The look in his eyes suggested that I was on the breakfast menu. I wondered where Jack actually was, considering he'd vanished. Perhaps he hadn't been as oblivious to these men as I'd originally guessed.

The eagle-man snorted when no reply came. "We already know you're a traitor," he snapped. "But I didn't know you'd turned into a coward, as well. What are you doing escorting humans through our territory? What are you protecting?"

His angry words echoed through the desert, and I jumped, but for some reason, words came out of my mouth before I could stop them. "What the hell do you want with him?" My voice held much more bravery than I actually felt. "He said he was exiled from you. State your purpose!"

My demanding words and tone surprised both me and the eagle-man. The wolves behind him snarled and snapped. The eagle-man let his gaze rake over me for a second before a malicious smile twisted his lips. "And who are you, I wonder, that he would protect you the way he did?"

I swallowed hard, but lifted my chin with stubborn defiance. "I'm a friggin' junkie. Who the hell are you?"

This, also, seemed to surprise him for he stared at me for several heartbeats as if he wasn't exactly sure how to respond.

I gave a flippant shrug. "You want an answer, you've got to give me something. I don't give information away for free." I folded my arms over my chest and spat on the ground. Who knows why? I was hoping to make myself seem more of a hard ass and less of the pathetic excuse for a frightened mouse I felt like inside.

The eagle-man's lips quirked in a small expression of amusement. "Name your poison, sweetheart."

Realizing he assumed I wanted drugs from him, I blinked and felt my face pale. Just the thought of someone bringing me a fix was far too tempting to me. It hadn't been enough time. The distance between me and my drug of choice was still not far enough. My mouth went dry, and I dug my nails into my arm in order to try and stay focused. "Well, answering my question would be a good start," I snapped. "Who are you and what do you want with Jack?"

His amusement seemed to grow. "What are you? His bodyguard?" He let out a loud laugh and his wolf lackeys began howling behind him, no doubt voicing their own delight. He shook his head and his eyes narrowed, growing cold. "Pathetic. This entire thing is pathetic. He betrays us for what? For human drug addicts? Something doesn't jive."

Before I could even blink, his hand was at my throat, squeezing. My eyes bulged, and I clawed at him as my airway constricted.

His golden eyes burned into mine. "Listen here, precious. I have no regard for your life one way or the other and you smell oh so delicious, so I would suggest you cooperate. Jack betrayed us for something. What was it? I need to know."

I croaked something incoherent and, in his eyes, I saw something besides rage and hunger. It was small, it was only for a millisecond, but it was there. A desperation that didn't match his cool demeanor. I recognized it because I had seen it before. I had seen it in my own eyes.

I was only able to concentrate on it for a second, though,

because a huge, powerful white tiger suddenly leaped through the air, knocking the eagle-man to the ground. I fell forward, gasping and choking, and the wolves turned on the tiger, attacking him en masse. The eagle shifted back into his bird form and, to my surprise, lifted his wings and took to the sky, abandoning both his companions and his mission.

I stared in fascinated horror as the wolves snapped at the tiger, tearing with their teeth and going for his throat with terrible growls. They were no match for the feline, even with there being three of them. Within only moments, all three of the wolves had been dispatched in a rather gruesome way. I had never seen so much blood, and I could no longer tell which pieces of the animals belonged to which. It would have made me sick, but before I could process everything that had just occurred, the tiger turned to face me. He let out a low, frightening growl, and I drew in a shuddering breath. Every inch of his body exuded raw power. Blood dripped from his fangs and there was no recognition in his icy eyes. The only thing I saw within them was hunger...and bloodlust.

"Jack," I whispered. "Jack, do you know who I am?"

He growled again and began to advance, his ears back, his teeth bared viciously.

I pushed myself up onto my knees and trembled as he approached, stalking me as any cat would stalk his prey. "Jack," I whimpered, tears forming in my eyes. "It's Reya. Please..." What was I supposed to say? How could I make him remember who he was? Who I was? He had told me it was almost impossible to reach the man in him when he was in animal form. And now that he had the taste of blood in his mouth... There was no way it was going to happen. He was going to kill me. It was as simple as that. They'd given him the anger, the fight, and the kill. I had no chance.

Knowing I was done for, I prepared myself as he approached. I was going to be murdered by the gentle man who had saved my life. It was the worst, most twisted kind of irony.

I closed my eyes as the tiger came near, his hot breath invading my senses while he continued to snarl. I bunched my hands into fists and waited for the inevitable when Jack's voice whispered through my memory. *You have no idea what kindness can do, Reya. It can change worlds and reshape men.*

I gasped and my eyes popped open, a strange idea burning through my mind. Kindness... It was what Jack valued, what he based many of his beliefs on. Kindness, goodness, the act of giving someone a second chance.

The tiger growled a low, threatening warning, and I met his icy eyes with boldness. I knew this was the one and only chance I had. I was going to die anyway if I didn't try. I had nothing to lose. The great cat made a snorting noise, obviously not liking the challenging look in my eyes. He crouched low, and his ears flattened.

I took a deep breath and slowly raised my hands up, keeping my eyes trained on his. His growl grew in volume, but I persisted. I moved my trembling hands forward. "Jack." My voice wavered. "Jack, it's okay." He let out a loud hiss that made me jump, but I forced myself to remain calm. "I know you can hear me," I continued. "I know you're in there. I need you to come back. I can't get to Pax by myself, and I'm sure there are many people who would miss you there."

The tiger let out one more warning growl and was about to leap at me when I sunk my fingers into the fur on his neck. He halted abruptly and made a roar that sounded crossed between anger and confusion.

I was shaking, but I remained where I was. I maintained eye contact and deliberately began to stroke my fingers across his fur, trailing them up to the top of his head and down the sides of his beautiful face. "Please, Jack," I murmured. "I know you can hear me. I know you don't want to do this. I believe in you... I believe in you like you believe in me."

The cat staggered back a step, hissed again, and sat down on its haunches, shaking its head violently. Gaining a small amount of confidence, I rose up on my knees and continued to stroke his face. Then, I slid my arms around the great predator's neck and embraced him. I felt his heart pounding, and he continued to growl low in warning, but I only held on tighter. I squeezed my eyes shut and buried my face in his soft fur.

I felt the coiled muscle of the tiger shift within my arms, shudder almost, and then begin to change shape. I held on, afraid to open my eyes, afraid that my death might still be imminent. It wasn't until the fur beneath my fingers changed to smooth skin that I realized I might be in the clear. The growling sounds changed to the noises of a man within in the throes of some kind of struggle, and I moved away to see Jack's familiar form in front of me. He had his head in his hands, his fingers knotted in his hair, and he was shaking almost as hard as I was. His eyes were tightly shut, and his jaw was clenched.

"Jack..." I breathed. Tentatively, I reached out and ran my hand down his shoulder and arm. The touch caused him to suck his breath in and recoil slightly, curling in on himself even more.

"Reya," he rasped. "What...the hell...were you thinking?"

I smirked at his usage of my catch phrase and some of my apprehension dissipated. I heaved a sigh, reached out to him, trailing trailed my fingers through his hair, and wrapping my arms around him in much the same way I had before. "Kindness can change worlds and reshape men," I said softly.

"I could have killed you," he whispered, but his arms came up to wrap around my back, his shaking decreasing.

"You were going to anyway," I argued. "I had to try something. Are you hurt?" I moved back enough to smooth his hair away from his face. I grimaced at the blood that still decorated his mouth, and I reached up to wipe it off with my sleeve.

He shook his head, then covered his mouth self-consciously. "I'm so sorry you had to see any of that. I couldn't have fought the three of them in my human form. I wouldn't have had enough power. I needed to shift. I thought I would be all right, but once I..." He shook his head again as if to dispel a memory. "The taste..."

He had an ache in his voice that I understood all too well. I leaned forward and rested my forehead against his. "It's irresistible, isn't it?" I questioned. "The power of just that one taste."

He exhaled a shaky breath and nodded. We sat like that for a few minutes before he gave a breathy chuckle. "When you said you weren't strong, Reya, you sure were full of it, weren't you?"

I laughed in spite of myself, but couldn't bring myself to move away from him. "I just didn't want to be eaten, Jack. It's called self-preservation."

"I wasn't referring to just what you did with me. I meant the way you handled the shifters, the way you handled Rigdon."

"Rigdon...I take it that was the big eagle guy?"

He nodded. "He is their leader. The way you challenged him..." He finally raised his head and looked at me. His eyes reflected silent wonder and admiration. "Reya, your courage..." He reached up and cupped my cheek in his palm, feathering his thumb across my skin.

I closed my eyes and my heart hammered out a peculiar rhythm.

"You tried to protect me." He said it as if he was surprised, as if the idea was foreign to him.

I smiled. "Of course. You protect me, I protect you. That's how it's supposed to work. I'm no slouch."

His lips formed into a stunning grin, and I let my eyes linger for a moment on his ferocious set of fangs. I knew I should be afraid of him, of what he was, but I wasn't. His situation was too familiar to me. A different kind of addict with a different kind of drug. That was all.

I reached out to smooth some of his wild hair again. "So, what did those shifters want anyway?" I queried. "I thought you were supposed to be exiled, that they weren't supposed to bother you."

A shadow passed over his face. "They're not. And the fact that Rigdon was delaying killing you because he wanted information was an interesting development. I'm not sure what it means, but I don't like it. I think we should make haste, get to Pax as soon as possible."

I nodded. "Are you all right?"

"Yes, I'm fine now."

I stood and gasped when I looked down at him. He had several gashes across one of his shoulders, and several along one of his sides. "Jack! You said you weren't hurt!"

He stood, as complacent about his nakedness as the other shifter had been. He glanced at his wounds and sighed. "I'll heal."

"But they could get infected!" I protested. "Please, let me wash them at least."

He flashed me a smile and reached down to capture my hand in his. "I'll tend them once we get to Pax. Reya"—he met my eyes with purpose—"thank you. You saved me from myself."

My heart melted at the tenderness in his voice, and I reached up to touch his cheek. He closed his eyes for a second before bringing my knuckles to his lips and kissing them briefly. The touch of his sinful mouth ignited my blood.

"Let's go," he said. "If we leave soon, we should be able to make it to Pax by nightfall."

Chapter Five

I was apprehensive as we continued to cross the desert. Jack was quiet and I kept expecting Rigdon to return with a bigger group of shifters that would slaughter both of us. As we plodded along, I replayed that morning's experience. For some reason, my mind kept returning to that look in the eagle-man's eyes as he'd tried to choke information out of me. That desperation was intriguing to me, especially when I took into consideration what Jack had told me about the shifters. He'd said they only thought about the hunger and the kill, and after everything that had happened, he had said that Rigdon's behavior had been unusual. I couldn't help but think that maybe the shifter had been searching for something more, something he could believe in also. I got the unmistakable feeling that the reason he had demanded to know what Jack had found out in the wilderness was because of something deeper than mere curiosity. Jack had turned his back on his entire life, on all of his brethren. Before he'd left, he'd tried to convince some of the others that the way they lived was not all there was. I had the hunch that Rigdon wanted to know what it was Jack had found that could be more fulfilling, more meaningful, than the hollow existence he lived.

But that was just my hunch. The only thing I had to go on was the look I had seen in the shifter's eyes, that desperate drive to dare to hope that maybe, somewhere, something else existed that was better, that was more.

The sun was setting when we reached a mountain range, but that, even in its expansive grandeur, was not that impressive. The mountains were just as barren as the rest of the land. Jack had still not spoken much, and I left him alone, knowing he was probably wrestling with a hundred different and conflicting emotions. Trudging along behind him, I kept his pace and tried not to complain.

I was lost in my own thoughts when his fingers around my wrist brought me to a halt. I looked up at him to see that he was grinning.

"Look down, Reya," he said, sweeping his hand outward. "Pax."

I followed where he gestured and made an audible gasp. Nestled between the rocks was a valley, green and gorgeous. The trees were thick and large and I could hear water running below. Fireflies twinkled amongst the leaves and I could just make out the structures of a village nestled within the heart of it all. It the twilight, it looked magical, and to me, that's about what it was. It was no less than a miracle. I had never seen anything like it in all my life.

I stared in wonderment and was aware of Jack watching my reaction. I saw him smile out the corner of my eye. For some reason, tears came to my eyes and I thought about my mother. I thought about how much she would have loved to see what I was looking at. I thought of how lucky I was to be seeing it for myself. I thought of how strange it was that, because of the awful course of life I had chosen, I had been thrown into Jack's path.

I turned my attention up to him, and he frowned thoughtfully at the enraptured expression that must have been on my face. "You have changed my entire existence in only two days," I said. "I can never thank you enough for what you have done."

His smile was gentle, and the light that came to life in his eyes was warm. He slipped an arm around my waist and pulled me up close to him. I drew in a soft breath, and my senses reeled with the feel and smell of him. I closed my eyes as he brought his mouth to my ear and his breath sent shivers down my spine.

"I believe I can say the same for you. You are unlike anyone I've ever known. Today you did what I thought was impossible. You reached me when I was blinded by the hunger and the hunt. No one has ever been able to do that. I am so grateful."

His humble, heartfelt words made my chest feel tight with emotion.

"All I have fought so hard for could have been destroyed. I never would have been able to set foot in Pax again if I had hurt you. It was bad enough that I had to destroy the shifters, but if I had hurt you..." He shook his head. "Pax is built on peace, on goodness. I could never have lived with myself. I almost can't live with myself now."

I wrapped my arms around his waist, overcome by his presence. I needed to touch him, needed to hear the furious pounding of his heart. I rested my head against his chest and basked in everything that he was, everything that he represented. "Jack," I said softly. "Please, you epitomize good to me."

He made a strange, startled noise, but I found his arms creeping around me as well. "You've been out in the sun too long. You see what kind of a monster I turn into. Nothing about that is good."

I shook my head and looked up at him. "You aren't a monster," I protested. "You're beautiful." Surprise flashed in his eyes, and I smiled. "And what makes you good is the fact that you defy everything you are, everything that is natural to you, to live the life you do. To believe in kindness when all you want to do is kill and destroy. To believe in this vision when all you want is to devour. You don't see that as goodness?"

He heaved a sigh and his arms tightened around me for a second before he dropped them and stepped away. "I see that as penance for the life I used to live." He turned, his demeanor suddenly aloof, reflective of the way he had been upon my waking in the hotel room. "Come." He walked past me and headed down the mountain toward the lush valley.

I stared after him for a minute, slightly baffled at his abrupt change of attitude, but I tried to shrug it off as I followed after him.

The mountain trail weaved down the rock face for about two miles before the trees began. As soon as we reached the outskirts of the forest, the temperature changed. It was no longer the sweltering, all-consuming heat, but cool and comfortable. The air filled with a tangy, crisp scent I'd never smelled before, but I attributed it to the foreign, spiny, needled trees we began to descend into.

Jack remained silent, and I didn't trouble him, but I did stick close to him as he headed through the forest and across a rope bridge that spanned over an enormous gorge of black rock. A wooden gate stood on the other end, guarded by two men who smiled, nodded, and waved both Jack and me through when we reached it.

Upon entering the gate, Jack stopped and glanced at me over his shoulder, a gentle smile playing around his lips. "Welcome to Pax, Reya."

I looked around, taking in the cabin-like structures interspersed throughout the trees. People milled around talking, laughing, working. I could see some men chopping wood, and not far off I could see fields being cultivated. The entire area exuded such complete peace. I'd never felt anything like it in all my life. No high I'd ever had could even begin to compare to the limitless beauty that surrounded me. It almost brought tears to my eyes for the second time.

"Jack! You're home!"

I turned at the sound of a feminine voice and saw a gorgeous redheaded woman run toward Jack with a bright grin. She flung her arms around him with a laugh, and he immediately returned her embrace with a chuckle. I tried not to pay attention to the twinge of jealousy that went through me. I'd only known Jack for two days. What right did I have to think I had any sort of claim on him?

I averted my gaze to the ground instead so I wouldn't have to look at how beautiful she was. Was I an idiot to think that maybe a man like Jack would be interested in someone like me? What made me think that he didn't have a woman waiting back at home for him? I felt like the world's biggest fool. No man would want to be with a junkie. Especially a man like Jack.

"Reya, I'd like you to meet my sister, Larissa."

Jack's voice snapped me out of my thoughts, and I looked back up at him in surprise.

My shock must have been evident because Larissa flashed her wide, warm grin at me and laughed. "Well, not by blood, but sometimes circumstance enables you to choose your siblings." She shrugged and patted Jack on the chest. "Blood doesn't always decide who your family is."

Jack smiled and leaned forward to press a chaste kiss to Larissa's alabaster cheek. "Do me a favor, Lara. Show Reya to one of the empty cabins and get her a change of clothing and a nice, hot bath. It has been quite a grueling few days."

She nodded and stepped forward to gently take my arm. "Come with me. I'll get you all settled in."

Instead of going with Larissa, I turned back to Jack. "Where are you going?" I asked. Was he just going to abandon me now that his mission was accomplished? I shouldn't be surprised and I shouldn't be offended. I had no right to be, but something about Jack... I'd thought we shared a kind of connection. I felt it. Maybe he didn't. Maybe I was just so grateful to him that infatuation was inevitable, but I couldn't help the way I was drawn to him. I didn't want to be away from him. I wanted more of his touch, more of his goodness, and more of his icy eyes.

He met my gaze and smiled genuinely, his eyes lighting up in a way I hadn't seen. "You go with Lara," he instructed. "I'm going fishing."

I blinked at him in bewilderment, and Larissa burst into laughter. She shook her head and started to guide me away and back down the path. "Always with the incessant fishing," she teased. "That man eats more fish than any shifter I've ever known."

I tore my attention away from Jack's retreating figure and focused on Larissa. "Are you a shifter too?"

She nodded at me with a smile.

"One of the civilized ones." I didn't think that there was an overabundance of once-savage shifters like Jack running around Pax.

She giggled and shook her head. "Jack..." she muttered with a sigh. "I would like to believe that we're all the same. Some of us just lost our way is all. Jack was able to find his way out of that pattern of rage and hunger. Others can too."

Her words made me remember Rigdon, and that strange look in his eyes. I shrugged, thinking of Jack. "I agree, but I understand why he is wary. You can conquer the addiction, but an addict is still an addict. There's always the chance of falling off the wagon. I imagine he doesn't want to take that risk."

Larissa snorted. "Jack hasn't slipped up a day since he was first brought to Pax. All he's ever done is protect and help our people. He needs to give himself, and others, more credit."

I fell into an unnatural silence that Larissa seemed to notice.

We came to a halt outside of a small cabin and she turned to face me with question in her eyes. "What is it?" When I didn't answer right away, her eyes widened as her mind put the pieces together. "Oh my gosh, Reya. Did he shift?"

I chewed on my bottom lip, wondering if I would be doing him a disservice if I told her what had happened. I didn't want to cause problems for him.

It didn't really matter, though. My nervous silence seemed to speak volumes and Larissa's eyes grew even larger. "He did!" she cried. "Why? What happened?"

"We were attacked by some shifters just outside of the No Man's Land," I finally relinquished. She gasped and I shook my head. "It was all my fault, actually. I was trying to bully Jack into telling me...well...anything, and I pushed him too far. He got upset and let out a growl that attracted the others. The next morning they had found our camp. They tried to get information out of me."

"Information?" This seemed to surprise Larissa as much as it had surprised Jack.

I nodded. "The leader wanted to know about where Jack was going, what he was protecting. I challenged them." My voice faltered at the look of utter shock on her face. Apparently the fact that I had stood up to the shifters was a really huge deal. "They attacked me. There were too many, so Jack shifted to fight them."

"Did he kill any of them?"

"Three of them."

Her look of shock started to morph into something crossed between wonder and horror. "And he was able to shift back?"

I swallowed. "Well...not really." I didn't elaborate right away, but she just kept staring at me with that same expression, so I continued. "He tried to attack me too, but I stopped him."

"Stopped him?"

Her voice went up, and I actually shrank back at the look of stunned terror on her face. "Um...yes?"

"How?"

"I..." I felt exceedingly self-conscious. "I just kind of, like, threw my arms around him and held on." She stared at me for so long I thought I might have to shake her out of her stupor. I tucked my hair behind my ears and frowned. "What? Did I do something wrong?"

She shook her head. "N-No, it's just...I can't believe you were able to do that. Jack has always been so disciplined. No one here has ever seen him shift while in a state of negative emotion." She placed her hand on my shoulder and looked at me intently. "We have all seen the other shifters, Reya. We know the way they operate. When they get that taste of the kill, of the hunt...I didn't think it was possible for them to be stopped." She stared at me a little longer in contemplation. "You are either extremely special, or you mean a great deal to him."

I snorted as a knee-jerk reaction and folded my arms across my chest defensively. "I'm a freakin' junkie. There's absolutely nothing special about me. And I've only known him for two days if you don't count the several I spent detoxing in the hotel. What could I possibly mean to him?"

Larissa raised an eyebrow and a knowing smile crept across her lips. "You were a junkie? And he brought you to Pax?" Her smile grew. "Well, that says you must mean something to him." She opened up the door to the cabin and went inside.

I frowned as I followed after her, but I couldn't stop my inquiry. "What makes you say that?"

She grinned at me. "Listen, Reya, Jack doesn't bring people with bad habits to Pax. He brings stable people, strong, steady people, people who present few risks. He must have seen something remarkable in you to bring you here. He must have been right, too. It is no small thing to be able to stop an aggressive shifter, no matter how much he thinks of you."

My frown deepened. "There's no reason he would think anything of me. He barely knows me." I kept denying Larissa's words because I wanted so badly to believe they were true, but couldn't afford to hope. My whole life had been based on disappointment and pain. Starting to hope now would only crush what was left of my jaded heart. Jack had been kind to me, yes, but that was his nature. He believed in kindness above all things. He had given me no reason to think that I was anything more to him than a new recruit.

Larissa put one hand on her hip and gave me a measured stare. "Reya, did Jack tell you what he was before he was brought here?"

I blinked at the sudden question. "He was one of the other shifters."

"He wasn't just any of them. He was their leader, their king."

My eyebrows shot up in surprise.

She nodded. "It was no small thing he did, turning his back on his people. Jack is the strongest, most disciplined person I have ever known, but he is terrified of hurting someone he cares about. Getting close to someone is too much of a risk for him. I'm surprised he is even as close as he is with me. Generally, he keeps to himself, is a very private man. He's not going to be the one to make the first move, even if he does have feelings for you. Jack's the kind of man that needs to be pushed a little."

I rolled my eyes. "Pushing him almost got me eaten in the desert."

She laughed softly and patted the foot end of a bed that was in the middle of the room. "This cabin is yours. There's a bathroom around the corner. I'll go see what I can find for you to wear. Get cleaned up and make yourself at home." She flashed me a warm smile. "This is your home now."

I felt a strange tightening sensation in my chest at her words. I couldn't even remember the last time I'd been able to call anything my home. I fingered the fringe on the end of a blanket, and Larissa patted my shoulder as she walked by.

"When you're finished, Jack's cabin is at the far end of the establishment. It's the one closest to the pond." At my questioning look, she gave a sly smile and shrugged. "I'm sure he'll want to explain to you what your duties here in Pax are going to be." She threw a wink at me, then disappeared out the door.

I heaved a sigh and sat down on the bed, exhausted and overwhelmed. The silence of the room seemed to close in on me, but strangely, it wasn't uncomfortable. It was peaceful. Smiling to myself, I lay back and stared up at the ceiling. I let my eyes drift closed and basked in the stolen moment of serenity. It was the first one I'd had in far too long.

Chapter Six

Jack was sitting on a small dock that jutted out into the water when I found him. He was shirtless, and looked tranquil in the light of the moon. Frogs and crickets sang merrily in the night, and I sighed. I stuffed my hands into my pockets and made my way toward him, anxious to see him and be near him again. I only hoped he didn't find my presence to be an intrusion.

"Catch anything good?" I asked with a smile as I approached.

He turned his head to look at me and grinned. He laughed softly. "Not really. I have been gone too long. I'm losing my touch."

I sat down next to him, close enough for our legs to touch, and pulled my sweater tighter around me to ward off the evening chill. I let my gaze wander off across the still black water of the pond and I sighed. "This really is the most beautiful place."

He smiled and gave a slight nod. "Did Larissa take good care of you? Did she feed you?"

I nodded and reached up to trace my fingers gently over the slash marks on his shoulder. "Did you tend to these?"

He met my eyes with an expression of mild amusement. "Yes."

I scowled. "Come on, I just don't want your arm to fall off or anything." His rumbling chuckle made me shiver. "Larissa is nice. How did you two come to be so close?" I absently swung my legs off the pier.

"Larissa took care of me when I was brought back here. She helped me come to terms with a lot of things, helped me cope with a lot more. She's the closest thing to family I've ever had."

I cleared my throat and reluctantly pulled my hand away from his skin. "How come you two never..." I let the sentence remain unformed and tried to sound casual, but my heart was fluttering in my chest.

"Never ended up together?" he asked. He made a face. "Larissa will make a wonderful wife and mother to some lucky man. I'm personally not for the caretaker, housewife sort."

I arched a teasing eyebrow. "Probably not edgy enough for an ex-aggressive shifter, right? Or is it just because you're a giant cat and cats are fickle?" He shot me a bland expression, and I giggled.

"No, you were somewhat right about the edgy aspect. I would be too restless with a woman like Larissa. If I was going to go after someone, she would have to have a little bit more—"

"Sass?" I interrupted playfully.

He glanced over at me again. "Something like that." He scanned my face briefly, and he looked like he was debating with himself on something. Finally, he said, "She'd have to be some kind of crazy woman who unabashedly challenges aggressive shifters while swearing and spitting at them."

My heart slammed against my ribs, and my breath came out in a shaky exhale at the force of his words. I stared at him, wondering if he was playing or serious, and daring to hope that it was the latter. His pale eyes were calm, but possessed a deep, burning intensity that made my stomach clench. "I didn't spit at them," I breathed, my gaze straying to his lips. "And I was scared to death the entire time."

He shifted his body so that he was facing me full on and he leaned in just a little. "Were you scared to death of me?"

"Especially of you," I whispered, transfixed by his gaze. "You could have snapped my head clean off my body in one bite."

He reached his fingers up and touched a wayward strand of my hair. "But you reached out to me anyway." A slow smile blossomed across his lips and it drew my attention to his fangs. "If that's not sass in its finest form, I don't know what is."

I shook my head. "I just didn't want to die...and I knew that you would have hated yourself afterward. I had to do something. I couldn't just sit there and let you eat me. It would have ruined both of us."

He sighed softly and took my face in his hands. "You understand much about me that others don't." He brought his mouth close enough to mine that I could feel his breath. "Even when you know less."

"It's because we're the same." I whispered it in a rush and took Larissa's advice. I couldn't sit there while he teased his breath across my lips and spoke to me in that velvety tone. My body came alive when he was near me. He'd had that effect from the minute I'd awakened to his silhouette in the hotel window.

I reached up, tangled my fingers in his hair, and crushed my lips to his in a bold kiss that set me on fire. The heat intensified tenfold when his hands on my face tightened and he responded instantly with the same kind of fervent passion. He tilted my head and parted my lips with his tongue, taking control of my mouth. I was more than willing to surrender and I wrapped my arms around his neck, pulling myself against his chest. His arms went around my back and held me tight to his unyielding frame.

He marauded my mouth until my lungs hurt for lack of air. He pulled away enough to let me gasp in a ragged breath, but his lips were on mine again before I could formulate any kind of thought. It was fine. I didn't want to breathe. Breathing only robbed me of his supple, perfect mouth. I was ravenous for his kisses, and for the first time since I'd left the city with Jack, my mind was completely free of all thoughts of my addiction. I only wanted to think of him, experience his touch, and die within the divine bliss that touch provided. It was black velvet, but so much more. His touch was safety, and comfort, and hot, all-consuming passion. I would gladly make Jack Snow my new drug of choice if given the option.

He reached up to cradle my cheek in one hand and sucked my bottom lip into his mouth. He bit down lightly, not enough to hurt, but one of his fangs grazed the inside, and I tasted the faint metallic flavor that let me know he'd drawn a small amount of blood. He growled low in his throat and kissed me with a savage kind of intensity. He ripped his mouth away from mine and began to trail hot, smoldering kisses along my throat and down my neck. My head spun, and I felt like I would incinerate.

He yanked my sweater down to expose my bare arms as I only had a tank top on underneath. His lips descended to my shoulder, and the haze of ecstasy I was experiencing came to a screeching halt as he bit down hard and his sharp teeth pierced my skin. "Ow!" I cried. "What the hell?"

I was more surprised than hurt, but my exclamation caused him to tear away from me and cover his mouth. He closed his eyes and drew in shaky, measured breaths. Bewildered, I reached for him, but he gently pushed me away, holding his hand out between us. I felt cold wash over me and I tugged my sweater back up. I waited, feeling foolish for crying out and ruining the moment.

He shook his head and let out a ragged sigh as he turned away from me sadly. "Even passion is forbidden to me."

I frowned. "What do you mean? You didn't do anything wrong." I slipped my arm around his shoulders in a pitiful attempt to offer comfort.

He gave a disgusted snort. "I just bit into your shoulder, Reya!" He looked at me with self-loathing reflected in his eyes.

"You just startled me, that's all."

He shook his head adamantly. "You don't understand. I wanted to bite you. Much more of that and I would have probably shifted."

"And I could have brought you back like before."

"It isn't that easy!"

I recoiled slightly at his outburst.

He sighed again and tangled his fingers in his hair, bracing his elbows on his knees. "Any kind of intense emotion is forbidden to me," he whispered. "You have to understand that. I am dangerous. I'm not safe for you and you're not safe for me. Please, leave me alone."

I flinched because his words hurt just as much as any kind of slap. "What?" I squeaked. "But...I thought you wanted me."

A deep groan reverberated through him. "I do," he all but snarled. He turned to face me with a wild, hungry look in his eyes that I didn't necessarily find unappealing. His gaze traveled over my body in such an erotic way I felt the heat from it. "I want to possess all of you, make every last inch of you mine. There's never been anyone like you in my life. You defy everything I've ever known. You rewrite carefully constructed rules, and you understand the inner workings of me better than people I've known for years. All I've wanted to do from the moment you awoke in the hotel was to touch you, touch you all over. I'm half animal. It's in my nature to dominate, to possess."

Why was none of this disturbing to me? I was pretty sure that he intended for this information to frighten me, to alert me to the wildness of his soul, but instead of afraid, all I found myself being was horribly turned on at the images he created.

"I can't be with you, Reya," he said emphatically. "You make my blood burn. Invoking that kind of emotional response in me is bad for everyone in Pax, as well as you. Stay away from me."

I blinked rapidly and shook my head. "Jack, you told me that everyone has a choice. You chose to hear my voice when I reached out to you in the desert. You chose to shift back and not kill me. You have more power over yourself than you think." I smiled and placed my hand on his arm. "I believe in you. I trust you."

He bristled and shook my hand off of him. "You shouldn't. I don't even trust me. I'm sorry, Reya, but I can't do this. I refuse to put you in harm's way. The risk is far too great. Please...go back to your cabin. I've done my job in bringing you here. I will return to the city soon to find more people to recruit. Until then, please don't seek me out again."

His voice was not cold, not angry. It was just flat, devoid of emotion. I stared at him for a long moment, but he wouldn't look at me. I bit my bottom lip in order to keep myself from crying and looking like a complete moron. Anger and sadness are emotions closely linked, and within moments, the hurt of being rejected and dismissed morphed into powerful fury.

I snorted and shoved to my feet, scowling down at him. "You know, for someone who spouts such complete BS about utopia and peace and how 'everyone has a choice,' you sure are a freaking coward." He lifted his gaze up to mine, his eyes stormy and moody. "You tell me how I have the ability to change my life to fit into your world, but when I try to do that, you decide to throw me out of it again?"

He frowned. "No one is throwing you out of Pax, Reya."

"I'm not talking about Pax, stupid!" I shouted. "I could care less about your idyllic paradise! The reason I came on this ridiculous journey at all was because of you! Not because I wanted to live in some kind of Garden of Eden! Because some weird shapeshifter bullied me into being clean and told me I didn't have to live my life of filth anymore. He told me I had a choice. He told me that he had made a choice. He led me to believe that all people had the ability to change their thinking and their course of life, that everyone was strong enough to do that. I was foolish enough to believe him because he was so convincing and so..."

My voice faltered and I looked away for a moment, trying to rein in my emotions. When I had gotten myself under control, I met his eyes with boldness. "Well, he was the sexiest thing I'd ever seen in my life." I saw a small flash of emotion reflect in his eyes, but I didn't give in and try to reason with him. I was too irritated. "Now all I see is a man who doesn't even live by the words that come out of his own mouth." I shook my head. "What a hypocrite."

He stood to face me, his eyes intense, his jaw clenched. "I am no coward and no hypocrite," he grumbled from between his teeth. "I'm only trying to keep you safe."

I rolled my eyes. "Oh get off it, Jack. I don't buy that crap for a second. You're just too friggin' scared that you might actually feel something other than your stone cold discipline. You're not afraid of shifting and eating me alive. You're afraid of your own feelings." I flung my hand into the air flippantly. "That's fine. Push me away if you want. Spend your life in solitude. Whatever. But I'll tell you something. Your words weren't hollow to me. They weren't meaningless to me. I took to heart what you said. I do believe that everyone has a choice, and depending on how badly the reward is wanted, people can overcome things much worse than your all-consuming fear of letting someone close to you." I stabbed my finger into his chest and narrowed my eyes in challenge. "I'll prove it."

I didn't say anymore. I just spun on my heel and strode away from him spurned, angry, and determined all at the same time. He shouted after me, but I ignored him. Jack may have pulled me out of my downward spiral and put me on the right path, but it was my ultimate choice. I was the one who had decided to follow him, to believe in him, to trust him. Jack was being an idiot, and his fear of being with me, of hurting me, was causing him to disprove everything he claimed to stand by. It wasn't going to happen. I had a nagging idea in the back of my mind, a suspicion that wouldn't go away. It was growing stronger with every minute and I knew I had to act on it.

It would show Jack that I was right and that he didn't need to be afraid.

It would show everyone.

Chapter Seven

The No Man's Land was a lot more intimidating when I was by myself. Several times, I had second thoughts about my idiotic plan and almost turned back while I still had a chance, but I had point to prove. Jack was adamant on doing the exact opposite of everything he professed to live by. I wasn't going to have it. I was going to show him that people could be different. He could be different. He'd already proved that on a number of levels, but I needed to convince him of just one more thing. I needed him to realize that he could get close to me without giving into the overwhelming desire to make me dinner. He could do anything he wanted to. I had more faith in him than he did.

It was strange when I thought about it. Two or so days before, he had set out to convince me of the very thing that I was now trying to convince him of. How we had switched roles I had no idea, but apparently being attracted to me was the worst thing that had ever happened to him and had altered his entire view on life.

I rolled my eyes. All right, so that wasn't exactly the truth, but rejection was rejection. It didn't matter the reasons behind it, it stung just the same. And every time I remembered the way he had kissed me, my heart fluttered in a way that threatened to take my breath. No one had ever wanted me. Not since my mother had died. And nothing had ever made me feel the same as I had in the memory of the black velvet. Safe, comforted, home. Only Jack had brought that back to me. I wasn't going to let him take it away now.

So I wandered, aimlessly, through the desert. I had no idea where I was going. I could only hope that the person I sought found me before one of his lackeys did.

I thought of Larissa. She had tried to stop me. She'd

spotted me as I'd stormed out of my cabin, heading out of Pax. I hadn't told her much. Only that Jack was being a bull-headed coward. I figured she would put two and two together when she spoke to him. I hadn't told her of my plan. That would have made her run to Jack, and I didn't need his lecture or his feline wrath. He'd told me to go away. So that's what I was doing. I didn't owe him an explanation.

I told Larissa that I just needed to be by myself to think. She was kind enough to not bother me about it. I'd slipped past the gate when no one was paying attention. It hadn't been difficult, and I remembered my way well enough to know how to get back to the No Man's Land.

It was strange, being there. I had camped in some random place overnight, trying not to listen to the frightening sounds of the wild and trying not to remember what it had felt like to sleep in the protection of Jack's embrace. I was stupid for feeling about him the way I did, and stupid for not just throwing my tantrum back in Pax where I was safe. This plan was almost suicide. But, then again, I guess I never had been all that great at thinking rationally. How had I dealt with my problems in the past? I'd gotten high. All I'd done was swap one drug for another. Instead of a poison that I pumped into my body, I was addicted to the sight, smell, and touch of a dangerous predator pacifist. And the thought of him pushing me away ripped my heart out. Even though we'd only known one another a few days. Even though there was still so much I didn't know about him. None of it mattered. I just wanted him. It was as simple as that. My heart reacted without restraint.

So I wandered the desert in order to prove my point, to prove I was right. To prove that I was worthy of him.

I felt his presence before I saw his huge shadow swoop down from the skies. It was like I could sense his golden eyes watching me from above. So it was no surprise when he landed in front of me and shifted into his human form. I did, however, find it interesting that he shifted with such ease. It helped prove my theory that the bloodlust an aggressive shifter experienced while in animal form could, in fact, be controlled.

"What's the matter, darling?" Rigdon inquired in a menacing yet silken voice. "You lose your escort?"

I raised my chin and tried to look fearless even though my hands started to shake. "No, I left my escort."

He raised an eyebrow and crossed his arms over his bare chest. "And why would you do a thing like that?"

"To come find you."

He frowned and stared at me long and hard. "That is a dangerous thing. Traipsing across shifter territory to locate their leader? You do understand that to be the leader of the shifters, one has to be lethal, predatory, completely ruthless?" He hissed the last word and took a threatening step toward me.

To my credit, I held my ground. I forced myself to stare him straight in the eye. "No, I didn't know that, actually. I really know next to nothing about shifters of any kind. I wanted to speak to you."

He snorted and began to circle me. "You are either extremely brave, or extremely stupid."

I shrugged. "I would be willing to bet on the latter." I heard him snigger just slightly, and heartened, I took a deep breath. "Listen, you said you wanted information about what Jack was protecting. Why did you want to know? What does it matter to you?"

He came to a stop in front of me again, casual, powerful even while doing nothing at all. He stared at me, studied me, for the longest time. Sweat dripped down the back of my neck and disappeared into the collar of my shirt. Vultures circled overhead. In the distance, a tumbleweed rambled across the parched desert ground.

Finally, he spoke. "Jack was the leader of us all, the most powerful, the most fierce. He was revered by his brethren. But he started to act strange, distant, not himself. And then one day, he came to us, called a meeting, and started spouting bizarre nonsense about being different than what we were. He said that we could have more meaningful lives, that we didn't have to be the savages we were. Obviously, this was insulting."

I swallowed hard at the vicious snap in his voice.

"We did what we know best. We attacked him. We dethroned him. I took his place."

He stopped there, and my eyes narrowed. "So why do you care then? What does it matter what he does? What he protects? He isn't one of you anymore."

"Exactly," he snarled. He surged toward me until his nose almost touched mine and I could feel his breath. "And yet, when I look upon him, when I see his traitorous face, I notice something I cannot ignore." He moved away and regarded me with calm malevolence. "He looks...peaceful." For the first time since seeing him, I noticed Rigdon's defenses drop just a small bit. He averted his gaze and his shoulders moved in a sigh. "I have never known what that feels like. All I know is—"

"The hunger. The hunt."

He looked back up at me, and a small bit of something I couldn't decipher flashed in his eyes. It gave me hope, whatever it was, and I continued. "I understand what you feel, Rigdon. I feel it too, on some level. When Jack found me, I was a drug addict, a junkie. All I ever thought about was my next fix. I think about it still. I imagine I always will, it doesn't just go away, but Jack said something to me that was so powerful, that made so much sense, I had to give it up. I had to turn my back on that way of life because it was meaningless, it was empty.

"For some reason, he saw something in me that made him stop and extend a hand to me. He wanted to help me make a better life for myself. He wanted me to experience the same thing he had...I saw the same thing in you. That's why I came here today. I saw in your eyes something that made me think you want more, too. If you do, I'm willing to share it with you. I'll show you what Jack protects."

I knew it was a gamble. He could lead the entire pack to Pax and slaughter everyone, but for some reason, I knew he wouldn't. If he'd wanted to kill, none of this would have mattered. This conversation never would have happened.

"I know you already have great mastery over your instinct to kill," I went on. "If you didn't, you wouldn't be able to stand here right now and have a perfectly civil conversation. And you wouldn't be able to shift in and out of your animal form so easily. Jack can't even do that. He almost attacked me while in animal form. You could help Jack. And you could help your brethren, the others like you who want something more than the bloodlust. Your skills would be invaluable." Because suddenly now I was an expert on Pax and shifters when I'd only been around them for a very short amount of time.

Yes...I was definitely stupid.

He eyed me warily and another long moment of silence stretched out between us before he said, "You would do this? Extend this kind of offer to me? A stranger? A monster?" His voice was low and carried a rasp that betrayed emotion he tried to keep concealed.

I shook my head. "If you're a monster, so am I. You're just an addict. Addicts can recover." I pulled a pocketknife from the back of my jeans and held it up. "But at any rate, I need to test you first. Can't go on blind trust, you know. That would be ridiculous. So, tell me, do you want to see what this place is for yourself? Do you want the chance to know the peace Jack does?"

So stupid, Reya.

He frowned and peered cautiously at the knife, but gave a solemn nod.

"All right, then master your craving for your drug the way I had to master mine." I pulled the blade open and poised it over my palm. I wasn't intending to do myself some kind of awful harm. I merely wanted to give him the temptation. The smell of my blood would set loose his instincts. I just hoped that he was serious about wanting to know about Pax. Otherwise, I was going to become a human sacrifice.

The rational part of my mind—small as it was—screamed at me to stop being so completely rash and impulsive. But I ignored it. As previously stated, I wasn't always the smartest person. All I knew was that I had an objective, and in order to accomplish that objective, I had to take a rather large risk. So be it.

I noticed Rigdon's eyes widen right as I was about to draw the blade over my skin, and he shouted at me. At that point, everything seemed like it happened in slow motion. The blade bit into my palm and I winced right as I registered what he had yelled.

"No, don't! I don't travel alone! I have guards!"

I drew in a gasp as warm liquid ran across my hand. I heard growls in the distance—horrible, voracious growls. I turned my head just in time to see two large, menacing figures leap in my direction. I saw vicious fangs. Then, nothing.

Black.

Chapter Eight

As my eyes opened and my hazy vision cleared, I thought I was back in the hotel room again. It felt the same. I was disoriented and felt like I had just been in some kind of battle. I glanced toward where I remembered the window to be, expecting Jack's silhouette to be there. It wasn't, and as my foggy mind became more alert, I recognized the earthy scent that was so unlike the dust of the desert and the stink of the street. I heard birds chirping merrily, and I took in the wooden structure that sheltered me.

With a frown, I tried to sit up. The sharp pain in my hand brought reality rushing back to me, as did the figure I suddenly noticed looming in the far corner of the room.

I sucked in a breath and collapsed back against the pillows, my head spinning in a nauseating way. I focused my gaze upon the eagle-man, now clothed, standing in the shadows like a foreboding statue, watching me intently with those all-seeing eyes. "Wh-what?" I stammered. I cleared my throat and tried again. "What happened? Where?" I glanced around and realized I was in my own cabin in Pax. "How did I get here?" The last thing I remembered was being attacked in the desert by several very hungry shifters.

With a sigh, Rigdon, looking stern as always, but weary, moved away from his shrouded corner and approached me with his arms crossed over his chest. "You are an extremely stupid woman."

I rolled my eyes. "Thanks a lot." But I didn't entirely disagree with him.

He smirked. "My men attacked you," he explained. "Knocked you down. You bashed your head on a rock when you fell."

I nodded. That explained the throbbing headache and the

nausea.

"They would have ripped your throat out if Jack hadn't been there."

My eyes widened. "What?"

"I don't know where he came from. I must have been too engrossed in our conversation to even recognize the fact that he was near, but when those shifters attacked you, he came out of nowhere. I pulled one of them off of you before he could sink his teeth in, but Jack was faster than I could even hope to be."

I stared at Rigdon for several uncomfortable heartbeats. "He was in his animal form?"

He nodded. "There was blood everywhere. His, yours, theirs. One of them managed to give him a pretty good fight while I took care of the other one. He was badly injured."

My chest squeezed tight and my heart hammered. "Is he all right?"

"He's resting." He scanned over me, and he sighed. "I had a difficult time with all of the blood. I did the best I could given the circumstances, but in the end, I had to take flight. Jack brought you back here by himself. I followed from the sky."

I blinked rapidly at the information Rigdon delivered. "Jack brought me? You mean he shifted back on his own?"

He nodded. "Rather effortlessly it seemed."

I forced myself to sit up. "Can I see him?"

He shrugged. "I don't see why not."

I frowned in thought as I swung my legs over the side of the bed, ignoring the wave of dizziness that passed over me. "Rigdon, why did you stay in here? Why did you watch over me? Why did you help me at all?"

His golden eyes grew the slightest bit warmer, and his lips twitched at the corners. "Had to make sure you pulled through. After all, you were the one who promised to show me this place. I don't intend to let you go back on your word. Besides, Jack's gone soft, and if you're going to run around in the desert like some kind of crazy woman trying to convert shifters to your cause, someone really needs to teach you how to fight." He smirked at me over his shoulder as he disappeared out the door.

I smiled to myself, elated that he was there, that he had

been allowed in Pax and apparently wanted to stay and learn more about what Jack and his friends were trying to do. At least I knew my idiotic stunt hadn't been for nothing.

My stomach twisted as I thought about Jack saving my life. How had he found me? How had he known? He'd been injured trying to protect me...again. Tears stung my eyes, and I shook my head, hating myself. I forced myself to stand and wobbled a little on my way to the door, but I wasn't lightheaded enough to stop.

It was twilight as I left my cabin, and it made me wonder just how long I'd been unconscious. I made my way down to the pond, where Jack's cabin was located, and I entered it without bothering to knock. My heart stopped when I saw him lying motionless in his bed with ragged, ugly gashes running down the length of one of his bare arms and across the side of his neck.

I approached tentatively, staring down at his sleeping form. His dark hair cascaded across the white pillow. His chest rose and fell evenly with his breathing. He was beautiful even in his sleep, even with the hideous wounds that I was the cause of.

Tears filled my eyes and I sat gently down on the edge of the bed, reaching over to take his hand between mine. I felt small, insignificant, and terrible. "My anger caused this," I whispered to myself. "My anger and my pride." I closed my eyes as two hot tears slipped down my cheeks. "Jack, I'm so sorry."

His fingers tightened over mine just slightly. "Don't forget that it was also your anger and pride that brought one of my brothers back to me...and more may follow. That is not nothing, Reya."

I drew in a sharp breath at the sound of his velvet voice. I looked up to see his eyes open, watching me quietly with their serene, pale depths. More uncontrollable tears cascaded down my cheeks, brought on by both my relief and my remorse. "Jack, I'm so sorry," I repeated. "You can't even know how sorry I am for what I pulled. I don't know what I was thinking."

He shook his head and let go of my hand, reaching out to touch my hair. "Shhh," he soothed. "You were thinking I needed an attitude adjustment." He smirked and reached back down to take my hand in his. "You were thinking that I needed to remember my own beliefs, and you were right...I'm sorry for what I said to you. I was afraid, a coward, just as you said."

I shook my head adamantly. "No, you were just trying to do what you thought was right. I was hurt. I was upset. I acted impulsively."

He let out a small, frustrated-sounding huff and forced himself up with his elbow. He winced and sucked in a breath.

I placed my hands on his chest to stop him. "You're going to hurt yourself."

He waved my hands away and gave me a stern frown. "I've survived worse, now shut up and listen to me."

I raised my eyebrows in surprise but couldn't stop my smile. He sounded like me.

His expression softened and he cupped my cheek in one hand. "Maybe what you did was impulsive, but it was also very brave. And you proved something, not only to me, but also to Rigdon, and all of the shifters here in Pax. It's something Larissa has been trying to get me to realize for a while now."

"Everyone has a choice," I murmured.

He nodded with a smile. "Yes. I professed that to you, and to many other humans I brought to Pax, but I never stopped to think that there could possibly be other shifters like me, who could make the same choice I did. They tried to kill me for that choice. How could I imagine that they would ever see things my way? I never gave them the credit they deserved as creatures with free will, as creatures with minds of their own. I never even gave myself that credit. You showed me, Reya. You showed me everything." He reached up to thread his fingers through my hair. "I knew I saved you for a reason."

I leaned into his touch, relishing it and his words. "How did you find me?"

"Larissa told me you were upset. I tracked you. I followed you."

"You saved my life...three times."

He shook his head and his expression turned somber, his eyes intense. "You saved mine."

I frowned in question.

"When Rigdon's men attacked you, I didn't even think. Not about where I came from, who I was, what the consequences could be if I didn't keep myself in check. I just shifted. Just like that. Not once did I feel the hunger. Not once did I see the red haze. Even with all the blood. I found something that was more important, more all-consuming than that desire."

I shook my head, not completely understanding.

He smiled softly. "You, Reya. All I could think about was keeping you safe, getting you back to Pax. Nothing else mattered to me." He took my face in both of his hands and feathered his thumbs across my lips. "I thought my life would only ever be three-fourths good. I had turned my back on the things that made me a monster, but the shadow was always with me. The demon inside always wanted out.

"I never felt like I would be able to control it completely. I pushed you away for fear that I would lose myself with you, like I did in the desert, and hurt you. That the passion you made me feel, the desire, the hunger, would be too much. It was a risk I wasn't willing to take. I never thought that you would be the answer. That the way I feel for you could overcome the beast within me. The aggressive shifters are said to be more animal than man, ruled by their instincts, and so, too, I thought, was I. You proved that wrong. When you are near me, the beast roars as it always does, but it roars in unison with the man. And both halves of me cry out for you."

His words brought on another bout of tears and I leaned forward to capture his lips with mine, being mindful of his wounds and not flinging my arms around his neck like I wanted to. He slipped his arm around my waist and pulled me up close to him, thrusting his tongue into my mouth in a demanding display of passion. I groaned and knotted my fingers in his hair.

He pulled me onto the bed, rolled me on my back, blanketed me with his body, and assaulted my mouth with searing, rapacious kisses that should have been outlawed. He trailed his lips down my jawline, nibbled on my earlobe and descended down my neck, which made me dizzy in a way that had nothing to do with my head injury.

I smiled and let out a breathy laugh. "Are you going to bite me again?"

He lifted his head and looked down at me with the most devilish grin I had ever seen. "If you want me to."

The last vestige of heaviness lifted from my heart and I kissed him again, gentler than the first time, showing him the emotion I felt and not just the passion. He matched me, coming to lie beside me, kissing me unhurriedly as he trailed his hand in lazy patterns across my side and stomach.

"Jack?"

"Hm?" He rested his forehead against mine.

"Do something for me?"

He pulled back to meet my eyes.

I gave a timid, unsure smile. "Can I see you in your animal form?"

He frowned. "You have already."

I snorted. "You were trying to eat me at the time. I didn't really get to appreciate it." I bit my bottom lip in apprehension. Had I gone too far? Asked too much? Would he push me away again? "Please?"

He stared at me for a few more seconds, then rolled his eyes and heaved what sounded like a playful, exasperated sigh. Before I could even comprehend what was happening, his body began to morph shape in front of my eyes. In only a matter of seconds, Jack the man had been replaced by the beautiful white tiger I had confronted in the desert.

I pulled back on instinct, but the cat didn't make any sort of move toward me. He just lay there, docile, his tail idly swishing, his icy eyes watching every move I made. I smiled and reached my hand out tentatively to touch his head. When he didn't try to snap my fingers off, I slid my hand along his sleek fur, marveling over the complete power and grace of him. I ran my hand in an exploratory caress down his neck and the length of his body, which drew a dark growl from him that sounded more aroused than hungry. I smiled and did it again, slower, and the great cat moved to rest his head against my shoulder. A tingling shiver went through me, exhilaration at being so close to such a fierce predator, and having him trust me the way he was.

As I continued to stroke his lithe feline body, I became aware of a deep rumbling sound that could not be mistaken. I glanced up at Jack just as he shifted back into his human form, his head still resting on my shoulder. His eyes were closed, and he had a small smile playing around his lips. "Now look what you made me do," he muttered. "I'm purring. I hate that."

I giggled and couldn't stop the blush that crept into my cheeks as I glanced down at his naked body. He'd been beneath the covers on his bed when I'd come in. I hadn't noticed anything past his wounds. I knew that, me of all people, should not be embarrassed or shy, but I was anyway. I had come to realize that the shifters had little regard for nakedness. It made sense considering their abilities, but it was still strange for me. Especially as he curled himself around me, covering me once again with his gorgeous, powerful body. I drew in a shaky breath and closed my eyes, trying to keep from burning up at the complete eroticism of it.

"You have more guts than any woman I've ever known," he said with a soft smile. "And you make me feel completely content for the first time in longer than I can remember. What am I supposed to do with that?"

I gazed up at him, and my heart melted. In such a short amount of time, one man had changed my life, my person, my outlook, and my whole world. I could never repay him and never thank him. All I could do was give him me, my heart. That was all I had to offer, and I gave it freely. "Deal with it," I stated.

He arched an eyebrow and chuckled. "Deal with it?" A radiant grin parted his lips. "Well, all right then." He lowered his lips to mine again and swept me away in his wild passion.

There were exactly two things I knew about shifters.

One was that they were to be feared. They were powerful predators, dangerous and strong.

The other thing was that they were human, even if they didn't always seem like it. They struggled with good and evil just as all creatures with free will do. They had a choice. Jack had made his choice, and I had made mine.

I chose the shifters, their ideals and their utopia, their vision. I chose to believe that the aggressive ones would, in time, come around just as Rigdon had, just as other addicts had when turning their backs on their drugs of choice. I chose to believe in a better life and a brighter future, in hope.

I chose to believe in black velvet.

I chose Jack.

Wings and Fire
By Brieanna Robertson

Chapter One

The entire household was in an uproar. It figured. She had stayed away from her home just long enough to return with her family in the middle of a crisis. Well, at least a crisis according to her younger sister, Penelope.

"I absolutely cannot marry that monster!" Penelope shouted, flinging down one of her finest dresses like it was nothing more than a rag. "Father is out of his mind and has no regard for me whatsoever!"

Steele heaved a sigh and tried to ignore her sister's whining by turning to the window and letting her attention drift to the rolling green hills of her homeland. She wrinkled her nose. No, that didn't make things any better. She missed the sea, and she missed the forest. The sprawling plains of Norden were not her cup of tea. Never had been.

"Do you know I had the worst nightmare the other night," Penelope went on. "I dreamed he had me tied to an altar and was going to sacrifice me to his dark gods! And he was a gruesome, hideous beast with scales and talons!"

Steele suppressed a groan and turned back to her sister with what she knew had to be a pained expression. "Penelope, please, the man does not have scales and talons. And I highly doubt he's going to sacrifice you to any gods."

Penelope stuck her lip out in a petulant pout and crossed her arms over her chest with a huff. "How do you know, Steele? You haven't even been here. You've never seen him, or met him. You've been off gallivanting on the coast with those ridiculous Ryffsalli scum." She snorted and waved her hands in disgust. "I can't imagine why you would want to help the creatures that used to be our enemies. It's a hairsbreadth away from betraying your own family."

Steele sighed in agitation. "The Ryffsalli never did a thing to anyone. Father just decided to attack them because they were different. They weren't our enemies at all until he almost annihilated the entire race."

Penelope sniffed. "I'm surprised Father didn't disown you when you ran off to become one of their knights."

Steele's lips twisted into a smirk. "He can't disown me. I'm the only one who can protect the Arshwyns. He's crippled and you can't even lift a butter knife without hurting yourself. The Ryffsalli respect me. I am one of their highest ranking knights. Because they respect me, they don't come and kill you all in your beds. I keep the peace. You should be thanking me for being one of their knights. Now, about this marriage—"

Penelope threw her hands up into the air dramatically. "He's a cruel, evil man, Steele! He practices the dark arts! I know he does because people in town say so!"

"Oh yes, and the people in town have always been able to be counted on for their accuracy," Steele muttered with heavy sarcasm.

"Father is sentencing me to death!" Penelope shouted, ignoring Steele. "How can he even ask this of me? He is willing to send me off to my execution just because my marrying Lord Venegoth will bring him more land and power!" She huffed. "Why can't *you* marry him, Steele? Why didn't Father ask you?"

Steele snorted and leaned against the castle room window. "Because he knows that if he tries to get me to do anything at all that I don't want to do, I'll just return to the coast and leave him with his wounded pride."

"But you are the eldest," she persisted. "Is it not customary for the eldest to marry first? At least you can protect yourself when he tries to sacrifice *you*. There's no hope for me!" She flung herself down on her bed in a melodramatic flourish. "The law states that you could take my place at my wedding. That during an arranged marriage ceremony, a sibling may replace an unwilling participant if they so choose."

She sat up and fixed Steele with a dark scowl. "But you won't. Never mind that I'm terrified. Never mind that he'll certainly kill me. All you care about are those bottom-feeding Ryffsalli wretches. Them and your ridiculous stubborn independence." She sniffed. "It's stupid, Steele. Women should not be allowed to become knights in any fashion."

Steele stared at her sister, and her brow crinkled in mild annoyance. "My mother named me Steele for a reason. Because she knew that someone in this miserable family had to have a little in their spine in order to survive. A woman should know how to take care of herself. Then she wouldn't have to be terrified of marrying a dark-arts-practicing warlock." She stood and walked over to her sister, bringing her fingers up to Penelope's face and curling them like claws. "With scales and talons," she mocked.

Her sister paled, and Steele fought a laugh. She left the room and heaved a sigh, making her way down the stone staircase and through the main hall of the castle.

"Steele!" her father's voice came after her.

She bristled. She'd been home for all of a day and she already couldn't wait to get away again. She'd thought it would be nice to take a leave to visit her family. After all, she'd been away for five years. Now she remembered why she'd left in the first place.

She made a slow turn to look at her father as he approached, hobbling on his cane. "In two days' time, we are traveling to the Venegoth keep for Penelope's wedding. You will be going with us."

She resisted the urge to roll her eyes. Her father still tried to act like he had some control over her, even though he hadn't had the slightest bit of it since she'd turned sixteen. "Well, obviously, Father. She is my sister, and I am here. Did you think I was just going to stay and feed the horses while you were gone?" She huffed. "Honestly, you people are giving me a migraine." She spun on her heel and continued to stride toward the door.

"Steele! You come back here! I want you in a gown! Not that horrific Ryffsalli knight uniform! You are a lady, do you hear me? I will not have you disgrace the Arshwyn name by you parading around in those treasonous colors!"

Steele ignored her father and continued out to the lists. If she didn't burn off some frustration soon, she was going to explode. Training for several hours ought to get the job done.

And she was *not* going to wear a gown.

The Venegoth keep was a dark, foreboding-looking place, and it caused Penelope to begin to whimper almost immediately. It stood alone, isolated, and a cold wind seemed to exude from it, chilling the skin and the soul instantly. This, of course, piqued Steele's interest right away. She had never been the type to shy away from dark things, or from dangerous situations. On the contrary, she seemed to seek them out and thrive on them. It had been her experience that the things that seemed the darkest often held the most amazing secrets.

Steele had never seen Lord Venegoth. She didn't even know his first name. She knew he had frequent dealings with the Ryffsalli, and he was respected tremendously by all of them. She had heard some of her fellow knights say that he was the fiercest warrior to ever take up a sword. She tended to find those tales a little bit more plausible than the ones of him sacrificing young girls and speaking in tongues.

Her family was admitted to the castle by a stoic guard, and they were led into the main hall where Penelope threatened to shake herself right out of her skin. Steele looked around the stone structure, admiring the intricately woven tapestries that covered many of the walls. They were beautifully dark, rich colors that shimmered from the light of the fire in the hearth and the torches on the walls.

"This place looks like a dungeon!" Penelope whispered in fright.

Steele frowned. Dungeon? Her sister was daft. The interior was spectacular. Although it was dark and slightly ominous in appearance, she felt almost at home in the room. The furnishings were not outlandish as one would expect of a rich and powerful noble. They seemed to indicate that the owner was refined, yet practical. A person with fine taste, but with no desire to flaunt his wealth.

Steele's attention was directed away from her surroundings by the echo of footsteps coming up the corridor. She heard her sister gasp in alarm, and Steele's breath hitched in her throat as the man entered the room. He was tall with broad shoulders and thick, dark hair the color of molasses. Power resonated from his frame, but his face remained expressionless. His eyes were a piercing amber color, and they settled on her for a split second before scanning over Penelope and then turning on her father. Shivers worked along Steele's spine. The touch of his gaze had a physical effect on her body. It burned like sensual fire. It made her heartbeat falter for one short second.

"Lord Arshwyn," he greeted, his tone neutral, almost cold. His voice reverberated with a resonance that made Penelope shake harder and caused the shivers to find Steele's spine once again.

Her father bowed his head courteously. "Lord Venegoth. May I present to you your bride-to-be, my daughter, Penelope." He indicated her with a sweep of his hand.

Lord Venegoth regarded her for a moment before taking her hand and kissing the back of it in greeting. Penelope whimpered and tried to recoil. Steele rolled her eyes and folded her arms across her chest in agitation.

"And this is my eldest daughter, Steele," her father continued.

Lord Venegoth turned his attention back to Steele, and the slightest hint of a smile touched his full lips before it was gone again. "I have heard of you, Lady Arshwyn," he said, taking her hand as he had done with Penelope. "A knight for the Ryffsalli."

His lips touched the back of her hand just for a moment, but her skin continued to burn long after he released her.

Steele's father scowled. "How do you know of the goings on of the Ryffsalli?" he snarled.

Lord Venegoth slid a cold, dark look to her father. "I trade with the Ryffsalli. I have heard your daughter's name spoken of with great admiration in their marketplace on the coast. I can't say that I am not surprised, you being such a fierce opposer of the Ryffsalli people."

Her father continued to look irate. "Well, I have never been able to have much control over that one." He jerked his thumb in Steele's direction with indignation. "After I took down the royal family of the Ryffsalli, she decided to run off and befriend the enemy."

"They were never your enemy!" Steele spat before she could stop herself. "They never did anything to you, Father. You hated them because they were different, with different customs and different traits."

"They are filthy abominations!" he roared. "Creatures crossed somewhere between human and beast! They should be eradicated!"

Steele felt her temper rise, and she turned to face her father. "It is people like you with your prejudice and narrow-mindedness that should be eradicated! What you did to the royal family was sickening! I fight for the Ryffsalli out of sheer guilt over the fact that I share your blood." The words that left her lips dripped with venom, and she heard her sister inhale sharply. Her father remained silent, but his face turned red with barely contained rage.

Lord Venegoth looked from her father, back to Steele, and his eyes narrowed when he took another glance at Penelope. "You two are like day and night in a number of ways, I imagine."

Steele looked over at her sister, with her blonde hair curled and flowing down her back, in all her finery. She looked like a doll. And she had the mental capacity of one, as well. Steele, on the other hand, was dressed in her knight's uniform, black pants with a green doublet and leather bracers on her wrists. Across her back was strapped her sword, her most treasured possession and dearest companion. Black boots adorned her feet and slender, toned legs, coming to a stop at her knees. Her black hair was pulled back into a sensible braid. Yes, she and her sister were like day and night. They even looked it. Although, if her coloring determined that she was the "night" half of that equation, Steele couldn't complain. The night was so much more soothing with the moonlight's pale glow and twinkling stars. She found the sunlight of the day harsh and hot, annoying. She had always been a fan of darkness in most of its forms, a creature of the night.

She returned her gaze up to Lord Venegoth's unnerving and breathtaking eyes, and she smiled. "You are astute in your observations, my lord."

He let his eyes linger for a moment before saying, "It is a

pleasure to make your acquaintance, Lord and Ladies Arshwyn. I am Lord Falcon Venegoth." He made the statement general, but his eyes remained on Steele. Finally, he turned his attention back to her father. "Supper will be in an hour." He glanced at Penelope. "We marry on the morrow."

Steele noticed a distinct hint of malice in his voice as he spoke to her sister, and she watched as he turned on his heel and headed down the corridor. He was a spectacular sight to behold. Power and grace... Dark beauty that called to her soul.

"Falcon!" Penelope snarled suddenly in a shrill voice full of terror. She spun and stared at Steele. "Did you hear that? His name is Falcon!"

Steele frowned. "And?"

Her sister scowled. "And? Falcons have *talons*!"

Steele heaved a sigh and tried to ignore the headache that began to form behind her eyes. She knew it was wrong to side with a stranger over her own flesh and blood, especially when her sister genuinely was terrified, but she really couldn't help but feel sorry for Lord Venegoth and what he was going to end up with in this entire arrangement. True, Penelope had a sizable dowry, but Steele didn't think that any amount of riches was worth the price of having to live with the woman every day for the rest of your life. She hoped the man had tremendous patience.

If not, a gag should do the job.

Chapter Two

Falcon resisted the urge to tear out all his own hair as he listened to Penelope Arshwyn ramble on at the dinner table. Good lord, the woman never shut up. She'd seemed genuinely fearful of him upon first encounter, but since then, she'd managed to lose her inhibitions and continued to complain and carry on like the spoiled, selfish little girl that she was.

"Is this meat cooked all the way through?" she queried, poking at her dinner tentatively with her fork. "I have a sensitive stomach. I can't eat raw meat." She pushed her plate away slightly and sniffed. "Only barbarians and animals eat raw meat."

"And things with scales and talons who sacrifice girls to their dark gods," Steele's voice taunted.

Lord Arshwyn inhaled sharply, and Penelope blanched before she stole a furtive glance at Falcon and inched away. Falcon forced himself not to show the amusement he felt. He glanced at Steele. She sat relaxed in her high-backed chair, absently cleaning her fingernails with a dagger. Her father had tried to scold her, but she'd ignored him completely. This was after she had devoured her entire meal, no questions asked.

She slid her gaze over to Falcon and smirked before she sighed, leaned over the table, and stabbed her dagger down into the meat on Penelope's plate. Penelope shrieked, and Lord Arshwyn choked on the sip of wine he'd been swallowing.

"Steele Arshwyn!" he sputtered in rage.

Steele inspected the piece of meat for a second, then wrinkled her nose. "Well, it's not bleeding. I'd say it's cooked." She put it back down on Penelope's plate, then sat back in her chair, and resumed what she had been doing.

"Besides, mine didn't kill me. Was pretty tasty, actually... I hear about you in the Ryffsalli marketplace, Lord Venegoth," she said, looking up at him from under her dark lashes.

Her green eyes were fierce, hypnotizing, and caused a momentary bolt of desire to flare through him before he quickly forced it away.

"They say you are quite a warrior," she continued.

He gave her a polite smile. "The Ryffsalli say a lot of things."

She arched an eyebrow. "They have great respect for you."

Falcon shot a look over at Lord Arshywn, whose expression showed extreme disapproval over the turn in the conversation. Falcon cleared his throat discreetly. "The Ryffsalli like the goods I give them when we trade. I am sure that is the origin of their stories and nothing more. I am a nobleman and a businessman."

Her eyebrows drew together in a curious frown, and he had the unsettling feeling that she could see straight through him.

"I don't understand why you deal with those sickening creatures at all," Penelope stated, slinging her blonde curls over one shoulder. "I wish Father had succeeded in killing them all off years ago. Hideous beasts, some of who can change their form into animals..." She shivered. "I find the entire idea repulsive."

Falcon felt anger boil within him, but Steele jumped in before he could formulate a rebuke. She flung her dagger down and leaned halfway over the table at her sister. "Penelope Arshwyn, you ought to be ashamed of yourself for speaking that way!" She stabbed her finger at her sister. "The Ryffsalli are nothing more than a different race. You have been listening too much to Father's ridiculous and biased speeches! Mother would be appalled!"

"How do you know?" Penelope spat. "You were only five years old when Mother flung herself off the parapets of the castle. You don't remember her any more than I do!"

Steele stood with force, overturning the chair. It crashed to the floor with a clanging ruckus. Her face turned red and her eyes turned deadly. "I was old enough to know that Mother did *not* fling herself off the parapets. She fell. And I was also old enough to know that she loved beings of all kinds. She told me stories of the Ryffsalli when I would go to bed at night." She slashed the air with her hands. "How she ended up with such a horrendous excuse for a prejudiced husband is beyond my comprehension." She shot a scathing look to her father. "And if she hadn't fallen off of the parapets when she did, rest assured she really would have thrown herself off if she'd lived long enough to see what a conceited, self-absorbed daughter she birthed." She shook her head. "I am ashamed to call either of you my family."

Falcon watched her leave, noting the graceful sway of her narrow hips and the confidence in her step. Again, he fought the smile that wanted to surface on his lips. He knew of Steele Arshwyn. He knew what she did for the Ryffsalli. She was their advocate, their champion—a strong, skilled warrior, and a woman unlike any other. She was fearless.

He slid his gaze to Penelope, who had dismissed everything her sister had said and was now studying the ends of her hair. Falcon sighed.

"You know, I hope that you aren't expecting me to sleep in the same bed as you," Penelope sniffed suddenly, turning her eyes up to him. "I won't be degraded in such a manner."

He stared at her for a second, felt sick to his stomach briefly, then felt his eyes burn with sinister malice. He knew his smile was wicked. "Of course I expect you to share my bed," he all but snarled. "In order for the marriage to be legal, it must be *consummated*."

She paled, and he knew he should leave it there, but the devil in him won out in the end. He reached his hand under the table and grasped her knee, changing the shape of his hand to that of a bird's claw with long, sharp talons.

Penelope gasped, then jumped when she felt his touch on her leg and looked down…

Her scream just about pierced his skull.

He winced and removed his hand, changing it back into its human form. He put his fingers to his ear and shook his head.

"Penelope!" Lord Arshwyn chided. "What has gotten into you?"

She screamed again. "He has talons, Father!" she cried.

Falcon couldn't take it anymore. He stood abruptly. "Really, Lord Arshwyn," he said. "How do you expect me to enter into a marriage with your daughter when she behaves like a complete lunatic?" He held both of his hands up. "Does it look like I have talons?" He shot Penelope a piercing stare. She retreated visibly. Seeing that she trembled brought him a small measure of satisfaction. "If these are the kind of manners both of your daughters were raised with, I am almost reluctant to enter into your family at all." He also felt satisfaction at the way Lord Arshwyn's face turned almost purple with anger and embarrassment. Falcon turned away from the table. "Excuse me, I find that I have lost my appetite." He strode out of the room and down the corridor, dreading the next morning, the entire marriage affair, and everything thereafter. The thought of having to be anywhere around that vile woman for longer than necessary was a fate worse than death.

He shook his head. He had to remember why he was doing this in the first place. It wasn't because he needed any more wealth. It wasn't because he needed any more power or allies. It was for his people.

It was for his family…

He slowed as he saw Steele standing out on the balcony. He allowed himself a moment to watch her. She stood tall, proud, and statuesque, looking every bit the knight that she was. Her ebony hair was bound in a braid and hung halfway down her back, gleaming in the sunlight. He let the smallest of smiles touch his lips and he sighed. "At any other time and any other place," he murmured to himself. "The indomitable Steele Arshwyn…" He appraised her for two more beats of his heart before he lowered his gaze and continued on his way. He had matters to attend to.

And his back…it ached tremendously. He needed to be alone so that he could be himself just for a second, if nothing else.

She saw her mother standing out on the parapets, the sun shining through her flowing golden hair. The summer breeze tossed it gently, and Steele blinked in bewildered wonder as she spotted two large black wings protruding from her mother's shoulder blades. She wanted to call out to her, *but she couldn't. She was frightened that if she did, she would be in trouble. Maybe her mother didn't want her to see that she had wings.*

She noticed there was something wrong as her mother tried to lift her wings and let out a cry of pain. She hunched over for a moment, and Steele could tell that she was crying. The wings hung limply and looked heavy and cumbersome. They didn't glisten and shine like the birds that Steele saw in the garden.

"I want to go home," Steele heard her mother say. "I can't stand it here one moment longer, in this prison. I want to take my girls and go home." She stood straighter and squared her shoulders in determination. "I can do it," she whispered. She stood on the edge of the parapets and looked down at the countryside below. She took a deep breath, closed her eyes, lifted her wings the best she could, and jumped...

Steele awoke with a scream lodged in her throat. Her heart was pounding, and panic gripped her. She sat up in her bed and looked around, trying to get a feel for her surroundings. Slowly, sense returned to her and she let her shoulders slump, putting her head in her hands. What a horrendous nightmare. She could kill Penelope for what she had said earlier about their mother jumping off the parapets of her own free will. Steele knew that she never would have willingly left her children behind, no matter how much she hated their father.

She swung her legs out of bed, her body still charged with adrenaline from the disturbing dream. She slung her thick, heavy braid over her shoulder and sighed, gazing out the window at the expansive countryside, pale and surreal in the moonlight. The sounds of night birds traveled on the soft breeze and she closed her eyes, trying to will peace to return to her. When her efforts proved futile, she decided that walking off some of her energy might prove beneficial.

She left the guest bedroom she had been put in and softly wandered her way down one of the meandering corridors of the castle. The stone was cold against her feet, but she found it refreshing. It brought her back to reality, which she preferred to that alarming and terrible dream.

She traveled the corridors for quite some time, studying the ornate tapestries, until she happened upon a room where golden-amber light spilled out into the hallway from a crack in the heavy wooden door. Curiosity getting the best of her, Steele quietly crept over to the door and peered inside.

Her eyes widened as she gazed upon the form of Falcon Venegoth sitting before a blazing fire in the hearth. He had his head in his hands, and he looked drawn and fatigued, but that had nothing to do with why Steele was surprised.

Coming from his shoulders were two large, coppery-golden wings that drooped and sagged like the image in the dream of her mother. The feathers did not shine or glisten like they should have. They were dull, weathered, and looked so very heavy. It made Steele's heart ache in her chest.

He was Ryffsalli. Wings were one of their distinguishing traits. They were a Ryffsalli's pride. When something un-speakable happened, or they experienced tremendous grief, their wings became broken, useless, no more than cumber-some objects that constantly taunted them of what they had once been. Lord Venegoth had been through, or witnessed, something awful.

Steele moved away from the door, concern mounting in-side of her. Her father and sister abhorred the Ryffsalli. Lord Venegoth would have some kind of strange abilities—the ability to change his form, or the ability to control the weath-er, something. It was only a matter of time before Penelope found out, no matter how carefully he tried to hide his race. When that happened, Steele's father would have him killed. There was no way he would allow his daughter to remain married to a Ryffsalli.

Falcon Venegoth was in terrible danger, and it made her curious as to why he would seek an alliance with the Arshwyn family. It was common knowledge that her father loathed the Ryffsalli. Why would he want to marry into that?

Steele frowned as thoughts buzzed around in her mind at high speed. First, her bizarre dream about her mother having wings like a Ryffsalli, and now finding out that Lord Venegoth was one? Something had to be done. She would not have Lord Venegoth's death on her conscience, no matter what it cost her father. He could stand to lose something for a change.

Turning on her heel, she started back up the corridor to her chambers, resolve and determination setting in. She was a knight of the Ryffsalli. It was her duty to protect the race at all costs. That was what she intended to do.

As she climbed back into her bed and readied herself for sleep, a vision of Lord Venegoth's piercing amber eyes flashed through her memory, and delicious, erotic shivers rippled along her spine.

Chapter Three

Just as planned, Steele wore her knight's uniform to the wedding the next day. She was pretty sure that her father had almost had a heart attack, and his face had turned its traditional mottled red and purple hue, but she would not concede. She was proud of her status as a Ryffsalli knight. Plus, she got tremendous satisfaction out of irritating her father.

No one attended the wedding. No close friends or family of any kind. It was more like a business transaction than a marriage celebration, and Lord Venegoth looked just about as enthused as a man going to the gallows for his execution. His wings were safely retracted, hiding his race and his sorrow. He was somber, stone-faced, and looked as if he wanted the entire affair over with as soon as possible.

Penelope, despite her protestations, was still dressed in enough grandiose finery to put even queens to shame. White flowers bedecked her golden aura of hair, and her train seemed to go on for at least a mile. She carried a bouquet of fat, healthy calla lilies, and a lone violinist played a melancholy tune as she walked down the aisle.

Steele's father was the only one who seemed happy about anything that was transpiring. He stood with his hands clasped behind his back and his chest puffed out, looking as if he was already counting the money he would come to inherit by being associated with Lord Venegoth. It made her sick. Between the overjoyed look on her father's face and the slightly sick one on Lord Venegoth's, she made her decision.

"Friends and family of Lord Falcon Venegoth and Lady Penelope Arshwyn, we welcome you here today," the portly minister began.

Steele frowned and looked behind her to see if she'd missed someone sitting in the shadows. Nope. No one there.

She sighed. By "friends and family," he must have meant her and her father, as well as the bugs hiding in the corners.

As the minister continued to drone on, Steele took the liberty of letting her eyes sweep over Lord Venegoth once again. His shoulders were strong and muscled and he stood with rigid determination etched into every sinew of his body. A muscle twitched along the hard line of his jaw. Steele turned her eyes to her sister. Penelope was dwarfed next to his towering frame. They looked awful together, and try as she might, she absolutely could not picture her sister giving birth to his child, or standing by his side at social events... Not that she'd ever heard of him attending a social event of any kind.

Still, the fact remained that he was dark and stoic. She was frilly and prissy and ridiculous. And she had the court etiquette of a cow in the field. *"I have a sensitive stomach. Is this meat cooked all the way through?"* She could just imagine her saying that at some important banquet and insulting the host.

Well, then again, Steele had been the one to stab her dagger into a piece of meat at the dinner table and then give her family a verbal lashing right in front of a stranger. She wasn't much better. However, she did know what proper manners were, and she could exercise them at the right time. That was more than she could say for Penelope, who would always be self-centered regardless of the time or place.

"Lord Venegoth," the minister continued, "you are now free to state whether or not you are willing to take this woman as your wife."

He nodded solemnly. Steele grimaced. The man was making a grievous error.

"Lady Penelope—"

Tears filled Penelope's eyes and she let out an anguished-sounding cry that made the hair on the back of Steele's neck stand up. She winced and the words flew out of her mouth of their own accord. "She is not willing."

A strangled protest escaped her father's lips, his face turned purple again—Steele partly wished it would just stay purple. It would save time—and Penelope's eyes filled with elation while Lord Venegoth's filled with irritation and the minister's filled with confusion. Steele sighed, resigned herself to what she had just done, and hoped the whole fiasco would be over soon.

"You *are* my sister!" Penelope screeched. "You do care about me!"

"What is the meaning of this?" Lord Venegoth's voice boomed. "What are you doing, woman?" He turned to Steele, anger stamped into his handsome features.

Steele was slightly confused at his apparent discontent. After all, she thought he'd only been marrying Penelope for her sizable dowry. Steele had a decent one of her own. Frowning, she continued. It was a little too late to go back now. "This was an arranged marriage against Penelope's wishes," she stated, striding forward with intent. "As her elder sister, the law states that, in such a case as this, I may willingly take her place."

Penelope took a quick glance from Steele to the minister, then to Lord Venegoth before she picked up her skirts and fled from the room faster than Steele had ever seen her move. Their father bellowed.

"Will you accept this arrangement, Lord Venegoth?" the minister asked.

He shot a contemptuous look to the minister, then turned his blazing eyes on Steele. "You had no right to interfere," he snarled.

Steele met his gaze unabashedly, even though the menacing growl of his voice sent wave after wave of warm desire through her against her better judgment. Was the man a complete idiot? Didn't he know that if he married Penelope, he would be killed? At least if he was with her, he would be safe. She furrowed her eyebrows. "Oh, I'm sorry. Did you have a blinding affection for my narcissistic sister? Must have missed that part."

She couldn't handle a man who had such beauty and such a demanding presence being killed because of prejudice when she could do something about it. He was someone the Ryffsalli had tremendous regard for. She would not have him die needlessly.

Lord Venegoth let out a frustrated and agitated sounding snarl, but did not dispute her words. He turned to the minister. "Can we get this over with?" he spat.

"This was not what we agreed on!" her father shouted.

Lord Venegoth's posture went stiff. He appeared to grow

tall in a way that seemed to make the entire hall feel smaller. He made a slow turn toward her father, and Lord Arshwyn actually retreated a step. "Yes, I am aware of this," he muttered, his voice all sinister fury. "Take it up with your headstrong and meddlesome daughter." He slid a deadly glance to Steele.

Steele frowned. All right, enough was enough. She yanked her sword free from the baldric on her back and deftly held it at the minister's throat. "I grow weary of all this melodrama," she drawled. The minister gasped and held his hands up. She narrowed her eyes. "Get on with the ceremony." She turned her gaze up to Lord Venegoth. "Before I start lopping off heads."

He arched an eyebrow, but it was not a gesture of amusement. It held a hint of curiosity, but mostly it was full of threat and challenge. "You will gain nothing from this," he muttered.

She studied his burning amber eyes and smirked. "Try me, Venegoth."

He snorted and shook his head. "You have ruined everything." He made a sharp turn back to the minister. "Get on with it!" he bellowed.

The minister made quick work out of the rest of the ceremony and Steele sheathed her blade. When they were pronounced husband and wife, a strange, sinking sensation settled in her stomach. Heavens above, what had she just done? She'd bound herself to a complete stranger with a less than cheerful disposition because...why? Because she didn't want her father to have him assassinated... Right. Why couldn't she have just interrupted the wedding, taken him aside, and explained her fears? Why did she feel the need to marry the man? She was a free and independent knight for the Ryffsalli, coming and going where and when she pleased! Had she lost her ever-loving mind?

"Um...law requires that you seal your union with a kiss," the minister's voice came, tearing through her thoughts and blinding her with the harsh reality of her situation.

She glanced up at Lord Venegoth, who looked so furious she actually felt a ripple of unease run through her. He took a step toward her, and his towering presence made her feel small and insignificant for probably the first time in her entire life. She swallowed hard and couldn't tell if the tremors she felt were of brazen desire at the sheer masculine beauty of him, or fear. She was not easily frightened. She was a warrior, strong and competent, but she couldn't ignore the fact that her hands shook as she stood there staring into the amber eyes that looked to slay her on the spot.

He grasped her by the upper arms and stared at her long and hard. "I know not what kind of game you seek to play, knight of the Ryffsalli," he muttered in a voice meant only for her ears. "I wish that you hadn't begun it at all, but now that you have, you had best hope you can finish."

Her eyes narrowed despite her apprehension, and she raised herself to her full height. "I always finish what I start," she stated.

He held her gaze in defiant challenge for several heartbeats before he gave a flippant shrug. "So be it. Wife."

The word left his lips with more than its share of spite, and he grasped her around the waist, pulling her roughly up against his unyielding frame and crushing his lips to hers in a searing kiss. She was sure that he meant it to be harsh and forceful, to show her his displeasure and rage, but the touch of his lips ignited a fire within her that started in a heady rush of warmth and spread throughout her body like an inferno. She responded before she could think better of it and matched him in his ferocious display, seeking more of the delicious heat.

His fingers dug into her arms fiercely and his tongue marauded her mouth in a way that made her dizzy and breathless. She reached up and tangled her fingers in his dark hair and felt his grip on her loosen ever so slightly. The ruthless force of the kiss ebbed into passionate play. One arm slipped around her shoulders to pull her closer and he nipped at her bottom lip, causing a sharp pain that he instantly soothed with a velvet stroke of his tongue.

Steele probably would have stayed there for the rest of the day, or for the rest of her life, soaking in his passionate fury and matching it with her own, but the minister clearing his throat brought her out of her stupor and reminded her of where she was and what was occurring.

She felt Lord Venegoth relax his hold, and she stepped back, opening her eyes to look up into his. She felt flushed and feverish, and he seemed so bewildered that she would have found it amusing at any other time. He blinked, then furrowed his brow as if troubled by what had just transpired. She untangled her fingers from his hair and brought her hands down, running the tips of her fingers along his neck and chest as she did so. She felt a blush creep into her cheeks at her bold display. Had she lost every single shred of sanity that she possessed? Maybe he really was a warlock and was working some kind of spell on her because nothing else made any kind of logical sense.

He turned, scowled at nothing and everything all at once, then slashed the air with his arm. "Everybody out!" he demanded.

"But," her father protested. "We have matters to discuss."

Lord Venegoth pivoted in that primal, frightening way again and, if it was possible, glowered even harder. "I said out," he hissed.

Her father got the hint, bowed to him, glared at Steele, and made his way out of the room, followed by the minister and the violinist.

Lord Venegoth tangled his fingers in his hair for a moment, closed his eyes with a frown, then let his breath out in a ragged sigh before he left the hall and disappeared down a corridor, leaving Steele standing alone.

Chapter Four

The moonlight bathed the entire countryside in a silvery sheen that Falcon would have found beautiful and peaceful if his emotions hadn't been in such turmoil. He stood before the window, staring off across his land, feeling numb and confused. His wings were out and strained against his back muscles with their heaviness.

He sighed and felt as if he could see all of his plans disappearing right before his eyes. Years of his life wasted on something that had been obliterated by one impulsive woman...

A gorgeous, tempestuous woman who made his heart beat faster and his body turn molten in spite of the cold, unfeeling barriers he had placed around himself as protection. In less than five minutes, she had infuriated him on a level he had never before experienced, then turned his blood to lava with a kiss. He couldn't wrap his mind around the way he had responded to her. It went against everything he was, everything he had trained himself to be. Not only that, but Ryffsalli only felt the fire in their blood when they had claimed another Ryffsalli as a mate. It never happened with a human. None of it made any sense. All he knew was that the taste of her had proved addicting, and regardless of how angry he had been and still was, he ached for more of her. He had ached for her ever since his eyes had fallen on her face.

"Someone broke your wings."

His breath caught at the sound of her voice, and he looked over his shoulder to see her standing in the doorway. He sighed. "Someone broke me. The wings are just the physical manifestation of that." His voice was flat. Not cold, but not warm either.

She came deeper into the room and stopped beside

him, gazing up at him while he focused his attention out the window. "It was my father, wasn't it?"

He swallowed hard and lowered his head.

"He did something awful to you, and you were going to use the marriage with Penelope to get back at him."

He heaved a sigh. "I am the last surviving heir of the Ryffsalli royal family. I'm not even blood related. The queen had no sons and her only daughter disappeared. I was a worker in their castle, a commoner. I became very close with the family. On his death bed, the king appointed me successor. I'm all that's left." He turned to face Steele as she came deeper into the room. "Long ago, when your father led his raid against my people, I watched him single-handedly slaughter my entire family. My parents, my sisters, my only brother. I saw it all with my own eyes." He almost choked on the words as the memories came unbidden to him. Visions of blood, death, destruction. "I managed to escape and I was able to make it to the coast with the other refugees... I was going to marry Penelope to get back at your father. I was going to keep her prisoner after the wedding, hold her for ransom until your father turned over every asset he had, all of his money and lands. I know it could never replace what my people lost, but I thought I could give them back some of the land they were driven from. With your father removed from his position of power, my people could return to their homeland without fear. Your father is a crippled old man now. He can do nothing if he can't command an army to do his dirty work for him." He shook his head. "For years I have planned this... Now it's all gone. Disappeared right before my eyes."

"I ruined your vengeance," she murmured.

"Yes," he said, his words etched with bitterness. "You did."

"My lord, you must believe, I thought I was doing good." She placed her hand on his arm and his skin burned at her touch. "Last night, I was wandering your halls because I could not sleep and I saw you in this room. I saw what you are. I knew that if my father found out what you were, he would have you killed!" She shook her head and looked down. "I thought I was protecting you."

He frowned and folded his arms across his chest, knocking her hand off of his arm. "I am not in need of a bodyguard," he almost snarled. "I am quite capable of defending and protecting myself."

"But you said you were only a trader and a business-man."

He snorted. "I kept my race a secret. Don't you think that there may be other things about me I kept secret, as well?" He glanced at her. "I do not need your protection, madam knight. Unlike my present company, I think things out all the way before I go barreling into them. I knew your father would try and have me killed once he found out I had taken your sister prisoner. I could very well have taken care of myself. You acted foolishly."

She adopted a defensive stance much like his own. "That may be, but my intentions were good, and I have done nothing to deserve your venom. Also, I am no longer 'madam knight.' I am apparently 'wife.'"

He recoiled a bit, but then gave a derisive snort. "You thwarted years of planning. That isn't worthy of my venom? I find myself saddled with a wife, and I have no idea what to do with her."

She scowled. "If you did not want a wife, my lord, why did you seek a marriage?"

"I was not in the market for a wife!" he cried. "I wanted a hostage! I can't very well take you hostage, now can I?"

She frowned. "Why not?"

Some of his anger deflated, and his air left him in a long, defeated breath. He ran his fingers through his hair. He snapped his eyes up to hers. "Because you would probably try to kill me in my sleep," he said dryly.

She smirked.

He shook his head and turned back to the window. "And no matter how infuriated I am with you, I could never be cruel to someone my people think so highly of." He sighed. "I see a lot from the marketplace. Even when people don't think I am looking. I have watched you interact with my people. They respect and revere you. I could never even pretend to do you harm." He scanned the countryside again, trying to regain some peace in his heart.

He found none. Only turbulent restlessness.

"Let me ask you something," Steele's voice came. "If you were in the market for a wife, what sort of woman would you go for? Certainly not someone like my sister." She gave a short burst of laughter. "She was convinced you had scales and talons."

He held his arm out without bothering to turn toward her and shifted the shape of it, first into a bird's claw, then into a dragon's. He saw her eyes widen, and he stifled a smile.

"Oh," she stated matter-of-factly. "I see."

He gave a wry chuckle.

She heaved a great audible sigh. "Well, from my standpoint, I see only one way to make any of this situation better."

He arched an eyebrow and slid his gaze over to her. Her green eyes were mischievous and glittering in a way that turned his insides molten.

"We cannot undo what has been done," she continued, "so I know of only one way to ease the unease and tension of this situation."

He frowned in curiosity and met her eyes.

She grinned. "Fancy a spar?"

Chapter Five

Steele collapsed in the dirt of the lists, laboring for breath. She threw her blade down and it landed in front of Lord Venegoth, who was down on one knee, leaning over and propping himself up on his own sword. He was breathing just as hard as her and his dark hair hung limply around his face and shoulders. "Draw," she rasped, flopping over onto her back. "Again."

"That's the third time," he puffed.

She stared up at the night sky, sparkling with its expanse of diamond-like stars. Slowly, her breathing returned to normal and the evening air cooled her skin. "Then I'd say we're just about evenly matched." She continued to watch the sky, and her breath hitched in her throat as Lord Venegoth's face came into her line of view as he leaned over her. She gave him a small smile. "Feel better?"

He arched an eyebrow. "Physically? No."

She giggled.

A smile graced his sensual lips and he shook his head. "Mentally and emotionally?" He met her eyes. "A little."

She held his gaze for a moment before asking, "Still hate me?"

He sighed and reached out to push back a rogue strand of hair that had fallen across her face. Her skin tingled at the touch. "I never hated you, Steele," he replied, his voice like warm satin. "I was just angry with you. Years of planning..." He shook his head. "I knew my path and now...I have no idea where to go. I'm lost."

"You can still regain your people's land," she said. "But you must take the throne. You can win back what is rightly the Ryffsallis', but they need a leader."

He frowned and shook his head. "I cannot bring more war to my people. They have seen enough as it is. If I took my place as king and led my people into a battle over land with your father, I would end up with an entire generation of Ryffsalli who couldn't fly. I can't do that to them."

She nodded and chewed on her bottom lip in thought, then looked up at him again. "I'll think of something."

A small bit of warmth came to life in his eyes and he sighed, reaching out to tuck another stray hair behind her ear. "You asked me before, if I was looking for a wife, what kind of woman I would be interested in."

She nodded.

He paused and continued to toy with her hair. "I imagine, if I had wanted to get married, I would have chosen a woman very much like you."

She took a sharp intake of breath and felt her body come alive at the way his intense, heated gaze swept over her. His eyes locked on hers and he lowered his lips to touch hers in the most deliberate, erotic caress. She shivered and felt fire ripple across her skin as he ran his fingers along her side.

He pulled back just slightly with a thoughtful frown. "You feel it too, don't you?"

She blinked in uncertainty.

"The fire."

She nodded. "Yes," she whispered. "I have felt it since the first time you touched me. What is it?"

He shook his head. "Unexplainable. It is something that happens when a Ryffsalli chooses a mate, but I have never known it to happen with a human... And I have never known it to be instantaneous."

She swallowed and knew that she would be lost forever if she continued to look into his mesmerizing eyes. "What do you suggest we do about it, my lord?"

"Falcon."

She frowned. "I beg your pardon?"

He grinned for the first time since she'd stepped foot into his castle. "My name is Falcon."

He whispered it over her lips, and she closed her eyes to savor the sensual sound of his voice and the feel of his breath on her skin. The firm press of his lips against hers ignited her blood, and her arms came up to wrap around his neck as she returned his kiss with ardent fervor.

He kept his kiss gentle at first, a stark contrast to the one he had given her upon their being pronounced husband and wife. His hand ran brazenly down her body, and she gasped at the sensation it created. Pure unadulterated, blissful fire that threatened to consume her in the best possible way. She opened her mouth, allowing him to deepen his kiss, and shivered in his arms as he moved his lips away from hers and down to her neck. He teased the sensitive flesh there, nuzzling and nipping, all the while memorizing her body with one hand while he cradled her face in the other.

Steele let out a soft sigh and let him do as he wished, far from minding the change in his attitude toward her. She had been attracted to him the moment she'd set eyes on him. She would be lying to herself if she said she hadn't entertained wicked fantasies about them while she'd been there. Even before she'd decided to destroy his marriage to her sister. It made her think that, subconsciously, maybe the real reason she'd stopped the wedding hadn't been what she claimed. Maybe part of her honestly couldn't stand the thought of him being married to a selfish snob like Penelope when she was the one who wanted the fire of his touch.

She felt his fingers move underneath her shirt and span across her stomach while he playfully nibbled on her earlobe. She grinned and couldn't help herself. "I thought you didn't want a wife," she teased, tangling her fingers in the silken strands of his dark hair.

He raised his head and met her eyes. His were dark, serious, and full of intensity. "You're right," he stated, "but if I have to have a wife, it may as well be a woman I want, and there really isn't any other I want as much as you. I won't waste any more of our time by lying to you about it." His fingers caressed across her cheek tenderly. "I have wanted you since the moment I first saw you."

She blinked in bewilderment at his confession, and she swore more than just her body burned. Her heart filled with a foreign kind of warmth that actually made tears prick her eyes. As the black sheep of her family, she had gotten used to most people not really caring if she was around. His words weren't only surprising and unexpected, they were something she cherished deep within.

"It was in the Ryffsalli marketplace," he continued. "Four years ago. I had heard of you but, naturally, was skeptical. You were an Arshwyn, after all. I thought you had to be some kind of spy. So I watched you from the shadows. I wanted to observe the way you interacted with my people." He continued to absently trail his fingers in lazy patterns down the side of her neck. "There was a group of children playing and one little girl hadn't figured out how to use her wings yet. She kept stumbling and falling, and all of her friends laughed at her because they could fly and she couldn't. They ended up leaving her there, crying her little heart out. You went over to her, dried her tears, and bought her one of those wooden swords the children like to play with." He grinned. "You spent the rest of the afternoon teaching her how to fight, and when her friends came back, one of the older boys was still getting a kick out of taunting her about her wings." He chuckled and shook his head. "That little girl took her sword and beat the tar out of that boy. He probably still has scars."

Steele giggled, remembering the day he spoke of.

"At that moment, I said to myself, 'Heaven help the Ryffsalli men because if this woman has anything to do with it, all of the females are going to be bludgeoning their mates.'"

He laughed, and Steele joined him, liking the way his eyes sparkled when he was joyful.

He gazed down at her and sighed. "I knew then, if any woman could ever touch my heart, it would be you... In a way, that day, you had already touched my heart. The only thing I have ever had love for other than my family is my people, and there you were, one of the enemy's family, teaching my people how to be strong. Now, here you are, delivered to me under the strangest set of circumstances."

She ran her palms up his chest and around his shoulders. "Are you disappointed? Wouldn't you rather have a hostage like you planned?"

His grin was demonic, and it stirred the fire between them into an inferno. "Maybe we can arrange something." He lowered his lips to hers again and gripped the fabric of her shirt. He gave it a mighty yank and rent the garment in two straight down the front.

She gasped as the cool night air attacked her exposed skin, but she didn't have time to dwell on it. His hands quickly replaced any chill with scorching bliss. Her fingers fumbled to remove his shirt as well, but he pulled away long enough to yank the garment over his head and discard it haphazardly before returning his lips to hers.

Steele pulled away from the kiss, causing a discontented frown to cross his face, but she just grinned and reached up to run her palm along the hard, stubbled line of his jaw. "Just stay still for a moment," she whispered.

He obeyed and she ran her palms over both of his strong shoulders and down the contours of his chest. She pushed herself into a sitting position and pressed soft kisses to the tawny skin of his shoulders and neck. Something about the tenderness of the gesture made him draw in a shaky breath and bury his face in the space between her neck and shoulder.

She smiled softly and ran her fingers through his hair, then down the back of his neck and along his spine. She saw the place where his wings emerged, and she brushed her hands over it, imagining that she could erase his pain and sorrow with a mere touch.

Falcon went very still for several seconds, then he shuddered, and he pulled her into his arms, holding her fiercely and kissing her with passionate turbulence. She could feel the intensity, as well as the uncertainty of his emotions. He had lost everything, everyone that was important to him. It had to be difficult for him to let her close. Not only that, but to have her know of his broken wings and accept them with ease. Broken wings were a Ryffsalli's greatest shame. They were viewed by many as a black mark, a symbol of weakness. It was believed that only those who lacked strength of character allowed a person or an event to break their wings. Having her run her hands over the place where his wings resided, showing him that she acknowledged and accepted them, had to be both difficult and touching. By his reaction, she could guess that the gesture meant a great deal to him.

He continued his assault on her mouth, and he pulled her shirt off the rest of the way. He swept his fingers over her skin and she drew in a shaky breath as he replaced the path of his hands with his mouth. Her body burned and pulsed with wicked desire under his onslaught. Before she could even comprehend what was happening, he had tugged off her boots and removed her pants as well.

She barely had time to catch her breath before the delicious flame of his touch returned and she lost track of time and reality while he explored her body. At some point, he managed to remove the rest of his clothing, and the feel of his bare skin against hers was the most arousing, addictive thing she had ever experienced. He was strong, powerful, all dominant male, but he touched her with tremendous gentleness in spite of the obvious level of his passion. He was all velvet fire, and as she gave herself over to him and allowed him to join their bodies as one, she knew in the deepest folds of her heart that she would never be able to be sated when it came to being with this man. To touch a fire that consumed but did not destroy was the most exquisite experience, one she would never be able to relinquish.

As he made love to her, he whispered her name. Her fingers dug into his shoulders while he continued to kiss her lips and neck. He reached up to grasp her wrists, stretching her arms out and pinning them above her head.

She laughed breathlessly. "Am I your hostage?" she gasped.

"No," he murmured against her ear. "You are my wife."

He took them both to the dizzying heights of their passion, and a hoarse cry was torn from her throat as wave after wave of smoldering pleasure crashed over her. He collapsed against her, his head returning to that place between her neck and shoulder. She reached up to stroke his hair as her breathing slowed and the night air cooled her heated skin.

"We just made love in the lists," she rasped.

He raised his head and looked down on her with a sardonic smile. "I guess that means we really are warriors," he muttered.

She laughed and smoothed back several locks of hair that had fallen across his face. He sighed and sat up. She did the same and studied his face, trying to gauge his mood. He looked serene, contemplative, and she frowned. "Are you all right?" She touched his shoulder gently.

"I didn't tell you the entire truth," he stated as he met her eyes.

Her frown deepened. "What do you mean?"

"I told you that Ryffsalli only feel fire between them when they choose another Ryffsalli mate. That's true, but..." He shook his head. "What I didn't tell you is that it doesn't happen to everybody. The chemistry between the two has to be perfect."

She inched closer to him, wanting to feel the warmth of his body. "So, that means..."

He took her wrist, pressed a kiss to the inside of it, then looked down at her. "That means you defy logic, and that means that, somehow, despite the shame I carry, despite my sorrow and my bitterness and my lust for revenge, I found my perfect mate...when I wasn't even looking for her."

Steele's heart leaped in her chest and threatened to take her breath away. "*I found my perfect mate.*" It should frighten her, to think of that kind of a bond between her and a man she barely knew, but it didn't. Falcon didn't seem like a stranger. They had known of one another from afar for years. Her body reacted as if it was meant solely for his touch. Her heart reacted as if it was meant only to be his.

She ran both of her palms up his chest, trying to bring some comfort and tenderness to him, for he looked confused and troubled. "I know this must be strange for you," she said softly. "Everything has happened so suddenly."

He let out a shaky breath. "I'm not like this, Steele. I'm not impulsive. I'm practical. None of this makes any sense." He looked up at her, and his eyes filled with tumultuous emotion. "The way I felt in your arms when we made love... I didn't think my heart was capable of feeling anything other than ice, but with you, I—"

She reached up and placed her fingers to his lips, silencing him. "Shhh," she whispered. She gave him a tender kiss and he closed his eyes, resting his forehead against hers. He let out a long, slow, calming breath. She wrapped her arms around him in an embrace, trailing her fingers across his back and the place where his wings were kept once again. He shuddered. "Falcon," she said, her voice hushed, "let me see your wings."

He pulled back and stared at her with a look close to horror. His brow furrowed and he averted his eyes. "You've seen them," he replied dismally. "They are useless."

She cupped his cheek in her palm. "Please."

He let out a ragged sigh of defeat and unfurled them, his expression holding so much sorrow she wanted to weep. Slowly, she went around behind him and studied the golden-copper feathers that must have, at one time, been magnificent. Fighting tears, she bit her bottom lip, and she tentatively ran her fingers along them. He let out an almost agonized-sounding groan, and she stopped. "Does it hurt?"

He shook his head. "Not physically."

Her heart ached for him, and she reached out to touch them again. She caressed and massaged, wanting him to know that she did not find shame in them.

"I used to fly with my sisters and brother," he murmured. "I loved the sky."

The pain in his voice stabbed at her, and she felt tears burn behind her eyes. "I am so sorry for what he did to you," she whispered.

He shook his head. "It is not your fault."

She continued to stroke his wings, pouring tenderness and compassion into her touch. Maybe it wasn't her fault, but Falcon had still suffered terribly because of her father. All of the Ryffsalli had. If she had wings, hers would have been broken at the sheer shame of having to claim him as her family. "You know, Ryffsalli can regain use of their wings, Falcon," she said softly. "You may be able to fly again one day."

He heaved a tremendous sigh. "Ryffsalli only regain use of their wings when they let go of their sorrow. I don't see how that could ever happen. Please, come here."

He held his hand out to her and she took it, leaving his wings and coming around to sit in front of him again.

"No more talk of depressing things tonight," he said, taking her face in both of his hands. "I have been blessed with a gorgeous warrior woman who sets my blood on fire. It may not make sense and it may be overwhelming, but that does not mean I want to discard it." He nuzzled her neck and pulled her close. "If anything, I just want to explore it...investigate."

She laughed and wrapped her arms around his neck. "Investigate," she muttered. "Right."

He pulled back and his grin was playful, erasing all former traces of sadness and pain from his beautiful features. "Would you like a bath?" he queried.

She arched an eyebrow. "With you?"

He chuckled and his eyes filled with warmth. "If you wish."

She sighed and felt herself slipping. Slipping out of her solitary, somewhat lonely lifestyle and straight into his heart...if he opened it enough for her. She hoped with all her might that he did.

Chapter Six

Steele was grateful that Falcon only had minimal servants and a couple guards taking care of his castle because she was not comfortable in any way, shape, or form, walking back from the lists with her shirt ripped down the middle. She had an ample chest, and while she didn't mind Falcon looking his fill, she certainly didn't want everyone in his household to get an eye full also. She really didn't know how she was going to explain to her commanding officer that she needed a new uniform either.

Falcon's grin was devilish as he looked back at her over his shoulder while leading them through the halls of the castle. Steele rolled her eyes and clutched her shirt tighter.

As they passed through one corridor on their way to Falcon's chambers, a large tapestry caught Steele's attention. She frowned in curiosity and stopped to study it. It was an intricately woven family tree with actual portraits of each person. They were remarkable, and she thought that it must have taken a tedious and long while to complete. "Falcon," she called.

He stopped and turned to look at her.

"What is this?" she queried.

He walked back over to her and studied the tapestry also. "This is the lineage of the royal family of the Ryffsalli. It was given to me when the king appointed me heir."

Steele let her eyes roam over it for a moment, and was about to turn away when one face caught her eye. She blinked rapidly and her heart slammed against her rib cage. "Who is this?" She pointed to the portrait of a beautiful, golden-haired woman.

"The last king and queen's only daughter, Dendra," Falcon replied. "She disappeared when she was only eighteen years of age. Her family believed she was abducted. No one ever found her. She was the last living blood heir to the throne."

Steele raised her shaking fingers to touch the woven portrait delicately. She felt like all the air left her body.

Falcon frowned. "Why do you ask?" He glanced down at her and his gaze became concerned. "Steele, what's wrong?"

"This—" The word came out like a croak and she swallowed hard. "This is my mother," she rasped. She shook her head and tears came unbidden to her eyes. "It wasn't a dream." She squeezed her eyes shut as the terrible vision assaulted her. "It was a memory. I saw it... I saw her die." She put her face in her hands, no longer caring about her shirt. It gaped open and she hunched her shoulders as a hundred pieces fell into place, creating a horrific whole.

"Steele." Falcon's hand on her shoulder was comforting and warm. "What are you talking about?"

She turned to face him, tears streaming freely down her cheeks. "This was my mother!" she sobbed, stabbing her finger at the portrait again.

He gently grasped her shirt and pulled it together discreetly in a kind way, holding it while she cried.

"I've been having this terrible nightmare, but I know now it was real. My mother died when I was five years old. I saw it happen." She shut her eyes again as if doing so could shut out the terrible memory. "She was Ryffsalli. Her wings were broken. She wanted to go home. She thought she could force herself to fly. She wanted to take me and Penelope and go home." Steele shook her head against the onslaught of emotion. "She couldn't fly. She fell." Grief unlike anything she had ever experienced welled up inside of her, making her chest feel tight.

Falcon gently pulled her to him reached up to wipe at her tears. "Steele, are you trying to tell me that your father is the one who abducted Princess Dendra?"

She looked up into his amber eyes. They were tender and caring and it killed her. "It's the only thing that makes any sense," she murmured. "I don't remember much about when my mother was alive, but I know she used to tell me stories of the Ryffsalli, and she hated my father. Even as a small child, I knew that."

Falcon frowned. "But your father loathes the Ryffsalli. Why would he take one as a wife?"

"Maybe he didn't hate them until Mother died." Falcon looked perplexed, but Steele knew the way her father worked. "My father has never been a good man, but maybe he really did want my mother to love him. She didn't. She wanted to go home. She died trying to escape. I bet my father turned his hatred toward the Ryffsalli because he didn't want to admit he was the one to blame."

Her thoughts spun at high speed and she didn't realize how badly she was trembling until Falcon wrapped her in his arms and held her close to his warm, unyielding body. She closed her eyes and relished his strength in that moment. She was strong, remarkably so, but in that moment, she felt like a frightened little girl. Her entire existence, her entire life, had been nothing but a lie. "I'm half Ryffsalli," she whispered.

"Not only that, but you're the heir to the throne," Falcon supplied.

He stated it so matter-of-factly that she pulled away and stared up at him in horror. Her? Heir to the throne? She was part of the Ryffsalli royal bloodline? Right about then, her brain just stopped working. It shut down, and she dissolved into tears. "My father broke my mother's wings." She sobbed. Regardless of everything else she had just come to learn, for some reason, that one fact seemed the most important.

Before she knew what was happening, Falcon had swooped her up into his arms. She buried her face in the crook of his neck and wrapped her arms around him as he carried her down the hall. He felt like stability. She'd spent all of her adult life, and even some of her childhood, taking complete care of herself. Her mother had died, and her father, the instant he'd realized she was not who he wanted her to be, stopped caring for her and, instead, coddled and babied Penelope. She'd grown so accustomed to being by herself that she'd stopped feeling lonely. Her Ryffsalli knight companions were enough for her.

She'd thought she'd outgrown the desire to be held or comforted. She'd mastered her emotions so completely that she'd even eradicated that basic desire from herself. Now, it came roaring back with a vengeance, and she desperately never wanted Falcon to let her go again. It was a strange and foreign feeling. It made her feel out of control, which she didn't like, but at the same time, it was nice to let go, let her defensive wall of iron slip. It was nice to know that she could cry. She could be upset, and he would be there to catch her. That was something she'd never had before.

Falcon carried her to his chambers and sat her down on his bed while he summoned a servant to draw a bath. He pulled a blanket around her shoulders, then tugged the tie free from her tangled hair and combed his fingers through the ebony strands, unraveling the braid it was bound in. He knelt before her and cupped her face in his palm, giving her a gentle smile.

Steele looked away and let out a shaky breath, feeling a stab of guilt over acting like such a weakling. She shook her head. "I'm sorry, Falcon. I'm usually not such a ninny—"

He frowned. "A ninny?" He chuckled and continued to move his thumb back and forth across her cheek in a soft caress. "Steele, you just found out your father not only kidnapped your mother but basically was responsible for her death. I think that merits you the right to show some emotion. Besides"—he reached up and smoothed her hair—"I enjoy being the one to care for you."

His voice was like a sensual, magnetic purr, and it made tingles course throughout her entire body. She met his bewitching gaze and sighed. Her heart felt heavy in her chest, and she knew that she had to go back to her home in the morning to confront her father. She needed answers. And she would need to claim what was rightfully hers and her mother's. Penelope, likewise, needed to know the truth. They were the last of the royal bloodline...

But all of that which weighed upon her mind receded just slightly at the gentle warmth that emanated from her husband's gaze. She cracked the smallest of smiles. "I can't imagine why a fearful warlock like yourself, with scales and talons and all, would want to care for someone like me."

He arched an eyebrow. "What, do my scales and talons frighten you? I could become something else, if you'd prefer."

She frowned as he stepped back and, in a sweeping movement, vanished right before her eyes. She blinked and her heart somersaulted in alarm, especially considering that all of the clothing he had been wearing a second ago was now in a pile on the floor.

Movement coming from that pile drew her attention closer, and she soon saw a tiny, pointed nose poke out from beneath the fabric. Morbid curiosity held her interest, and she jumped back in surprise when a small opossum made its way out of the cloth. It looked up at her with familiar amber eyes, then made a mad dash up onto the bed and into her lap. She shrieked in surprise, then started to laugh as the furry animal climbed up her arm and onto her shoulder. It started to rub its nose against her neck, and she screamed, half in delight and half in complete distress. She tried to move away and pushed at it with her hands, squirming both at and away from its touch.

Within seconds, the rodent had scampered off of her and was back on the floor. Within just a few more, it was back to being Falcon, who was now completely without apparel and grinning like a mischievous little boy.

She shook her head and shuddered. "That is so unnerving," she stated.

He chuckled. "What, you've never been around one of the form-changing Ryffsalli before?"

"Not one who pops in and out of shape right in front of me, and I'm telling you now, I am never going to be able to see you as a frightening creature ever again now that I've seen you in the shape of an opossum."

His smile grew tender. "Good. I never want you to be afraid of me."

She returned his smile. "I never was." She frowned in thought. "Well, except for a split second right after I destroyed your wedding to my sister and you were scowling down at me as if you could turn me to dust with your eyes alone."

He chuckled. "Was that only earlier today? It seems like a lifetime ago." He shook his head in a gesture of mild disbelief, then met her eyes. "You have turned my world upside down in a very short amount of time, madam knight."

She sighed and a twinge of sadness went through her heart. "It's the same with me, Falcon. I just found out I am next in line for the Ryffsalli throne."

The servant girl returned with the bath water then, got completely flustered over Falcon's state of undress, and dropped half the water on the floor. Falcon rolled his eyes, pulled a sheet around his waist, and they waited for the girl to come back with more.

When the bath was ready, Falcon thanked the servant girl, who made an awkward curtsey, then stumbled out the door. Falcon sighed and looked at Steele, who laughed. He dropped the sheet, then went over to her and pulled the blanket away from her shoulders. He smiled, then bent to the task of removing all of her clothing for the second time. He picked her up into his arms again and carried her to the bathtub, where he gently set her in the steaming water.

Steele closed her eyes and luxuriated in the feel of the hot water against her skin. It had been a long day and was well into the middle of the night. She had gone through a gauntlet of human emotion and felt exhausted and confused. Falcon's hands came up to caress her neck, and he placed a row of slow, tender kisses along the curve of her shoulder.

"You know something?" he whispered in her ear as he gently rubbed the dirt from the lists off of her back and shoulders. "I am beginning to think that my vendetta was a stupid idea."

She frowned and leaned forward to give him better access to her back. "Why is that?"

He sighed and stopped touching her for a few minutes while he climbed into the tub behind her. He pulled her up close to him and she settled against his chest contentedly. "Because if I'd gone through with it, I would have spent the rest of my natural existence feeling nothing but rage and sorrow." He wrapped his arms around her waist. "Steele, I've spent so much of my life thinking only of revenge. I forgot what it felt like to laugh, to tease." He stroked her hair absently. "I forgot what it was like to care. If I could fly as I once did, I would show you the stars. You make it so easy to smile."

Something in his words, as well as the unadulterated sincerity in his voice, made her heartbeat falter. Tears stung her eyes once again, but she held them back. She turned, slipped her arms under the water, wrapped them around him, and she held him close. She listened to the rhythm of his heart, strong, resilient, and slowly, the warmth that surrounded her lulled her into sleep.

Chapter Seven

Falcon paced restlessly across his balcony until he thought he might wear a path right across the stone. He wanted to go after her, the headstrong woman, but he dare not leave his home unguarded. He had a terrible uneasiness sitting in the pit of his stomach, something that warned no good was coming his way.

Why? Why had she disappeared on him while he was still asleep? He would have gone with her. The fool woman probably still thought she was protecting him. He knew she'd gone back to confront her father. It was the only place she would have gone.

With an agitated sigh, he went to the railing of the balcony and gazed as far as he could across the countryside. It wasn't a long ride to the Arshwyn keep, several hours at the most. If she had not returned by nightfall, he was going after her. He didn't trust her father. Not in the least.

He took a deep breath and tried to force some calmness into himself. *Steele is a warrior*, he reminded himself. She was no stupid, impulsive girl. She was a knight. She was a brave fighter. She had taken care of herself this long. He should trust her to be able to take care of herself now. He'd only been married to her for a day. That barely merited him the right to suddenly be her lord and master.

But that was the trouble. He didn't want to control her. He just wanted to keep her safe. She had no idea what havoc she'd wreaked on him in such a short amount of time. The night before, she'd fallen asleep against him in the bathtub. He'd lifted her out and taken her to bed, then had spent at least an hour just staring at her perfect body and mane of gleaming ebony hair. She was gorgeous, and so strong. She defied her family and fought for the Ryffsalli, which took a tremendous amount of courage. Not only that, but in one day's time, she had married a man she barely knew, discovered she was half Ryffsalli, was the rightful heir to the throne, and that her father had, more than likely, kidnapped her mother. That was the kind of day no one sane would wish to have. Her entire world had been destroyed.

Yet, even though she'd cried, when her emotional outburst was over, she accepted the information. She took it in stride and moved on, and still was able to make him laugh and smile.

That was the thing that amazed him the most. There was something magical about Steele in her ability to send such light streaming straight into his heart. Light and fire. Light that made him remember what happiness felt like, and fire that set him ablaze with desire for her. He'd been so alone and so cold for so long. With one impetuous move, she had altered his entire existence. And try as he might, he could not find fault with it. He should still be angry with her for ruining his plans, but he wasn't. Far from it. He was grateful. She had kept him from going down a path no better than her father had taken. Kidnapping and cruelty. That was not what the Ryffsalli were about. His people did not pay back hurt with hurt. They were better than that. He was better than that.

He closed his eyes as he recalled the way her soft yet strong body had felt against his as she slept. He'd wrapped his arms around her, had held her close to him in the hopes that he would not wake up and find the entire day just some torturous dream. He'd gotten used to living alone, to existing in solitude. He had long ago given up his desire for a woman by his side. He'd been two breaths away from a completely blackened and jaded heart. She'd changed everything. She'd sauntered into his castle with no fear. She'd given her body to him in reckless abandon, not shrinking from the slight roughness his starvation for passion and feeling had given him. She'd matched him, just as she had matched him in the lists when they fought. She did not shrink from him. She embraced everything he was.

He wanted her back. He wanted her back with him forever.

If she didn't return by nightfall, he was going after her.

Steele's boots echoed on the stone floors of the hall as she entered her father's home with purpose in her step. Her uniform had been ruined, so after some searching that morning, she'd found a shirt of Falcon's. An old shirt with the crest of the Ryffsalli royal family embroidered on the front. It was large on her, as Falcon was much taller and broader in stature, but it suited her purposes well enough. She was trying to make a statement. She had most of the excess material tucked into her black pants and her sword was, as always, strapped to her back.

She stopped in the main hall and took a deep breath. She dreaded the confrontation that was coming, but it was inevitable. It had to be done. The truth had to be known. A vision of Falcon asleep in his grand bed as she'd made her escape that morning flashed through her mind. She'd hated leaving him there and sneaking out like a thief when all she wanted to do was remain in bed with him all day, exploring more of his delectable body, sharing more heated kisses, and pretending like the world outside did not exist.

Unfortunately, the world outside did exist, and it needed to be dealt with immediately.

"Father!" she bellowed at the top of her lungs, adopting her defensive soldier's stance. It took only several minutes for Penelope to come running down the stairs.

"Steele!" she cried. "Oh, have you managed to escape that horrible man's clutches?" She rushed to her and gripped her arm. "Did he harm you?"

Steele sighed and shook her sister off of her. "No, he did not harm me. Where is Father? It is urgent that I speak with him."

"I hope it is to discuss the money and property Lord Venegoth told me he would be giving me upon his marriage to my daughter," her father's voice came.

Steele glanced over to see him hobbling out of the corridor and into the main hall. She swallowed and squared her shoulders.

"How was your wedding night, *daughter*?" her father leered. "Did Lord Venegoth teach you some manners?"

His chuckle was wicked, and it made a shiver run up

Steele's spine. She raised her chin in defiance. "Oh, yes, Father," she sneered. "He made me scream *several* times."

She got satisfaction out of the way he blanched.

"My wedding night was probably much better than yours considering you kidnapped Mother and forced her into being your wife."

Her father went rigid, and all traces of humor left his face.

Penelope gasped. "Steele! How can you say such a thing?"

Steele gave her sister a sympathetic look, dreading the next part of the conversation. She took a deep breath and pointed to the crest on her shirt. "Did you know that Mother was a Ryffsalli princess when you abducted her?" she asked her father.

Penelope blinked in bewilderment. "Ryffsalli princess? What?" She laughed. "Father, what is she talking about?"

"Where did you get that?" her father snarled, stabbing his finger at the crest.

Her eyes narrowed. "From my Ryffsalli husband."

Penelope gasped again. "Lord Venegoth is Ryffsalli? Father! You were going to marry me to one of those disgusting creatures?"

"I hate to tell you this, Penelope, but you *are* one of those 'disgusting creatures.' At least half, anyway," Steele supplied. Penelope paled and stared at her in horror. Steele sighed and met her sister's gaze. "Mother was Ryffsalli, Penelope."

Penelope stammered for several stunned seconds before she scowled. "You're lying!" she shouted. "Father, tell her she's lying!"

Lord Arshwyn didn't even acknowledge Penelope. He was too busy trying to murder Steele with his eyes in much the same way Falcon had tried to do the day before. "I'll have you know, I never kidnapped your mother," he snarled. "I never forced her. She came willingly."

Steele held his gaze without fear. "Oh, I see. So you charmed her, made her think you were something you're not, then kept her prisoner here until she was so miserable that her wings ceased to function. You wanted her all for yourself, is that it? Were afraid that if you allowed her any freedom at all she would desert you?" She snorted. "No doubt she wanted to when she found out what kind of a man you really were." She folded her arms. "That's why you waged war on the Ryffsalli, wasn't it?"

"She loved those wretched people more than her own family!" her father bellowed, veins protruding from his neck with his barely contained rage. "She died trying to get to them! She would have abandoned you, as well!"

Steele shook her head. "You're wrong. I saw it happen. I saw her fall. She wanted to take Penelope and me and go home, back to her people. She died trying to fly when you had already broken her wings. You killed her."

Penelope shrieked and stumbled backward a few steps, putting her hands over her mouth. She shook her head violently. "Y-You're lying!" she cried, balling her fists at her sides and stomping her foot.

"Of course she's lying!" her father shouted. "Lord Venegoth has bewitched her! He has poisoned her mind! He deceived her just as he deceived us!"

Steele turned to face her sister. She looked mortified. "Penelope, listen to me," she said, trying to keep her voice level and calm. "There is a tapestry of the Ryffsalli royal bloodline in Falcon's home. Mother's portrait is on it. I saw it with my own two eyes. She was the only daughter of the king and queen that Father killed." She turned a deadly glower to her father. "Our grandparents." She looked back at Penelope. "We are half Ryffsalli. We are of the royal bloodline. Father has been lying to you all this time." She took a step toward her sister.

Penelope staggered back, shaking her head vehemently as tears coursed down her cheeks. "I don't believe you!"

"Don't believe her, Penelope!" her father ordered. "She is feeding you lies! She has been tainted by Ryffsalli thinking! She is lost to us now."

Steele saw Penelope glance over her shoulder and gasp in alarm. It raised every hair on the back of her neck, and just as she turned to see what it was her sister found so frightening, something heavy came down and hit her hard on top of the head. She fell to the floor and colors swirled in strange patterns across her vision.

"Father!" Penelope screamed. "What are you doing?"

"She must be kept from doing harm to herself, or to others," her father's voice drawled in a very cold tone. "Guard, take my daughter to the cellar and lock her in there."

"What are you going to do with her?" Penelope whimpered, her voice wavering.

"Rid her mind of the poison Lord Venegoth has infected it with. If that does not work, I'm afraid she'll have to die."

Penelope gasped. "But, Father!"

Steele tried desperately to cling to consciousness, but she felt sick to her stomach with the way her head was spinning.

"Silence, Penelope, or else I will put you in there with her!" he barked. "Guard, when you have finished with my daughter, send a regiment of men to Venegoth keep and exterminate the man that lives there. I will not have him spreading anymore treachery."

Steele's heart slammed against her ribcage and a scream lodged in her throat. *Falcon! He's going to be killed! I have to get to him!*

Suddenly, she found her body being hoisted up, and her delicate hold on consciousness slipped from her grasp. Darkness descended.

Chapter Eight

Steele snapped awake as if someone had poured water on her when she heard noise on the other side of the cellar door. She gasped and blinked rapidly to get her bearings, ignoring the throbbing pain that stabbed through her head. Everything inside of her tensed as she heard the bar slide away from the outside of the door and she grasped for her sword, but it was nowhere to be found.

The door burst open and she jumped up, ready to defend herself, but it was only Penelope who came in. She let out a breath. "Penelope," she breathed.

Penelope cast a furtive glance behind her, then shut the door and made her way over to Steele. She carried Steele's sword in her hand.

"How did you get in here?" Steele questioned.

"I knocked out the guard," Penelope replied breathlessly.

Steele raised an eyebrow.

Penelope shook her head and gave her a pained look. "Is it true, Steele? Is what you said true? Mother was really Ryffsalli?"

Steele's heart softened at the genuine confusion and torment she saw etched into her sister's innocent face. She nodded. "It's true, Penelope. I kept having this dream, only it wasn't a dream. It was a memory. Of Mother falling as she tried to fly. I saw her wings. I saw that she was Ryffsalli."

"Why didn't you ever say anything until now?"

She sighed. "I told you, I thought it was just a nightmare. It wasn't until I saw Mother's portrait on that tapestry that any of it made sense."

Tears filled Penelope's large blue eyes. "Do you think Father really kidnapped her?"

"He said he didn't, but Father has said a lot of untruths."

Penelope bit her bottom lip. "You say her wings were broken. What does that mean?"

"It means that Mother went through something so painful that her wings, the pride of her race, stopped working. It is a Ryffsalli's greatest burden and greatest shame."

"You think Father was responsible for that?"

Steele met her sister's eyes, feeling sad for her at having to learn such awful things about their father when she had always been his pet. "I know that Father was responsible for a lot of bloodshed back when he was trying to annihilate the Ryffsalli. I know that he was responsible for killing all of Falcon's family right before his eyes. I know what he is capable of, Penelope. More so than you do because he always took such precautions to shield you. I do not doubt that he caused Mother great sorrow."

Penelope averted her eyes right as a fat tear rolled down her alabaster cheek. "He was going to kill you," she whispered. "He said if he couldn't rid you of your tainted thoughts, he would have no choice but to kill you." She met Steele's gaze again with fear and anger burning in her eyes. "What kind of a parent would kill their own child?"

Steele heaved a sigh, and her heart filled with sudden affection for her little sister. It was the first time she had ever heard Penelope voice her own thoughts and not blindly repeat the rubbish their father spouted.

Penelope made a sharp, sudden intake of breath. "Father sent a regiment of men to Lord Venegoth's keep," she stated. "He's going to have him killed!"

Fear rippled through Steele as she remembered hearing that unsettling order right before she blacked out. Falcon was strong, and more than capable, but one against a hundred? True, most of the soldiers were unskilled peasants, but it didn't matter how unskilled they were when they outnumbered him so amazingly. She looked at her sister with force and took her by the shoulders. "Penelope, do you trust me?"

Penelope nodded, more tears brimming in her eyes. "I believe you. I trust you. I'm with you, sister."

Steele had honestly never thought she would hear those words come out of her sister's mouth, but she was grateful for them now. "I need you to be brave," she said.

Penelope swallowed. "I am braver than most give me

credit for." She handed Steele her weapon.

That was truth. She never would have expected her prissy little sister to render a much larger man unconscious just to help her escape. "I need you to ride to the coast, to the Ryffsalli city. I need you to tell the knights what is happening and have them deployed to Lord Venegoth without delay."

Penelope's eyes widened in fear. "I can't do that, Steele! The second they find out who I am, I'll be killed!"

Steele shook her head. "Nonsense. I am an Arshwyn, and they have not killed me yet." She stood and strapped her sword securely across her shoulders. "Tell them you are sent as a messenger for me. Before they start asking too many questions, tell them both Lord Venegoth and myself are in terrible danger."

"Do they know Lord Venegoth?"

Steele nodded. "He kept his race a secret from us, not from them. The king appointed him heir to the throne right before he died. Technically, he is their prince. They will protect him at all costs." She started toward the door and through the passageway that lead outside.

"How long of a ride is it to the coast?" Penelope questioned as she followed after Steele. "What if I get lost?"

"You're not going to get lost. Just ride south and keep going. You'll run right into it. It should take half a day at the most. I will see what I can do to buy time once I get to the castle. Once you reach the coast and deliver your message, the knights should fly to Lord Venegoth's keep. That will make up some time." She turned and faced Penelope while they left the castle and reached the stables. "Is Father with the regiment?"

Penelope nodded.

"All right. Can you do this for me, sister? Can I trust you?"

Penelope's eyes filled with tears again and she looked terrified, but to her credit, she tried to hide it. "You can trust me. I would never betray my own sister the way—" She swallowed and averted her gaze. "The way Father betrayed us."

Steele gave a curt nod. "Good. Ride like the wind, Penelope. With luck, I will see you again soon." She went to her horse, led it out of the stables, and mounted it, not bothering to put on the saddle. She didn't have time for that. She could ride bareback just as well as saddled. She glanced back at

Penelope, who was readying her horse, and hoped she was up to the task Steele had given her. It was a lot to ask, but Penelope was her only hope. Steele could not be in two places at once, and she needed to help Falcon.

She spurred her horse into a fast gallop and they took off across the countryside. The regiment would probably already be approaching Falcon's castle. She just hoped he could hold them off and survive long enough for her to get there. *Please let him be safe,* she thought to herself as she rode. She had just found her husband. She was not ready to lose him so soon.

The regiment had already reached Falcon's castle by the time Steele arrived. Her horse was lathered, and her legs ached from the strain of holding herself on without a saddle. She stopped on top of a nearby ridge and scanned Venegoth keep from afar. At first, nothing seemed amiss and she could see nothing resembling a battle anywhere, but as she kept looking, she saw a group of soldiers off to the side of the castle. Upon closer inspection, she saw that all of them were circling Falcon, who was moving with lightning-like speed as he defended himself against the attack.

Steele's heart went into her throat, and she spurred her horse down the hill toward the castle. She had no choice but to jump right into the fray. It wasn't as if she could sneak up on anyone. There were men swarming everywhere. There was nowhere to hide and nowhere to run, and Falcon desperately needed some assistance. He wouldn't be able to hold everyone off forever.

She pulled her sword free as she rode right into the thick of the group, mowing men over with her horse to get to the middle.

She was off her horse and swinging her sword before anyone could prepare an attack. She caught a few men off guard and was able to dispose of them rather quickly, but it wasn't long before she was just as overwhelmed as Falcon.

"Steele!" Falcon shouted at her over his shoulder. "Where have you been?"

"I'm sorry!" she cried back as she fought. "My father

knocked me unconscious and locked me in the cellar! I'm pretty sure he was going to kill me!"

"What in the name of all that's sane is going on? I have guards, but I sent them to the south weeks ago because they are more useful there than here...usually."

"I confronted my father about my mother and told Penelope the truth about our heritage." She ducked as an axe hurtled toward her head.

She heard Falcon let out a derisive snort. "I take it things didn't go so well?"

She gave a dry laugh. "Whatever gave you that idea? Where is my father? Have you seen him?"

"No," he muttered with sarcasm. "Forgive me, I've been a little busy."

She smirked. "I bet you wish you had your reinforcements at your castle now." She dispatched several persistent men who had been gaining on her. She glanced over her shoulder to see how Falcon was faring. He looked exhausted, and there was no way he could be in every direction at once any more than she could. "Falcon!" she called. "Back to back!" He quickly fought his way toward her and got himself into formation. At least back to back they would not have to worry about who was sneaking up behind them.

Steele inhaled sharply as Falcon's body aligned with hers. Time seemed to slow, and fire blazed along every place that his body touched. She could feel his heartbeat, could hear it thrumming in her ears. It synchronized itself with hers as if they were one person. She became acutely aware of her breathing, of his breathing, and she felt a strange, surreal calm come over her. Her hands gripped the hilt of her sword and, as if compelled by a power unknown to her, she began to move with swift, fluid grace, dodging and thrusting faster than she ever had in her years of training. She and Falcon moved as if they were one cohesive unit, all flowing elegance and deadly accuracy. They continued that way for an unknown length of time. It could have been seconds. It could have been hours. Steele could no longer tell. All she knew was that, fighting that way, they were the deadliest force she had ever seen.

Suddenly, the blade of a sword slashed its way across Steele's upper thigh. She gasped and let out a yell, shattering the strange connection she and Falcon had been sharing. He called her name and she shook her head, ignoring the searing pain in her leg. "I'm all right!" she shouted back. She glanced around in terror, and panic gripped her heart. There was no way they were going to make it out of this alive. The more men they dispatched, more replaced them. "We need to get out of here!" she cried. "Is there somewhere we can hide?"

"You would rather run and hide than fight, madam knight?"

It sounded like he was making a weak attempt at humor, but she didn't find him particularly funny at the moment. "I would rather run and hide when all staying and fighting is going to get me is buried in a shallow grave!" Her arm was aching and starting to get heavy with exertion. She wouldn't be able to keep up this pace for much longer. She had no idea how Falcon was, considering he'd been fighting before she'd arrived.

"I know a place!" he called back to her. "But there's only one way we can get to it. I need you to trust me."

"I do trust you!"

"All right, on my signal, I'm going to throw my sword to you. Take it, then wrap your arms around my neck, and hold on!"

"All right!"

"Ready... Now!"

Steele spun and caught his sword just as he shapeshifted into an enormous golden dragon. He took out half the men with a swing of his tail alone and sent the others running in fright. It gave them a small window of opportunity, and Steele wrapped her arms around his neck as he made a powerful leap into the air. His talons dug into the castle wall as he scaled it, sending pieces of stone crumbling to the ground below. She squeezed her eyes shut and held on as he made his way to the top tower.

A shout from below caught her attention long enough for her to open her eyes and see several men launching spears in their direction. She shrieked and buried her face against Falcon's body. She heard one of the projectiles pass by much too close to suit her, and she gasped as she heard Falcon let out a roar of pain. She raised her head to see that one of the spears had lodged itself into his shoulder. She took one of the swords she held and poised it in her hand to throw. She peered down at the only man left holding a spear and got him in her sights, then sent the sword hurtling to the ground like a missile. It found its mark.

Falcon shifted back into his human form right as they reached the tower window, as he was too large to enter as a dragon. Both he and Steele tumbled through the opening and onto the cold stone floor. He got to his feet quickly, let out an enraged scream, and yanked the spear out of his shoulder, flinging it to the ground.

"Falcon," Steele murmured, scrambling to her feet and going to him. "Are you all right?" She placed her hand over his, which was holding his wounded shoulder.

He met her eyes and tender warmth emanated from them as he reached up to cup her cheek. "I'm fine." He shook his head. "I can't believe we're still alive."

"We were lucky. Father's army is not made up of trained soldiers. Most of them are enslaved peasants who barely know how to use a sword."

He snorted in disgust. "Innocent men dying...for what? One man's bloodlust?"

Steele felt the same shame and sadness his voice held, and she hung her head, wishing she'd been born into any other family. Her father had caused so much pain and suffering.

"Come on," Falcon said suddenly, taking her hand in his. "We have to get to safety." He led her to a door hidden beneath a stairwell and pulled her inside, grabbing one of the torches that illuminated the castle passageways as he did so. That door led to a narrow, spiraling staircase that went downward for a great long while before ending in a room barricaded by a heavy oak door. Falcon slid the bar back and ushered her inside. It had double bars on the inside and he handed Steele the torch while he slid both of them into place.

Steele held up the torch and peered into the dark room. It was small with no windows, and it was sparsely furnished. Lining one wall, however, were supplies, foodstuffs, blankets, and clothing. She raised her eyebrows. "What is this place?"

Falcon came up behind her and took the torch, making his way around the room to light several more on the walls. "As you know, I was not born into royalty, and though I was named heir, the Ryffsalli royal palace was destroyed by your father. For many years, I lived amongst the refugees on the coast. My family was killed, so I lived with the king's advisor, who had also managed to survive. It was he who helped me set up my trade business, which has, in effect, brought me great wealth. In my quest for vengeance, I wanted to move back to the country of Norden. It was, after all, rightly the Ryffsalli's homeland. When I went looking for a place to call my own, I happened upon this castle, which had been vacated by the previous lord. I bought it from him and made it my own. This room used to be a dungeon, but I converted it into a safe room of sorts. For events such as this one. It will take the men awhile to find and a long while to break down the door as they will not be able to cart a battering ram all the way down the staircase." He pointed to the wall of supplies. "I have this regularly stocked by my servants. There is food, water, blankets. Even a few weapons." He went over to a pile of blankets and unfolded one, wrapping it around his waist, as he was naked from shapeshifting.

"Why didn't you come in here when you knew the army was approaching?" Steele asked.

He turned and fixed her with a primal, deadly look, as if he was offended that she'd asked. "I didn't know where you were!" he exclaimed. "Why would I run in here and save my own hide when you were out there and in danger?"

Steele felt her heart soften, and she went to him, placing her hands on his muscled chest. "You could have been killed."

The torchlight reflected in his eyes and made his gaze look feral. "So could you," he all but growled, taking her by the shoulders. "I never want you out of my sight again. Understood?"

She arched an eyebrow and stepped back, putting her hands on her hips. "You may be the appointed royal heir, but the last time I checked, no one had died and made you my commanding officer. I have been a knight for as long as you have been in the revenge business. I know what I'm doing."

He snorted. "Said the woman who was locked in a cellar."

She narrowed her eyes and stabbed her finger at the ground. "Sit down and let me dress your wound," she commanded. "I'm going to have to stitch it."

He obeyed as she went over to the wall of supplies. She grabbed some cloths, needle and thread, something that looked like it might be a salve, and something that, upon closer inspection, she realized was alcohol. She gathered the items and made her way back to Falcon.

"The least you could have done was wake me up and tell me where you were going," he groused. "Instead, you left me sleeping and vanished into thin air. I could have gone with you. I could have protected you."

She rolled her eyes. "Said the man with the hole in his shoulder," she grumbled.

He heaved a sigh and reached around to grab the hand that was cleaning his wound. "Steele, for the love of—" He guided her around to face him, then pulled her down onto his lap. "Listen to me. I am a proud man. I do not admit weakness lightly, but I was afraid, all right?" His gaze burned into hers and she saw the sincerity in his eyes. It made her heartbeat falter. So did the way he reached up to cradle her face in both of his hands. "You cannot barrel into my life and obliterate every defense I own in one night, then turn around and go gallivanting off to who knows where and expect me to sit idly by and not care."

His gaze was unnerving and his words made a strange feeling creep into her chest. Looking away, she swallowed and frowned.

"I spent all day worrying about you," he admitted, his voice soft and hypnotizing. He reached up to stroke her hair. "Steele, I have felt nothing but cold, black hatred for so long. Last night, you brought me laughter. You brought me tenderness. You brought me light when my soul has been starving for it for ages." He lifted her chin with his finger so he could look into her eyes. "Do you really expect me to just give that up now that I have it?"

The strange feeling in her chest moved up to coil around her heart and squeezed so tight that she almost choked. She couldn't remember the last time anyone had needed her. Never... No one but the Ryffsalli as a whole, but that gave her little fulfillment. She was one knight in an army of knights. The Ryffsalli needed knights. No one had ever needed *her*. "I'm sorry, Falcon," she whispered. "I am used to doing things on my own."

He nodded. "I know, so am I. I understand that independence in you, but I did not like and will not stand for another day like today. All I did was worry while your father locked you up so he could kill you."

She arched an eyebrow and gave him a sardonic stare. "And then he sent the army to come annihilate you. Today has not been a good day."

He snickered and shook his head in agreement.

She sighed. "Not many couples I know spend their honeymoon in an old dungeon."

He snorted. "I have no idea how we're going to get out of this. The soldiers will find this place sooner or later. Your father won't give up." His eyes turned stormy, as if he was recalling a horrid memory from long ago.

She placed her palm against his cheek. "I know. We just have to hold them off until reinforcements arrive."

He blinked, and a small remnant of hope came to life in his eyes. "Reinforcements are coming?"

"With any luck. Now let me go so I can finish fixing your shoulder."

He smiled, slipped an arm around her waist, and pulled her up against his chest. He lowered his lips to hers in a slow, deliberate kiss that robbed her of breath and made her dizzy. Her heartbeat stumbled and faltered before it synchronized itself to his. That strange, surreal connection took its hold once again and she could hear the beat of his heart, could feel every breath he took. Her body burned.

"What is that?" she gasped as she pulled her lips away from his.

He met her eyes and shook his head. "I don't know," he whispered. "Something extraordinary."

"Is it that Ryffsalli connection you spoke of before?"

"It has to be." He trailed his fingers down her neck. "I do not know the specifics of it as I have never found my perfect mate, until now."

His gaze locked on hers again, and waves of molten desire flowed through her. She wanted to stay there forever, drown in the burning intensity of his eyes, and lose concept of time within his embrace. But she forced herself to move away and tend his shoulder. She couldn't afford to have it get infected. That would threaten Falcon's life, and regardless of how short of a time they had been together, she couldn't picture her life without him now. She didn't want to. She didn't want to remember what it felt like to be completely alone, didn't want to remember how life had been before his fiery touch and his scorching gaze, didn't want to remember what it had felt like before she'd been someone's perfect mate.

Chapter Nine

"Ugh, what is this stuff anyway?"

Falcon smirked as Steele poured alcohol over his wound one more time to cleanse it after she'd stitched it shut. "Ryff-salli liquor," he replied. "It's got two important uses. To prevent wounds from getting infected and to make the person with the wound so intoxicated they can't feel the pain."

"It smells like it could kill a horse," she muttered.

He chuckled. "It probably could." He glanced at her while she took a tentative smell, then threw back a drink.

She sputtered and wiped her mouth. "Yes, it could."

He grinned.

"You didn't even flinch while I was stitching you," she remarked as she went to put the supplies away.

He nodded. "I suppose the burden and pain of my heavy, useless wings has given me a high tolerance for discomfort." He watched her over his shoulder as she swaggered back to him. He grinned devilishly. "Do I get a kiss for bravery and sheer manliness?"

She stopped in her approach long enough to shoot him a bemused expression and roll her eyes. "You're ridiculous."

He chuckled and warmth stole through his entire body as she came to sit next to him with a sigh. He closed his eyes and basked in the glow of companionship. He hadn't realized how much his solitude had pained him until Steele had come exploding into his life. "Did you tend to your wound as well?" he queried.

She nodded. "It was only a graze. I cleaned and bandaged it."

He let his eyes roam over her as she let out a heavy sigh. He could see her weariness in the way her shoulders slumped and he reached out to touch her face tenderly. "Were you hurt?"

She looked up at him in question.

"When your father attacked you? Did he hurt you?"

"No," she muttered. She reached up and rubbed at the back of her head with a frown. "He did bash me a good one in the head, though. Or, maybe it was his guard that did that. I'm not sure. I didn't see it coming."

"How did you escape?"

"My sister." She smiled when she saw the surprise in his eyes that he couldn't hide. "I know. I was just as stunned, trust me." She looked away and her wry smile faded as she shook her head. "I wish I had been born into any other family," she confessed quietly. "I try to handle things as they come at me, change what I can, accept what I cannot. I am having a very difficult time coming to grips with the fact that my father is outside of this castle right now, intent on killing you. And when he finds me, he'll kill me as well. He won't even bat an eye. When he finds out Penelope helped me, he'll probably kill her also."

Falcon hated the sadness in her voice and did not like her slender, proud shoulders looking burdened. He reached out to run his hand down her back in a gesture of comfort.

She looked up at him and gave him a small, pained smile. "Was your family close? Were they good people?"

His heart squeezed tight in his chest at the mention of his family and he averted his eyes, nodding slowly. "Yes, they were. My mother and father adored one another. My family was full of love..."

"I'm sorry you ever had to come in contact with my abominable family," she said softly.

The raw ache in her voice as she spoke made him pull her into his arms. "Steele," he whispered, "we cannot control the things that happen to us any more than we can control the family we are born into. I am not sorry for what has happened."

She met his eyes, complete bewilderment reflected in hers.

"I miss my family. Do I hate your father for being responsible for their deaths? Absolutely, and if I could do to him what he did to them, I would not hesitate, but because of my desire for revenge, I went seeking out your father, and it was because I sought him out that I was able to arrange the marriage with Penelope. If I had not done that, I may have never been put in your path, and that would be a great tragedy in itself." He gazed down into her green eyes, full of awestruck emotion at his words. "Steele, it does not matter where you come from, or where I come from. All that matters is who we are now. I will be your family, and you will be mine." He caught a tear as it made its way down her cheek, and he brought his lips to hover over hers. "The past is gone," he whispered. "It cannot be changed. What matters is how we live to shape our future."

Fire ripped through his body when she threw her arms around his neck and fused her lips with his. An all-consuming fire a hundred times hotter than anything else he had experienced thus far. He trembled with the force of it and clutched her close to him, never wanting her out of his arms again. He didn't know how he had existed so solitary all this time. When he held Steele, the thought of being without her made him feel so empty it hurt.

He cradled her in his arms and brushed the wild wisps of her hair away from her face, pouring gentleness and kindness into his kiss and his touch. He explored her mouth languidly, without hurry, and delighted in the way she melted against him. She went soft, pliant, and ran her hands down his shoulders and arms in the most delicious of caresses.

Steele Arshwyn, knight of the Ryffsalli. So strong, so unbreakable, yet she was pliant in his arms. The woman who defied and fought against her own family. The woman who had fought more men in one battle than he had ever seen a single person take on. She put her trust in him. It was overwhelming and wonderful.

Without realizing he'd done it, he found his fingertips dropping her shirt to the stone floor. She moved back just enough to let him discard it, then was back in his arms, kissing him again.

He shivered at the feel of her bare, supple skin against his. She was a warrior, full of lithe muscle, but she still possessed the soft curves of a woman that he adored. She was the best of everything he loved. She was the best of everything in his life.

He pulled away from the kiss enough to make her frown, and he chuckled. "Just one moment," he said, running his fingers across her jaw line. "I want to do this right this time."

She blinked as he stood and went over to the wall of supplies. "I didn't particularly find anything wrong with the last time."

He grinned. Yes, he knew her passion could match his, but he didn't want this to be rushed. He wanted to take his time with her, explore and worship her the way she deserved. While there had been something raw and primal about making love in the lists, he wanted this time to be slow and sensual. He wanted to explore the extent of their connection, and see how long the fire would go before it burned out.

He grabbed several blankets and went back over to her, dropping the one he wore around his waist as he did so. Her heated gaze raked over his body, then met his eyes with a hunger that just about laid him flat. Never in his life had he thought a woman would look at him like that. Steele's eyes held a thousand dark promises, and he wanted to know each and every one.

He spread the blankets on the ground to make the cold stone as comfortable as possible, then laid on his side and pulled her back into his arms. "Maybe one day we'll graduate to a bed," he muttered.

Her laughter lit up her face and his heart. He wanted to keep her laughing for all time. He lowered his lips to hers and kissed her in an unhurried display until both of them were breathless and his heart was pounding so hard he thought it might burst.

He turned his attention to the rest of her body, removing her boots and pants and taking the time to seek out every delicate line and luscious curve. He worshipped her body, tasted every inch of her until he thought he would become intoxicated. She was perfection, as if she had been created just for him. Nothing had ever felt as good as her soft skin against his hands. Nothing had ever sounded as sweet as the noises of pleasure he could elicit from her. Nothing had ever looked as beautiful as her face in the torchlight.

He kissed his way up her body and smiled as she tangled her fingers in his hair. He turned his face against her arm and nuzzled her wrist, placing soft kisses to it as he made his way to her palm. He pressed several kisses there as well, then placed her hand over his heart. Her tender touch set fire to his skin.

He held her close as he joined himself with her, not wanting to relinquish one inch of her warmth. He closed his eyes in pure bliss at the feel of her and wondered how he had gone his whole life in such cold desolation. After his family had been killed, he'd thought revenge would be the only thing to ever bring him joy or satisfaction. How very wrong he had been. He'd experienced more joy in the short time he'd spent with Steele than he probably ever had.

She drew in a shuddering breath suddenly and clutched him close to her. He went very still for several seconds as his ears filled with the rapid pounding of her heartbeat, and he felt her ragged breathing as if it was his. The intensity of his pleasure doubled, and judging by the way she dug her fingernails into his upper arms and groaned, hers did as well. He lowered his lips and pressed hot kisses to her neck. She brought her legs up and wrapped them around his waist, almost sending him into convulsions. He moved against her and they both cried out. Never in his life had he ever felt such dizzying, all-consuming pleasure. It wasn't just physical. He felt it inside and out, like something was taking hold of his heart and gripping it without mercy.

His breath started to come in shallow gasps and raging fire spread across his back to the point of pain. His head spun in an almost nauseating way, and he started to tremble. A series of visions that replayed his entire life barraged his mind. Familiar, unrelenting pain stabbed at his heart, and he squeezed his eyes shut to try and block the memories that came unbidden to him. He saw his family. He saw the war, the battle that had cruelly taken their lives. He saw the Ryffsalli refugees. He saw years and years of painful, black solitude.

Tears stung his eyes as he tried to push the memories away, but they were relentless, forcing him to relive every terrible tragedy he had endured. Just when he thought he could no longer take it, he saw Steele's face. He saw her in the Ryffsalli marketplace, proud and stoic. He saw her in his home, fearless, undaunted. He saw her in his arms, laughing, her green eyes sparkling like jewels. The sight of her and the remembrance of all the beauty she'd brought into his life in such a short time drove out the cold darkness and pain of the other memories with the force of an explosion.

White-hot pleasure and fire tore through him, and he

screamed her name. His back arched and his wings shot forth from his shoulders as billowing waves of delicious, overwhelming heat passed over him. He cried out again, his voice mingling with hers, and he went limp and collapsed to the ground shaking.

"Falcon!" Steele cried. "Are you all right?"

She placed her hand on his shoulder and he pushed himself into a sitting position. He reached his trembling fingers to his cheeks, which were wet with tears, and he blinked in bewilderment.

"Oh my gosh, Falcon," Steele gasped. "Your wings!"

He looked over his shoulder, and his heart slammed against his chest with shock. What had once been nothing more than two heavy, tattered burdens were now full of thick, shining, copper-golden feathers. They arched out of his shoulders with an elegant curve and felt light and free.

"They're so amazing," Steele whispered, running her fingers along the feathers.

Falcon closed his eyes and relished her touch in the deepest part of him. He felt more tears burn and he grabbed Steele by the wrist, hauling her back into his arms and pressing kisses all over her face and lips. "Steele," he breathed. He rested his forehead against hers and sighed. "My beautiful Steele. You restored my wings." The words caught in his throat as emotion threatened to choke him. "You have given me everything."

Her arms came up to pull him close, and he snuggled into her hold. She buried her lips against his neck and kissed him with such tenderness it gave him chills.

"Come lay next to me," she murmured. "We should rest and I want to be close to you."

She didn't need to ask him twice. He would follow her straight out of his world and into a different realm if she asked him to. He crawled back over to the blankets, retracted his wings, and lay down, pulling her into his arms. She pillowed her head on his bicep and pressed herself close to his body. He tugged one of the blankets over them and closed his eyes. He enjoyed the quiet, intimate moment, and he enjoyed the way she felt against him. Most of all, he enjoyed the way his heartbeat synchronized itself to hers as he drifted off to sleep.

Chapter Ten

"Break it down or I will see to it that you never see the light of day again!"

Steele was jolted awake by the indistinct voice, followed by the sound of splintering wood. She sat up with a start and looked over to the door. "Falcon," she said, shaking his shoulder. "Falcon, wake up!"

Something hit the door with such force it sent the bars rattling. Steele gasped and scrambled to her feet, locating her clothing and pulling it on.

"What's going on?" Falcon asked as he sat up. "How long have we been asleep?"

"Too long," she replied. "They're trying to break the door down."

"With what?" he questioned as he went to the supplies to locate some clothing.

"It sounds like an axe. Will they be able to get in?"

He snorted. "The door is made of wood. It's only a matter of time." He tugged on a shirt and some pants, then grabbed a sword from the limited supply of weapons. He came to stand next to her, and they faced the door as the pounding and hacking at it continued.

Steele swallowed. There was no way they would be able to fight off the entire army pinned in like they were. This was a death trap. She stole a sidelong glance at Falcon, whose face was grim. Her heart twisted. She wasn't ready for it to end this way. She had so much left to see of life with Falcon.

She jumped as the head of the axe made its way through the door, splintering the wood. Her heart started to hammer, and she gripped her sword tight. She would not go down without a fight.

"Steele," Falcon whispered.

She looked over at him. His face was stoic and emotionless, but his voice betrayed his fear.

"I have something I need to say to you."

"No," she interrupted before another word could come out of his mouth. She could sense what he was going to say, and she couldn't hear it yet. Not right now before they stared death right in the eye. He turned to meet her gaze, sadness reflecting in his amber eyes. She went to him and put her palm on his cheek. "Tell me after this is over," she said with resigned determination. "Take me to the stars and tell me then."

He held her gaze for a long time before a small, baleful smile twisted his lips and he nodded, turning his face to press a kiss to her palm. The axe rent more of the wood away from the door, and Falcon trailed his hand down Steele's arm until his fingers were twined with hers "Back to back," he said softly.

She tightened her hand on his. "Always."

They turned to face the door as the axe shredded enough of it away for a boot to crash its way through.

"It's about time. Now, move out of the way!" a voice shouted. A voice that sounded familiar to Steele. She frowned thoughtfully just as a figure plunged through the ragged opening in the door.

Steele felt the color drain from her face, and her heart tripped over itself as her eyes fell upon the vision of a woman in battle armor with golden hair still flowing down her back. She swallowed hard. "Penelope?" she rasped.

Penelope followed Steele's voice over to where she stood with Falcon, and her eyes widened. Her harsh demeanor crumbled, and she put her hands over her mouth. "Steele!" she screamed. "Steele, you're alive!"

Steele staggered backward as Penelope flung herself into her arms.

"I thought you were dead!" She buried her face in Steele's shirt and sobbed.

Steele felt tears sting her eyes as she dropped her sword and wrapped her arms around her sister. She looked over Penelope's shoulder as the room filled with several Ryffsalli knights. Relief washed over her like an ocean wave.

"I really thought you were dead," Penelope whimpered.

"We couldn't find you anywhere. Even after the regiment had retreated. It took us all night to find this room, and this was our last hope."

Steele swallowed and pulled back so she could look down at her sister. "Penelope, where is Father?"

Her blue eyes filled with new tears.

"Lord Arshwyn fell in battle," one of the knights stated. "He was trying to kill Princess Penelope."

Steele blinked. Princess Penelope. There was something nightmarish about putting those two words together.

"I stopped him from killing one of the knights." Penelope sniffled, casting a glance over her shoulder at the man who had spoken. "When he saw it was me who had stopped him, he..." She looked down as more tears filled her eyes.

"He tried to strangle her," the knight finished, sweeping a kindly gaze over Penelope. "It is our duty to protect the royal family and she saved my life." His voice grew soft for a moment before he returned to the business at hand. "We dispatched him, Princess."

Grief tugged at Steele's heart, but she didn't allow it to plague her for long. If they had not killed him, he would have destroyed everyone. "You told the knights about us?" she asked Penelope. "About our lineage?"

"It was the only way I could get them to listen to me." She pulled away from Steele and glanced over to Falcon, who had remained silent and still. She bit her bottom lip and threw her arms around him, as well. "I'm so happy you're alive! I'm so sorry I treated you so badly! I was awful to you!" She squeezed him hard around the shoulders, causing him to grimace with pain.

Steele's eyes widened. "Penelope, the man has a hole in his shoulder!"

She gasped and let go immediately, looking horrified. "I'm so sorry!"

Despite the seriousness of the situation, Steele had to stifle laughter at the mortified expression on her sister's face. She had to stifle laughter at her sister in general. She looked ridiculous in battle armor, and she really appeared to be on the verge of hysteria. Steele had to hand it to her, though. Penelope had demonstrated more bravery and courage than Steele had even thought she possessed.

Falcon gave Penelope a warm smile and pulled her back into his arms, gently. "It's all right," he soothed. "You didn't hurt me, much."

She gave a sort of half-crazed sounding giggle that made Falcon grin and he met Steele's eyes

Steele smiled and shook her head. She put her hand on her sister's shoulder. "You did well, Penelope," she whispered. "I'm very proud of you. You saved us all."

"Ryffsalli knights, salute!" one of the knights commanded, causing all of them to drop to one knee with their right hand in a fist over their hearts.

Steele raised her eyebrows in mild surprise and Falcon touched her on the shoulder. "You are royalty now," he whispered.

She looked up into his eyes and warmth stole through her, chasing out the coldness and sorrow at the events that had occurred. Being royalty didn't matter to her. She was just happy that she wasn't about to die. Their greatest adversary was gone. The Ryffsalli were safe and could return to their homeland if they chose. Steele would give them back their land. Penelope had proved herself to be much better of a person than Steele had thought possible. Penelope had an entire army at her command.

But none of that mattered to her half as much as knowing that she had Falcon.

And nothing that had happened, however life-altering any of it was, seemed to be nearly as important as the fact that her beautiful Ryffsalli husband had regained use of his gorgeous, amber-golden wings.

Steele heaved a sigh and rubbed at a sore spot in her neck as she made her way down the long corridor to Falcon's chambers. It had been a long and exhausting day. The bodies of the slain had to be taken care of, and the Ryffsalli knights had to be fed, bathed, and given places to sleep. Steele found herself suddenly having to give out orders, even to her commanding officer, and she found the entire experience overwhelming at best. She was used to being a soldier. She was not used to being in a position of power.

She'd put Penelope to bed almost immediately, as she did not want her sister to end up losing her last vestige of sanity. She was having a difficult time coping with everything that had occurred, and she felt tremendous loss at the death of their father. Steele could understand. Penelope had been his favorite, and she'd had no idea what kind of a man he actually was. Finding out she was Ryffsalli royalty, and then having her own father try and murder her, had hit her hard.

Steele knew she would be all right after she had time to rest and think. Her sister was much more formidable than she had given her credit for. Plus, the Ryffsalli knight she had saved from her father's blade was taking extra time to make sure she was comfortable and cared for.

There was a mountain of work that needed to be done, but Steele didn't want to think about any of it right now. She just wanted to retreat into the sanctuary of her husband's arms and rest there.

She opened up the door to find Falcon standing shirtless on the balcony, gazing out across the moonlit countryside. She smiled and went to him, wrapping her arms around his waist and snuggling against his back. "What are you looking at?" she asked.

He placed his hands over hers and sighed. "Freedom. I can barely remember what it felt like. We're free. My people are free."

She hugged him tighter, and he turned to face her, lifting her face and lowering his lips to hers. She closed her eyes and lost herself in the kiss as tingling flames leaped along her skin. "Falcon," she whispered as he pulled away.

"Yes?"

She looked up at him and smiled. "You told me before that you had something you wanted to say to me."

He frowned thoughtfully. "Oh yes, I did, didn't I?"

She nodded.

He tightened his arms around her and sighed. "Well, I wanted to tell you that the buckle on your boot was undone. I didn't want you to trip over it in battle."

She blinked rapidly and felt as if someone had slapped her hard across the face. "O-Oh..." she stammered. She frowned. "Well, I guess that would have been beneficial for you to tell me back there."

He gave a lazy shrug with only one shoulder and arched an eyebrow. A taunting smile played around his lips.

Her frown deepened, and she looked away, feeling her face flush with humiliation at what she'd assumed he would say to her. She suddenly felt very awkward and stupid.

Falcon's rumbling chuckle brought her gaze back up to his, and her body burned at the light that shone in his amber eyes.

"Steele," he said, "I'm joking."

She scowled. "I see," she muttered. "So your people are freed from the clutches of their greatest enemy and suddenly you turn into a comedian?"

His grin, despite her annoyance at his teasing, caused warm desire to blossom within her. He pulled her close and lowered his mouth to her ear. "Hold on," he whispered.

His voice was sinful, and she closed her eyes, wrapping her arms around his neck. She heard his wings unfurl and his arms held her tight as she felt them slowly ascend into the sky. She opened her eyes and gasped as the cool night air touched her face and they hovered high above the castle. She looked up at him and grinned.

His smile was tender and he touched her face with gentle fingers. "Steele," he murmured, "you have shaken the very foundation on which I stood, and I am grateful to you for it. You have given me everything, and you *are* everything. I love you with every single beat of my heart."

She felt tears sting her eyes, but for the first time in too long, she knew they were tears of joy. "I love you too, Falcon," she whispered.

His gaze raked over her with molten adoration. "Take the throne," he urged. "We will rule our people together. Be my queen. Be my wife."

She grinned. "Back to back?"

He ran his lips along the column of her throat. "Side by side."

She tangled her fingers in his silken hair and delighted in the tendrils of fire that seemed to travel back and forth between their bodies. "Even though I am an Arshwyn?"

He held her close and feathered his fingers across her face and neck, gazing into her eyes with the deepest and most profound love she had ever seen. "You are no

Arshwyn," he breathed. "You are all Venegoth." He kissed her again, slow and languorous, robbing her of air and stoking the fire into a blazing torrent. He kissed along her jaw until his lips were against her ear. "Do you want to see the stars?" he whispered.

She grinned and nodded.

His eyes sparkled with joy. "Hold on tight."

She obeyed and wrapped her arms snugly around his neck as he changed his form back into the golden dragon he had been during the battle. The only difference was that this dragon could fly.

And fly he did until they disappeared into the clouds, and all anyone could hear was the echo of Steele's unbridled and joyous laughter.

A Walk With Lilly
By Tex Leiko

So there I stood on the suspension bridge in Lynn Valley, Canada. She looked me in the eyes and smiled; the wind blew tempestuous, making the bridge sway. Rain fell heavy and hard, soaking us to the core, and lightning danced, illuminating the sky. Sirens blew in the distance and we could see spotlights narrowing in on our position.

"So, tell me, what did you even come for?" she said to me.

"I'm on a pursuit of happiness," I said.

"Oh, and did you find it?"

"I don't know. But I do know, whether I live or I die, I lived life to its full," I said to her, rubbing my aching head. The giant lump I'd acquired earlier in the eve was throbbing, but in this moment, I didn't care.

"Well, there's always tomorrow, Ares," she said, holding out her hands.

The bridge blew, rocked hard, and she stumbled into my arms. I heard dogs barking by this point and knew that the authorities were close at hand.

"Yeah, I know. Now go and be free, but before you do, tell me. What's your name? I never got it." I caught her and stabilized her body against mine.

"Lilly," she said as she leaned forward and kissed me soft and gentle on the lips.

It was sweet, innocent, and refreshing. The kind of kiss most people don't have anymore...

"This is when we broke away from each other and your bloodhounds rounded the corner. So, want me to back up?"

The officer just stared at me.

"I take your aggravated silence as a yes, geez...just say so then," I said, smiling sheepishly with my hands behind my back. "Well, it goes something like this. I arrived in Vancouver early in the day. It was unusually warm for the beginning of March. Spring had just started, but typically winter still brought rain and dreariness to the city as long as it possibly could.

"The clouds were all but scared away by the sun, and the pavement radiated heat below my feet. I walked from where I parked my car to the hotel with the usual bounce in my step, despite carrying three bags and a suit. I usually didn't pack like that for a week-long trip, but I had no idea what may come my way.

"So I walked in through the double doors of the hotel to be greeted by Jennifer. She was a cutie too—long brown hair and soft brown eyes to match her skin. She had some sort of accent I wasn't familiar with and she rushed over to help me with my bags. Guess I was struggling more than I had thought.

'Thank you, you guys are all so nice,' I said.

'Us guys?' she questioned, arching her eyebrow at me.

'You know, Canadians,' I said nervously. I hadn't meant anything bad by it. I think she took it racially. Like I said, she probably wasn't from Canada judging by her accent, but I had no idea what nationality she may have been. Feeling like a dope, I handed her only the suit to take because I didn't want to seem like a total jerk. She just shook her head as she walked behind the desk and hung up my suit.... Am I boring you with details?" I asked the officer with a straight face.

"Yeah, why don't you try telling me details that actually pertain to the case we are investigating, you punk?" the officer said gruffly.

"Fine then... So I went to this place called Sharks and Hammers to buy a souvenir for myself while in the city. I know, totally lame and touristy, but I just thought it would be cool to get a little trinket, so I did. Plus, it is a totally independent shop and I like supporting those types."

The officer just eyed me suspiciously as I continued my narration of the events leading to me being handcuffed behind his table. I could tell by his grim expression and the hate in his eyes that he wanted to beat me until I gave him something credible. Really, I had nothing, and he was going to listen to my story whether he liked it or not.

"Trust me, this all applies. It's a little bit of cause and effect. Maybe you can follow the smoke in the breeze and get new leads with these details. Help me help you, officer," I said, dry and sarcastic.

He didn't so much as crack a smile or show any emotion at all, and I continued.

"So there I met a fellow named Joshua. He was really neat and I told him about how I had found his company on the Internet and thus set a quest for myself to go and purchase something from his humble little shop. He thought it was pretty cool that I did that and, like me, he traveled alone to many places himself. So we chatted about that for a bit and related some stories. Finally, when I could sense our endless banter was annoying the customers behind me who wanted to purchase some things, I said, 'So, any recommendations on where to go if you have never been here and you just want to go somewhere where something might happen?'

"He said, 'Sure,' as he grabbed one of his business cards and began writing down locations on the back. He slid it over the counter to me and said, 'Try the middle one first,' and then winked..." I wiggled a little in my chair and eyed my left back pocket the best that I could. "The card is still in my pocket," I said, then continued the story.

"I picked it up and read the back. On it was written Six Acres, The Diamond, and L'Abatoir. I thought to myself Six Acres sounded too much like a sports bar and L'Abatoir sounded too stuffy—stinkin' Frenchies. But The Diamond? I liked the ring of that one, plus he had said it was located above another store and that I would have to travel into an alley and up a stairwell to find it.

"It sounded like an old fashioned speakeasy to me and I liked the image that conjured in my mind. Plus, I just plain like alleyways. It's like opening the mystery box on a game show. You never know what is going to be in an alleyway. Sometimes, you find a gem, other times just hobos doing unsightly things.

"So I left once again with a spring in my step over to The Diamond. With his directions, it was pretty simple to find, however, without them, I would have been totally lost... Is any of this helping you?" I asked the officer with a wink.

"I think you're trying to break me, kid. Trouble is, I've seen far worse than you in this line of work, so try your best. In fact, have fun with it. You're not changing where you spend the night tonight with this fanciful tale."

"It isn't a tale, I assure you. I left enough of an impression everywhere I went that I am sure you are going to be able to trace this back and confirm it all the way. Anyhow, I'll finish as quickly as I can. I can tell you're irritated, Mr. Grumpyface...

"So I pulled up a stool at the bar of The Diamond and struck up a conversation with the bartender, Taylor, seeing as there was nobody else around to talk to just yet. I mistook him for having an accent, but he just sorta mumbled like Brad Pitt in *Snatch*. He was from Vancouver and was filled with lots of helpful information, the bits I could make out anyway.

"After a few hours of chatting and drinking, the bar was finally filling and I was feeling a bit...festive. By this point, everyone at the bar was my friend, they just didn't know it yet. I must have been pretty inviting in the way I was joking with everyone around me because a cute little Chinese girl parked her tush right next to me and started chatting it up. *Great, a call girl*, repeated in my mind. But I figured I'd let it play out and that I'd be safe as long as I didn't follow her into any alleyways or back to my room or any other. She was interesting and clearly a little bit more festive than myself. We talked a bit and then she decided that she wanted to show me a Gelato shop.

"So I paid my tab, tipped the bartender well, and thanked him for the Trinidad Sour he made me. At that, we hurried down the stairs and out to the main street. Once there, we walked and talked, she asked my name, and I gave her a fake one. I also didn't tell her what I really did for work. I figured I'd never see her again, so she didn't need that info.

"We walked for blocks and she told me about all the things to watch out for in the city. I was wrong; she wasn't a call girl, just another bold soul like myself. Unfortunately, one of the most uninteresting souls I had ever met. A total material girl. We couldn't get to Gelato quick enough.

"At last, we arrived at the shop and, seeing as they offered free tastes of each flavor, I tried about thirty before deciding. It was a place that truly catered to my fickle nature. Finally, I settled on two flavors, Espresso and Chocolate.

"Anyway, I shoveled that stuff down as quickly as possible while listening to her drone on and on about all the things she wanted to buy. I yawned and decided to call it quits.

"She asked if I wanted company back at my hotel room. I said no in the kindest fashion I could muster. Really, she was cute enough, but about as boring as a plank in a wood fence. She insisted I get her number and call her the next day so she could be my tour guide. I took it, but I've never once thought about contacting her.

"So, yeah, all of that area of the story you may not want to try to track down. I mean, I don't even remember the name of the Gelato shop. It wasn't very good and I don't recall her name, though her email address may still be in my front pocket if you care to check." I said the last part with a lisp.

The officer, once again, wasn't amused by me at all. In fact, I think he wanted to bash my head in with his night stick, but that would have been terrible PR and he may have just blown open this lump that was already formed on my forehead.

"I'll continue," I said.

He nodded.

"So I told you the rest of the story to tell you this part. But before I do, I just have to say this. Had I never gotten into Vancouver at the time of day that I had, this may have never happened. Had I never gone to Sharks and Hammers, the story may not read this way. Had I never taken a chance on The Diamond, I may not be in this interrogation room. Had I never met the most ugly, boring, materialistic soul ever and shared a treat with her, this may have never happened. But I did, and so what happened next is a result of a butterfly effect, so to speak.

"So there I was, walking back to my hotel, still buzzed from the drinks the bartender had mixed me. He must have made them stronger than I had thought. Either that or I really did lose count of how many I had.

"Two blocks up and two blocks left, there would be my

hotel and I would crash my head onto a pillow only to prepare myself for the next day. Alas, my prior decisions led me to something I hadn't planned.

"I heard a girl giggle just behind and to the left of me. I looked over and she had shining brown eyes that glimmered in the dead of night like diamonds. Her long brown hair resembled tree roots and flowed down to between her shoulder blades. She was dressed in a simple hoodie and she had ear buds in bumpin' some fat beats that even my ears were picking up.

"I glanced at her and she smiled nervously. She did a double-take, looking away then back and in one motion, pulled her ear buds out, and let them dangle between us. Feeling merry, I threw my arm around her shoulders and faced us forward saying, 'No worries, let's walk.'

"She laughed and said, 'Let's. Sorry, I just giggled because I saw your walk and couldn't help but think to myself, that is the happiest and nicest guy I've ever seen.'

'Really?' I questioned.

'Yeah, you just look so carefree and happy. I wish I could be like that. Plus, if you don't wanna find yourself in danger, you may wanna pick up the pace if you're walking with me,' she said.

"I recall thinking that she was just joking when she said that. So I made light of it and said, 'Oh really? Who's gunna hurt me, little girl? You?'

'My guards,' she said with a smile.

'Guards?' I questioned.

'Yeah, I ditched them for a second, but I'm never free really...' She trailed off.

'Oh yeah? So what do you do 'round here?' I questioned her, changing the mood.

'Nothing much. I'm headed to a location where I'm supposed to demonstrate my talents, then after that I'm going to my home in Phoenix, Arizona.'

'Oh yeah? So you live here and Phoenix?'

'Well, I have homes everywhere really, here, Switzerland, Arizona, and many others.'

"My mouth agape, I looked at her and said, 'So, like, you're rich, or some sort of really big stuff then, huh?'

'You could say that,' she said with a sigh.

"It was then that we rounded the corner of the block. Despite ditching her guards, she was still walking to where she was destined to go without deviation. I had forgotten that she even mentioned them, but there they were, in suits, with guns, headed toward me.

'You know them?' I questioned as I felt her body stiffen under my arm.

"My guards, and we are headed to that place,' she said, pointing to a tall building with a neon sign that I couldn't quite read.

"In shock, I stared into her eyes. 'You're serious about that!? I seriously thought you were joking!'

"She giggled again. I glanced to the guards. They were closing in quick.

'If you hate this life, why not get rid of them?'

"She mustered a smile at me and said, 'It isn't that simple.' Then she grasped a collar that was hidden beneath her hoodie and wriggled it over it to show me. She tugged on it twice and the smile disappeared from her innocent face. She said, 'I can't get rid of it and it hinders me from ever escaping. Now get lost and forget me before you're hurt.'

"Words escaped me. I had nothing heroic to say, nothing insightful, just the buzz that I had fleeing quickly and the sharp burst of reality and danger thumping in my chest. *She is really serious*, I thought to myself. I heard a guard yell, and I took off running.

"I darted across the street and almost got struck by a speeding car. He had the green light. That would have been a horrible ending to this tale, but it isn't, as you already know. So I ran as fast as my legs could carry me and disappeared into an alleyway.

"I had run a couple blocks in a different direction than the building she had pointed out to me and, by now, I had no reason to believe that her guards were still pursuing me. She probably covered for me and, really, all I knew was that I didn't know anything other than she was in a bad situation.

"The night was warm and the scent of flowers blooming from Queen Elizabeth Park wafted through the night air. I had never thought I would be in a situation like this before. I didn't know where it would end, but it was in this moment that I was reborn.

"All the ideals I always preach in stories and on my pro-verbial soap box were what I was about to become incar-nate. I liked writing about heroes, but had never thought of myself as one before. But this night, I would become one. This night, I would stand tall. I would stop shrinking back from the things that I was afraid of. I would face demons, and yet, I didn't know what they would be. I was scared, I was excited, I was nervous, and I was bold. I was all at once but none of it at the same time. I was just ready to be what I needed to be when I needed to be it.

"I scrambled down the alley and headed back to the building that they were taking the mystery girl to. It probably took me five minutes to get to the alley behind the building, but it had felt like only seconds. Adrenaline and fear coursed through my veins as I shed my coat and prepared for any-thing.

"For a brief second, I thought that maybe the threat and danger would all be in my head and that she really was jok-ing. I had thoughts that maybe she was just some spoiled celebrity who got off on playing jokes on people. But I had to find out.

"There I was, climbing up the fire escape of the building where I knew she was supposed to perform whatever this talent was that she spoke of. I had reached the third story when I peeked in a window and caught a glance of her.

"There she stood in the middle of a room with seven armed guards all in black suits and white shirts with pale green ties. It was just her, surrounded by them with three ranking officials from the UN seated against the wall. I rec-ognized them from the news.

"There was a pot filled with topsoil at her feet, but noth-ing else was in the room. One of the men stepped forward with a key and removed her collar. At the same time, the other six guards raised their automatic rifles and aimed them at the mystery girl.

"She raised her hand over the planter and a green aura flowed forth from her hand and into the dirt. As if I were dreaming, a vine shot forth and coiled around her body. It ex-ploded in a cloud of green, and moss sprung up everywhere in the room. I could barely see what was happening because of the aura and what looked like pollen swirling in the room.

"It settled, but then from the moss and vines that entangled the room, there began to spring lilies of every shade imaginable, along with orchids, belladonnas, peonies, poppies, and amaranths, as well as many little wild things skittering about.

"She glanced over to the window I was peeking in and caught sight of me. In a moment of quick thinking on her part, she cast the vines from herself and entangled everyone in the room. That quick little maneuver was followed by the flowers bellowing out vast amounts of pollen as if they were incense pyres.

"She ran toward the window and leapt forward. I didn't have the smarts to step back. I was in shock and awe. She smashed through the glass and collided into my body. What looked like chlorophyll dripped from her cuts and scrapes as she knocked me over.

"There was screaming coming from inside the room as my head made contact with the side rail of the fire escape, thus explaining this nasty lump on my melon. Our bodies hit the steel grating of the fire escape simultaneously and we glanced into each other's eyes once again.

'You came back for me, didn't you?' she questioned with a quivering voice.

'And you broke free because of it, didn't you?'

"We could hear the men screaming for backup, unable to do anything themselves. Judging by the strength of the vines that entrapped them, they wouldn't be cutting free anytime soon. We both quickly jumped to our feet without her answering me. It really wasn't the time for a deep conversation.

"She touched the rail I had knocked my head on and a vine formed. I motioned her first and she grabbed onto it and slid down. I stood watching the window, waiting for the worst of it to come barreling out at me at any moment, but it never did. After she was down, I slid down and met up with her.

'C'mon, Let's go!' I said, grasping her hand and dragging her with me.

"She was crying. Women, always crying at times when they should be laughing and vice versa. I glanced at her and exclaimed, 'You want to be free or get caught?'

'I…I don't know where to go next,' she huffed as she followed behind me.

'Let's just get back to my room and we will decide. They don't have any way to track you anymore now, do they?'

'No,' she answered as we disappeared into the darkness.

"We made it back to the hotel pretty uneventfully and we were both short of breath from running, so we didn't converse much until we got to my room. I stood hesitantly outside the door before swiping us in. Thoughts of them finding us and waiting for an ambush were racing in my head.

"I slipped the key in—red light, blink, double green, and a click. That was followed up with a slam of the sole of my boot into the door, causing it to fly open. I sprang forth into the room and flipped the lights on. Nobody was in there and, in retrospect, I am sure I looked like a total moron, but hey, that's how I roll.

"She followed behind me and I closed the door. She sat on the edge of the bed in the room and I hadn't noticed earlier, but I noticed now. She had shed her hoodie and was wearing a simple white camisole-styled shirt, the kind of white I didn't think existed. Along with that she had a simple long, flowing, bright green skirt. It made her look like a flower.

"She was flushed from the running, her head was hung in defeat despite the great escape we had just pulled, and her hair masked her face, keeping me from catching sight of it. She still breathed heavy and I was puzzled. I had gotten my breath back already and she seemed to be in better shape than me.

'Do you have a glass of water?' she asked, looking up at me.

"Her face had gone from the rosy sight of a goddess to something scary and withered. Her face had turned a light brown and resembled tree bark. It appeared as if this was spreading throughout.

'Sure!' I exclaimed as I grabbed both the cups in the bathroom and filled them to the full.

"I rushed back to her and she drank the first one quickly. The second she just sipped. Her skin began to return to normal and she got her breath back. She smiled and just stared at me. 'I was right. You really are the nicest person I've ever met,' she stated as matter-of-factly as possible.

'Well, I get the sense that you don't meet a lot of people.'

'But still, you have yet to run away in fear or judge me

even at the sight of what you've just been a witness to. I'm sorry for that. My powers really take it out of me.'

'Yeah, about that,' I said, tripping on my words, not knowing if it was up for discussion or not. But I proceeded. 'What are you? No offense, but I don't know many people with a green thumb quite the same as yours.'

'Simply put, I'm a planter. I don't have many memories except those of the men testing me, studying me, probing me, and checking for results. I asked once; they told me that I died at birth as a human. A lab named Polyhelix purchased my remains from my parents and they used my raw genetic material to create what I am. I asked once why I can't remember anything until I around age ten.

'I was told it was because of the DNA they spliced into me. Something to do with the botanical DNA that kept my brain from developing quite the same as a regular human. They never called me anything except Planter One. My powers were kept in check by the collar they made me wear and I tried to escape once when I was eleven... They tortured me for weeks after that. He kept saying sorry over and over again. I knew he meant it. He tried to help continuously, tried to tell me which way to go, what to do. I'm sorry, I am beginning to ramble. The man I'm talking about is the one who created me. He was good, he loved me. I loved him. I didn't listen. Anyhow, I was too scared to ever try escaping again. But when I saw you, my heart grew warm and I told myself, if you came back, I'd try again.'

'Ha,' I said, smirking. 'I ain't that special, just a guy who doesn't know when to quit.'

'That isn't true. I'm sure you'll make a difference on some level someday. Take some pride in that. Stop selling yourself short or else you will wind up the loser you claim to be. It's springtime, it's time to grab hold of that and sprout like a sapling changing into a mighty Baobab.'

"I just shrugged bashfully. I didn't really believe her.

'So why did they make you?' I questioned.

'At first, the head researcher of my experiment had good intentions. He planned to create me to heal the earth, along with a few others. We can create rapid generation and re-generation of plant life. He estimated that in just a few years, we could be used to turn the entire earth into a paradise, however...' She trailed off.

'However what?' I asked, clinging onto her every word.

'I remember that day well. I was fifteen when it happened. Some officials from the United Nations came to see the project. I was progressing rapidly, and by this point, I came to enjoy my life. The mishap when I was eleven was simply me trying to run from fear, not from any mistreatment prior. However, when those men came, they got the idea to turn me into a weapon. They thought I could go and conquer for them while turning the places I consumed into beautiful places to live rather than the desolate wastes that bombs and weapons leave behind.

'I caught wind of their plan and began faking setbacks in my abilities. However, since then, they removed the man who was in charge of creating me and replaced him with someone cruel. Someone who starved me of water and soil and wouldn't let me grow. Someone who treated me the way man's governments treat the environment. That was my life from fourteen to nineteen. They had me leashed too well. I couldn't do anything. But I knew when I saw you that my day had come. I knew that if you came back for me, you could be a catalyst to something great! I was scared when we got here. I was thinking, what should I do? But it's clear now!" She lit up as she exclaimed her words in an abundance of excitement.

'Oh yeah?' I asked.

'There's a rainforest outside the city, in the Lynn Valley. Take me there and let me be free and I can change things, and they'll never be able to do me any harm. I just know it," she said, grinning as if she had never experienced anything hurtful in her life... You see, officer. You never take a risk, you never find something great. Sure, sometimes you find heartache, headache, or something overall unpleasant. But isn't it made up for by all the times you find something truly amazing?" I asked, pressing my chest into the table and leaning toward the officer, pausing from my telling of the evening's events.

"I've never had anything like that happen to me," he said abruptly.

"And why do you think that is?"

"I'm sure you're about to tell me."

"Nah." I leaned back and shrugged. "But tell me, if you were me in that hotel room with that information, just having seen what I had seen, would you have stopped running with her?"

"Shut up, tell me what happened then."

"I looked at her beaming face. I didn't know if someone had drugged me back at The Diamond and I was just hallucinating all of this. I didn't know if I had made it to the hotel and was dreaming all of this. It was unreal, but regardless, I knew how I wanted it to end.

'Let's go,' I said, extending my hand toward hers.

"She grabbed hold and I pulled her to her feet. We made haste down to the street and skipped along to the parking lot where I had left my car. We hopped in and I proceeded to drive it like it was stolen. I didn't know if Polyhelix was still looking for us or not.

"I pulled out on to the street, tires squealing. I must have run a dozen red lights and sped past twice that many officers in the direction of the Lion's Gate Bridge. As we approached it, we could see a roadblock. I was speeding toward it, worried that this would be our end, but she kept telling me not to worry and to keep driving.

"Vines sprang forth from the road and carried off the cars. The officers were smart enough to get out of my way. We were traveling at roughly one-hundred-fifteen miles per hour. By the time we got over the bridge, something hit me.

"I hadn't felt like this in ages. I wasn't really sure what it was, but I felt as if I had love in my heart. I didn't know if it was for the girl sitting beside me, for the great adventure, or just for life in general. But I noticed that in the midst of the chaos, I regained a feeling I had long thought dead.

"As we whizzed down the highway, we sat in silence. It was unusual. I usually blasted the radio to just about any genre other than country. But all we could hear was the rumbling of my tires on the pavement, the body of the vehicle parting the air like a knife through butter, and the faint sound of sirens in hot pursuit.

"She glanced over at me and asked, 'Aren't you going to miss this? The cars, the asphalt, the concrete and steel structures you live in?'

"I just smiled, shrugged, and said, 'Nah. Besides, if we just put our heads together, we can figure out how to make things similar without draining the environment. Cars, trucks, homes, roads. Everything could be made without drain to the earth, and yet, man does it. Why? Greed. That's why. There are prototypes of machines we use today run solely off of solar power that were created in the seventies and yet, we still use gas! Why?' I continued to ramble on and on for at least three to four minutes about all the things my simple mind could think of that was wrong with this world. She was an angel, and all she did was listen, and criticize where needed.

"In the finality of it, all she just nodded and said, 'Agreed.'

"Finally, we made it to Lynn Valley Park. We could hear the sirens, and now there were helicopters circling. We parked the car and ran into the forest. We stopped on the middle of the suspension bridge and she raised her hands to the air. That was when the storm broke out.

"She glanced at me like a sly vixen and said, 'That will make them have to land sooner or later.'

"The spotlight reflected off of the two of us and we just stood staring for a moment. We both knew this moment couldn't last forever, and soon it had to end. However, I do have to admit I was pretty perplexed as to how she would escape at this point, but as the rain fell harder and harder at her commission, I was comforted and realized there was nothing out of her power.

"This was the part where the wind picked up. You know, as I described earlier. The dogs yapping and growling. The bridge swaying, her falling into my arms. The look we gave each other.

"This was where we finally discovered each other's names. When she told me hers, I gave her an odd look and she added, 'It's what I call myself. It sounds better than Planter One, don't you think?"

'Hell yeah,' I said.

"Then the kiss. Maybe that's the wrong order. I'm not entirely sure. Everything was happening quickly. What I do know is this. What came next was the spotlight disappearing. The helicopter had to land, as she predicted. The dogs barked and yapped, the sirens blared, and the wind howled as she stood up on the steel cable that held the bridge we stood on.

"With the grace of an Olympic gymnast, she stood on the swaying cable, keeping her balance without so much as slipping. Then, she jumped. I gasped and looked over the edge in time to see her hit the water of the river below.

"You know, a normal person would have drowned, but I saw her resurface with grace and agility and bob down the river to a little clearing. Lightning flashed and illuminated the forest as I saw her make it to shore and run into the woodlands.

"It was then at this moment your expertly trained mutt bit me square in the crotch and the other my forearm. Seriously, that is the most painful thing I think I've ever had the chance to experience, but still...tonight was worth it. So, officer, can I go now or not?" I asked, smiling sheepishly.

"I've heard enough of this crap," he said, standing and exiting the room.

"Aww! No fair!" I shouted behind him. "You haven't even given me an ice pack for my junk! It hurts, I swear!"

Again, the officer was unamused.

After a few hours, a nice little lady cop came into the interrogation room. She was way too little to be a police woman. She was about four-foot-nine inches and maybe seventy pounds dripping wet. She took her position behind me, and the man who had been interrogating me stepped in through the doorway.

"Ares, today is your lucky day. From what we can tell, your only crime was driving way too fast—a felony, by the way. You would have to post bail, but a Mr. Smith dropped by a moment ago and paid it in full. He also provided the best lawyer in the city if this charge ever reaches the courts. You have some powerful friends, don't you?" he questioned as he stepped over to the table.

"I guess now I do," I said matter-of-factly, following with, "And probably even more enemies."

"What was it you said your line of work was again?"

"I thought I was no longer under interrogation?"

"You aren't. I just wasn't sure if I heard you right at the booking."

"I write fanciful stories until they become real," I said with a wink.

"Right. Release him, Emily. We have a mountain of paperwork to file after tonight. He's small compared to it all."

Freedom was what I felt when the cuffs came off. That and severe pain in my groin and forearm. They still hadn't provided me with so much as an aspirin or an ice pack. I hobbled out of the room and back to reclamation. There I gave the man at the counter my social security number and he gave me back my possessions.

I gimped over to the station's exit with my police escort, who was making sure I didn't retaliate out of anger for what they had done. I wasn't mad. They'd done their job, I'd done mine. Easy as that; however, I'd never want their job for anything.

As I exited the building, a man with little round glasses, white hair, a big nose, a grey, surly trench coat, and a bow-ler hat approached me. I was worried this would be the end of me and my heart raced.

The streetlight danced off of the playing cards stuck in his hat and I spotted the ace of spades in the brim. I was trem-bling at the thought that he would leave that placed on the chest of my corpse and leave me in the rain. Instead, he presented an umbrella and said, "Walk with me."

I did.

We made it about three blocks before he piped up. "The name is Tex. I gave the police the name and identity of Brian E. Smith, then I presented your bail. Thank you for releasing Planter One. She was my creation." As he finished his sen-tence, we came to a dead halt.

The air hung heavy between us. There was a tension, but it was a good one. I was just in shock. This was all really too much. Finally, I broke the silence and said, "Well, she goes by Lilly now."

He smiled, winked, and said, "Thanks, I've got my eye on you, kid." At that, he lifted his hands and a flash of smoke blew forth.

It only took a second or two for the rain to clear the smoke, but in that time, he had disappeared. I continued walking to my car, twirling the gifted umbrella in my hand as I enjoyed the pitter-patter of the spring rain falling upon the nylon spread between shoddy steel.

As I approached my car, I looked to the ground. There was a crack in the pavement and between it were growing several lilies. I don't know today, the same as I didn't know that day, but I wondered if she had put them there for me.

I left the keys on the hood of my car, for someone who wanted it more than me. Then I walked back to my hotel. On the way, I felt baptized in the warm spring rain and like my life would never be the same.

Every now and then, I'll find some hit in the city in which I live that proves that she is still about. Spreading growth and new life across the globe. That was merely three months ago, and when I turn on the news, there are always baffling stories of forests popping up overnight.

If the climate keeps changing like this, starvation will be a thing of the past. Food will grow so plentifully that all we will need to do is harvest it. I don't know if I'll ever see her again, but the evidence is always there.

As for me, I'm looking for my next big adventure. Maybe this time, I won't hesitate if I find a mysterious stranger in need of help. Maybe, someday, I'll see the hero she saw...

Sunrise of My Soul
By Brieanna Robertson

Chapter One

"Daelynn! I need your help! This is an emergency!"

Daelynn looked up as a large, loud woman burst through her door with the force of a hurricane. She winced as her door slammed against the frame with a boom resembling a clap of thunder. She arched an eyebrow and looked up from the papers on her kitchen table. "What is it, Lena?" She suppressed a sigh. Knowing Lena, it was one of only a few things. Man trouble, someone had irritated her in the marketplace, man trouble, she'd stubbed her toe on something and thought she was going to die, or man trouble.

Lena stood in front of Daelynn on the opposite side of the table and braced her hands on the surface. "You will never believe what that no-good son of a troll said to me last night. Do you know that he had the audacity to forget my birthday? The most important day of the year! And then he honestly thought I was going to sleep with him after that!" She snorted and put her hand on her hip. "So I ripped him another one, of course. Like I'm gonna let him get away with that kind of behavior. Please, not in this lifetime." She huffed. "I just don't know if he's worth my time or my trouble. And you know, contrary to popular belief, I'm not a whore!" She leaned over the table toward Daelynn, her low cut blouse showing more than its fair share of looming and swaying cleavage. "Plus, I have this weird rash...you know...down there."

Daelynn let out a long-suffering sigh and sat back in her chair while Lena continued to go on and on about her bodily functions and her sex life. When she had finally exhausted her air supply, Daelynn gave her the best advice she could for her problems, but she felt worn out by it.

She put her head in her hand when Lena finally seemed satisfied. "Lena, I don't mean to be rude, but...can you pay me for this today?"

Lena blinked at her and a sympathetic expression crossed her face. She reached across the table and took Daelynn's hand in hers. "I can't today because I just had to pay to get my hair done up with all these pretty braids for the queen's visit and the spring celebration. Not to mention this gorgeous henna tattoo." She held up her right arm in a showy display of the vine-like design snaking up to her shoulder. She all but pouted at Daelynn. "I promise I'll pay you as soon as I can, all right? You know I will. If nothing else, I'll at least have you over for dinner." Without bothering to wait for Daelynn's reply, she waved and flounced back out.

Daelynn sat there for a second, soaking up the silence that finally descended on her small home, and she sighed. The tension in her shoulders started to dissipate and she turned her attention back down to the papers she had been working on. She smiled and poised her quill back over the parchment.

"Daelynn!"

She jumped as her door burst open again and her quill smeared ink halfway across her page. She scowled and flung her quill aside. "What is it?" she snapped. She glanced up to see a man she knew almost as well as Lena. Despite this being her profession, she, Lena, and Wilbur had all been childhood friends. And sadly, over the last twenty or so years, the two of them had grown very accustomed to taking advantage of her.

He retreated a step and looked apologetic. "I'm sorry, am I interrupting you?"

"Well, I was working on something and I haven't been able to finish it because people keep coming in here." She knew she sounded witchy, but she didn't care. Not this time. She felt frazzled and exasperated. She just wanted to get this scene down!

"Oh...that stinks." He waved his hand as if in dismissal. "Anyway, I really need someone to talk to. I've been feeling so depressed lately." He practically whined, and Daelynn resisted the urge to claw her own eyeballs out. He wandered over and plopped himself into a chair in the corner. "I feel so much darkness and I just don't know what to do with it. Connie keeps playing games with me and I can't seem to get over Anna—"

Daelynn swore she felt her eye twitch. "Wilbur." She splayed her hands on the table top and stood up. "I'm sorry, but can you pay me today?"

He looked perplexed. "You know I can't, Daelynn. I don't have any money." He sounded super indignant—typical. How dare she ask him to do something for her? "And besides, don't you remember that time I paid for you to go to the north and visit that shapeshifter clan you were so in to? You wanted to do some kind of weird research or something? Anyway, I paid for that, remember?"

She closed her eyes for a second and tried to locate her usual overabundant reservoir of understanding. "Yes, Wilbur, I remember. That was a year ago. And, actually, that was my money. All you did was send the courier to make the reservations at the—never mind. The point is, you have been back here every day since then—every day—and I haven't charged you anything. I do need to get paid. You understand this?"

He looked even more confused than he had before. He got out of the chair and approached her table. "Dae-Dae, I need your help. I just feel so dark and—"

"Tragic?" she spat out. "You always feel tragic, Wilbur. Every bloody day you feel tragic. And you come in here and you tell me about your sad life and how horrible it is and how everyone you ever loved left you and that's why you're so messed up, right?" She rounded the table to come face to face with him. "Well, newsflash! The only reason you even say that much is because you are regurgitating what I said to you two years ago!" She put her hands on her slender hips and started to back him toward the door. "Let me ask you, Wilbur, in all the years you have been in here wasting my time and my care, have I actually helped you cure anything? One thing?" Her voice was raising. That wasn't good. She advanced on him. "I have listened to your sad, catastrophic tales of 'woe-is-me' for longer than I can even comprehend. And what has it accomplished? You coming in here whining at me about all the things you are too cowardly to fix—because then you might actually have to take responsibility for your own life—and me not getting paid!" They had reached the door now and she shoved it open. "I. Am. Done! Do not come back to me again unless you can give me some kind of compensation!" Out of the corner of her eye, she saw a tall, dark-haired man standing close to the door, his arm raised as if he had been about to knock. She ignored him so she could stifle the tears that were threatening in her eyes.

"Sorry, I thought we were friends," Wilbur grumbled. "I didn't think people charged for being a good friend these days."

"Oh gimme a break!" Daelynn spat. "If you want a friend, don't come to my place during business hours or I am going to freaking charge you like I charge everybody else! You are not special! Also, the last time I checked, good friends returned the favor and I don't think you have ever once appreciated or listened to anything I've had to say. Get out of here. I can't even deal with you right now."

Wilbur still looked shell shocked. He held his hands out in entreaty. "Dae-Dae, please..."

"Stop calling me that!" she shouted. "You only call me that when you want something and I am tired of all of your drama! Just leave me alone!"

She must have screamed it with the right amount of force because he waved his hands in the air like he was annoyed and stalked off.

Fighting tears, Daelynn turned to the man at the door. "What?" she cried.

He arched an eyebrow and cleared his throat, then lowered his hand. "Um...I'm looking for the healer."

She rolled her eyes and went back into her house.

He followed her. "Who was that guy?" He jutted his thumb in the direction of where Wilbur had gone.

"Wilbur," she muttered as she went back to her table.

He snorted. "He was a jerk."

She heaved a sigh and looked at him full-on. "Did you need something?" He was tall, taller than she'd realized outside while she had been yelling at Wilbur. And broad-shouldered. His brown hair hung in careless, roguish waves around a face that was all masculine planes and angles. He was wearing an insanely bright purple patterned tunic that was garish even by fairy clan standards. Oddly, however, it seemed to suit him while not making him look less manly. She cleared her throat and folded her arms over her chest.

He wandered into the room, still looking over at where Wilbur had vanished, then turned to face her. "I need some herbs for pain. I have a back problem. Old injury. Someone ran me over with a horse. Can you believe that?"

"I'm not that kind of healer," she bit out.

He raised an eyebrow. "I'm sorry?"

"I can't fix broken bones and stomach problems or...whatever."

He frowned. "Then what do you fix?"

"Hearts. Souls. People's issues." She still seriously wanted to cry, and she wanted this stranger to leave her alone so she could do just that. She felt at her wit's end with...everything.

He studied her for a moment then came further into the room. "People pay you for that?"

"Sometimes!" she spat. "But not nearly as much as they should! Now, if you need medicine, you're going to have to go to the next village over. We don't have a regular healer here. Just...me. It's not all that far. Maybe twenty minutes on foot."

"Wait, wait a second." He grabbed the chair from the corner and dragged it over so it was opposite her table. He plopped into it and regarded her. "So, you, what? Read people and figure out what their problems are?"

She rolled her eyes. "Sure, gimme your palm and I'll tell you how long your lifeline is. No! I'm not a psychic. I just listen." Her anger seemed to deflate out of her and she sunk into her chair. "I listen to people. They tell me their problems and I offer advice. I'm good at figuring people out and I'm good at making assessments."

"And they only pay you for it sometimes?"

She shot him a glower. "Yes, only sometimes. A lot of the rest of the time they just tell me they are going to and they never do! Or better yet, they never tell me they are going to at all. They just tell me, 'you're a life saver. I don't know what I would do without you,' then leave me to figure out how I'm going to feed myself next week!" She shoved away from the table and stood again, pacing a few agitated lines. "I give and I give and I give to these people, trying to help them, trying to make their lives better, listen, be a good person. And at the end of the day, all I end up with is a migraine. Everyone I 'help' goes on about their oblivious lives while I am here alone at night with a bottle of brandywine."

He snorted. "Well, that's stupid."

She stopped pacing and looked over at him. Was he serious? Yeah, insulting her profession and her desire to help people was going to do wonders for the mood she was in. Why was she pouring her heart out to a total stranger anyway? She must have lost her mind. She ran a hand through her long black hair then slashed at the air with said hand. "Look, I told you, I don't have any medicine. Please leave."

He stood, languidly, like he had all the time in the world, and gave her a mischievous smirk before he started to take a tour around her living room. "Well, it is stupid. There is a line you should draw at being a nice person. Like, not getting paid is a definite line." He perused her bookshelf and wandered around toward her side of the desk.

She put her hands on her hips as she watched him. "Taking inventory, are you?"

"There's nothing wrong with caring about people, especially ones who honestly deserve it. But putting yourself in the position to be taken advantage of just because you have a bleeding heart doesn't make you a healer." He glanced over his shoulder at her and his startlingly blue eyes met hers. "It just makes you a doormat."

She stared at him for a second, unable to formulate words to combat his blunt, caustic delivery. Finally, she shook her head and scowled. "I don't remember asking you for your opinion in the first place—"

"What's this?" He descended on the papers on her desk like a swooping vulture.

"Not yours!" She tried to snatch them from him, but he was quicker and held them just out of her reach.

"Ah ha, a reaction like that is worth investigating." She grasped for them again, but he held them back and wagged his finger at her like she was a naughty child. "Tell me what they are and then I'll give them back to you."

She blinked so rapidly she felt like her eyes were spasming. Probably her brain trying to process anything that was currently happening. "N-No! I don't even know who you are!"

He held his free hand out to her. "Demetri." He waited for her to put her hand in his. "And you are?"

"Uh...Daelynn."

He shook her hand and flashed a grin that should have been outlawed. "Now we know each other." He waved the papers tauntingly at her.

Daelynn felt like she had just been rendered stupid by this entire day, and she was still reeling from the effects of this odd man's gorgeous smile. The combination made it so that she just didn't want to argue anymore. Too much more of this and she would probably forget how to verbalize at all. "It's a scene. I dabble in writing short stories and plays, all right? Now give them back!"

"How about that? So do I."

She frowned. "You write?"

He nodded. "Poetry. I'm a bard."

She looked back down at his flamboyant tunic. "A bard. A traveling entertainer? Everything suddenly makes a lot more sense."

He reached into a pocket inside his tunic and pulled out some rolled up parchment. He held it out to her. "I'll show you mine if you show me yours." He punctuated his statement with a wink.

She eyeballed him with skepticism, but relented, and tried not to think about the fact that a total stranger—who had since hopped up onto her desk and made himself quite at home—was reading her rough draft of a romantic kissing scene. She unrolled his parchment and began to read through his work, surprised at how well-crafted it was. His words flowed beautifully, and she found that she wanted to keep reading even after the poem was finished.

"This is good, Daelynn," he finally said with no hint of sarcasm in his voice. "You have a lot of skill."

She felt her face flush and she shrugged self-consciously as she handed his poem back. "Thanks. It's just a hobby of mine. Yours is amazing."

He chuckled and stuffed the parchment back into his

pocket. "Well, thank you, but I get the feeling you are saying that just to be nice."

She shook her head. "No, I mean it. I'm part of a fairy clan. A lot of us have arts and creative things we occupy our time with. Given my occupation, I have listened to a lot of people gripe about their crafts. Let's just say, I've read a lot of bad writing over the years, so I'm rather difficult to impress. Yours was exceptionally good." She hated that her cheeks burned slightly at this admission.

He gave her an almost bashful nod and soft smile before his playful, confident expression returned. "Again, thank you." He handed her papers back. "A word of advice, you should stop being everyone's personal 'heart healer.' You should make this your life's work instead. I imagine it would be much more fulfilling."

His gaze captured hers and all of her previous frustration and anger from Lena and Wilbur melted away like it had never been. Who was this man? He'd barreled into her house like he lived there himself, delivered tactless honesty, had insulted and complimented her at the same exact time, and had slain her with a smile? What was going on with this day?

A knock sounded on the door before a brunette woman poked her head in. "Demetri, are you in here?" she called. "The sign out front says this is the healer." She spotted him and grinned. "Oh there you are." She walked in, followed by a redhead and a blonde. "We've been looking everywhere for you." They sidled up to him, crowding around Daelynn's desk and all but pushing her out of the way. All three were dressed in what looked to be a uniform of some kind.

"We need your assistance," the redhead said with what she must have thought was a cute pout.

Demetri sighed and stood. "All right, ladies. Let's go." He glanced back at Daelynn with a roguish smirk. "Please excuse me. Duty calls."

She arched an eyebrow and ignored the sick feeling in her stomach. "By all means," she grumbled. She watched him and his passel of drooling females leave and she tried to shake off the effects of the bizarre encounter. She glanced at the clock. She didn't have time to think about it anyway. She had to meet her brother for lunch. She would just chalk this day up to being strange on all accounts and leave it at that.

Chapter Two

Charlon was late, but that was all right. He sometimes got slammed over at the tavern and couldn't meet her exactly on time. She wandered through the forest with the picnic basket that held the lunch she had made, and she took the time to marvel over the lush green foliage and spring blossoms that decorated the trees. Sunlight spilled down through the leaves and cascaded across the moss that grew on the forest floor and the blooming wildflowers. Daelynn loved the spring. Winter was dark, cold, and oppressive. Spring always felt to her like a new beginning, not just for the plants, but for life as well. It was a time for endless possibilities.

She set her picnic basket down and twirled in a slow circle, making herself smile and feel silly. Her thoughts meandered to the play she had been attempting to work on before her peculiar encounter earlier, and she wandered through the trees as she let her mind work out the scene. She lost herself in it, as she often did, and started to mutter the intended dialogue under her breath. Soon, she was acting out a complete scene, playing all the characters at once, lost within the boundless expanse of her own imagination.

"And here I thought I was the only one who did that."

Daelynn let out a startled shriek and spun around at the intrusive voice. Her heart, which had already been hammering from the shock, did a strange kind of somersault as her gaze fell on Demetri in a small clearing, sitting on a large boulder while the sun beamed down on and around him like some kind of majestic painting. "How long have you been there?" she wheezed out.

He shrugged nonchalantly. "A while."

"What are you even doing here?" Her voice was high and screechy. She tried to tell herself to breathe. It was important to do that.

"I was gathering herbs. Pain. My back. Remember, we

had a conversation about this not very long ago."

She ignored the blatant taunting in his tone and crossed her arms. "You said you needed to ask a healer."

"I didn't say I had to ask a healer. I am well aware of the herbs I need and can find them on my own. I was apprentice to a healer for a while when I was younger. I just didn't necessarily want to go forage for them if someone already had them and could give them to me. I am a busy man, you know."

His merciless smirk reminded her of how he had left her home earlier and she gave him a flat expression. "Of course. What happened to your minions anyway?"

He arched an eyebrow before he stood and approached her. "The girls? Oh, I teach them."

She rolled her eyes at him. "I'm sure you do."

He crossed his arms, mimicking her posture. "They're no one. They're under me is all."

She stared. She couldn't have formulated a retort if someone had waved a bag of gold coins in her face.

He unleashed his devastating grin on her. "In rank." He stated it simply, as if he had never meant the subtle sexual innuendo his previous statement had held.

She cleared her throat and frowned, trying to concentrate on anything other than that scandalous smile of his. "So...are you a bard, or a healer, or a teacher of some kind?"

"I'm a military commander."

"A what?" She shook her head, wondering if it was possible for her to be even more baffled by this man. "For what army?"

"The royal army. I train the new recruits. The queen's procession arrives in a few days. A small band of us came early to make sure everything in your village was safe and ready for her arrival."

"So, you're a military commander who trains new recruits, knows medicine, and moonlights as an entertainer? So, a jack of all trades, master of none?"

"Oh no, jack of all trades, master of *all*." He made a sweeping bow then straightened and smirked down at her like he was having the time of his life.

"And so humble too," she muttered.

"One of my finer qualities."

To her own dismay, a giggle bubbled up her throat and out of her mouth before she could stop it.

Something in his expression softened. "So, what are you doing out here acting out scenes all by yourself anyway? Not that there is anything wrong with that. Why aren't you back at your home, 'healing' people?"

She snorted. "Why do you say it like that? With such condescension? I'm trying to help people. I'm good at it. I know that I shouldn't let them walk on me. I'm aware of that. Just...sometimes people need someone to listen."

"Yes, but who listens to you?"

She met his gaze to see if he was teasing her, but he wasn't. There was sincerity in his playful blue eyes.

He smiled softly. "Come to the tavern with me."

She swore her brain operated on a different frequency than this man's. A soon as she started to absorb one subject, he bounced off to another. "What?"

"Come to the tavern. Have a drink with me."

She shook her head. "I can't. I'm meeting my brother for lunch."

"So? Bring him too."

How was it possible for everything to be so easy for one person? His nonchalance was giving her anxiety. "I...no. He works at the tavern. I really doubt he would want to eat there. Besides, I meet him here every day."

He arched an eyebrow. "So structured. I took you for wilder than that... Pity."

She opened her mouth to protest, feeling offended.

"Well, if you change your mind, you're more than welcome." He didn't give her a chance to respond, but sauntered off. She watched his broad shoulders disappear into the trees—she had a brief, foreign, fleeting thought that she wanted to know what it felt like to be sleeping up against that kind of impressive back, but she shook it off—and she felt confused, although she didn't really know why. His blunt honesty, overbearing charisma, and roguish charm were doing a number on her usually collected thoughts. Not to mention the fact that, other than Charlon, no one usually gave one iota about how no one listened to her or gave anything back. It was just her job. And everyone else was too selfish to care about the toll it took on her listening to everyone's problems all day long. So long as they slept at night, what did it matter?

"Who was that guy?"

Daelynn swore that if one more person startled her, she was going to have an all-out heart attack and drop dead. She put her hand to her chest and tried to catch her breath as the familiar form of her handsome brother wandered into the clearing. She waved her hand after where Demetri had vanished. "Oh...some military commander-teacher-healer-writer ...interesting...Demetri...person," she muttered.

Charlon cocked an eyebrow. "An 'interesting Demetri person,' huh?"

She rolled her eyes and tried to shoo it away with an erratic hand gesture. "He's some man who came to my house earlier today thinking I was a medicinal healer." She started to tromp back over to where she had left the picnic basket, wanting to be away from this conversation.

"What did he want right now?" Charlon continued, following after her.

"He wanted me to go get a drink at the tavern with him."

"Whoa! Hold on a second." Charlon grabbed Daeylnn's arm and turned her to face him. "Why didn't you go?"

She frowned up at him. "Because I was supposed to meet you."

The expression on his face made it look like he had smelled something awful. "You meet me here every day, Daelynn! It wouldn't have killed me to miss one! I would have understood! You should go! It's not like you have much of a social life." He took her by the shoulders and gave her a small shove as if to accentuate his point.

She staggered and then turned to face him with an annoyed expression. "Come on, Charlon! The man just saw me acting out a scene by myself in the forest! He probably thinks I'm completely crazy!"

"You *are* crazy!"

The wave of hurt that washed over her was almost a physical pain in her heart. Charlon was her only family, and the person that meant the most to her in the world. He thought she was crazy too?

As if reading her thoughts, his expression softened and he put his hands on her shoulders. "Daelynn, name me one person you admire who isn't crazy. One artist, of any genre.

All of those people from the royal city you love to read about. The shapeshifters in the north. Creative people are crazy. And that's what you are. A creative person. You make your living as this 'heart healer,' but what you are and always have been is a playwright. A writer. An artist. All great artists are crazy. It's about time you realize that and embrace it." He nudged her playfully and smirked.

For the second time today, she felt tears threaten as she stared up into her brother's clear blue eyes. He understood her on a level that didn't make sense given the amount of communication they actually had. While they were close, they never usually engaged in in-depth, soul-searching conversation. Charlon was very lively and spontaneous. Things came easy for him also. While he was the kindest person she had ever known, he didn't always put his inner heart out in the open, so it always surprised her when he read her the way that he did. Most of the time, she thought she hid her feelings and desires pretty well too. Maybe she wasn't as slick as she imagined. She leaned forward and rested her forehead against his chest silently.

He sighed and wrapped his arms around her. "Stop thinking so much, Daelynn. And stop trying to be so sensible all the time. At some point, you have to stop telling everyone else how to live their lives and you have to live your own." He took her by the shoulders again and held her out so he could see her face. "Seize your own day. Isn't that what you're always telling people? Make the most of the moments you have. You're the most responsible person I know, but you work *too hard*." He spun her around and gave her a little nudge again. "Go to the tavern. Talk to that guy. I'm not stupid. I know you want to." When she didn't move out of feeling misplaced guilt she didn't understand, he wrapped his arms around her again and gave her a gentle squeeze. "You deserve to live your own life as much as anyone, sister. Stop worrying and go and do it. You only live once...unless you're a river troll."

He released her and she didn't think—for once—because she wanted to go. For some reason that made no sense, Demetri made her want to push the boundaries of her own comfort zone. Let's face it, she had been bursting to do so for so long. But her life was routine and safe. Blah.

She wanted something else, she just didn't know what.

She wanted...

She just wanted more.

She wanted to listen to more of his bizarre, brutal truth. She wanted to read more of his amazing writing. She wanted to see more of his ridiculously beautiful smile.

And with her brother's encouraging words ringing in her head, she felt like maybe she could actually take the risk.

He was relaxing at a table in the corner with a pint when she entered the tavern. She squared her shoulders and started toward him just as a young brunette decided she was going to make a beeline for him also. Daelynn caught her eye and shot her a scathing look that had the girl turning on her heel and going the opposite direction before she took two steps. Daelynn briefly wondered what in the world was the matter with herself. The man had rattled her brain entirely in the course of a few hours.

She stood in front of him and crossed her arms.

He smirked. "Change your mind?"

"No, my brother changed it for me after you baited me. And I will have you know that there is nothing wrong with structure. I have to be structured. I am surrounded by insanity and chaos all day long. If I don't keep some kind of order, I will end up just as crazy as everyone else. And not even the good kind of crazy that Charlon just called me either. The real lunatic kind." She tapped her finger against her temple to emphasize her point. "I spend all my time trying to solve people's problems, and most of the time it doesn't even work, so I don't really know what kind of healer that even makes me. A bad one, I guess. But at the end of the day, if nothing else, I want my own life to feel like I have at least that much under control." And now she was rambling. Wonderful. "So don't presume to know me. Because you don't. You only know one little part."

He said nothing. Just regarded her for a moment before he pushed his ale across the table toward her.

Daelynn grasped the mug and took a healthy swallow before she set it back down and flopped into the chair across from him with a sigh.

"It's not your responsibility to try and fix people who don't want to be fixed," Demetri finally said. "I'm not saying you shouldn't care. But if you let people affect you so much that you aren't sure where you end and they begin, you need to reevaluate your profession. You let me read your writing. I can tell just by that small sample that you are a passionate woman, but you seem to be bogged down by everyone and everything else to the point that you don't have time for you. You *should* be out in the middle of the forest acting out scenes. You shouldn't be trying to squeeze in time to do what you love while village idiots barge in your door all day demanding that you fix their owies. You're not everyone's mother and people shouldn't expect you to be. And if they do want a bandage and a hug, they should at least give you something in return for it, considering it is your occupation."

Daelynn gave him a weary, meager smile. "You sound like my brother... How could you possibly know all of that in such a short amount of time? You don't even know me."

He smiled enigmatically. "I'm good at reading people too."

She traced the patterns of the wood grain on the table with her finger and shook her head. "I don't know how it got to be the way it is. I used to enjoy helping people, and I felt like they appreciated it. Somewhere along the line, people just started taking advantage of me instead while they demanded even more of my time. Charlon, my brother, is right. I have always wanted to be a writer. I've always wanted to create things. But I lost all of that somewhere under some sick sense of duty. Now I don't even know what I am. Just some misplaced, broken woman."

He shook his head. "That's not what I see."

"Oh yeah?" She raised an eyebrow and gave him an incredulous expression. "And what would that be?"

He leaned across the table slightly and held her gaze with his. "I see a beautiful and majestic snow leopard that's been locked in a cage for far too long. You just need someone to set you free and show you how to run again."

She stared at him, which seemed to be her reaction of choice when dealing with this man. She tried to speak, but squeaked instead. She cleared her throat loudly and tried to ignore the wave of heat she felt wash up her neck and cheeks. "And who do you suppose is going to set me free? You?"

He grinned wickedly. "I'm good with animals." He sat back in his chair, looking roguish and smug.

Her flush intensified and she shook her head. She pointed at his ale. "I need one of these."

He signaled a tavern wench, who Daelynn was sure tried her best to make sure her enormous breasts actually oozed out the top of her corset every time she came to serve Demetri...because she really was only serving him. Daelynn was happy the woman's bosom stayed where it was. If her breasts had broken free, she was pretty sure Demetri would have smothered. She'd never seen one man attract so much attention...except maybe Charlon. It made her wonder briefly what had happened to her own charisma. She'd had some once, she was sure of it.

"So...what fairy clan are you from?" she asked, trying to steer the subject away from herself. She felt too confused at the moment.

"Oh, I'm not a fairy," he stated.

She frowned up at him. "But you said you are in the royal military."

"I am, but I'm not a fairy. I'm a shapeshifter."

Daelynn almost overturned the table in her excitement. "You are?"

He sat back in his chair, obviously to avoid any flying beverages, and raised an eyebrow. "Yes?"

She tried to contain her excitement and sat back down. She folded her hands. "Sorry, I'm just really interested in them."

"Any particular reason why?"

She shrugged self-consciously, and was happy when the barmaid brought her ale. She downed a healthy swallow. "I don't know. They—you—" She glanced up at him and cleared her throat. "Are interesting. So wild and free." She stole a glance up at him and swore his blue eyes were sparkling. "I went to visit one of the clans a few years ago. I...had an idea for a play..." She shrugged, feeling stupid. He was going to think she was stupid.

He sat quietly, regarding her, before he gave her a soft smile. "Did you ever write the play?"

She felt her cheeks flame. "I'm...working on it." She took another long drink. "I just don't have time—"

"Was that part of what I read today?"

She glanced up at him. "Yes," she answered meekly.

"Too many village fools taking up your time," he stated simply. "Do what you want."

He was so blunt. She didn't know what to do with it, so she changed the subject. "What...uh...what animal do you change into, if I can ask?"

His blue eyes may as well have devoured her for the way he was staring into her like he was. The intensity of his gaze intrigued and frightened her. More intrigued...she liked getting to the bottom of people.

"Wolf," he stated.

She drew in a soft breath as a vision of him in wolf form flashed through her mind. Somehow, she imagined him white—strong, powerful, magnificent. "Shouldn't you be with a pack? Not...you know, a bunch of fairies?"

His smile was slightly sardonic. "I choose my own pack."

She didn't know what to say, so she stared at him...again. For all of his playful nature, there was something else beneath that surface. Something cautious, guarded...undeniably wolflike.

Tingles raced down her spine.

"So," he said, his unflappable nature taking over once again. "Tell me more about this play of yours."

She and Demetri fell into a lively conversation that soon had Daelynn's overactive mind quieted. She couldn't overanalyze everything when he had so many interesting stories to tell, and when he wanted to know about the stories she created.

They spoke roughly about their lives, to an extent—she noticed he didn't want to elaborate much on his beyond the basics. They spoke about their writing, her plays and his poetry, and she found him amazingly easy to talk to. Time vanished, the sun set, and people filled the tavern ready for dinner and entertainment. Still, they talked. And by the time there was a small lull in the conversation, she was leaning across the table with her hands over his, enraptured by any words that might leave his lips.

She realized the placement of her hands and drew them away as she felt her cheeks burn. Blaming it on the few pints she had consumed, she decided it would probably be best if she left. She didn't even know what she was doing here, going on and on to this stranger.

"Don't," he said softly, reaching back across the table to capture her hand with his. He gently brought it back to rest over his. "That was nice."

She glanced up at him and her heart did something funny at the genuine, kind light sparkling in his eyes.

At the same time, a couple of local musicians decided to kick up the revelry a notch and began to play a lively traditional song that most of the fairy clans knew. Secretly, the music made her want to reveal her wings, which female fairies of her kind only did when they were really in an extroverted mood, but in all reality, she couldn't remember the last time she had actually done so. Male fairies of her kind didn't have wings, but females had retractable gossamer ones. Showing one's wings was announcing one's presence, and she had become comfortable with her anonymity. Her family, close friends, and those who sought her assistance knew who she was. She was fine with that.

She jumped when the man across from her suddenly started singing out the words of the song the musicians were playing loud enough that half the tavern heard him and cheered in encouragement.

Daelynn stared. How could he be like that? So unbridled? She didn't even remember how that felt. Weren't wolves wary creatures? She had seen that in his eyes earlier, yet here he was, bellowing away. He grinned at her as he finished up the first verse of the song and she giggled and shook her head. "You're an interesting one," she teased.

If it was possible, his grin widened even further and he stood. He offered her his hand. "Dance with me."

She blinked and glanced around. No one else was out of their seats. "No one else is dancing," she whispered.

He shrugged. "So?"

She bit her bottom lip, feeling self-conscious and stupid. "But everyone will be watching."

He cocked his head to the side and gave her a quizzical expression. "What does it matter? You should just have fun."

Charlon would have done it, she knew. But Charlon was...Charlon. He was free-spirited, carefree, full of life. She was... She didn't even know anymore. She was so full of everyone else's issues, she had lost her own person.

Demetri took her hands in his and gave her a smile that was none of the relentless taunting he had given her thus far, nor the devouring, aloof one he had glimpsed at her earlier. It was warm, gentle, and made her heart melt. "Tell you what. I'm going to dance. I don't care if anyone is watching. When you feel comfortable, come join me." And with that, like he had no qualms about anything that had ever existed in any realm in the universe, he backed away from the table, went to the dance floor, and just started moving his body to the beat the musicians supplied.

She watched him for a few moments, watched his unbridled zest for life, his enrapturement of the music, and his careless abandon, his disregard for everyone's prying eyes. He didn't care that the whole tavern was watching him. He didn't care what they thought. He just knew he wanted to dance. He wanted to enjoy himself.

And as everyone else in the tavern started to clap and sing along in encouragement, she realized that was why he had such a magnetic charm. Because he was free. And he was so comfortable with that, he drew all others around him. Most other people didn't know how to be that free, and they all wanted to sample some of his light. Her brother was the same. She understood it now where she never had before.

And suddenly, she was tired of sitting in the back, observing. She wanted to bask in that light. She wanted some of it for herself. So she took one more long drink of ale, sucked in a deep breath, and propelled herself out of her chair. Before she knew it, she was on the dance floor with him. She felt foolish. She felt exposed. She wanted to hide, but he grabbed her hand and held her captive with his laughter and the radiant light he exuded.

From the bar in the back, she heard the unmistakable hoots and hollers from where her brother was working. She squeezed her eyes shut and laughed, really laughed, and just let herself get caught up. In the music. In the man with her. In the moment. It had been far too long.

She wasn't sure how long she and Demetri danced. There were a few more pints involved and a lot more songs.

Daelynn's inhibitions vanished and she laughed like she hadn't in years. Demetri was fun, and she realized that was something she hadn't had in a while either—fun.

She spun around with reckless enthusiasm, but then stopped abruptly when her fist made contact with something. She turned to see that she had just accidentally clocked a barmaid. "I'm so sorry!" she cried.

The barmaid shot her a scowl, but continued on her way.

Daelynn turned to Demetri. "Oh my gosh!" she shouted. "I just punched a barmaid!"

He frowned. "You what?" He obviously had not been paying attention.

"I punched a barmaid! She was walking by, and I apparently can't control my arms when I dance, and I went like this—" She gestured, and her fist made contact with something else. She squealed and spun back around to see that she had seriously just belted someone else. Without stopping to assess the situation, she just screamed, "I am so sorry!" and put her hand out to console her victim. It was only after a few moments of horrifying silence from everyone but the musicians in the tavern that she realized she had socked the big-busted barmaid from earlier...and now had her placating hand right on her giant breast.

The barmaid just stared at her, unamused.

Daelynn looked up and tried to get her mouth to work, but it wasn't cooperating.

"All right, then!" Demetri's voice came. He grasped Daelynn gently by the arm. "I think it's time we took a break, huh?" He guided her back over to the table.

"I cannot believe I just did that," Daelynn said, exasperated.

"Which part? The dancing, or groping and assaulting the tavern staff?"

She glanced up at him and burst into laughter. "Both!" She continued to laugh, not caring if she was making a scene, not caring if she was a little bit drunk, just genuinely enjoying herself.

Demetri chuckled, then reached across the table to grasp her hand in his. He brought her fingers to his lips, and the sparkle in his eyes made Dealynn's heart stutter. She couldn't help but feel like she had been stagnant for so long...

Until this man blew in like the wind and brought her back to life with his fire.

Chapter Three

Daelynn awoke with a start, with wild didgeridoo music blaring into her ear. She grunted in protest, raised herself off of what she was lying on—seemed to be several stacks of grain—then chuckled as she tried to get her bearings. She rubbed at her eyes and saw her brother messing around with his musical instrument, and Demetri next to him, laughing.

"What...why are you doing that?" she mumbled, still trying to wake up.

Charlon chuckled. "You fell asleep in the supply room after you and Demetri danced yourselves into the ground."

She blinked as she sat up. "I did?" That didn't sound like her. "How? Why was I back here?"

"You said you needed to use the loo," Charlon stated. "Apparently afterward, you decided to take a nap."

"The six pints you had probably had something to do with that," Demetri joked.

She briefly remembered decking a barmaid and then groping her. She groaned and glanced up at where Demetri was standing casually. "Why are you still here?"

"Well, it's not like I was just going to abandon you. I'm a lot of things, but I'm not *that* rude. After you fell asleep, I just shot the breeze with your brother. You were safe back here."

Daelynn ran her hand through her hair. "Geez..." She cast a sheepish glance up at Demetri. "I'm sorry."

He shrugged, his devil-may-care smile ever-present. "No worries."

She smirked up at him. "You danced me to death," she teased.

He shot her a wink. "What I'd really like to know is why your brother brought his didgeridoo to work with him." He cocked his head in Charlon's direction.

Charlon raised his eyebrow as if he was confused that

someone would even ask that question.

Daelynn laughed lightly. "He's always playing something. He collects musical instruments from all over the realms."

"Well, now that you're done hanging out on the hops, I need to close up the tavern," Charlon said.

Daelynn yawned and stretched. "Kicking me out, huh? Thanks a lot."

Demetri smiled and held his hand out to help her up. She stumbled a little, her head still foggy, and bumped into him. His hands went to her waist to stabilize her and she suddenly found herself pressed against his chest, staring up into his dynamically beautiful blue eyes. "Thanks," she murmured, feeling her cheeks flush.

His gaze scanned over her face for a moment before his lips quirked in a mischievous smile. "If you wanted to get close to me, all you had to do was ask." He winked.

She giggled and his lips split into his breathtaking grin. She stabilized herself and took a step away from him, messing with her rumpled hair some more.

"I'll walk you home," he offered.

The sky was lightening with a pink-purple hue as Daelynn stepped out of the tavern. She drew in a breath. "Oh my goodness, it's dawn!" Birds were chirping, greeting the new day, and she stopped for a second to stare at the sunrise. She smiled softly, then glanced over her shoulder at Demetri. "I've never been up till dawn before."

He smiled at her. "You danced the night away."

She felt stupidly giddy, and she didn't know if it was the lack of sleep, the drink still in her system, or...maybe just the man behind her. She didn't care. For the first time in so long, she did not care.

She turned to Demetri. "Thank you for last night," she said. "It was really nice to get out of my routine for once."

He stared at her with his all-knowing eyes again, as if assessing her person. Ice blue...wolf eyes.

"Why are you alone?" she blurted suddenly.

He arched an eyebrow.

"I mean, why do you have no pack?"

"I told you, I choose my pack."

"But...is that how it really works?"

He regarded her for a moment, his features guarded, but

then they softened somewhat and he sighed. "Sometimes, we don't fit in our designated pack. I've never fit anywhere. I've been a lone wolf for a long time. But I have friends I consider my pack now. And they fulfill me better than the one I was born into."

She nodded slowly. She could understand that. Although, it made her somewhat sad to realize, other than Charlon, who was her family, she couldn't say she felt that way about anyone in her life. She had people, like Lena and Wilbur, who she had known forever and who said they were her friends, but if she was left to her own devices in a "pack" with them, she'd probably never survive. Actually, none of them would because they wouldn't know how to do anything for themselves and she would die trying to help them.

She heaved a disgruntled sigh.

Demetri flashed her a slightly concerned expression. "Are you all right? If you're going to upchuck, please do it elsewhere."

She waved her hand. "No, I'm not going to upchuck. It's nothing. Come on, let's go home." She caught her mistake in phrasing almost immediately and turned to him. "My home, I mean. Like...I mean, I need to go home."

He chuckled and casually slipped his arm around her shoulders. "Yes, let's get you home."

She didn't want to admit that she leaned into him, but she did. And she didn't want to admit that the way his arm felt around her seemed natural, but it did.

She didn't want to admit that she liked Demetri, because she barely knew him and that was weird and so unlike her because she was *not* impulsive...

But she did.

The queen arrived at sunset the next day and the entire marketplace and surrounding forest was abuzz with activity. Everyone in the village had turned out to watch the procession. Torches had been lit along the roadway and colorful paper lanterns and glittering streamers decorated the trees. The queen visited every spring, and it was always a cause for celebration that usually lasted long into the night.

Daelynn was tired, considering the previous night, but truthfully, she had never felt more alive. Demetri had walked her home like a gentleman, then left her with the image of his beautiful smile and sparkling eyes. She couldn't remember ever having such a wonderful night. She hadn't seen him today, but that was all right. She knew he had a lot to do, and he didn't owe her anything anyway. In her mind, he had already given her much more than anyone had in far too long.

She stood with Charlon as they waited, and a hush fell over the crowd when they heard the beginning strains of a piper in the distance. The air was charged with excitement, and as the music grew closer and more instruments joined in, the crowd started to cheer and throw flower petals along the roadway.

The musicians were the first to appear in the procession, followed by dancers wielding colorful streamers to the lively melody. Behind them marched the royal army, where Daelynn spotted the three women who had been in her home the day before. She bristled involuntarily and looked around for Demetri in the group of soldiers, but couldn't see him anywhere.

She glanced around at the cheering crowd. All of the women had their wings out and they flickered and gleamed in the lantern light. Daelynn had dressed up in a flowy, sea foam green gown with sheer sleeves that tied at the elbows, and she had adorned her long black tresses with white flowers, but she still felt amazingly reserved somehow amidst all the revelry. And while she usually rejoiced in the fact that she could disappear into the shadows, tonight it made her feel oddly out of place.

More dancers and acrobats preceded the queen, and then she came into view, carried by river trolls on a litter with white and gold glittering, shimmery drapery all around her. She smiled and waved regally, as was her way. Her king sat next to her on one side and Daeylnn's heart tripped over itself when she saw who was sitting just behind them. Dressed in, not a military uniform of any kind, but bright teal that was almost as outlandish as the purple tunic of the day before, was Demetri. She wondered how it was possible for him to get away with wearing such bright, flamboyant colors and still seem so undeniably masculine.

She watched him for a while, then giggled and shook her

head. "I guess he wasn't full of donkey dung after all," she said to her brother. "He really is with the queen's army."

Charlon smiled at her over his shoulder then did a double-take and turned to give Daelynn a shocked expression.

Daelynn's cheeks burned and she looked down shyly, giving a small shrug. Over the course of the procession, she had decided to reveal her wings, caught up in the carefree excitement and energy around her. It had been so long since she had done so, Charlon had probably forgotten she even had a pair.

"Well, look at you, big sister!" he teased.

He pulled her against his side in a rough, playful hug and she laughed softly. She watched as the procession passed by and she sighed, remembering her evening of dancing and laughter with Demetri. How strange that one person could make so much of a difference in her life in such a short amount of time. Yesterday, she had felt haggard, exhausted, older than her years, and here she was tonight showing off her wings.

Maybe she could force herself out of her regimented routine after all. Maybe she could loosen her controlled grip on her life and remember how to dance through it like Charlon and Demetri did. Maybe there was more than being responsible and listening to people gripe to her about their problems all day long.

Maybe there was hope for her after all.

The revelry lasted well into the night and was showing no signs of letting up when Daelynn finally escaped the marketplace and snuck out through the forest to the cliffs and sea beyond. While she had enjoyed herself, she needed a moment of solitude, of quiet.

She settled herself down on the soft sand and sighed as she watched the powerful waves crash up onto the shore. The moon was full and bathed the entire landscape in a peaceful silver glow. The queen would stay for a day, visiting her subjects and making sure everything was all right in the village. Then she would go off to the next village to do the same, taking Demetri with her. Daelynn didn't imagine she would get to see him between then and now. He would be busy with his duties. While she knew that he had been a chance encounter and would never be a permanent fixture in her life, it saddened her to think that the person who had made her realize so much so quickly, who had changed her outlook in only a day, would more than likely never see her again.

She was grateful for the encounter, very much so, and felt privileged that her dreary existence had been graced by such a beautiful soul, but it was bittersweet.

"Hey, big sister! Whatcha doin' out here?"

Daelynn looked over her shoulder to see Charlon stagger over carrying a bottle of brandywine. She snorted out a laugh. "I was trying to get away from drunkards like you," she teased.

He made a face at her, took a swig out of the bottle, then frowned and tipped it upside down. No liquid came out.

"Congratulations, Charlon, you drank the whole thing," she said.

He held the bottle up and wavered a little. "I will have you know, this is the second one."

Daelynn raised her eyebrows and Charlon accidentally dropped the bottle. It landed on her shoulder with a *thunk* before rolling into the sand. "Ow! That was my shoulder, you idiot!" she spat as she rubbed the stinging spot on her arm.

He laughed and stumbled again. "Sorry, sister."

She rolled her eyes. "Tomorrow when you feel like you are on death's door, I'm going to scream in your ear until your head feels like it's going to split in two."

"It's gorgeous out here," he said with a sigh, ignoring her jab.

Daelynn turned her attention back out to the sea. "Yeah, I just needed to get away from all the noise for a while. Needed to think, you know?" When Charlon didn't answer her, she glanced back over at him and frowned quizzically. He was muttering to himself, but she couldn't make out what he was saying.

Suddenly, he let out a huff and grumbled, "Forget it, you only live once."

Daeylnn opened her mouth to ask him what in the world he was talking about when his clothing all but exploded off of his body. She had never seen anyone take their clothes off that fast. How he managed to do it with so much finesse in his inebriated state was a mystery to her, but he did, and then went charging out into the ocean waves in nothing but his skin.

Daelynn arched an eyebrow, trying to wrap her mind around what she had just witnessed, then collapsed backwards onto the sand in laughter as she watched her brother emerge from the water, wave his arms, and give a few hoots and hollers.

"Come on, Daelynn!" he shouted.

She propped herself up on her elbows and shouted back at him. "What, you want me to come in with you? Are you insane?"

"The water's not that bad!"

"Of course not! You have the liquor burning in your belly to keep you warm!"

He dove back under the waves and she squeezed her eyes shut as she got a full-on look at his naked white backside. There was absolutely no reason she should ever have to see that much of her brother. She glanced up at the cliffs and decided she would go up there to think. As much as she enjoyed Charlon's free-spirited antics, her mind was spinning with things she needed to sort out.

"Come on, Daelynn!" he encouraged again. "Live the dream!"

She laughed softly as she stood up. "I'm going up to the cliffs!" she called back. "Don't drown!" She knew he wouldn't. He spent every single morning of his life playing in that water, had practically since the day he'd been born. Besides, she knew if he did get into any trouble, the mermaids would be more than happy to assist him.

She made her way across the beach and up the narrow path that led to the top of the cliffs. The waves sounded thunderous from up there, crashing against the cliff base and sending salty spray into the air. She closed her eyes and took a deep breath. She thought of her life, of Lena and Wilbur and the others who had come to her for "help" when all they'd really wanted was someone to whine at. Who'd claimed to be her "friends," but never paid her when they knew she depended on the income. Who never really even bartered with her. Even that would have been okay. Who only took and took until there was nothing left of her to give, but never gave anything in return, not even the friendship they claimed. She was tired of it. Utterly spent. She had given so much of herself to everyone else for so long, she barely had anything left for her. She didn't even know who she was anymore.

At one point, she had been more of a free spirit. Maybe not quite as much as Charlon or Demetri—she was pretty sure she had come out of the womb responsible and sensible—but she had been less concerned about everything. Somewhere along the line, she'd lost the part of herself that didn't care who was watching while she danced, that didn't care how she looked when she danced, that wanted to dance. The part that had been devoted to her craft, her art, and not her occupation, the part that was uniquely hers. It had been bogged down by everyone else's issues, and with every person who came to her and drained her of all her care while never reciprocating in any fashion, she lost another little piece of herself.

Demetri was right. She had gone too far over the line of being a good person. And Charlon was right. She needed to take her own advice. She didn't know how many times she had told people they needed to live each day to its fullest, seize opportunities, and never take a moment for granted. She had dished those words out while living the opposite. When had she become afraid of the life she'd used to think was beautiful? She needed to seriously reevaluate some things.

She heard some rustling in the underbrush off to her left and glanced over to see a man hoist himself up over the cliff edge. Her eyes bulged when he stood and she saw it was Demetri. He was wearing much more subdued clothing of black and gray, and he brushed himself off as he started toward her.

"D-Did you just climb up here?" she squeaked.

"Of course," he said, like she was out of her mind for even asking. "How did you get up here?"

She jabbed her thumb in the direction behind her. "I took the trail!"

He shrugged. "Why take the trail when you can climb?"

She shook her head in bafflement. "You are a crazy man." His grin undid her and she had to look away because her heart twisted painfully at the thought of never seeing it again. She looked back out toward the inky water turned silvery in the moonlight.

"I saw you during the parade today," he said.

"I saw you too," she replied. "You were wearing bright turquoise. It was impossible to miss you."

He chuckled and took a step closer to her. "I saw your wings."

She hunched her shoulders self-consciously and shrugged. "Everyone else had their wings out. Seemed like the thing to do at the time." She knew it had been much more than that. She knew he knew too, but he didn't press it.

"You didn't feel like participating in the festivities?"

"Oh no, I did," she said. "I just slipped away for a while. And then watched my drunken brother run naked out into the sea." She giggled at the memory.

"Yes, I saw him out there, cavorting with mermaids it looked like. He's the one who told me you were up here."

She frowned thoughtfully and turned to meet his eyes. "You were looking for me?"

He smiled and reached out to tuck a strand of hair behind her ear. "You sound so surprised."

She looked down at the sandy ground and felt her cheeks grow warm. "I'm just not used to people looking for me unless they want me to fix them."

"Do I seem like someone who needs to be fixed?"

She glanced up at him and shook her head.

"Then I must have been looking for you for a different reason." His blue eyes seemed pale in the moonlight, gray almost, matching the color of his tunic. "In the last day, I have had more intriguing conversation than I can remember having with anyone in a very long time. Daelynn, you are a breath of fresh air to me."

She knew her expression had to reflect the "what in the nine fairy realms have you been smoking?" feeling that shot through her at his words. "What is the matter with you? I'm nothing special at all. I'm forgettable. I'm insignificant."

He shook his head and put his hands on her shoulders gently. "You listen to me, you appreciate me. Not many people really do. You understand my poetry. You accept me for who I am blindly. That is unusual," he murmured. "You're not like a lot of other girls. You're not a girl at all. You're a woman. You're not forgettable and insignificant. You're a snow leopard, remember?"

She sighed and looked away. "Trapped in a cage."

He ran a hand down the length of her hair in a slow caress that made her shiver. "No, you're free. You have been for a while. You just need to remember how to run."

Silence stretched between them while she tried to figure out how to get her heart to return to some kind of normal rhythm. She didn't think it would happen while he kept stroking his thumb back and forth on the inside of her arm. His touch did something to her. Something insane. His touch and his words combined were enough to level her. It made her thoughts cloudy and nothing seemed to make sense anymore. All she wanted was more of his words, more of his touch, more of his lunatic spontaneity and zest for life, more of his candid honesty, more of him...

She looked up into his eyes and lost herself there. She was fine with being lost. She never wanted to be found. His face was beautiful, his heart even more so. "I may steal a kiss," she whispered. She barely even recognized the words as her own. But what did she have to lose, really? She needed to be more like Charlon. Just dive on in. Exposed. Who cared?

His smile was soft. "I may not stop you."

She didn't think. She didn't want to. She just leaned up on her toes, wrapped her arms around his neck, and pressed her lips to his. It was a gentle kiss, tender in its approach, but the way he held her made her world tilt, like she was precious, cherished, above all others. She felt that in his embrace. She felt that in his heart. His words may not have said as much, but his touch did.

"Daelynn," he finally said when she pulled away. He didn't speak again until she met his gaze. "Come with me."

"What?" she practically screeched.

"To the other villages as the queen travels. Come with me."

"Why in the world would you want me to come with you?" She staggered back a few steps, away from his searing touch and that sparkle in his eyes she didn't know how to handle. Reality suddenly came rushing in on her and she felt confused, out of her element. "I'm nothing like you, Demetri. I'm not impetuous or outgoing or anything like that. I'm cautious, I'm sensible, I'm methodical. I plan things. I think of all the consequences before I make a choice. I think...all the time!"

"Daelynn, you just kissed a near stranger. You don't call that impetuous?"

She shook her head, feeling out of control. She hated feeling out of control. "I-I...we're just too different, Demetri. I would never fit into your world."

His brow furrowed in disapproval. "Why would I want someone exactly like me? How does that make sense?"

She stopped and looked at him in bewilderment.

He approached her again and took her hands in his. "It's the differences in people that make us learn. That makes us grow. How boring would it be to have someone exactly like me by my side? Anyone who would want such a thing is not an adventurer. He is a coward. Because, truly, an adventurer wants the terrain they don't know, that they don't understand. No one who wants a familiar course could ever call himself a true adventurer."

Daelynn stared up at him, true to form, and her heart did something strange. It reached out to his, bound itself to his, in a way that didn't make sense. She wasn't sure she even wanted to make sense of it.

"Come with me, Daelynn. Let's explore uncharted territory together. Every adventure has a risk. I think you're worth the risk."

Something foreign bubbled up within her, something dormant and sassy. She backed away and cocked a hip, putting her hand on it for effect. "Oh, I'm definitely worth the risk, sir. Let's see if you survive the journey."

His grin was magnificent as he walked toward her. "Does that mean your answer is yes?"

Daelynn smiled as his hands circled her waist. How could she say no to him? The man who had brought more clarity and beauty in two days than she had experienced in a lifetime? He was like a sunrise in her soul. He was offering her everything. All the adventure, all the excitement and wonderful things she could imagine. He was the only one to offer her anything in so long.

She looked up into his blue eyes and she saw her future there. She wasn't entirely sure what that future was, but she knew he was a part of it. And she would be stupid to deny it.

Epilogue

Charlon had a raging hangover as he made his way to his sister's house. He didn't want anything from her. No remedy or cure-all. After all, it was his own fault he had drank that much. He just wanted to know what had happened with the royal "interesting Demetri person" on top of the cliffs. He knew she liked him, and he knew the man was making an effort. He just wanted to know whether or not his sister had enough courage to follow her heart and not her brain.

As he got to her home, he was surprised to see that the normally "open" sign on her door was turned to "closed," and all the lights were off. He would have been concerned except, under the rock where the extra key was, there was a note. For him.

"Charlon,
I will always love you and always look out for you. You are the one who made me see my own course. You are the one who made me take this chance. You saw in me what I was trying to deny. I have found the sunrise, Charlon. The sunrise in my own soul. I love you always, little brother, and I will contact you soon. I've done what I said. I've seized my own day.

Big Sister"

He read it, then read it again because he couldn't believe what he was actually seeing.

Responsible, regimented, no-nonsense Daelynn had run off into the night with a member of the royal guard.

He did the only thing that made any logical sense at that moment.

As joy for his sister boiled up inside of him, he threw his head back and he laughed.

Falling
By Tex Leiko

Preface
By Brieanna Robertson

As I sat down to figure out this compilation, I started with just my stories. I had a few rogue shorts lying around that needed to be published, but then I realized that my late husband—AKA Tex Leiko—also had some shorts that had never found their way to anywhere. And I went digging for buried treasure.

It's no secret that my late husband was a writer, but he would dabble in things without intent, just to get his ideas out. Where writing is lifeblood to me, it was a hobby and passion to him, but not something he would invest his soul into. Which is probably why it was so annoying to me that he was so inherently good at it.

But it was one of the many things that connected us—our love of the written word.

I remember when he first wrote this piece. It was right after we had met one another. He had initially written it for a writing competition. I had all but forgotten it existed.

When I found it and read it again, I was destroyed in the best kind of way. Because this piece reflects *so much* of what my husband believed in.

I entitled this compilation "Extraordinary Creatures" because all of the pieces have had a fantasy element to them. This one doesn't, but I still think it's the most poignant piece out of all of them.

Because sometimes, the most extraordinary creature of all can be a human being. A good man.

To this day, the most extraordinary creature I have ever known was the author behind this piece.

I love you.

The Only Chapter

As I stood on the podium, I took a deep breath and looked across the audience at the sea of faces. Some old, some young, some there just to support me, some because they had known my father. Some of the faces in the audience I had seen just three years earlier when Mother had passed.

Her slip had said "Dementia," so we all had known just how she would go. When she turned sixty-seven and started forgetting things, we knew it was coming. Before long, she didn't know who we were and was convinced there was an airplane on the tarmac coming to pick her up.

She would wake at night screaming in terror. When we would come into her room, she would ask, "Is it still there?"

Every night, every twenty minutes like clockwork, I would undoubtedly say, "Is what there, Mama?"

"The plane! The plane that's going to pick me up! Is it still there?"

The answer of "no" would send her into a fit of crying until her brain reset and she would ask the same question. If you answered with a "yes," you would receive a sigh of relief and a request for her to be taken outside. Inevitably, I would say to that, "Okay, let me just gather some things first."

She would just lie in bed, content with a smile on her face, for twenty minutes while I was outside the room "gathering things." Her brain would then reset and she would be screaming again soon.

It was tiresome, but between father, my sister Emile, and myself, we each picked a night and rotated. It made it more bearable. Nobody ever thought Mother would pass first, but once again, the machine made fools of us all and proved us all wrong.

I was nervous. I had done this before at my mother's funeral. But my father's eulogy would be a bit more difficult to tell. His story was a bit less predictable, even if we had always known the end. I cleared my throat and began.

"Garret Winston Kabos was known and loved by all. We are gathered here today to share a loss, the loss of a great man. Many of us here remember him well. Some of you knew him before I did, though I would like to think I know my own father better than even his closest friends.

"We all know him as a risk taker, as a wild card, as the cat with nine lives. I want you to know him as something more. I want you to know him as a caring, loving, devoted husband and breadwinner. Also, as an extraordinary father to both myself and my sister. But also, as a man who truly loved life.

"I see many in the audience shaking their heads, or by your faces, you beg to differ with my latter statement. However, I assure you that Emile and I will mourn his loss greater than anyone else living possibly could. Sure, there were fights growing up, with us, with Mother, but that wasn't the point. The point is, he was a man who truly loved life and nothing...nothing would ever change that for him.

"Not a stupid slip of paper, not a machine, not a God damned blood test! I have had mine done; it says 'car accident,' my sister, 'stroke.' Many would say that I follow in my father's footsteps because I haven't given up driving. The point my father proved to us all is that just because the machine says something, it leaves out a lot as well.

"It doesn't say when the accident will happen. It doesn't even say I will be in a car. I could be in my living room for all we know, enjoying my favorite TV show, when some drunk teenager plows through my living room, killing me on my couch.

"As we all know, Garret had always been a very fit, healthy man. Judging from the photos of his youth, it was important to him from the time he was a young child all the way until he died at the age of seventy-two. He was an explorer at heart. He should have been born in the fourteen-hundreds, for then he would have died a legend that would be read about in history books.

"Instead, he had to be born in the era of the 'silver death' or 'fate-o-matic.' Yes, the two-edged sword known as the Death Machine. Garret took his test when he was twenty-one years old on a drunken dare. The machines were everywhere then, just as they are now. Its display lit up and it made its campy little noises and out it spit, just a single black and white sheet that said, 'falling.'

"His friends all gasped; they weren't surprised. By this time he had already proven himself to be quite the risk taker. He had climbed Jumbo Love only two months prior, and was ready for something more difficult. So, naturally, when his slip spit out the fate of falling, his friends all concluded that he would stop his outdoorsmenship, his rock climbing, his bow hunting in extreme areas of the wilderness... His life.

"Even his close friends and associates believed he would give up his life over a little slip of paper that told him how his story would end. His close friend Brady did. After seeing my father's fate, he hastily took his own test. It read, 'climbing accident.'

"Brady died two years later. He was my father's climbing partner until the day they had both taken their tests. Brady quit that night; my father didn't. He told me once when I was grown what had happened. My father was still a bachelor living his life, spending most of his days in the wild. Brady had left him.

"Brady was worried that if he kept climbing with my father, he would meet his demise early. He knew the machine was always right, that sooner or later he would go, but he didn't want it to come early. Not now that he had a fiancée. Brady, in the two years that passed from the night they got their blood tests, never once joined my father in the great outdoors.

"He forsook all that was meaningful to him from that time onward. My father would always invite him. He would laugh, ridicule, and mock my father. Even told him one time, 'If you want to go and get yourself killed early, then fine! But stop trying to drag me down with you!' Dad stopped inviting him after that.

"Brady didn't think twice, though, when his fiancée asked him to climb on top of a ladder and paint the trim above the doorway to the home they had just purchased together. He did so willingly, happily...and in that one moment...his life came crashing to an end. He fell from the top rung, a mere loss of balance. When he landed on the ground, he hadn't put his hands out to catch himself. His neck snapped at the cervical levels one and two. It severed his nerves and he died en route to the hospital.

"His fiancée called Dad from the emergency room scream-ing and crying. She wanted him to know his best friend was dead, but mostly, she wanted to blame it on him. It wasn't rational; it didn't make sense even to her, but she was hurt-ing. She questioned why Dad was alive, taking all the risks that he had been taking, and why her fiancée, who played it safe, was dead and to be cremated by the end of the week.

"Tragic? Yes. What was my father's response? He took some time; he consoled her the best he could. He made sure to do right by her and see to it his best friend's love was tak-en good care of. However, it didn't stop him from living!

"At twenty-five, he still had not stopped doing anything that he loved to do. He climbed every summer in Yosemite. During the winter and off season, he went bouldering in are-as around our home out here in Tempe, Arizona. If it was too wet to go out, he went to the gyms to climb.

"However, he met someone he didn't expect to meet. Ida, my mother. The two quickly fell in love in a whirlwind romance. Within three months, they had moved in together. Six months later, she was pregnant with me. To keep the parents all satisfied, they got married quickly thereafter. They had never discussed how each other was going to die...that is, until after I was born.

"They had been married for seven months and I was just a week old. They were drifting off to sleep, as my father told me, when she sprang it on him. 'I'm going to be old,' Ida had said matter-of-factly.

"'Old when what?'

"'When I go. My slip, it said dementia. Young people don't get dementia.'

"'Oh,' he said, trying to shrug it off, hoping my mother would go back to sleep.

"'What does yours say?' she asked him suspiciously.

"'Falling,' he said hesitantly. He battled internally whether or not to tell her. He had told me many times he almost lied that night.

"That night was the first time there was ever an argument about the matter between him and her. She tried to convince him to stop. He stood his ground and told her no. She cried and told him he was selfish; the same as many of his friends, relatives, and associates had told him and would tell him.

"Mother was so sullen about his firm standing that he quit, but only for about four months. As a final demonstration of just how confident he was that he wouldn't go young, he stole me for a climb without her knowledge. He knew I would die in a crash; they had me tested young. What he didn't think of was that I might die from shaken baby syndrome brought on by a fender bender on the drive up to the rock face.

"Sure, it was far-fetched, but Mother didn't stop at that scenario when he returned home, me strapped to his back, climbing gear in hand and photos as evidence of what he had done. From how he always told the story, Mother just about ended his life that night. He said, of all things she was angry at the most was the fact that he had belayed himself on the climb.

"After Brady had quit on him, he always did prefer to belay himself. He knew then if the fall was because of a mistake on the part of the belayer, the mistake would be his own. He always told her it was just as safe as having a partner...that was a lie.

"Life continued on. Dad continued to climb and, by now, I was in my late teens. I picked up many habits from my father and being an outdoors enthusiast was one amongst many of them.

"I was sixteen; he was forty-one. I didn't fear climbing much. I always knew I was going to die in a car accident. Hell, I feared the wrath of my mom knowing I went climbing with Dad more than I feared anything else.

"But there we were, standing at the face of Half Dome Snake Dike. It was only a five-point-seven rating on the Yosemite Decimal System of rating. It would be easy for Dad, but for me...it was my first real outdoor climb. It was also the day I thought I would see my father die.

"We were on the fourth pitch when it happened. He was climbing ahead of me, placing our safeties as he always did. I was behind, giving slack and always ready to catch him by keeping up the slack. Of course, if he did fall, he would still fall to the next safety, take a good whipper, recover, and continue the climb. Now not many of you may know this next story. Mother did; Mother almost divorced him over it…she didn't, as we all know, but she was close.

"There we were; he had placed a safety then climbed another fifteen feet. He was in the process of shoving a Camalot into a crack he had found as our next safety point when he slipped. He fell the fifteen feet to the safety he had placed earlier. This had happened many times in our years of climbing together. Nothing out of the ordinary to take at least one fall. Especially when he was over confident.

"However, this time, when he reached his safety, it did not stop him. It was poorly placed, or the granite crumbled, neither of us knew for sure which it was. The point is, he fell roughly another fifteen feet and the rope snapped to the core. It was frayed and for the only time in my life, I saw fear in my father's eyes.

"For the first time in his life, that little death slip that said, 'falling' meant something to him. His falling had slingshot me up and we were pretty well eye to eye; he had tears in his. I had tears in mine. I was scared, scared of losing Dad, scared of dying myself.

"In that moment, I had forgotten what my slip said. I forgot I was to die in a car accident, but he remembered. He swung himself back to the rock face and grabbed on. He looked me dead in the eyes and he said, 'Hey, only one of us dies of a fall. You die in a car accident, right? And unless someone parked right under us, which isn't likely, that isn't how you go. As a matter of fact, it isn't how I go either. Now, pull yourself together. We need to get to the next pitch to rest and gather our thoughts.'

"That is what we did. We placed safeties and latched ourselves to the rock face. Father cut the rope and singed it where it had frayed with a lighter he always carried; the rope, being nylon, melted over and it formed a new end. We knew we had to be more careful, that we had lost about forty feet of rope, but we had something to work with and we made it to the next pitch.

"When we did, we realized it was time to swallow pride. We had one damaged rope to rappel back down with and he didn't trust it. I was so shaken up I didn't trust myself. So he got out his emergency phone and called in an S.O.S. We waited up there for what seemed like forever talking about stuff. Talking about how mad Mom was going to be.

"We returned home; Mom and Dad fought the way we had discussed up on the climb. Mom left for a few days and said when she came back she was going to take everything, including my sister and myself. We all thought she was serious. For the next several days, we said our 'we will see you on weekends' goodbyes to Dad. When Mom returned, she was a lot cooler over the situation.

"She told him she didn't mean all that she said. She even said she knew she couldn't persuade him to stop climbing or hiking or doing any of the things that he loved, so she wouldn't try. She told him she knew she would live a long time and, if he died early, she was strong enough to raise us kids on her own.

"She truly was; she was a strong woman, but it never came to that. Years passed and finally, in his sixties, Dad gave up climbing. He still hiked, hunted, and fished. He was still a trailblazer. In fact, he would even go white water kayaking from time to time. Thank God Mother never factored in that him going over a waterfall could have been the 'falling' that the card had predicted.

"Mother turned sixty-seven and Father, seventy-one. He saw her into her old age and death. He never stopped the things he loved, despite everyone opposing him and calling him insane. He didn't die early.

"He didn't die in some tragic accident; he didn't die from stupidity; he didn't die regretting that he didn't enjoy the years he had despite the machine telling him the ending to his tale. He died at seventy-three, good, old, and accomplished. He told me just weeks before that he believed he just may be the only one who would prove that device wrong.

"Maybe he jinxed himself? Who knows? But the one thing I can say for sure is that he taught me an important lesson. The machine writes the end of the story. It is up to us to make the rest something worth telling. Whether it be while we are alive, or while our friends tell it around a campfire.

"I mean no offense when I say we can be like Brady, and die the same as was predicted only to be full of regret, full of lost opportunity, or to die like Garret, without regret no matter the age. Living life to the full and doing the things that we love. He also taught us life doesn't turn out the way we expect it, nor does it turn out the way others do either... It just plays out. Our stories just unfold.

"I will tell stories about my dad until the day I die; his grandchildren both from myself and from Emile will do the same. He still lives in that sense and has been my greatest inspiration. I am now forty-eight; I still drive a car. There are even times I drive fast on windy roads because I love it. I have yet to die. I don't get cocky and think I am invincible, nor do I drive recklessly, but I realize I just as well may be struck as a pedestrian the same as I may run myself off the road.

"Life, even in the certainty of death, is still unpredictable. That is all I wish for you to take away from this. That and that I am proud of my dad for being a great father and teaching me this lesson I only hope to pass on to my children."

My eyes were full of tears by the end when I walked off the platform. Before I did, though, I stole a glimpse of the audience. Many were with me on the scale of emotion. Crying, weeping, sobbing or just "had a grain of sand in their eye." The point was, I wasn't alone in the emotional impact my father had on my life.

We walked out as a crowd to a ledge overlooking the desert. The service had been outside near a cliff Father and I had climbed many times as a child. I scattered the ashes over the side and encouraged all that had come to go and read his obituary, to go and see for themselves.

It was framed in glass sitting on a white tablecloth atop an oak table. Its pale green trim contrasted the colors of his photograph, nicely bringing out his green eyes. It was as if Michelangelo himself had painted a portrait of my father's death. Everyone who didn't know the circumstances of his death read it before they left; even some who already knew in full detail had to read it again after hearing my short speech.

"Garret Winston Kabos died at age seventy-three inside his home today. This loving father of two apparently fell to his demise off of a step ladder while hanging a portrait of his beloved family on the wall of his living room. He will be missed by his friends and family members."

Tex Leiko:
March 3, 1987-April 6, 2016

About the Authors

Brieanna Robertson

If someone were to ask me what I am, it could be summed up in one, simple word: Dreamer. Ever since I was a small child my imagination has run wild. I have been telling stories for as long as I can remember, creating grand worlds in my head and going on adventures that were invisible to others around me. Am I eccentric? Yes. Am I proud of that? Absolutely.

I write about the things that inspire me, both in this world and in realms only seen with the imagination. My heroines are sassy and strong. My heroes are sometimes shy. I have an obsession with music (and musicians) and a fascination with wings. I believe true love does exist, and sometimes it is found in the strangest, most unexpected places. I also believe that family and close friends are the glue that hold people together.

Above all things, I believe in being true to yourself and seizing the day. Life is an amazing gift. Make your experience as beautiful as you possibly can.

Tex Leiko

Tex was born in a factory in Detroit, MI. Little is known of Tex except he doesn't care to be a part of society or even seen by many. After being exposed to a drug known as TXZ-

871 he began to exhibit many abnormal signs of being a "Dreamer."

Sometimes, his mind brings to life creatures and events better left behind; alas they manifest and wreak havoc upon those around. As a Dreamer, he is constantly on the run from "Nightmares." One such Nightmare is Seamus, who constantly seeks to destroy and bring down what he creates.

www.ingramcontent.com/pod-product-compliance
Lightning Source LLC
Chambersburg PA
CBHW020046180626

46812CB00006B/2213